MW00605051

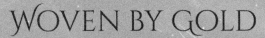

WOVEN BY GOLD

BEASTS OF THE BRIAR
BOOK TWO

ELIZABETH HELEN

LUNA FOX
PRESS

Published by Luna Fox Press

First Edition published June 2023

Interior Design © 2023 by Elizabeth Helen

Cover Design and Illustration © 2023 by saintjupit3rgr4phic

Proofread by Andra Kapule of sinfulalohaediting.com

Identifiers

ISBN: 978-1-7388279-3-0(eBook)

ISBN: 978-1-7388279-4-7 (paperback)

ISBN: 978-1-7388279-5-4 (audio)

This book is dedicated to our passionate, welcoming, and wonderfully twisted online community of Roses. May all your ever afters be happy.

TRIGGER WARNINGS

Woven by Gold is the second book in the multi-book Beasts of the Briar series. It is a why-choose romance that ends on a cliffhanger. It contains mature themes, explicit sexual content, and is intended for audiences 18+. The following paragraph contains trigger warnings. **Please note these warnings do include a spoiler for the book.**

Trigger Warnings: Fantasy violence and gore; on-page death of a parent; mentions of physical and emotional abuse in a previous relationship

PART ONE
BANISHMENT

I

ROSALINA

It's been four months, and the rosebush is still frozen. Winter has turned to spring, warm rain has washed away the snow, pastel flowers sprout up from the hard earth, and the rosebush is still frozen. Crystallized red petals glimmer like jewels in the dusky pink light, while shadows—long and inky—dip between the thorns, casting fingers of darkness onto the forest floor.

Fiery rage crawls through my body as I dig my nails into my palms.

I *hate* him. Hate him all the way to my core where the anger simmers like a wild thing. Hate him in the deepest way. The way you can only hate yourself. Because despite everything, that is what he is. A part of me, woven into my very being.

Keldarion. The High Prince of Winter.

My mate.

I hadn't known what a mate was before I found my way into the Enchanted Vale, home of the fae. The place where I'd spent every day researching mates, trying to find a way to break the four fae princes' curse.

A humorless laugh bubbles within me. I'd been the answer—at least part of it—all along. Kel's mate...

I clutch at my chest, gripping the fabric of my sweater. An ever-present ache. The bond that awoke when I saved Kel's life. I know he felt it, too. But instead of accepting me and breaking the curse, he'd forced me back here.

To the human world. To Orca Cove.

This way is closed to you forevermore. His kiss still echoes on my lips, a tingling of frost that will never melt.

The rosebush shudders, chunks of ice falling off and breaking apart on the ground. Out crawls Papa. He gives me a wide smile, dusting off broken briars and dirt.

Going through the thicket doesn't take you to the Enchanted Vale anymore, just ten feet behind to another cluster of trees. I would know. I've crawled through it more times than I can count these last four months.

My father's brown hair is mussed, and dirt streaks across his nose. "I got a good one this time, Rosie."

"That's nice, Papa."

He carefully wraps a frozen rose blossom in some cloth, then tucks it in his large backpack. "Come on." Papa casts a glance back at me. "Let's go home."

But Orca Cove isn't home anymore. Home is waking to cherry blossoms floating in my room and tea with Marigold and Astrid. Home is being surrounded by books so old the pages are stiff, and the sweetest smile peering out from behind them. Home is the smell of salt and sea, and a laugh so joyful it always brings out my own. Home is the softest touch over my body, safety behind what others fear.

And home is arguing with a stupid icy bastard across a dinner table and pelting him with bread rolls, as my friends—my family—laugh with me.

I trail behind my father out of the forest, my mud-caked boots sinking in the damp soil.

Keldarion took that home from me.

And I hate him so much I think it's going to burn me alive.

2

ROSALINA

I t's springtime in Orca Cove, and everything is gray.

It's not like that's unusual. Heavy clouds hang overhead, covering any remnant of the rising sun. They look so full of rain they might burst.

That's how I feel, too. Gray and void on the outside but exploding within. Like there's something in me clawing to get out.

I can't let it.

But it's not only the thick clouds overhead making Orca Cove void of color; the people seem ashen; the wooden buildings dull. Like I've forgotten all the colors I've just learned how to see.

Papa and I walk down the street toward our little cottage on the outskirts of town. He vibrates with energy, a near skip in his step. He doesn't care about the side-eyes we get at his booming voice, or the way people cross the street to avoid walking near us. I don't care either. Not any more.

"Are you listening to me, Rose?" Papa waves a hand in front of my face. "First, we can grind the rose petal into the tonic from that tablet I dug up in Romania, or we can try the lullaby and dance from the children's book. We'd need to choose a good tree. You've got excellent intuition. Which tree should we pick?"

I nearly laugh out loud. My intuition has been nothing but wrong.

"Papa," I say, "I'm not skipping around a tree dancing and singing like I'm from some cursed musical."

He narrows his bright blue eyes, then sighs. "Fine. We'll try the tonic first."

A pang of guilt simmers in my gut, and I hold on to his arm and lean my head on his shoulder. We walk in step. Gulls call from the harbor, and I inhale the rich smell of pine. "Let's take the long way home past the willow tree."

If there's any silver lining to my gray world, it's that for the first time in my life, I feel connected to my father. I'd spent my twenty-six years feeling nothing but resentment for him, for leaving me alone while he went on his wild quests to enter the fae realm. Now, I'm his accomplice.

After Keldarion sent me away from the Enchanted Vale and closed my only way through, I stumbled back to my first home. The home before Castletree.

I expected it to be empty. For Papa to have sold my belongings and be off on one of his adventures.

What I found instead was the physical manifestation of grief.

The cottage was a mess: a torn-apart hovel littered with strange artifacts, unwashed cups of congealed coffee, and empty cans of beans. But George O'Connell was there, his usually full face gaunt, his tall form hunched over the kitchen table, hands shaking as he marked squares off a map of Briarwood Forest.

"Papa?" I whispered as I crept through the unlocked door.

His bloodshot eyes held mine. And he did something I'd never seen him do. He fell to the ground and cried.

I cried, too. For the father I left alone the same way he'd left me throughout my life. For the guilt of falling in love with a new world. For the sorrow of losing it.

The next day, all I'd wanted to do was stay huddled in bed, but Papa hadn't let me. Now, he had proof. And he had me. "Covered in fae magic, that's what you are," Papa had said. "Plus, if the residents of Castletree are as good-hearted as you say, then that connection will lead us back."

I'd been eager at first. So what if Keldarion had sent me away? He also claimed books were boring and made some sort of deal with the Prince of Thorns. He obviously wasn't the sharpest icicle in the cavern. And once the other princes discovered I wasn't at Castletree, they would come for me. Papa had said Keldarion sent him back to Orca Cove using the magical mirror inside Castletree. If the princes could use the mirror to connect to the human world, then it was only a matter of time before they found me.

But then the days turned to weeks, the weeks turned to months.

Keldarion didn't change his mind. The snow melted from our little yard, the ice on the lake cracked. Winter gave way to spring, and he didn't change his mind.

No one came for me.

I don't cry when I think of them anymore. Not even when I think about the way Farron would raise his eyebrows, glasses too low down his nose. Or the rush of warmth through my body when Dayton trailed a hand up my back, the giddy delight in wanting so much. Or the rough-spun fabric of Ezryn's cape that I clung to when the world seemed too big for me, or how in that moment I was grounded and sheltered and safe.

Or how I'd kissed Keldarion and known in every essence of me that I belonged to him. That he belonged to me.

"Hey, is that you, Rosalina?" A gruff voice tears me from my thoughts.

"Keep walking," Papa says. "Don't stop."

We're passing the *Seagull's Gullet Book Emporium*, my old place of work. Richard, my former boss, is writing on a chalkboard sign in coarse, boxy letters. Not like the care I'd spend thinking of book puns and doodling literary characters.

"Rosalina!" Richard calls. "I left you a couple of voice messages. Thought you might want to pick up some shifts. You can even do a few of the orders. Rosalina?"

"Sorry, Richard. Too busy."

He swears under his breath. "Chasing pixies with your father now, eh?"

"Faeries, actually," I say without looking back at him. "You should try reading a book for once."

Papa chuckles and ushers me down the road. I couldn't go back to working for Richard after living at Castletree. Not after I spent months with Astrid, Marigold, and the other staff and experienced what it was like to work with people who respect you. Who care for you.

Or at least I thought they did.

Why wouldn't Marigold and Astrid ask the princes to come for me? Don't they miss me like I miss them?

I don't even feel slightly bad that Richard is overwhelmed and the store's falling to shit. I'm done with his underpaid-overworked job. Keldarion sent Papa home with jewels, and he's been driving to the city a few hours away to pawn them off at various shops.

Keldarion gave me something precious, too. The necklace I wore to the Winter Solstice Ball.

The necklace that belonged to Keldarion's mother. I'll never sell it.

My throat grows tight. *They don't want me in the Enchanted Vale. Fine. But I have to give that necklace back. And I have to tell them goodbye. On my own terms.*

My father makes a clicking sound with his tongue. "The damned building looked better when it was closed up."

I take a deep breath, not wanting to look, but also never able to look away. The abandoned building I used to stare into every day isn't abandoned anymore. It's been purchased by the Poussin family. They're turning it into an Orca Cove gift shop for the summer tourists.

A huge red "GRAND OPENING NEXT MONTH" sign hangs on the door. Though the building is dark, I spot the merchandise: Orca Cove hoodies in every color, Poussin Hunting Lodge ball caps, and a creepy whale stuffie named Orky who will be the town's mascot.

It's fine. I could never have turned it into a library anyway. And besides, what library could compare to the one with bookcases so tall you needed a ladder? With maple trees growing among the stacks? With the golden-eyed man with the sweetest smile?

"Let's go," I whisper.

"Yes, let's go—Oh shit!" Papa pushes me to the side of the building.

I recognize that tone of voice. I quickly press myself against the wall and try to appear as unnoticeable as possible.

Headlights on full brightness careen down the road, going too quickly for our quiet town.

I know the rumble of that truck anywhere.

But to be sure, I peek around the corner. Lucas Poussin has his head out the window and looks right to left, his mouth in a scowl, red brows lowered.

I flatten myself back against the building and hold my breath, willing myself to be smaller, to be invisible.

When the roar of the truck ebbs away, Papa creeps out. "He's gone."

"Good spotting." I pull my sweater tighter around myself. "I don't have the energy to deal with him today."

I didn't really care when Lucas found out I was back in town and showed up at my door. I didn't even care when he gaslit me about the goblins, saying we both must have fallen and hit our heads. Whatever —if that's how he deals with the existence of fae and my father being right all these years, then good for him. I was even over the fact he'd left me for dead ... Which he also denied, saying he never would have left me, and how dare I think so little of him?

At that point, there was nothing left in me to give to Lucas at all. No hurt. No sadness. Just numbness.

But then he tried to shove the engagement ring on my finger.

A visceral thing, something like fear and disgust and rage all mixed together, burned in my chest. I snatched my hand away.

I can still hear the anger in his voice. The desperation to make sure he was still in control. "What are you doing, Pumpkin? Give me your hand."

I wish I could say I threw the ring at his face. That he didn't spend each night driving around town looking for me. That he feared me the way I feared him.

My right hand slowly drifts over my left wrist, feeling the raised scar where he once marked me. Then down to my sweater. The heavy engagement ring wears a hole in my pocket.

"I-I need more time. I'll let you know. Soon."

That's all I could manage. And what I've said every time he finds me walking down the street or in my yard. Papa does a good job of putting him off, but there's nothing Lucas loves more than the hunt.

I can practically imagine my head on his wall beside all the deer and elk and wolves, my eyes as glassy and dead as theirs.

I take a minute to shake off the memory, willing my heart to calm. I want to get out of here. Our cottage is on the horizon, small and dark. A little den for a prey animal to scuttle away into. A perfect place for me.

When I finally look up, I see my reflection in the dusty window.

Who am I?

Dark shadows creep under my eyes. My skin is pallid, hair limp. It's not the person I remember who lived at Castletree. The woman who made a bargain with the High Prince of Winter without fear. The woman who stood up to the most powerful fae in all the Enchanted Vale.

What is it about Lucas that makes me so afraid?

And what was it about Castletree that made me so strong?

I can't look at my reflection any longer. This half person. This shell, with only that visceral thing trapped within my ribs, frenzied and caged.

"It's okay, Rose." Papa touches my back and urges me to start walking. "Let's go home."

I nod, but I know I can't go home. *Vengeful. Escapist. Coward. Traitor.* The princes had been cursed for these sins. But am I any better?

Am I anything more than a terrified beast?

"This is a good tree, isn't it?" Papa says musingly. He stares at the willow tree, the one he stood before in my favorite picture of him and my mother.

Its branches are starting to fill with green leaves that blow like ribbons in the wind. "Yes, Papa," I say. "It is."

It's true. I know good trees.

3

ROSALINA

How do you return to somewhere that's not supposed to exist? How do you find your way to a place that feels more like a dream than reality?

My father and I have gone over it a thousand times now. When Papa crossed into the Enchanted Vale, and Lucas and I followed hours later ... Why had we been able to pass through? What was the difference?

Papa had told me he'd tried to return after Keldarion sent him back, but there was no path through the rosebush anymore. But I will find a way, if only to quell this ever-present ache in my chest.

I told Papa about my research in the Enchanted Vale and trying to find the princes' mates. I even explained how I know, heart and soul, that I am Kel's mate. And when the only evidence I presented was the burning feeling beside my heart, that invisible tug to him ... My father hadn't scoffed or called me crazy. No, only a deep understanding shone in his blue eyes.

Our cottage is a jumbled mess of papers and books, a testament to Papa's relentless pursuit of answers. Every surface is covered with his research notes. Shelves overflow with dusty tomes and ancient manuscripts. I used to feel resentment every time I saw them, knowing that his obsession with the fae robbed me of a normal childhood.

But now as I sort through his notes, I feel excitement. Perhaps this is how it had to be all along. Now it's not just his coffee cups and tins of beans that litter our workspace, but also my Diet Pepsi cans and Pop-Tart wrappers. Papa and I are in this together.

Keldarion closed that portal, but surely there are more portals in the world. That logic was why my father was always traveling, trying to find another way in. The Enchanted Vale is vast, but we don't have time to search every far corner of the world. If I can't help my princes before the roses in Castletree wilt, they'll remain beasts forever.

"What about placing the necklace Kel gave me outside during a full moon?" I ask, looking up from my book. "Perhaps it'll charge with magical energy."

"Good idea, Rosie." Papa adds some rose petals to a concoction he's brewing over a burner.

The current plan: open our own way to the Vale. That means using all the magic and folklore the human world has available.

A boom echoes through the cottage, and a puff of black smoke envelops my father. He coughs. I leap from my chair, seeing the flash of flame on his scarf.

"Papa!" I grab my glass of water and douse the small flame.

He gives a chuckle, face covered with soot. "Why, thank you. That one got away from me."

"What were you even trying to do—" My voice trails off as he unwinds his scarf, and something flashes in the light. "Mother's necklace."

"Ahh, yes." Papa takes off the necklace and places it in my hands. "She wore this always."

An ethereal hum flows through me. It's a moonstone necklace in the shape of a rose.

I've seen this symbol before. On the door of Castletree.

My fingers carefully slide along the edges, and I think of the necklaces worn by the princes. The glittering shell that brought me to the warmth of the Summer Realm, the golden leaf that helped me escape the rebellion to the safety of Castletree. A small wooden square, a crystallized snowflake. This can't be and yet...

My nail grazes a hidden seam, and with a small click, it opens. Inside is a mirror.

A wave of hope and joy washes over me like a burst of sunshine in my chest. The weight that's been smothering me lifts.

"A locket," my father says. "I never knew it opened."

"This could be it, Papa." And though I try to not let it, hope quivers its way into my voice. "All the princes had necklaces like this that returned them to Castletree."

"Can you make it work?"

I pull back my brown hair into a messy ponytail. My heart races, and everything sharpens to a new clarity. When I was in Castletree, the magic responded to me. The memory of a dangerous voice flickers inside my mind: *Trust your own instincts above all else.* Maybe the Prince of Thorns had some wisdom in his twisted words from the ball after all.

Carefully, I hold out the locket the way I'd seen Farron and Dayton do. Papa's gaze widens with my every move.

A loud knock sounds at the door, shaking the whole cottage. I cry out and flinch, and the locket flies from my hands.

"No!" Quickly, I throw myself to the ground. I snag the necklace and hold it protectively against my chest. "It's alright. It's alright."

The walls shake with another resounding knock. "Rosalina! I know you're home. Open up."

Lucas.

Papa pulls me up. "Don't fret." He leads me into my room. "I'll get him to leave."

More knocks rattle the cottage. I clutch my elbows, trying to stop myself from shaking. "I'm so stupid." Did I really think the locket would work for me? The High Princes are the most powerful fae in the Enchanted Vale. I'm a human. "I can't do *anything.*"

"Don't say that." My father casts another anxious look at the door.

"I don't understand. This isn't me." Tears flow down my face. "I was never afraid to speak my mind to the princes. When I thought I was trapped, I never stopped fighting."

Papa places a reassuring hand on my back.

"The fae princes are so powerful, but when they made me angry, I would tell them. I stood my ground out there—" I pause, gasping in air. "I don't understand why I can't do the same thing now. Why can't I tell him to leave? Why can't I tell him I don't want to marry him?"

My father gives me a soft expression, even as the knocking grows to a frantic pace. "Because you are afraid."

"But Lucas is only a man, and they were beasts."

"Perhaps your heart knows what to fear and what is safe. And it's hard to see a monster when he's proclaimed a hero."

My father's words settle deep within me, and I wipe my eyes. "I just wish I wasn't so scared."

"Your flame may simmer now, coals in a hearth. But it is there, of that I have no doubt. Do not be afraid of the fire within."

"I can't let you go out there for me."

"Nonsense. That's what fathers are for." He puffs out his chest. "I haven't always done right by you, but this I can do."

He closes the bedroom door behind him, and I let him face the battle I can't. I reach into my pocket, touching the ring. Even the thought of it near me feels so wrong.

I can't help but pull up my sleeve. There, carved into my arm: the scarred letters that go from forearm to wrist. The name Lucas.

I yank down the fabric, hiding the shameful secret. One I've kept from everyone in my life.

Only Lucas knows, and he'll never let me forget it.

But I'm not that girl he branded. Not anymore. The locket feels heavy in my hands. Maybe it won't work for me, but I have to try. Something led me to Castletree in the first place. Something inside me responded to the magic in the Enchanted Vale. And this locket is my best chance. Even if it doesn't work, I'll never stop trying.

But I can't have *him* here.

Papa and Lucas's argument drifts through the door. I know how it'll go ... They'll fight for a few more minutes, then Lucas will storm out. Then in a few days the whole thing will repeat, like watching a play I hate, but I'm strapped to my seat. I can't leave when the curtain goes down.

Unless somebody ends it.

Unless I end it.

I clutch the moonstone locket in my hand and leave my room.

4

ROSALINA

Lucas's eyes gleam as he takes me in, gaze sharpening, like I'm a frightened doe he's lining up in his crosshairs.

But he will not take me down. Not today. Not when I finally have a lead on how to get back to where I belong.

"We're busy right now," I tell him, hating the shake in my voice. The quirk of his smile when he hears it.

"There she is. Finally." Lucas runs a hand through his dark red hair.

My heartbeat quickens and nausea roils in my gut. I wish Kel, Ezryn, Dayton, or Farron were here.

"It's rude to avoid your fiancé." Lucas moves closer. My father tries to step in front of me, but Lucas pushes him.

I shove my free hand into my pocket, feeling the ring. This is it. I pull it out and stare down at the golden band, the gaudy diamond. "My answer is no."

He snorts a laugh, but there's no humor in his eyes. It's hard for me to believe I ever thought he was attractive. "Don't you see, Pumpkin? That's not a choice you get to make." He grabs my wrist, holding tight over my long sleeve, atop my scar. I cry out in pain as the pressure of his grip forces my hand open. My moonstone necklace falls to the ground, tinkling against the wood.

"Let her go!" Papa reaches for us.

Lucas ignores him and tugs me closer. "Ring or not, you've belonged to me since the moment I pulled you out of that frozen lake."

Saving someone's life does not grant them ownership over it. Keldarion told me that. After we saved each other. After my mate bond awakened.

"You know nothing of belonging to someone!" I snarl, yanking my arm away.

And maybe I don't either. But I am going to do everything in my power to find out. And that means returning to Castletree. To my princes.

I step back and throw the ring at Lucas's face.

He blinks, stumbling, but before he can regain his composure, Papa winds his fist, then delivers a sharp blow across his cheek. "Stay away from my daughter, you insufferable cur!"

"Fuck you, old man." Lucas slams my father so hard he falls across the table.

But Lucas never takes his eyes off me. His pupils darken with hunger and desire, a hunter stalking his prize. I will never give in to him again. He approaches me relentlessly until the sharp crunch of glass sounds across the room. He pauses for a moment and looks down at the broken necklace before kicking it away, sending pieces of moonstone skittering across the floor.

My hope destroyed under the heel of Lucas's boot.

"Come now, Pumpkin. This is getting ridiculous," Lucas says.

As I look from the broken necklace on the ground up to the face of the man I once thought I loved, something shatters inside me too.

No...

Ignites.

Warmth floods my chest. Call it fire. Call it power. Call it a wild beast, even. But with the power of a tempest, I look Lucas in the eyes and say: "Leave. Get out of my house. Get out of my life."

He flinches. "W-what's wrong with you…"

Cold sweat covers me as my body shakes, fear writhing inside my chest like a trapped animal. But it will not consume me today. I prowl forward. "I don't want to see you again."

He backs up onto the porch, blinking wildly, unsure what to say. A cold wind whips inside, wrapping around me like an embrace.

"Goodbye, Lucas." I pick up the ring from the ground and toss it right at his chest. "And I *hate* the name Pumpkin."

5

ROSALINA

"Careful. Careful!"

Papa shushes me. "I've got it. Now, I need a splinter. Triangle shaped. Quarter of an inch long. Do you see it?"

"This?"

"Atta girl."

My father's hands are steady as he uses tweezers to pluck the small fragment of moonstone from the tray where we've gathered all the broken pieces. Taking a deep breath to calm my shaking hands, I apply a bit of Super Glue to the tip of the shard. Papa adds it to the patch-work necklace.

I can't even bother to chide myself for how ridiculous we are right now. We're *Super Gluing* a possibly ancient, magical artifact back together. It's absurd. It's foolhardy.

It's my only hope.

My skin still feels on fire after the altercation with Lucas. Maybe the woman who came alive in the Enchanted Vale isn't so lost after all. Maybe there's something to having a bit of a beast inside you.

"It's taking shape," Papa mumbles. "All these years, I never knew it was a locket..."

"It belonged to Mom." I take a seat beside my father and place a hand on his arm. Gently, he sets his tools down. "Why did she have an item from the Enchanted Vale?"

He shakes his head. His brown hair is graying at the sides, his face weathered from wind and sun and lack of care. "You know we met on the archeological excavation in Cairo. She was the anthropologist assigned to our site and had a hell of a career before we met. Made me look like a greenhorn." He chuckles, and it's almost like I can feel a warmth radiating from him as he talks about her, like the long dormant coals of his soul spring to life. "Anya was a bit of a collector, or a packrat, as I liked to call her. She kept all sorts of things: gifts from the people she worked with, paintings from local artists, strange jewelry."

"But you told me she wore this every day," I urge.

He nods. "She said it was her first treasure."

I look down at the gleaming locket. All along, the key to the Enchanted Vale had been around my father's neck. Like the necklaces the High Princes always wore, this might be able to create a portal home.

My father picks up his tools and begins to work again. But I can't sit still. My knees shake, and my fingers tap on the table.

"Rosalina."

"Sorry." I clasp my hands in my lap to still them. "It's just … It's too much of a coincidence, isn't it? We're both drawn to Castletree, and Mom had this necklace all along."

"Indeed," Papa says, not taking his eyes off the broken pieces he glues back together. The swaying light above us buzzes and flickers. "In fact, I'm fairly certain it's the only reason your dear friend Keldarion imprisoned me."

His name sends shivers up my spine. "What?"

"He was quite intent on me leaving the castle until he saw my necklace." Papa narrows his eyes as he fits a tiny sliver back into place. "Perhaps he knows something we don't."

"That's Kel, alright. Thinks he knows everything."

"Reminds me of something your mother once told me." Papa's voice is even, focused. It's like I see him clearer than I ever have before. "Within the depths of knowledge, we find the vastness of our ignorance, and it is there that true wisdom begins to unfold."

"Papa," I say tentatively, "how come you're so certain Mom was taken by the fae? Ezryn said the fae don't steal humans. It's forbidden. She could have wandered into the Vale by accident and not been able to get out but—"

He closes his eyes, his rough hands too big for the delicate tools. "We lived in this very cottage, and Anya was so happy. She glowed with the radiance of the sun. She loved her work: adventuring, learning languages, studying different cultures. But she loved you above all else."

My eyes brim with tears. How different could my life have been if Anya O'Connell raised me? Papa didn't mention her much when I was growing up, but when he did, he would talk about her brash laughter, her sureness, her stubbornness. Well, I got the last one, but I wish I had some of the confidence.

"She disappeared the night of your first birthday. She seemed strange all day. Unlike herself. I thought it was just the emotions of her baby turning one. And right before midnight, she said she was going for a walk and would be right back. But I had a feeling. It's hard to describe. Your mother and I ... We would joke it was like we had a psychic connection; we were so in tune with one another. I could tell something was wrong. So, I followed her."

"I hope there was a babysitter," I joke. "Otherwise, you're admitting you left a one-year-old by themselves."

"Nanny Eve was with you at the time, rest her soul."

My childhood nanny passed away when I was five; though I don't remember much, I know I spent a lot of time with her in those five years while my father was away. "What happened when you followed Mom?"

He closes his eyes. "What I saw has been burned into my mind ever since."

I take his hand, silently encouraging him to continue.

"I watched your mother walk deep into the Briarwood Forest. She loved to walk among the boughs, but it was so late at night. At one point, I thought I lost her. But then, just barely visible in the light of the full moon, I saw her kneeling on the ground. Before her was a single red rose."

Red roses ... like on the thornbush that led me to the Enchanted Vale. "And then?"

"And then it was like the moon had fallen from its perch in the sky." My father's voice grows deep and haunted. His eyes close, and I squeeze his hand to let him know I'm here. "A luminous glow erupted, so bright I could barely see. It was all I could do to stay standing. In that burst of light, I caught sight of it."

My father screeches his chair back and storms to the window. "For a single moment, I saw a being of terrible power, one not of this realm. And then your mother was gone."

My heart thuds. I know better than most mortals the horrifying capabilities of the fae. But what would one have wanted with my mother?

"I must have passed out because I woke up at dawn. All that was left of your mother was that single rose and this necklace." He looks back to the broken moonstone.

"I'm sorry, Papa."

He shakes his head. "No, I'm sorry. Sorry you never got to know her. She was magnificent." A soft, sad smile creeps up his face. "You're a lot like her."

"No." I get up and walk over to him. "I'm sorry for never believing you. For never standing up for you. But I have your back now." I feel that thing inside my chest, that tightly wound courage I unleashed on Lucas. It draws me toward the necklace. "And we're going to return together."

Papa nods and sits down, immediately getting back to work. "I was no father of the year. You deserved better than I gave you. You still do."

"Enough mushy stuff," I joke. "More gluing."

Papa laughs under his breath, but before he picks up his tools, his eyes grow distant. "Rose?"

"Yes, Papa?"

"I know I haven't done anything to gain your trust, but please..." His voice cracks. "Trust me when I say I know your mother is still alive. I *know* it. In here." He thumps his heart.

"I believe you." And it's true. Because there's something in that exact space telling me I *need* to get back to Castletree. Even if no one wants me there.

But as much as I want my dad and I to get the answers we seek; I can't give myself hope yet. Even if Papa crafts the necklace back together, the princes each wielded their own magic that is connected to Castletree. *But that magic answered to me too. Castletree showed me the memories hidden within its bark.*

I need to try again.

Another few tense moments go by before Papa says quietly, "Okay. Everything's reattached."

I hover over his shoulder, staring down at the glittering relic. Though it's cracked and dripping with glue, it's still beautiful in a broken way.

"It has to be you, Rosalina," Papa whispers.

"I know." My eyes squeeze shut. "I need to give myself as good of a shot as I can."

With careful, delicate hands, I build an altar of magic: everything I have that once belonged to the Enchanted Vale. First, I lay down Keldarion's mother's necklace, remembering who I was when I last donned it. *The Lady of Castletree.* Then I carefully place the thorn crown, a gift from the Prince of Thorns, the fae man draining Castletree of its magic. But his thorns had answered me: they helped me save Keldarion's life. I run a gentle finger over the dagger-sharp thorns. The crown had become a dagger when I needed to break the ice but had returned to this shape.

My only remaining items are the ones I wore on my back the day Kel banished me: Ezryn's old clothing we'd found in his cache when we took shelter for the night. I bring the shirt and pants up to my nose, inhaling deeply. Despite the many months, I can still smell him: the earthy scent of the Briar, deep and woody like a dense forest, tempered by a gentle sweetness.

I look out the window. Dandelions burst under the late morning light. Green grass has fought and won against the frost. I even saw a crocus out back two days ago. Winter is gone, and spring has come.

I do not know how I will face a new season without them.

"Are you ready, Rose?"

I nod, and my father carefully places the rose-shaped locket into my hands. I sit on the floor before my altar and close my eyes.

Carefully, I open the locket. "Castletree," I whisper, "if your magic can reach me here, please send it. I need your help." I let my body empty. Everything except that smoldering in my chest. "I need to see them."

Let my body be your vessel. Let your magic run through me. Let me do this thing, just this once.

With one hand, I hold out the open locket. With the other, I drag my fingers over the smooth jewels of the necklace, the jagged edges of the crown, and the rough fabric. My hands catch on the clothes, and I bring it to my chest. Tears stream down my face, and I inhale deeply. Wet earth and rain and the Briar. I smell the Briar ... I smell him.

"Rosalina." My father's voice.

I blink my eyes open. A shimmering light appears before me, a soft glow emanating from the very air itself. I scramble forward as the light coalesces into a shape, a pool of liquid silver. The edges of the light take on definition forming...

Forming a window.

And staring back at me, rain ringing off his silver armor, is Ezryn.

25

6

ROSALINA

I s ... Is this real?

Is Ezryn, High Prince of Spring, actually in front of me right now? The glowing light shimmers at the edges, but the middle is clear as a window. Looking down, as if peering at me from above, is Ezryn.

"Ez..."

He tilts his head, and though I can't see his true face behind the silver helm, I feel his confusion. "R-Rose?"

The sound of my name in his raspy voice—tinged with the metallic reverberation of his helmet—is all too familiar. All too right.

I pitch forward. "Ez!" My fingers grasp the shining light—and scrape against the image. An invisible barrier blocks me from the fae realm.

"What's wrong with it?" I turn to my father. "It's supposed to be a portal."

My father only gulps and shakes his head. "I-I don't know! Could be the moonstone isn't a strong enough conduit now that it's cracked. Or the magic isn't right—"

I fling myself to the window, palms flat on the unseen barricade between us. Home. Home, home, home, it's through here. And Ezryn is *right* in front of me, and I can smell him, and I know what it would feel like to have his warm hands caress my skin.

"How is this possible?" Ezryn's voice grows more frantic, and he looks back and forth, grasping for me. His gloved hand bangs against the barrier. "Where are you? Are you in danger?"

"No," I cry, eyes welling with tears. "I'm safe. I'm home."

Ezryn gives a shaky laugh, a sound I've never heard from him before. "You're home? Stars. Okay, wait for me. I'm not far from Castletree. I'll head straight there. When did you get back? Doesn't matter. I'm coming—"

"No." My heart rages within my chest. "I mean, I'm home in Orca Cove."

His fingers scrape down the barrier and his head falls forward, as if his helm is suddenly too heavy. "Oh."

Images flash through my mind: his warm hands healing my ragged flesh, him sneaking chocolate muffins underneath the table, his steady presence as he named me Lady of Castletree before Kel's vizier. For so long, I thought he'd been avoiding me. Or that he hated me. But the night of the ball, I swore … I swore I was so wrong about everything.

"Why are you tormenting me?" he whispers, his voice a broken rasp.

"Tormenting you?" My hands fall from the barrier. Tears stream down my face, but I don't care. "Why didn't you come for me? I thought you would keep me safe."

His whole body shudders. "You left. Keldarion said—"

"Keldarion *banished* me," I half-sob, half-snarl. "He wouldn't even let me say goodbye. He sent me away. I've been trying to get back to you and everyone at Castletree, but I can't figure out how—"

Ezryn goes still. Stiller than I have ever seen him. For a second, I think the image beyond the window has completely frozen, and I've lost all connection to the Enchanted Vale. But then a rumble more beast than fae erupts from him. "Keldarion did *what?*"

"Ezryn." His name on my lips is the only thing keeping me together. I feel like I'm in the Briar with him, the rain pounding upon my skin. "I want to go home."

"Rosalina, I—" Ezryn reaches forward, and for a second, I clutch the tip of his leather glove. Then a sputter sounds, and the light bursts into blinding white, before fizzling out altogether.

Mist trails up from the cracked moonstone, and my body suddenly feels weak.

But I look at my hand, wet with rainwater. And I know deep within that smoldering place inside me.

I will tear apart the veil between our worlds to get back to them.

7

EZRYN

My body is entirely numb, mind void of thought. I have to push everything down, at least for a moment, or else I will shatter.

The pond is dark and empty where only a moment before, her face had rippled in water and light. At first, I'd thought it was just my mind playing tricks on me again. How many nights have passed where I've heard her phantom voice calling to me from the dark?

I thought you would keep me safe.

The tears streaming down her face … The broken sound of her voice. She thinks I abandoned her.

I *did* abandon her.

Keldarion banished me.

I can do it no longer. I can't keep the feelings at bay. A guttural howl looses from my chest, and the Briars quiver with fleeing animals. My wolf strains to break free from my flesh, but I keep it contained with pure stubbornness.

I want to see Keldarion's traitorous face with my own eyes.

Dark clouds swirl overhead, making it appear nightfall in the Briar, though I know the sun is somewhere behind the storm. Rain pelts down upon my armor but I can't feel the cold or the wet.

There is only rage.

Every reckless decision, every deceitful act, every moment of apathy, I have stood behind Keldarion. Made excuses for him. Protected him. Forgiven him.

Farron's quiet voice plays in my head: *"Kel … Where is she?"*

"Gone," Kel had said. *"She'd had too much. After she learned the truth of the Enchantress, she said she couldn't stay here anymore. She wanted to return to the human world and forget the fae. I took her back where she belongs. We must honor her wish and pretend she never came into our lives."*

Another feral yell reverberates from beneath my helm, and I snatch out my sword, swiping uselessly at the briars. My pace quickens, mud squelching beneath my gait.

I can't think of her huge brown eyes wavering. The way she said my name. The way I left her broken and deserted.

Because I trusted Keldarion.

My cape snaps in the harsh wind, and sharp thorns scrape against my armor. I push out of the thicket and stare up at Castletree. It's been months since I've been home; I couldn't stand the silence, or the dullness in Farron's eyes, or watching Dayton self-destruct again and again.

Thorns crawl across every inch of the bridge as I storm toward the door, but I barely notice. I've been living in the Briar for so long now, they are familiar company.

But the ice cracking beneath my boots … That's new. Looking up at the condition of the castle, I don't feel empathy.

I feel disgust.

That selfish bastard.

I throw open the door and stride into what used to be home. It's so dark and cold, it makes me want to bring the whole cursed place to the ground. It's nothing less than the master of Castletree deserves.

A familiar face pokes around the corner into the entrance hall. Marigold's eyes widen. She's wearing her usual pink apron, but it's stained and dirty. "Your Highness! My goodness, you're back! It's been months. I'll prepare your room straight away—"

I walk past her with barely a glance. "I'm not staying."

My heavy boots ring upon the glistening floor. A few more eyes poke around as word passes to the servants that the High Prince of Spring has returned. They all crouch back, none so brave as Marigold to approach me. I don't blame them. I can only imagine what I look like.

A towering being of dark metal, scarred by monsters and stained with blood, with vengeance in each step.

I start up the stairs when a quiet voice breaks through the echoing silence. "Ez? Y-you're back."

Farron stands at the top of the landing. He's a mess. There are dark circles under his eyes, and I swear he's wearing the same tunic he was when I left months ago. A scraggly bit of scruff covers his jaw.

Deep within my chest, there's a part of me that wants to grab him and pull him to me. Apologize for leaving him here in the cold alone. Tell him it's going to be okay.

But that part is too buried beneath the scorching rage.

"Ez?" He stands in my path when I don't answer.

I don't even think. I shove him in the chest, causing him to stumble. I keep walking toward the Winter Wing.

"Well, well," a voice slurs, "if it isn't the long-lost faceless wonder."

Dayton leans against the entrance to the Summer Wing. Like usual, he wears only a patterned wrap low on his hips and nothing else. Stars, he's thin. At least by his standards. His chest, usually broad and bursting with muscle, seems narrow, his normally tanned skin pale and sallow. *What happened to us?*

But I know what happened.

And I know whose fault it is.

Ice shatters beneath the force of my boots; I am a spring gale. I am the thunder and the lightning. I am a reckoning.

Winter has taken Castletree.

It is time for Spring's melt.

Idly, I notice Farron and Dayton following me, and behind them, two of the staff. Marigold and Astrid.

I fling open the door to Keldarion's chambers. Despite it being day, a giant white wolf lies before me, its head down, eyes closed. If possible, it's even more of a monstrosity than I last saw it: bright blue icicles jut out from the shoulder blades, and the ice covering the floor is marred with long claw marks. Clouds of mist form in the frigid air around its nostrils, the only sign it's still alive.

"Keldarion," I roar. The audience behind me, even the two High Princes, tremble.

The white wolf barely raises its head, cracking open a single glowing blue eye, then lowers its head again.

My comrade. My best friend. My brother.

My traitor.

For all else, I have turned my gaze. But not for this.

Not after what he did to her.

With the raw frenzy of a spring storm, I grab the wolf by the fur of its back and throw. The massive white beast sails through the air, breaking through the huge glass window, and lands in a heap below in the gardens.

Dayton and Farron cry out and grab my arms, but I tear loose.

Outside the window, the wolf gives a shudder, its body receding, shimmering into that of a fae man. He struggles up to his forearms and glowers at me through a curtain of white hair.

I stride over to his bed, reach underneath to retrieve the discarded Sword of the Protector, and chuck it out the broken window.

"Ezryn," Dayton cries, "are you mad?"

"What are you doing?" Farron asks.

I turn to my brothers and hold each of their gazes. I know they can't see my eyes, but they can feel it. The determination. The vengeance. "Kel sent her away."

8

DAYTON

He sent her away. Kel fucking sent her away.

Fury and despair mix inside of me. I can barely see straight through my ale-blurred vision, but I glimpse Ezryn. His metal body thrums with anger, shaking as if he's about to jump out of his own skin.

He sent her away.

"So, she didn't want to leave us?" Farron asks softly, the first whisper of hope I've heard in his voice in months.

"No." Ezryn storms out the door. "Rosalina used magic to speak to me. I don't know how. She said she's been trying to find her way back to us."

"Gods Below." I tangle my hands in my hair, doubling over. Nausea roils in my gut.

"Get up." Farron grabs me under the shoulders and the contact of his arms on my bare chest has me reeling. How long has it been since I've had him? My mind feels foggy. Weeks? Months? "Snap out of it, Day!"

He snatches something off a dresser, and suddenly I'm drenched in a spray of cold water. Well, that's a shock to the system. I squeeze my eyes shut and take a deep breath. "Okay, okay."

Farron and I dart into the hall after Ez. It's harder to get around with the huge number of new briars that have grown in the last few months. Fuck the Prince of Thorns.

Ez is almost to the main staircase, taking strong, deliberate steps. He pauses as he passes a huddled Astrid and Marigold. "Grab the master's clothes. I will not fight a naked man."

Farron and I exchange a look before following Ez out the main castle door to the grounds. Immediately, I'm hit with a wave of sleet and cold wind. Winter's last attempt at the coming spring. The clouds are so dark, I almost think it's night. But of course, it's not. I'm a man, not a beast.

We circle Castletree. I glance at Farron, and I'm pretty sure those are tears mixed with the rainwater on his cheeks. "Ez just threw Kel out a window, and you're smiling?"

He wipes his face with the heel of his palm and grins up at me. "Rosie didn't leave us. She doesn't hate us. Aren't you happy?"

I … I don't know what to feel. Because I honestly don't know what I've been feeling these last four months. In fact, I've been doing everything in my power to not feel at all.

Because when Kel returned without Rosalina, and I knew I'd never see her again … That pierced something so deep inside me I thought I was going to die. And equally heartbreaking was watching Farron. For the first week he didn't read, didn't do anything, just stared glassy-eyed at the wall. Then he started going over everything, every moment that may have led to her leaving us. I wanted to help him. Really, I did. But when he said stuff like that, the ache in my chest started to grow.

It's better to feel nothing at all.

We round the corner and see Kel kneeling on the ground among the overgrown topiaries and briars. His long white hair falls in messy strands over his muscular shoulders. The Sword of the Protector lies untouched before him.

He's a man.

I can't remember the last time I've seen Kel as a man. He's been the white wolf day and night since she left.

Not left. Since he sent her away.

Behind us, Marigold and Astrid scurry up, bundles of cloth in their arms. Ezryn grabs the fabric and tosses it at Kel's feet.

Keldarion gives a long sigh. "Fuck." Then he stands, tugging on a pair of thick leather pants and a loose black shirt.

Kel runs a hand through his wet hair, then stares at us all in turn. For someone who was recently flung out a window, he doesn't look angry. Only exhausted, a bone-deep weariness.

Ezryn's grip tightens on his black sword. Now there's anger, and I can't even see his goddamned face. "Why did you send her away?"

No expression passes across Kel's hard features before he turns away from Ez, voice rough from lack of use as he mutters, "I did what you all could not."

Ezryn grabs Kel's shoulder. "You took away our choice. You took away *her* choice!"

Kel simply brushes his hand off. There's only the ringing of rain clinking off the Spring Prince's armor.

"Rosalina found a way to contact me. The magic of the Enchanted Vale calls to her," Ezryn says. "She wants to come home."

Kel stills at that. His shoulders tense. "She is home."

"No, not yet." Ezryn turns away from Keldarion. "But I'm going to get her. Brothers, are you with me?"

He looks at Farron and me.

I blink, stunned. Ezryn has never disobeyed Keldarion. Not even when he should have, like during the War of Thorns.

But he's forging his own path now.

For Rosalina.

The answer blazes in Farron's golden eyes, and it's the same one radiating through my entire being. "Of course we are," I say.

A crystalline sound rings throughout the gardens, the long echo of cracking ice, and I look past Ez to Keldarion. He's picked up the sword Ezryn threw before him. He hasn't held that sword in twenty-five years, but he's holding it now, and damn if he isn't a scary-ass motherfucker.

The ice blade shimmers blue in his hand, casting sharp lines over his jaw and white hair. The rain around him turns to shards of ice as he snarls: "I will end everyone in the Vale before allowing *her* back here."

Fear courses through my body, and Farron grips my arm. But Ezryn holds no such compunction and raises his sword. "Then you'll have to start with me."

Kel shakes his head, then rushes forward, and the sound of steel meeting steel reverberates throughout the gardens.

"We've got to get in there," I groan.

Farron's eyes are wide as he takes in the scene. Kel and Ez move almost too fast to track, swords clashing, feet moving as they dance across the grounds, neither giving an inch.

"What are we supposed to do?" Farron shakes his head, long wet strands of brown hair falling in his face. "Kel is—"

"Come on, Fare. It's three against one. There's no way we can lose." I grip tight to his shoulder. "For Rosie."

His throat bobs, then he says, "For Rosie."

With that, he digs into his orange tunic. "I'm certain I put a good spell in here." He pulls out a soggy piece of paper and murmurs a low chant. A dancing spiral of leaves and wind swirl from his palm. They slam between Kel and Ezryn, jolting them apart for an instant before falling to the ground in a sodden heap.

"Oh fiddlesticks," Farron mutters before pulling out more soggy paper from his tunic. "I thought that was a better one."

Each High Ruler learns a way to channel the vast amount of magic we're blessed with. Ez and I usually manifest ours into physical strength. Farron prefers to use spells, either from within himself or using written incantations as a conduit.

But Keldarion...

Keldarion's a master of both.

"Guess it's my turn." I reach for my swords before realizing they're back in my room. I only have time to mutter a quick curse before a torrent of hail and sleet strikes me in the chest, and I fly into a hedge.

"Get out there and fight!" Soft hands push me up. I blink to see Marigold huddled in the bushes, Astrid beside her. "You've got to bring her back."

I gently touch my aching head. "But I don't have my swords!"

"Are you a gladiator of the Summer Realm or not?" Astrid narrows her red eyes. "I want my best friend back, so don't give up, okay?"

My head whirls as I stand. Ez and Kel move like flashes of lightning. Farron's doing ... I don't know what the fuck he's doing. Discarded pieces of paper lay littered on the ground, along with red mushrooms and strange spiky twigs.

I rush past him. "Lose the paper, Fare. Feel for your magic."

He gives a frustrated sigh, running up beside me. "It's not so easy."

At least there are no signs of Farron's beast coming out. That thing could end us all.

Farron rushes up to stand beside Ez, and I twirl behind Keldarion. I could probably hold my own against him if I wasn't so drunk. And if I had my swords. But I guess it's going to have to be fists and praying that all the instincts of fighting in the Sun Colosseum come back to me.

Kel's sword flashes blue as it clangs against Ezryn's obsidian blade, sending chips of ice sparkling into the air.

"Let us leave, Kel!" Farron abandons his incantations and instead swipes his palms through the air: a line of fire ignites in a whoosh, but it's doused by the rain as quickly as it came.

Keldarion doesn't spare him a second glance, his attention solely faced on the mountain of metal in front of him.

Perfect. He's distracted.

I strike, landing a powerful blow against Kel's back. At least, I mean to—but he dodges, pushing both Farron and Ezryn away in a gale of ice before spinning to face me.

The Prince of Winter pauses for a moment—a moment where I should be able to strike, dodge, do bloody *something*—but my mind is so muddled I can't think. Kel gives a dissatisfied grunt and knocks me on the side of the head with the hilt of his sword, grips my shoulders, and heaves me through the air.

I smack against the ground hard, rolling until I land in a pile beside Ezryn and Farron. Kel's frozen their feet in a patch of ice.

37

Ezryn gives a mighty yell and brings his sword down, shattering the ice.

"Get me out of here!" Farron gasps, trying to pry free.

Stars cloud my vision. "I don't have a weapon. I don't—"

Ezryn charges, his great sword held high. Keldarion deflects the blow. "You don't know what you're doing, Ezryn."

"What I know," Ezryn lands a cut along Kel's arm, "is the Vale calls to her!"

Kel glances down from the cut on his arm to Ezryn. "You think I can't feel that?" His speed increases, a strength and fury in his movements like none I've ever seen. "You think it does not haunt me day and night?"

Ezryn tries to match Kel's new pace, but I see it. Ez's slowing, his movements growing sloppier as he tries desperately to stop Kel's advance.

Then Kel lands a punishing blow. Ice and snow and magic erupt from him, and Ezryn's sword clatters to the ground. Kel grabs him, holding the glittering ice sword to Ezryn's neck, right between the gaps of his armor.

"If you want to stop me," Ezryn's metallic voice echoes through the mask, not a trace of fear, "you're going to have to kill me."

Kel's ice-blue eyes flash with something so feral, so utterly primal and unhinged, I think he might just do it.

But in the end, he releases a long sigh and drops Ezryn to the earth in a heap. He takes one step away before his whole body shifts into the massive white wolf. "If you truly care for the girl," he growls, "then you will leave her be."

Ice trails behind the white wolf's every step as he prowls back into the castle.

Ezryn stands, then looks at Farron and me sprawled out on the ground. "Well, are you coming?" he asks. "We're going to get our girl."

9

ROSALINA

Dancing around the willow tree in the middle of town at dusk on a Sunday is not exactly how I imagined my life going. But after you've spent months living in a castle with a bunch of shapeshifting faeries, at some point, you just have to say fuck it.

I prance around my father's beloved willow tree, wearing a woven crown of daisies and daffodils. At the base of the tree is my backpack full of our Enchanted Vale possessions. I carry a wicker basket filled with a mixture of ground mushrooms, dried lavender, and carrot seeds, and sprinkle it like I'm the most cursed flower girl you could possibly imagine. I'm also wearing my favorite 'This Shirt Glows Blue When Orcs Are Near' hoodie, but that's for my own aesthetic, and has nothing to do with the ritual. Maybe Mom's necklace, tucked under my shirt, will help.

"My legs are getting tired," I say in a sing-song voice to my father, who's prancing right in front of me with his own basket.

Most of the various experiments we've tried over the last few months have been based on ancient folklore from across the world. This is from some creepy children's book Papa found on one of his visits to the countryside of England. But at this point I'll try anything.

Even if that anything means practically every resident of Orca Cove has gathered to point and whisper as Papa and I continue our ridiculous display.

"Keep going!" Papa looks back at me with a wild grin. "We're powering this tree with fae magic!"

This morning, I would never have submitted myself to such humiliation or such foolish hope. But now, I don't give a damn who's watching or how stupid this might be.

I saw Ezryn. And he saw me.

Was it my own foolish hope that he'd sounded happy to see me? Relieved?

What exactly has happened at Castletree since I was there?

I take a deep breath of the early spring air, remembering the sight of him, his huge frame like a sentinel. At least he was still a fae; the curse hasn't taken them yet.

Out of the corner of my eye, I catch the disgusted looks of the townsfolk. My old boss, Richard, has his hands on his hips and shakes his head. One lady quickly ushers her young daughters past us. *Go ahead and stare,* I think. *I've seen colors you can only imagine.*

But one color emerges out of the crowd, a face red with anger. Lucas shoves through the onlookers and stomps toward us.

"Keep dancing, Papa," I say. "Don't stop."

My heart hammers, and my throat grows tight. I sent him away earlier. I can do it again.

Lucas blocks my path and yanks the wicker basket out of my hand, tossing it to the ground. The face I once thought so handsome is marred by a bruise across the cheekbone where Papa slugged him. "Stop right now. You're humiliating me."

"Then leave," I say.

"I will not have my future wife prancing about like some sort of hippie heathen," he snarls.

"Good thing I'm not going to be your wife then." I reach for my basket.

Lucas slams his foot down on it, breaking apart the wicker.

"Get out of here, boy," Papa bellows. "She told you once. She told you twice. If she has to say it again, I'll remove your useless ears."

"Careful, Papa," I whisper, but it's too late.

Lucas turns to the town. "For years, we've forgiven this man's delusions. We've always thought of him as just a harmless old eccentric. But this morning, he did this!" He points to the bruise on his face.

The trapped coals within me light ablaze again. "You deserved it!"

"This man is a danger to himself, to Orca Cove, and to his daughter." Lucas's fiery gaze lands on me. "We must separate them for her own safety."

I stumble away from Lucas, but he grabs me by the back of my neck. My whole body goes rigid, his touch paralyzing. The flower crown falls from my head.

"You can't talk to her like that," Papa roars. He charges toward us, but two of Lucas's hunting pals step out of the crowd and grab his arms. "Rosalina!"

"Get off of him!" I scream. "Someone help!"

But all of Orca Cove looks down, their faces shrouded in shame. Because of Lucas? Or because of the embarrassing O'Connells?

"Listen to your fiancé, Rosalina dear," a woman calls. "He'll take care of you."

"He's not my fiancé," I snap and drive my foot down onto Lucas's. He yelps and lets me go. I quickly grab my backpack and sling it on. I won't let him destroy these items like my basket.

"Run, Rosalina!" Papa cries, struggling in the grasp of the two burly men. "Run!"

Breath comes ragged from my throat as I sprint away. Lucas swears behind me, and I hear him give an awkward chuckle. "She's worn herself out caring for her father. I'll make sure she's okay."

I barely get five steps before Lucas yanks the back of my sweatshirt, then throws a powerful arm over my shoulders. To the crowd, it probably looks like an embrace. But inside, it feels like he's clamped chains around me.

"Enough, Rosalina," Lucas whispers. "You are *mine*. Agree to marry me and put on the ring in front of all these people."

"Never."

Lucas pulls me tighter against him. I feel like I'm pressed against thousands of worms. "Do you see those two men holding your father? That's Laughy and Aldridge. Old buddies of mine."

"I know them," I spit. "No better than thugs."

"Yeah, well, those thugs beat the shit out of a guy who cheated me in cards. Imagine what they'll do to your father."

Tears prick my eyes. "You wouldn't."

"I fucking would." All the time, he keeps looking up at the throng of people, plastering on a smile. They probably have deluded themselves into thinking he's whispering sweet nothings into my ear. Can't they see my face? Can't they hear my cries? Or do they just not care?

I look at my father, getting pulled further and further away from the crowd toward the Poussin Hunting Lodge. No ... I can't let him get hurt. Not because of me.

"Accept the reality," Lucas says, his voice an eerie whisper. "There is no one else for you. You'll always be my little Pumpkin."

I close my eyes. There's no choice to be made. I'll do anything to protect my father. I take in a shaky breath—

A murmur trembles through the crowd and a couple gasps erupt. I blink my eyes open and stare. The crowd has parted. And walking down the street toward me, the blaring sun at their backs, are three towering men.

"Who the fuck are they?" Lucas snaps.

I squint against the sun. Who *are* they? I can't make out their faces yet, but there's something odd about them.

They're dressed like they walked out of the nineties.

The tallest one on the left looks like he just left the slopes, wearing a ski suit of vibrant purple, pink, and green. A matching neon ski mask covers his entire face, complete with huge orange goggles with tinted lenses.

The one on the right wears baggy acid-washed jeans, topped with a huge shirt covered in colorful squiggles and geometric shapes. His face is totally covered in shadow from his oversized holographic bucket hat, but I see auburn waves peeking out from underneath.

But all eyes are on the one in the middle. Even Lucas is squinting and staring at him. He's wearing the tightest jeans I've seen in my entire life, the denim hugging his huge thighs. I swear I could see more, but a leather fanny pack covers his hips. A fucking *fanny pack*. Who are these people? A black turtleneck envelops his torso, complete with a gold chain.

I should use this distraction to get away, but I'm as entranced as everyone else. I squeeze my eyes shut, then open them, fighting against the sun's glare.

Then it comes into focus.

Not my vision, but my heart.

These are not just three weirdos with totally outdated fashion.

These are *my* weirdos.

"Ezryn! Dayton! Farron!" My voice carries crystal clear through the air.

They look up from the crowd.

I see them so clearly now: Farron's golden eyes sparkling in the fading light, his mouth half-open, my name upon his lips. Dayton in the middle, a strange, genuine smile breaking across his mouth, strands of blond hair falling loose from his long ponytail. And Ezryn, face still hidden from view, but the stance of his body changing, his gloved hand reaching for me.

They came.

The High Princes of Castletree came for me.

10

FARRON

I'd thought it really was the end. Castletree had held onto a bit of hope for the last twenty-five years, but that hope disappeared when she did.

But as I stare at her now, her messy brown hair trailing across that beautiful face, it's like the sun has dawned again.

Rosalina. Our Rosie.

"Who the fuck is she with?" Dayton growls under his breath.

"I told you I should have brought my sword," Ezryn says huskily, his voice clearer out of the fabric mask than his usual metal helm.

"You know what Marigold said," I whisper back. "We have to blend in."

We'd been ready to take the mirror to Orca Cove right after the altercation with Keldarion, but Marigold had chastised us: "You think you three are going to waltz into the human world dressed like you walked out of one of Rosalina's storybooks? You should at least *try* to fit in."

None of us have ventured to the mortal realm since the curse, over twenty-five years ago, but Marigold found some garments from the last journey. Though looking around now, these humans certainly have lost their penchant for color.

I give my head a shake to better focus on what the other princes are saying, I've been too caught up in the shimmer of Rosie's eyes as she looks at each of us. But then I see it.

A man has his arm around her.

Anger burns hot and bright inside of me, like a flame fueled by a gust of wind. She's obviously in distress, cheeks stained with tears. "Get off her," I yell, but it doesn't come out in words, but a primal growl.

"Easy, Fare." Dayton touches the back of my neck. The feeling is electric, one of the few times his skin has been on mine in months. "We'll handle it."

"I. Want. My. Sword," Ezryn says on his other side.

Dayton sighs. "When did I become the reasonable one?" He raises his hands before him. "We'll break his nose and be on our way."

We run, the crowd doing nothing to stop us. They merely stare at us agape; I wonder why these strange humans find us to be of such interest. I mentally file these observations away for further study. Out of the corner of my eye, I notice a tall older fellow in a brawl with two younger, burly men. I think of helping him, but he seems to be holding his own just fine.

The man with his arm around Rosalina notices us. Rosie screams for us again, but he throws a hand over her mouth and drags her behind a boarded-up building to the right.

Dayton lets out an animalistic growl. "Fine, I'm with you. This guy dies."

Breath comes ragged out of my throat. All this time, I thought she'd wanted to leave us. That she would be safer in the human world. But now I see...

Humans are just as monstrous as the fae.

"He took her in here," Ez says, waving us behind the building. The human onlookers are scattering. I'm not sure if we've made them nervous or they've lost interest now that the red-haired man is out of sight.

Behind the building, there's only a wooden door with a big brass knob. Ez tries it. "He locked it."

"Get a little creative," Dayton snaps. He places both hands on the knob and pulls. His shirt is so tight, I can see the muscles bulge.

With a terrible *creak*, the old door yanks from the hinges. Dayton tosses it away, and we run in.

The building is dark, the only light drifting between the slats of the boarded-up windows. It's one big room, covered in half-opened boxes and partially set-up shelves. I recognize the stuffed replica of the majestic orca whale, but this is a terrifying version, the eyes gaping at unseen horrors.

Standing in the middle of the room is Rosalina and the red-haired man. His face looks nearly possessed, a demon of wrath and violence. He's so focused on her and his rage, he doesn't even notice us, despite the sound the door made.

Rosalina … My heart clenches, and I stagger forward, knees weak. She appears almost unfamiliar, scared and shrunken. I've seen her afraid at the Winter Solstice Ball or when my wolf nearly tore her leg off. But I've never seen that look of surrender on her face.

My breath feels too full for my lungs, my blood too hot. That's not my Rosalina. What has this man done to her?

What have we done to her? We've left her. I believed Kel over myself. Even though I knew, deep within my heart, Rosalina wouldn't want to leave Castletree, her friends, her work.

Wouldn't want to leave me.

But I'd been afraid Kel was right. Too afraid to question it.

A vicious snarl tears from my lips, my body shaking with the raw power of my anger.

The man's got her left wrist clasped in one hand and a knife in the other. "You don't want to wear my ring? Fine. I'll brand you another way."

Ezryn steps forward, voice gruff and haunted. "You have a choice. You can walk away now, or we'll rid you of your ability to walk at all."

Rosalina stares at us. Tears shimmer down her face. "You came."

For a moment, I can see through the fury. "Always, Rosie," I whisper back.

"I don't know who you three think you are," the red-haired man rasps, "but this is between me and my fiancé."

"Oh-ho-ho." Dayton throws his head back in a humorless chuckle. "So, you're the famous fiancé who's unable to satisfy a woman?" Dayton strolls over, each movement laced with swagger. He grabs the wrist of the hand holding onto Rosalina. "Don't worry. I took care of her for you."

The man curls his lips over his teeth, but Dayton squeezes. Hard. A *crack* sounds through the dark room. The man howls and yanks his limp wrist back toward his chest. Rosalina immediately staggers to Dayton's side.

"You fucking broke my wrist!" the man screams.

Dayton shrugs. "Count yourself lucky. I took the hands off the last guy who touched our girl."

Rosalina glances frantically between the two of them. "Leave, Lucas. Just go."

The man—Lucas—looks like his skin may melt off his bones. "Who do you think you are? Rosalina doesn't know you. Get the fuck away from us!"

He raises the knife, a beam of sunlight gleaming off the tip. In a single fluid movement, Ezryn punches him in the gut. He snags the falling knife while Lucas doubles over, coughing.

"Last chance." Ez holds the knife up to examine it. "Leave. Or we'll make you leave."

Rosalina trembles like a fall leaf beside them, her brown eyes frantic. Dayton and Ez have this demon. She needs me. Needs me to tell her it's okay. We've got her. She's not alone anymore.

But I can't because every nerve in my body is alight. Like there's no movement I can make, because if I even so much as blink, every piece of me will burst into flame. *I should have come for you. I should have known. I left you alone.*

Shame floods me, but it changes to fury. She should never have been in this position.

Why wasn't I strong enough to stop it?

The anger bubbles up inside of me like a noxious potion, filling my veins with heat. Even the surrounding air seems to grow thick, and I'm breathing too much oxygen, giving too much fuel to the inferno within. *Stay calm, Farron. Stay calm.*

Lucas looks up at Dayton and Ez. He isn't aware of my presence. "Fine. Take your fucking whore. Just know she'll come back to me." He grins too wide. "She always does."

I have but a single moment for one last thought: there's nothing I can do. Farron is about to disappear.

And when he wakes up, he'll have to live with what he's done.

Excruciating pain rips through my body as the beast tears its way from my flesh and lunges straight at Lucas.

PART TWO
UNINVITED GUESTS

II

ROSALINA

Everything is happening so fast; I barely have time to let loose a scream as Ezryn flings me to the ground and crouches his body over mine.

"Fuck!" Dayton snarls. "Farron!"

But it's too late. The wolf rips its way out of the Autumn Prince. The massive beast lunges across the floor and tackles Lucas to the ground. Lucas releases an ear-shattering cry.

I stagger up, and bile rises in my throat. The wolf, brown fur embedded with rotten leaves and brittle twigs, has Lucas pinned beneath its claws. His chest is ripped open, flesh falling away like pages of a book. And he's screaming, screaming, screaming as the wolf's teeth clench upon his head—

Ezryn reaches into the neckline of his neon ski jacket and yanks out his necklace: a wooden square carved with floral designs. It clicks open into a locket, and he shines the light right beside Farron's wolf. A shimmering portal erupts from the space. Ezryn turns to Dayton. "Deal with him. We'll meet you out front of the castle."

Dayton's mouth is a thin line, eyes dark. He nods, and then his own skin melts away, replaced by the golden wolf. The beast lopes forward, snagging Farron by the loose skin around his neck.

I cover my ears, unable to take Lucas's screaming or Farron's howls. Ezryn still perches over me, holding Lucas's knife toward Farron. Dayton yanks hard, and the Autumn wolf recoils from Lucas, his maw red and dripping.

"Go!" Ezryn cries.

The last I see is the brown wolf swiping with a bloodied claw before the two monstrous beasts shimmer out of sight.

I can't think. There's no time to revel in how my life has changed in minutes. Lucas is lying on the ground, his wails now a guttural sputter. With trembling hands, I crawl closer. His pooled blood splashes around my knees.

His insides are outside, eyes glassy and unseeing. Each breath sounds wet.

He's dying, I think. I feel nothing, not sorrow or pity. Just a fact. *Lucas is dying.*

But I can save him.

I sense a presence behind me and look up to see Ezryn. Regardless of this strange outfit, he has the aura of a knight in shining armor. "Help me," I breathe. "I owe him a life-debt. Please. Ez."

For once, I'm glad I can't see Ezryn's face. By the way his body stills, I can only imagine his disapproval. And why not?

Lucas is a monster.

But Farron isn't. If Lucas dies, Farron will never forgive himself for killing someone. I can't let him live with that.

"Ezryn," I whisper, "you can heal him."

Ezryn snarls under his breath in a language I don't know, but I'm pretty sure he's cursing me out. But he tugs off his gloves and places his hands straight inside the gaping wound. "I need something to staunch the bleeding. Hurry."

I look around the hideous gift shop and jerk a couple of brightly colored Orca Cove hoodies off the racks and run them back to Ez.

A feeble green light shimmers around his hands as Ezryn holds the fabric to the ragged flesh.

Lucas's blood seeps through my leggings as I kneel beside Ez. *Ezryn came for me. They all did.*

Well, not all of them. Tears spring anew to my eyes, and I hastily wipe them away.

I don't want to distract him, but I can't help myself. I reach out and touch his brightly colored jacket.

"What are you doing?" he murmurs.

"Making sure you're real," I whisper back.

He turns and looks at me. My throat clenches. His goggles are too darkly tinted to see his eyes, but I feel the intensity of his gaze.

He reaches out a hand, his fingertips shimmering with magic and blood, and touches my arm.

"What are you doing?" I ask.

"Making sure you're real."

"Rosalina? Rosalina!" a voice booms, and we both turn to the doorway. A man charges in, gasping for breath.

Immediately, Ezryn lunges for the knife, but I fling a hand to his chest. "That's my father!"

"Oh." Ezryn releases it and turns back to Lucas.

Blood runs down a gash on my father's temple.

"Papa!" I rush to him. "Are you okay?"

"I may be old, but I can hold my own against a couple of thugs." He practically puffs out his chest. Then his eyes leave mine. "My god, what happened here?" He's not looking at Lucas dying on the floor or the large man in nineties ski wear with his hands literally inside Lucas's body.

He's staring at the shimmering portal.

"This is Ezryn. Remember I told you about him? He's my ... friend." The word sounds odd, too intimate and distant all at once.

"Yes, yes, High Prince of Spring, how do you do?" Papa mumbles but walks closer to the portal, holding a hand up to it. It licks at the edges of his fingertips.

Ezryn doesn't respond. The ripped skin on Lucas's chest has knitted back together, but his breathing is shallow. The hoodies are wrapped like a tourniquet around his torso. Ezryn heaves him up over his shoulders. "My magic is weak in the human world," he says. "I've stabilized him, but we'll need to take him to Castletree if he's to recover."

I nod, not letting myself think too hard about what that means.

Ezryn strides to the portal and looks between my father and me. "Alright, O'Connells," he says smoothly. "Let's get you home."

12

ROSALINA

T he sharp sparkle of magic wraps around me as we leap through the portal. I grip Ezryn tightly; it's so strange to feel the shape of his arm beneath a jacket when he's usually covered in armor.

My sneakers hit solid ground, and I take a deep breath. I know with just a taste of the thick air: *I'm back. I'm here.*

Home.

I blink as my eyes adjust. We're on the bridge outside Castletree. My heart races with memories. The spires soar among sturdy tree branches, those cursed thorns snaking up the side. But there's something different, something that wasn't here before, and certainly shouldn't be here now that spring has crested.

A thick layer of ice smothers the tree. Icicles drip off the turrets and swirling frost clings to the windows.

What has happened to Castletree?

Ezryn carefully sets Lucas down on the stone bridge. Beside him, my father positively vibrates with excitement. You'd think the man would be a little more cautious, figuring he was thrown in the dungeon last time he was here.

"He's stable for the moment," Ezryn says, standing. His nineties ski gear looks even more out of place in the Enchanted Vale. "We've got bigger problems to deal with."

"Tell me about it," a cocky voice says.

Dayton leans by the door, a fae man again. He wears loose pants, with only his seashell necklace gracing his muscular chest. But there's a deep red gash across his skin, and a slice along his right eye.

"Day." I throw myself at him. His arms wrap tightly around me, and I burrow into his body. "You're hurt."

"Ahh, Blossom." He presses his lips to the top of my head. "You're here. I could take on an entire army."

I lose myself in his warmth, the scent of salt and sunshine. "Farron?" I pull back slightly, gently touching the side of his face.

"Got him in the cell. He's fine." Dayton shrugs. "If I didn't know better, I'd say that damn beast is getting stronger."

"He couldn't stand seeing Rosalina in danger." Ezryn steps toward us, casting a disdainful look down at Lucas.

I'm sure he'd love to have left him there. Deep inside, there's a part of me that wishes that, too. But I couldn't just leave him to die.

I push my thoughts away and—without letting go of Dayton—reach out to grab Ezryn's gloved hand. "Thank you for helping him. For bringing me back. Both of you."

Something sparks inside me, and I double over, clutching my chest.

"Rosalina!" Ezryn, Dayton, and Papa all reach for me, but I wave them off.

"No, I'm fine," I mutter and stand, glaring at the castle. "Kel knows I'm here."

It isn't a question, but Dayton answers me anyway. "Yeah, he knows we left to find you. Wasn't exactly all sunshine and rainbows about it."

"It's time to deal with that bigger problem you were talking about, Ezryn," I say.

"I agree." Ezryn glances toward the sky. The sun dips below the horizon, and the sharp crackle of magic ignites around us.

Papa gives a gasp of surprise, but I am not afraid of the golden wolf with glittering shells and seaweed in his fur or the black wolf covered in moss and bone. Both step close to me, bowing their heads, and I brush my fingers over their soft fur.

"Stay with Lucas," I tell Papa. "I'm going to tell the master of the castle I'm home."

Ezryn and Dayton walk on either side of me as I open the door to Castletree and step inside.

I told Keldarion I'd find my way back, and I did.

I found my way back to my mate.

13

ROSALINA

As I step inside of Castletree, a great weight lifts from my heart ... replaced by a sinking sense of dread. Something is terribly wrong.

This is not the Castletree I remember. A thick, dangerous layer of ice covers the entire entrance hall. Icicles hang from the rafters like stalactites. Thorns pierce through every surface, creeping along the edges and weaving across the ground in such abundance that the marble floor is obscured from my sight. *What happened here?*

Everything feels heavy, like a suffocating blanket has been draped over this once vibrant place. The air carries an acrid scent, and the sickness of Castletree lingers on my tongue. The princes' magic is weaker than ever.

My legs shake, and I clutch Dayton and Ezryn's fur to keep steady.

An electric shock surges through my body, and my gaze snaps to the top of the grand staircase, where I see his silhouette. The giant white wolf, pacing and snarling. He's bigger than I remember, a layer of frost covering his fur, blue fire dancing in his eyes.

"You shouldn't have returned." His deep growl reverberates through the air.

"I promised I would," I snarl back, lacing the words with my own sort of venom.

The wolf shakes his head in anger before prowling down the stairs, jagged shards of ice shooting up with each step.

Ezryn and Dayton both bare their teeth, but I gently run a hand along their heads. "Thank you for coming for me," I whisper. "But I am not afraid."

I step out from the protection of my cursed princes. It's true; the gnawing terror I'd felt back in Orca Cove has vanished from my being entirely. Castletree gives me courage. The Enchanted Vale gives me strength.

This is my *home*. I belong here.

The wolf halts in the middle of the entrance hall, a frozen tomb of his own creation. I step closer, observing his massive teeth as long as my arm, the giant maw, the whirl of emotion in those icy eyes.

Maybe I should feel fear or anger or betrayal, but as I stare up at the Prince of Winter, a human girl in a silly sweater and sneakers, there's one feeling more prevalent than all the others. Tears flow down my cheeks.

"I really missed you," I gasp before throwing my arms around his neck and burying my face in his fur.

The embrace of winter hits me immediately, and a fire blazes inside my chest, relieving an ache that's been tearing me apart for the last four months. "I fucking hate you, Kel."

Then I'm falling, crashing to the floor, braced against a hard chest as arms wrap around me so tightly, I can barely breathe.

Kel ... Kel is a fae man. Even though it's night. Like when we shared the cave together. He tucks his head into the crook of my neck. I want to touch every part of him. I run my hands over his muscular shoulders and tangle my fingers in his hair. A gasping sob escapes me.

"My Rose," he murmurs into my hair.

Slowly, I pull back because I need to take him in. Yep, he's completely naked. And I'm in his lap, my legs wrapped around his torso.

Dayton and Ezryn slowly creep closer to us, each step wary.

Kel's heart beats frantically as I press my palm to his chest. I trail my gaze higher to take in his face. In classic Kel fashion, his wild, white hair looks like it hasn't been washed in months. His eyes are half-lidded, as if he's taking me in the same way I am him. However, my focus is drawn to his lips, remembering how they felt against my own. "You kissed me."

A rumble resonates in his chest. Does he remember what it felt like?

But another growl sounds as Ez prowls forward. Even with the wolf's features, I can tell he's surprised. "How is this possible?"

The answer is so clear now. So clear now that we're pressed together, two pieces of the same star, my heart beating in time with his.

"Because," I say, "Keldarion is my mate."

Ezryn scrambles back as if the very words have pierced him. Dayton waves his head back and forth. "Kel, is this true?"

I stare across at my mate, knowing he cannot deny it now. Not with this magic blooming between us like a star igniting.

Something passes over his features, hard and unreadable. He pushes away, and I land on the icy ground. The moment he's no longer touching me, there's that crackle of magic, and he shifts back into the giant white wolf.

"Kel?" I gasp.

"It is true," his deep voice drips with ferocity, "and I could not have asked for a crueler fate in all the stars. The Enchantress's curse is nothing compared to the utter torment of being mated to *you*."

And with that, the Prince of Winter prowls from the room.

14

ROSALINA

"Ooh, that's a little shivery," Dayton says.

I dip my finger into the healing ointment and run it over the gash along the golden wolf's eye. "Come on. Aren't you a brave, strong gladiator of the Summer Realm?"

"A big, strong gladiator can still get shivery."

A laugh bubbles out of me, and I wipe my hands on a cloth. "Hey, I think I'm getting pretty good at this healing wolves thing."

I cork the lid back on the ointment bottle. Dayton and I are in the healing chamber of Castletree, a place I've never visited. It's located in the Spring Wing, and flowers bloom from the floor and trail up the walls between the dark purple thorns. The healing chamber is vast and airy, filled with plush chairs. In the middle of the room is a trickling fountain, its waters shimmering with a soft pink light. There are several beds covered by soft pastel curtains with dried flowers and leaves hanging off each bedpost, filling the room with a strong floral scent.

I approach a shelf of intricate glass vials filled with fae potions. Each one shines with a different color, casting a glow across the room. I scan the labels, trying to decipher their uses. Did Ezryn make all these, or did he bring them from the Spring Realm? It was the medicine in one of his caches that helped heal Kel after goblins attacked us.

I walk back to my patient: the giant golden wolf, his fur littered with rotten seaweed and shells. Ez had been too weak to heal him tonight, and he'd mentioned they have a harder time accessing their magic in their wolf forms. So, it's up to veterinarian Rosalina to heal my Summer Prince.

Lucas is unconscious but stable. Ez will continue his healing tomorrow and hopefully get him back to the human world in the next day or so. Now, Ez has gone with Papa to get him settled. Though, I hope he's prepared for Papa to ask a million questions about every leaf and root throughout the Spring Wing.

Running my fingers down Dayton's golden fur, I ask, "Are you feeling any better?"

"Oh, this? This is nothing." He gives a wolfy grin. "Not when I've got such a cute nurse."

"When you're like this, I'm a vet." I can't help but smile back, but it fades quickly. "Farron did this to you. Is he…"

"Don't worry. He's fine. Well, physically." Dayton looks down. "I was as gentle with him as I could be."

My fingers knot into my leggings. "He's in the dungeon, right? Do you think it would help if I went and—"

"No." Dayton cuts me off. "Don't get anywhere near him, Rosie. It doesn't matter how strongly Farron cares for you. When he's like this, he doesn't know friend from foe. Trust me, we've tried."

I nod, my heart breaking for my poor Autumn Prince. I can only imagine the guilt he'll feel in the morning for hurting Dayton, the fae I'm pretty sure he's in love with.

"So," Dayton eyes me with his teal gaze, "I shouldn't have doubted your ability to find our mates. At least one of them. Did it feel as sparkly and magical as you described to me?"

"Yes," I reply. "Like a fire bursting from my chest. When I was next to Kel, I felt his dreams as if they were my own. But it was all happening so fast, I didn't really put it together until I was back in Orca Cove."

Dayton shakes his head. "I can't believe it. He must have known you were his mate, and he sent you away. No wonder Ez is fuming."

"Ez is mad?"

"Ezryn's parents were mates. If anyone understands how strong that connection is, it's him."

I wasn't sure what I expected when I reunited with Kel. But the way he held me like he never wanted to let me go ... For a moment, I thought maybe he realized he was wrong to send me away. I should have known better. I chew my bottom lip and try to focus on the positive. "But this is good, isn't it? It's proof that there are mates out there. There's hope for you to break your curse."

Dayton doesn't even seem to register my words. There's a bitter edge to his voice as he spits, "I'd never have done what he did. Sending you back there. Back to *him*."

I look to the closed pale green curtain.

"I don't get it," Dayton says, following my gaze to where Lucas sleeps. "Why bring him here? He's a dick. He doesn't deserve your help."

I'd told Dayton about Lucas when we'd traveled together to the Summer Realm. How he'd asked me to marry him. At that point, a part of me still thought I'd return to Lucas. The idea sends a wave of nausea through me now.

"Why did I save him..." I whisper, still rubbing my wrist. "Because I could."

Dayton narrows his eyes at me, and I continue, "Because he might not deserve my kindness, but if we can help someone, shouldn't we?"

The golden wolf shakes his head, and murmurs not unkindly, "You're too good for this world, Rosie."

"I know now," I say, staring at the pale green curtain, "after Lucas heals and we send him back, I never want to see him again. Ever."

"Agreed. But hey, I warned you not to marry a man who wouldn't even go down on you."

It flashes in my mind: my legs flung over Dayton's shoulders, his tongue brushing against me. But I shake my head and flick him on the snout. "Okay, fine, you told me so."

He nuzzles closer to me, and I wrap my arms around his neck. Some of the rotten seaweed in his fur comes loose. Carefully, I pry it free, leaving behind only the glittering seashells.

Dayton squints at me. "How did you do that?"

"It just felt loose." I smirk. "If you're a good boy, I'll give you a brush next."

"I did not think you calling me a good boy would be such a turn on."

"Can you not flirt with me while you're like this? It's weird."

But the wolf playfully knocks his entire giant head into my stomach. "I don't think I could stop flirting with you if I tried."

A gasp sounds at the doorway, then a voice smooth as honey says: "Well, butter my biscuits! Aren't you a sight for sore eyes?"

"You're back! You're really back!" a higher voice squeaks.

In the doorway stands a brown raccoon and a small white hare.

A sob stutters up my throat. "Marigold! Astrid!"

I fall to my knees in front of the animals. Astrid and Marigold leap into my arms, and I hug them with everything I have. "I'm so happy to see you."

Finally, after an eternity, I let them go and sniff back the last of my happy tears.

"We heard the princes brought you home," Astrid says, her red eyes glistening. "Thank you so much for finding her, Prince Dayton."

"A little trip to the human world was nothing," the golden wolf says. "I'd descend all the way to the Below to get Rosie."

My heart jumps at the words, said so casually and yet like he'd said them with his whole heart.

"I'll let you girls catch up." He brushes past but stops and gives me one last look. There's something in his turquoise eyes, a promise. I know what it means. He's not going to let me go again.

I smile at him and then turn back to my friends. They're both giving me a knowing look.

"Well, he's certainly happy to have you back." Marigold somehow waggles her brows, even in raccoon form.

I put my hands behind my neck, letting out a breath and tugging on my hair. "That's just Dayton being Dayton."

Astrid wiggles her nose. "We haven't seen him like this in months."

"Really? You'll have to tell me everything."

"Of course, dearie," Marigold says. "But let's get you back to your room. The master ordered your dinner brought there."

My room! I've missed my room so much. But then I scowl at the rest of her words. It seems *the master* still wants to micromanage my entire life despite me being the worst thing that's ever happened to him. I shake my head. I don't want that icy prick to ruin my reunion with Astrid and Marigold.

I follow them down the familiar halls of the Spring Wing, tempted to take off my shoes to feel the moss under my feet. Maybe I would if the dark thorns didn't curve up so often.

My fingers trail along the wall, touching the soft bark of Castletree. When I stroke the thorns, they shiver beneath my fingers.

When Kel was drowning, I swore I'd controlled the briars to save him. But then he'd told me Caspian was the only one who could do that.

But there was a feeling inside of me like the briars had moved at my command.

"We're here!" Marigold chimes, throwing her paws against the door.

I nearly squeak with excitement as I take in my room, with the cherry blossom tree growing out of the wall, my wardrobe filled with beautiful dresses, and the four-poster bed—guarded by the stuffed winged lion Dayton bought for me in the Summer Realm. I rush to my window overlooking the Enchanted Vale: the briar patch as far as I can see, the mountains, the forests. I'm home, I'm home, I'm home!

Though I can't help but notice a bit of Winter's frost has even crept into my room, a few of the cherry blossoms crystallized.

Astrid hops on the bed, and Marigold pushes over a little stool so she can reach the wheeled cart I hadn't noticed before. She lifts off a lid, and the delicious scent hits me immediately.

Food in the human world is nothing compared to this, especially considering Papa and I have been living off of toast and frozen dinners. I sit on the edge of my bed and dig in.

"This is just the best darned day ever," Marigold says. "Not only are you back, but on our way to the healing chamber, we passed the most delicious tall drink of water walking with Prince Ezryn. Very distinguished looking."

I nearly drop my fork. "No! Marigold, that's my father."

She gives me a wink. "All I'm saying is I know where you get your looks from, girlie."

I can only laugh and dive back into my dinner. I savor each bite of the juicy portobello mushrooms, paired with a creamy avocado sauce and a side of crispy kale chips. As I eat, Marigold and Astrid fill me in on the last few months.

My heart aches for the princes and residents of Castletree. Dayton drank every day, Farron barely spoke, Ezryn lived out in the Briar, and Kel confined himself to the Winter Wing, his frost slowly creeping out with each passing day.

I wonder what the roses in High Tower look like now. They'd been so wilted when I last saw them. How much longer do my princes have?

"It's been terrible for us without you," Astrid says. "When you were here planning the ball, you gave the staff purpose. Hope. Even just seeing you in the halls made us all smile, but since you've been gone..."

"Everything's taken a turn for the worse," Marigold says, carefully taking my empty dinner plate in her little paws and putting it beneath the cart. Then she slides a small dessert bowl under my nose.

"I didn't want to leave," I say, digging into a rich chocolate mousse. "Wow, this is terrific. It was all Keldarion's—"

"Your mate!" Astrid peeps, her long white ears going straight up.

"Oh honey, I've been waiting for us to dish about that juicy little development of yours." Marigold heaves herself up on the bed.

So, all of Castletree knows about Kel and me. I lay back on the fluffy pillows, the hare on one side and the raccoon on the other.

"A mate who doesn't want me." I sigh. Thinking of his words cuts me like a physical blow.

"The master has always been secretive," Astrid says gently. "Perhaps there's a reason he didn't want you near."

"How can I be so disagreeable that he doesn't even want to try to break his curse? At times, he looks at me and I swear there's something there. But most of the time, it's just..."

"His scary, frosty face?" Astrid says, and Marigold barks a laugh.

"That's it!" I'm so grateful for them. Even in my worst moments, they're able to make me smile.

"Well, whether or not he sees it," Marigold says, "I've known there's something special about you from the moment you walked in here. We all did."

"Everything feels better now that you're back," Astrid says.

"That it does." Marigold creeps off the bed, followed by Astrid. "But it's long past time we let you get some rest."

I sit up. "I'm not going to give up. I'm going to break this curse. If Keldarion wants nothing to do with me, fine. But it doesn't mean I can't help the other princes."

"Thank you, Rosalina," Astrid says, hopping after Marigold. "I can feel it. There's a change in the air."

Alone again, I spend some time reacquainting myself with my beautiful room. I go to the wardrobe, change into a long-sleeved pale-blue nightdress, and let my hair out of my ponytail. But as I snuggle deep into my bed, something doesn't feel right.

A great uneasiness settles in my chest. I know both Dayton and Ezryn are asleep, resting after such an exhausting day. Keldarion is probably wallowing in his own torment from being the worst possible stink-faced, blue-balled icy fae male in existence. But Farron...

Farron is hurting. Not physically, but *inside*. He's terrified.

I throw my legs out of my bed. The stars are still out, but I know what I must do.

I must find the Autumn Prince.

15

ROSALINA

I traverse the thicket of coiling thorns that wind their way up the staircase to the dungeon tower. On one of my first evenings within Castletree, I dared to climb to the dungeon and rescue the prisoner held captive there. But I'd been ignorant of the terrible curse that plagued the princes—a curse that condemned Farron to become a ferocious wolf at nightfall. It was then I realized the true reason he was locked in that cell. For when the moon rises high and the beastly form emerges, he hungers not for freedom but for flesh.

Unlike the others, Farron has no control over his beast.

I clutch a book. It was one I'd left in my room before Kel forced me back to Orca Cove. Farron had recommended it to me, a collection of ballads and love stories from the Autumn Realm. Somehow, I know he's in torment. It's a silly idea, but maybe my presence will soothe him.

The door to the dungeon is a massive slab of iron with rust coating its surface. From beyond it, I hear deep growls and the thrashing of chains. My heart careens in my chest, but I force myself through. The creaking hinges groan as I push it open, revealing a dark and musty chamber.

My feet tread quietly on the stone as I grow closer to Farron's cell.

I thumb open the book, trying to see the words in the flickering light of the torches.

"'As I traverse the forest with my dear companion, the world takes on a wondrous hue of cerulean. The leaves rustle with the gentle caress of the breeze, and the soft ground beneath our feet sings with the sweet melody of our footsteps.'" My voice is barely audible over the clinking chains. "'"Twas in that verdant grove that we chanced upon the will-o'-wisps. Or, I should say, they chanced upon us.'"

The chains groan as I near his cell. The torch nearest is burnt out, and all I can glimpse is a dark mass of fur and the shine of sharp teeth in the moonlight from the window.

"'The elusive creatures appeared as if from nowhere, their ethereal glow illuminating the emerald foliage.'" I swallow in a dry throat and blink back down at my pages. "'They laid upon us, alighting my bosom and hers, revealing the depth of our intimate bond. In that fleeting moment, it was as if they could see into the very souls of our beings, and—'"

The chain rattles relentlessly, my presence sending the wolf into a deep frenzy. It bounds into the moonlight. Twigs, mushrooms, and branches are matted into the brown fur of the beast, as if the forest itself has woven its way onto the creature. I struggle to comprehend how the horror that stands before me could be my sweet Autumn Prince. The wolf's eyes lock onto mine, and I feel as though I am staring into the depths of an endless abyss.

I know I should turn and run, but my feet are rooted to the ground. The beast lunges, jaws wide, and bites the bars separating us. They creak, shaking at the base—

I scream, jumping back, as my book falls from my hand.

A sound like thunder echoes through the dungeon as an enormous form leaps in front of me. Keldarion howls, and his massive paws slam onto the ground, spreading ice along the prison. The Autumn wolf's growl descends to a whimper as the ice touches its paw, and it slinks back to the corner of its cell, curling into itself.

My heart bleeds with fear and pain and sorrow. Then the giant white wolf turns his frosty gaze to me. "You shouldn't be here."

"I—"

He shakes his head before snatching me in his massive jaws. Great, so we're back to this again. The white wolf carries me to my room, depositing me on my bed. And I hate that every part of me aches to reach out for him to stay and aches to return to the Autumn wolf in the dungeon.

Keldarion doesn't say another word before he leaves.

I curl into a ball, knowing something deep within me. I have to save Farron.

Save him from himself.

16

KELDARION

A thin line of light glitters along the horizon. Dawn will be here soon. I feel the man within me aching to be free of this cage of flesh and fur.

Rosalina is safe now. I'd felt her fear like a drum beside my heart. I had no choice but to follow her to the dungeon. She should have known better than to provoke the beast. Then again, she should have known better than to return.

Though my chamber looks carved of ice itself, I can't feel the cold. Every part of me is numb, and for that I am grateful.

Every time my mind wanders to the feel of her arms around my body, I force myself inward. To the cold. To the numbness.

Claws scrape against ice, and I feel his presence like a looming shadow. "So, I'm not the only one who can't sleep," I say without turning.

His silence is deafening.

I knew my decision to send Rosalina away would break me.

I didn't realize how much it would break them, too.

"Have you come to ambush me in my chambers again?" I ask when he still says nothing. "Or perhaps to explain that other human scent I smell?"

"An accident occurred during our visit. The human will be gone as soon as he's healed," Ezryn says flatly.

I let out an annoyed huff. I recognized Rosalina and her father's scent as soon as they stood on the castle grounds. This other wayward human is of no concern to me.

Finally, Ezryn sighs and strides in. There are bones tangled throughout his dark fur, little bird skulls cracked by fungi and covered in moss. Yet, his dark brown eyes shine brightly, flashing nearly yellow in the light.

Are they the same as the man's? I wonder. Long have I yearned to look upon the face of my closest friend. Perhaps this is one small blessing from the curse. I get to see his eyes.

"You lied to us, Kel," Ezryn says, the wolf's voice deep and rumbling. "You knew she was your mate, and you hid it."

I turn away from him. "I did what I had to. For all of us."

"You don't get to make those calls. We should have had a say—"

"I am the master of Castletree," I roar, baring my fangs.

He rushes up to me, his incisors exposed and dripping. "And we are a family!"

"You don't understand, Ezryn." My body shakes. "Every decision I have made and continue to make is for her best interest."

Ezryn gives a growl of frustration and knocks his snout against my shoulder. "She is your *mate*, Kel. You do not get to hide from this like you have your throne or your people. You have a duty to her."

"Do not speak to me of duty."

Ezryn digs his paws into the ice and his hackles rise. "My father and mother were mates. I saw their bond with my own eyes. They *needed* each other. When my mother d-d... Without my mother, Father is—"

"Rosalina isn't dead," I say. "She will find a way to live with joy and contentment. I will sleep peacefully knowing that."

Ezryn lunges at my neck, wrestling me to the ground. "The bond cannot be broken. You are her mate. You gave up *everything* for him and yet you will give nothing to her?"

Fury ignites within me, and I shove Ezryn off, now tackling him to the ground. "I am giving everything up!"

"Traitor. Always a traitor. You could save your realm right now. Free yourself from this curse. And yet, you betray your people again. Betray Rosalina. Betray yourself!"

Ez wants to speak to me about being a traitor?

My teeth sink deep into his flesh, and he roars in pain. "I'm finally doing what is right, Ez," I say against his skin. "Trust me."

He jerks up, throwing me off balance. "You have become the very thing that nearly destroyed you."

The sentiment makes me throw my head back and give a half-laugh, half-howl. "Is that how you see me, brother? Then fine. Let the Vale mark me as a villain. But I would lay waste to every realm, cover every field and mountain in an eternal winter, and keep you and Dayton and Farron and every being in Castletree cursed if it meant saving her."

Rage alights in his gaze, and he tackles me. I am pinned on my back, and the entire weight of the black wolf pushes down upon me. "Tell me the truth of your bargain with Caspian," he roars. "Tell me what it has to do with Rosalina!"

For a second, I see him behind the primal rage of the wolf. My brother, my friend. *He wants to help me. He wants to keep me safe.*

But I cannot tell him this truth.

For if I did, the burden would fall on him, too.

I would so much rather be his enemy than let him carry the weight of this decision with me. I tried to rest in his harbor of safety years ago. Tried to trust him with a secret.

A secret he betrayed.

And there is something much darker in my heart, something I can't even bear to think of. Because I know what course of action Ezryn would take. An action that would either end his life or the life of...

Caspian's words haunt my mind.

Kel, we both know if you were capable of doing that, you'd have done it when I first betrayed you.

I stay silent, even though my bones are crushing beneath his weight, and his incisors are dangerously close to my jugular.

Light shivers through the window. His body trembles over mine, the curse fading for another day. Immediately, I close my eyes as I feel the warm touch of his skin instead of fur.

I could open my eyes right now and look upon his face. Bring about the greatest shame any royal of the Spring Realm could endure. That would stop him from questioning me.

But I place a hand over my eyes. We breathe together, skin against skin. "There's a helm in the wardrobe," I say.

"I know," he mumbles.

He presses on my chest to stand, and I wait to hear the clink of metal before I open my eyes. He braces his hands against the wardrobe, body muscular and tan. I've kept the helmet in this room precisely for an instance like this when he may need it. The down-turned visor makes him look disapproving, a suitable expression. "I don't care what your reason is, Kel," Ezryn whispers. "You can't treat your mate like this. You can't treat *her* like this. If I were—"

"If you were her mate?" I growl.

He intakes a sharp breath. "She would never wonder for a moment that I would seize the stars from the sky for her if she asked."

"Well, that's where we're different, Ez." I fall back to the icy ground, staring up at the ceiling. "I'm doing it without her asking."

He shakes his head and strides to the doorway, naked besides the helm. My chest grows tight, and I want to call out for him to stay.

I want to crack myself open and admit that I've destroyed my world for her, and I'd do it again, but it's *hard*. Because I miss Ezryn.

"Ez," I croak.

He turns to me.

"I need your forgiveness."

He stands rigidly in the doorway, the muscles of his back tensing. "Not for this, Kel," he whispers. "Never for this."

I lay there on my back for a long while after he's gone. For the first time in so long, I feel cold. The ice beneath me seeps through my skin and into my bones. I wonder if I were never to move, what would happen to me? Would I turn to ice like the castle? What would they find when they came looking for me—a skeleton of hoarfrost?

Though I don't suspect anyone would come looking for me at all. And who could blame them?

Perhaps I shall just wait for my winter to freeze me—

Two dark shapes skitter on the edge of my chambers. Slowly, I turn, trying to keep them in view when something cold presses against my throat.

A dagger.

17

ROSALINA

L ucas looks like a little boy. I stroke a finger along the raised
scar on my left wrist. When he's asleep, I remember the
feeling of being pulled from the ice and falling into his arms. I
can almost pretend he's innocent.

It's morning in the Enchanted Vale, and dappled sunlight trickles
through the windows into the healing chamber, dancing across the
walls like butterfly wings. Of all the things I've wanted to do since
arriving back at Castletree, being with Lucas is the very last. But I
needed to make sure he was still alive, for Farron's sake.

Lucas is in the bed closest to the window. Ezryn was already here
when I arrived, sitting in a chair nearby. He's got one hand on Lucas's
chest and one hand on his head. I've been standing still for about ten
minutes now, watching the mellow green glow of his magic spread
over Lucas's skin.

Finally, Ezryn leans back. "He'll remain asleep until he's recovered.
As soon as I'm certain his body has healed, he's gone."

"Thank you."

Ezryn walks over to the fountain and begins rinsing his hands. I
hover awkwardly behind him, swishing my skirt back and forth.
Marigold has dressed me in a soft pink dress that flows over my hips

and cinches at the waist. I feel like a cherry blossom drifting through the wind.

Ezryn's barely looked at me.

I bite my thumbnail. He's been quiet this morning, quieter than normal. Last I saw him in his fae form, he was dressed like a Ski Fun Ken Doll—which I've since learned was Marigold's idea—but now he's back in his usual gear. Sunlight glints off the elaborate vines and floral embossment on the dark gray helmet. He's not wearing as much armor as usual, instead a tunic in a rich earthy shade with a thin leather chest piece. His brown trousers are loose and far more comfortable looking than the metal tassets he normally sports. Maybe it's the buttery light of dawn amidst the healing chamber, but for once he looks soft.

"I really appreciate you helping him," I say, because I can't stand the silence.

Ezryn walks to the marble counter and picks up a cloth to dry his large, tanned hands. He says nothing.

"He doesn't deserve your help. Or mine. But I kind of owe him a life-debt. And now ... I feel free. You know?"

Ezryn nods.

My heart rattles in my chest. I'm used to Ez's reservedness but there's something different about him this morning. With us alone in the healing chamber, I thought we might talk about when I contacted him through the mirror. But he seems like he'd rather spend time with half-dead Lucas than me.

He turns to another counter and picks up a mortar and pestle, then shakes in some herbs from a jar. I stand beside him.

"I'm thankful you came. I ... was really lost without you guys." My words sound stupid, all trembling and jumbled up. But it's like I'm not even present, and I can't help feeling like he's angry with me.

He drops the pestle with a thud and walks across the room to a basket filled with linens. He begins tearing them into strips for bandages. I follow right on his heel.

"I'm sure I freaked you out when I randomly appeared. I built this altar of all the things I'd collected from the Enchanted Vale, and I had some of your clothes that I got from the cache and when I smelled them—"

He drops the linens. Walks back to the counter and begins mashing the herbs in the mortar with surprising intensity.

"Well, they smelled just like you. And it's about spring in Orca Cove and I thought, how am I going to see the flowers rise and the birds call when I never got a chance to really say thank you for all you've done? Then you came for me. You came for me, Ez, and now I have even more to tell you—"

His hands drop to firm fists. Oh my god, he is mad. He probably hates me for bringing Lucas here. Or for wanting to come back at all. Maybe he agrees with Kel, and I really am a nuisance.

Ezryn storms off to the side of the room, yanking open a door into a small walk-in pantry. It's filled with rows upon rows of jars, each labeled in delicate calligraphy. I wonder if it's Ezryn's writing. He goes to close the door, but I push my way in. The door clicks shut behind me. It's dark, except for a single lit lantern on a shelf, causing the room to glow with orange light.

"I'm aware I've kind of uprooted you guys' entire lives, but I really need you to know that when I saw you there, it was like everything fell back into place." I gesture wildly as I talk, though the pantry is so small with the door closed, I keep accidentally smacking Ezryn in the chest. He stumbles, jangling the shelves. But I can't stop talking. "Like my upside-down world was shifting and everything was coming back into focus. And I missed you, Ez. I really missed you."

My throat grows tight. I look up, staring into the dark T-shaped visor of his helmet. "Are you mad at me?"

A beat of silence passes between us, full and aching.

"Damn the stars," he growls. Then his left arm flings out, smashing the lantern. I jump at the sound, the pantry now pitch-black.

"Ez?" I whisper. "I can't see anything—"

"I know."

There's the heavy *clunk* of metal hitting the marble floor.

And I'm swept up in his arms, his hands lacing behind my back.

He pushes me against the wall, and jars clatter and tinkle off the shelves, but I don't care. Ezryn emits a purely male sound, and he kisses me.

Ezryn *kisses* me.

My heart flutters, and my hands instinctively fall into his hair. Oh my god—it's so thick, curling at the nape of his neck. So, he's got wavy hair. I store this information away like its treasure.

He kisses me harder, his mouth tender soft and crushing all at once. Stubble scratches against my cheek, and I tear a hand away from his hair to caress his jaw. I want to—need to—memorize every piece of him. That space between us that always felt so vast suddenly feels imaginary, like my body has clicked right into place against his.

His hand tightens around my waist, and his arousal presses into me. My stomach loops, and giddy lust makes my core grow hot. More, more, more. My hands can't get enough, needing to feel the sharp point of his ears, to scratch down his neck.

He groans into my mouth, capturing my bottom lip and biting lightly before crashing against me again. My fingers dip down to the edge of his tunic, and I pull upward—

Ezryn straightens. Without his touch, I suddenly feel hollow, carved out. "Ez..." I hear a shuffle then the *ting* of metal. Light blinds me as he opens the door. "Ez?"

Without a word, helmet back on, Ezryn walks from the pantry and leaves the healing chamber.

18

FARRON

He's getting stronger.

Or maybe I'm getting weaker.

Regardless, the wolf is winning.

I sit on the hard stone steps leading up to the dungeon tower. Dawn has long since risen, and Rintoulo, the butler, has let me out of the cell. But I can't make myself go downstairs and face the others.

I should be happy. Rosie's back. She's safe.

But each time the wolf takes over, he steals another piece of me. I knead the bridge of my nose. Is this because we're running out of time to break the curse or am I just becoming more like the beast?

I can't even imagine what would have happened if Dayton and Ezryn hadn't been there yesterday. Rintoulo told me there's a human in the healing chamber—so I didn't murder Lucas. The thought fills me with relief, even though that man deserves nothing but agony. I don't want any blood on my hands because of the beast's wild rage.

What would have happened after the wolf finished with that piece of shit human? He would have gone for the next prey.

He would have hurt Rosalina. *Not he. I. We are one and the same.*

I pound an angry fist down on my knee.

"FARRON!"

A bellow sounds from down the staircase. Keldarion. Why would he scream my name?

I sprint down the stairs, taking them two at a time. I don't think Kel's ever asked for me directly in all the years we've lived at Castletree. I rip open the last door and slide into the entrance hall.

Keldarion stands at the top of the grand staircase as naked as the day he was born. It would be a fine painting, truly: the majestic Winter Prince in all his glory, body sculpted, and long white hair falling over his shoulders. And a look of absolute murder in his eyes ... which I can only assume is meant for me.

His bellow has attracted the others. Ezryn runs up from the Spring Wing, and Dayton stumbles out from Summer. He's got a huge gash over one eye.

My knees feel like they're about to give out. I did that. I did that to him.

Rosalina follows behind Ezryn, her face bright red. "What's going on?"

But Keldarion turns around and throws two things down the stairs. Two *people*.

They tumble, thudding on each step, before landing in a heap at the bottom.

I rub my eyes. It's not possible. The two people Keldarion haphazardly chucked down the stairs are princes of Autumn.

My little brothers.

"Dominic!" I cry and rush forward. "Billagin! What are you doing here? *How* are you here?"

Astrid runs from the Winter Wing and hands Kel a pair of fabric trousers. He yanks them on unceremoniously. "These miscreants sought to perpetrate my demise within the confines of my chamber."

"What?" I fall to my knees and skid across the floor until I'm at my brothers' side.

Dayton and Ezryn flank Keldarion. A show of unity, of strength. Despite the constant infighting between them, the idea of an outsider attempting to murder the Protector of the Realms...

But Kel can't be right. My brothers aren't assassins.

"Dom. Billy." I touch their shoulders. How long has it been since I returned to the Autumn Realm? Since before Rosalina left. Months.

The boys sit up, and there's a hardness to them I've never seen before. The twins share my unwieldy hair, though theirs is redder, their faces splattered with freckles. I imagine in Rosalina's eyes, they would appear no more than teenagers, sprites on the cusp of manhood.

"They snuck into my chambers and tried to assassinate me." Kel holds up a dagger, the handle clearly carved of Autumn's red oak. He chucks it down the stairs toward them, as if to show how truly futile their attempt was. Billy snags it, quickly tucking it into his boot.

"No, no." I touch each of their faces, trying to find the answer in their eyes. "They wouldn't."

"We did," Dominic says. "And we'll try again. No prison will keep us."

"Stop that," I scold. "What's gotten into you two? How did you even get here? The way between Castletree and Autumn was shut a long time ago."

"We went on foot," Billy says. "We've been traveling for weeks."

Breath catches in my throat. Who are these boys before me? They're dressed in tight-fitting garments of maroon, with knee-high boots made of sturdy leather. A belt around each waist holds various knives, whips, and what could be a vial of poison. They look like warriors, not my little brothers. "You went through the Briar? Stars above. You could have been *killed*. What would Mother say?"

"We did this for Mother," Dom snaps. "For our people."

"Why would they want you to hurt Keldarion?" I breathe.

Billy shakes his head, his eyes shocked. "You don't know?"

Everyone's staring at me. Even the staff are poking out from the hallways. "Know what?"

Dominic stands in a defensive position and pulls out a shining dagger from the holster on his belt. He stares up at Keldarion, fearless despite being incapacitated by him only moments ago. "A frost has

84

come to the Autumn Realm. It's killing everything: our trees, our crops. Our people. And it's *his* fault."

A collective gasp utters through the entrance hall.

"No," I whisper. "Kel would never do that."

Rosalina drifts over to Kel and places a hand on his arm. "Tell them you didn't do this."

Kel sets his jaw. "I don't know what's happening in Autumn, but I assure you, I have nothing to do with it. My death will garner you no freedom from this terror."

Though Castletree is covered in Kel's frost, I know in my heart he's speaking the truth. He would never do this.

Dom stabs his knife through the air. "If that's true, you better figure out who is causing it."

"And quickly." Billy stands beside his twin. "Because Autumn is preparing to go to war with Winter."

METAL CLINKS as Keldarion finishes chaining Billagin to the staircase banister.

"Is this really necessary?" I mutter. Both my brothers have their wrists bound in steel, not that they seem to mind. They're staring wide-eyed around the entrance hall, taking in the thorns.

"They traveled all the way from Autumn, navigated the Briar, and snuck undetected into my personal chambers intending to assassinate me," Keldarion says gruffly. "They stay chained."

We stand in a semicircle around them. My stomach twists. Rosalina appears almost nervous, glancing over my shoulder, keeping a watchful eye on them.

"What are you thinking?" I whisper.

She tucks a curl behind her ear. "I'm meeting your family for the first time. It's a big deal."

I give her a smile I can't feel. Nothing seems real right now. My little brothers are assassins. My realm is preparing for a war on Winter. And all the while, the briars twist deeper into Castletree.

Dayton smacks the boys on the shoulders and grins. "All that way only to get your asses handed to you! Come on, lads. When this pesky misunderstanding is cleared up, I'll teach you how real warriors fight. Give you moves that will even take down the great Protector of the Realms." His cocky smile gives no hint that Kel had completely defeated all three of us only yesterday.

Dom and Billy gaze up at Dayton with adoration, eyes wide and shining. My stomach twists, remembering all the times our families got together in the past, how Dayton used to wrestle with them, how all three would prank me and then laugh like it was the funniest thing in the world.

It was a simpler time, even if our relationship had been no less complicated.

Ezryn steps forward, hands on his hips. "You realize that an assassination attempt on a High Prince is punishable by execution."

The twins' faces, so warm and light looking at Dayton, both swivel to Ez. "Then kill us," Dominic growls. "War is coming between Autumn and Winter, anyway. The murder of Autumn's princes will only quicken the act."

"No one's murdering anyone. Right?" Rosalina looks between all of us. "Right?!"

Kel gives an exasperated growl. "Tell me of this frost."

"It started two full moons ago," Billy says. "Initially, we only saw signs of it in the borderlands, between Autumn and Winter. A crawling blue rime. First, it took out the maple groves east of the Rucklewood. Then it took the potato and pumpkin crops in Appleclove Valley."

Dom sets his jaw. "Originally, we thought it was just taking our vegetation. But then the frost kept growing. It reached the villages."

"Hundreds of people," Billy says quietly, "turned still as statues. Frozen in these terrible poses, mouths still gaping in fear."

It's like the frost has caught me too. I feel it creeping up my legs, weaving through my lungs, making it harder to breathe. "How come no one sent word to me?"

Dom and Billy look down.

I grab their shirts and pull, my voice frantic. "How come no one sent word?"

"Mother did not think you could be of assistance," Dom says finally. "She said it should be handled by people who spend more time in the Autumn Realm than with the Winter Prince."

I stagger back. My mother was High Princess before she passed the rule to me. I'd left her as steward for the last twenty-five years. *She doesn't trust me. She has no faith.*

An awkward silence passes over the entrance hall. The other princes don't look at me, and it's almost worse than their stares.

"Well, it's simple, isn't it?" Rosalina says, hands on her hips. "Obviously, Keldarion isn't causing the frost, so there's no need for a war."

Keldarion has turned away, knuckles white as he grips the banister. "So, the steward of Autumn didn't think to send word to Winter before she sent her youngest sons to assassinate the High Prince?"

"She sent word to Winter," Billy sneers. "Every letter unanswered."

"Perth would have received those letters," Kel breathes. "He should have brought it to my attention."

The name sends shivers up my spine. Perth Quellos, Keldarion's vizier and steward of the Winter Realm. Rosie stiffens at his mention, and Ezryn quirks his head toward her.

"That guy's got the deepest icicle up his ass," Dayton drawls.

Kel ignores the remark. "I will send for him at once. Surely, he has some idea of what's going on."

Dom and Billy exchange a glance.

"What?" I whisper.

"It's too late," they say in unison. Then Dom stares me straight in the eye. "Mother's amassing the army. Unless you can stop this frost now, there will be a full-out realm war. And she won't stop until Keldarion answers for the lives his magic has taken."

Keldarion looks over his shoulder at them, then stalks up the stairs and into the Winter Wing.

Dayton sighs and rips the handcuffs off the boys. "Come on. We'll get you set up in a room in the Autumn Wing. But I'm taking your knives."

"That's fine," Billy says. "I can make a shiv out of a splinter and a shard of glass."

"Fascinating." He pushes on their backs, leading them up the stairs.

"Let us reconvene this evening to discuss our next course of action." Ezryn turns to me, and I can feel the severity through his helm. "You are High Prince of Autumn, Farron. Decisions will need to be made, and soon. Only you can make them."

I stumble away, pushing myself out of the castle and into the open air. Rosalina calls my name, but I don't stop. "I just want to be alone," I mumble.

Out on the bridge, the cool air and earthy scent of the Briar wafts over me. I can't catch my breath, my whole body trembling. My hands reach out to grasp the railing, but there are thorns everywhere. One slices into my palm, and I retract, holding my wrist as blood oozes down my hand.

For a second, I'm grateful for the pain. It reminds me I'm real. The last few months without Rosalina have felt like a haze. I haven't even checked in with my family.

I squeeze my hand into a fist, and the blood seeps out between my fingers. My people are suffering. My family has forsaken me.

Autumn deserves a true High Prince, not the shadow of one.

19

ROSALINA

My heart aches for Farron, but I need to respect his wishes and give him the space to sort out his thoughts. As much as I'd like to avoid Keldarion, there are things more important than my pride.

First, I check the Winter Wing, which has become an ice rink. I navigate by clinging to the banisters or hanging off the thorns. Hey, they might as well be useful for something.

Where are you?

And then I feel it: a glittering string bursting from my chest, urging me forward.

The mate bond.

It takes me to the door of the High Tower. Carefully, I tug on the handle. Unlocked.

The stairway is a patchwork of thorns. Caspian created them, and the princes say they're sucking the life from Castletree. That's part of the reason Kel sent me away. *Caspian wants you.* I don't buy it. He's tormented me, sure, but with the intention to antagonize the princes. What would the Prince of the Below want with me?

I pause at the entrance to the chamber, and Kel turns to face me.

He's dressed now, wearing a fitted black tunic. His white snowflake necklace glimmers on his chest.

"You might as well come in," he says.

Sunlight blazes through the stained-glass panes, making the chamber appear painted by an artist's brush in vivid red, blue, orange, and green hues. Yet, the briars grow thicker here than anywhere else in the castle. They ensnare my gown, carpet the floor, and stretch up toward the ceiling as if they are the very bones of Castletree.

The tiled floor, barely visible beneath the thorns, depicts a breathtaking mural of a starfall. Amid the tiles, four roses flourish from a small patch of fertile earth. One for each of the princes: a rose of pink, turquoise, orange, and blue.

Their wilted petals are scattered on the floor.

"I just want to talk." I walk up beside Keldarion.

"Do you think it's me?" he asks. "Freezing the Autumn Realm?"

Kel's magic has spread across Castletree. If it's that wild here, then why not across the realms?

"No," I say after a breath. "I don't."

He looks down at me, face filled with weariness. "Well, thank you for that."

Something catches my gaze at the back of the room, a small piece of stainedglass peeking out from the thorns. I walk toward it, then quietly mutter under my breath, "Would you mind moving a little so I can see the picture, please?"

The thorns obey and slither down to reveal a stained-glass picture.

Kel looks around wildly, as if looking for someone. But Caspian's not here. I study the picture. It's the sigil of a rose about to bloom—the same shape as the emblem on Castletree's door. The same emblem as my necklace. I pull it out of my shirt and study it.

"That's how you contacted Ezryn?"

"Yes," I say, studying the moonstone. "It belonged to my mother."

"I recognized the sigil on your father's neck when he first came to the castle. The symbol of the Queen who abandoned us." Kel's rough hands touch the necklace, then my hand. "I intended to question him. But when you came..."

"You'd rather have had me as your prisoner," I say dryly. I don't dare move, not with his rough fingers still grazing my palm. "My mother was an anthropologist. Perhaps the Queen lost it in the human world."

He quirks his head, but he's not looking at the necklace anymore. His blue fire gaze is entirely on me. Flushing, I continue, "My father and I think it could be why one of the fae took my mother. Maybe they thought she stole it from the Queen."

"The Queen hasn't been seen in five hundred years," Kel says slowly. "Her name is still revered, and there are disciples who worship her, but I can't imagine any so radical as to steal a human woman."

"It's only a theory." My words have lost all sound, turning into nothing but breath as Kel's hand slowly drops the necklace and glides past the planes of my chest, over my neck, and cups the side of my face.

I draw nearer to him, but my gaze catches on his rose in the ground. So wilted, ice-blue petals littering the dirt below. I kneel beside it.

"Shouldn't it look better?" I chance a look up at him. The hard expression returns to his face. "I mean, the Enchantress said to break the curse you have to find your mate, and that's... that's me."

Whether he likes it or not.

"I guess," I continue, "we can assume the curse isn't broken because you're still a wolf at night. When I touch you, it turns you fae ... But I suppose that's just holding off the curse for a bit. I really need to make some notes with Farron on all this."

"The curse is not broken because we have not completed our mate bond," Keldarion says.

"Oh, like, we have to have sex?" I stand and say bluntly.

He stares at me.

I stare at him.

Then I crumble over, hiding my burning face in my hands. "Oh my gosh, I can't believe I just said that."

"Completing the mate bond is more than sex, Rosalina. It's the union of two souls into one. The sharing of every moment, every joy, every pain, every breath. It's the ultimate expression of love, a bond that transcends time and space, a connection that no other can understand." His eyes blaze with an intensity that takes my breath away. He's not speaking, but it's like I can hear his words in my mind, words I so desperately wish he'd say: *I want that bond with you more than anything.*

Hearing him speak about this connection, it's like my whole body aches for him. I stare deeply into his ice-blue eyes. *Let me show you all the ways I could love you.*

A muscle feathers in his jaw, and he swallows a growl. Almost like … almost like he heard me.

Then he turns away. "It's clear that the others cannot stand to exist without you. I will no longer ignore your wishes. You may continue to live and work in Castletree and help them find their mates. But do not think that because you are now aware of our bond, it will change anything between us."

I want to stab his stupid eyes out. "When did you know, Kel? When did you know I was your mate?"

He stills a hand on a thorn. "The moment you stepped into Castletree."

I remember him looking down at me, such fury in his features. I shake my head at the realization of it all. "You knew I was your mate, and you kept me in the *dungeon?*"

He growls and paces, the flicker of his wolf wanting to break out. "I did not want to keep you at all."

"Why not? Didn't you want to break the curse?"

"If you must know, I thought when I first met you that merely having you near might be enough. The Enchantress mentioned love and accepting our mate bond, but I was willing to try regardless." He shakes his head. "As I got to know you, it became clear that nothing in this world could persuade me to complete my mate bond with you."

His words are arrows, sharp and piercing, tearing at the fragile hope that has been growing within me. I try to mask my pain, but my eyes betray me, brimming with unshed tears. "Because I'm a human?"

He shakes his head and gestures to all of me. "It's nothing so defined as that."

I try to push my pride aside, the desires of my own stupid heart. "But can't you see? It's so much bigger than you and me. We could … we could try to break your curse right now. You could get your full magic back and help heal Castletree. Maybe even stop the frost in Autumn—"

He gives a scoff, as if the fate of Castletree and the realms are meaningless to him.

I grit my teeth, holding back the urge to hit him in his big, broad, stupid chest. "I know I'm not exactly what you wanted. But you care about me, at least a little. You protect me and feed me, and you sent me home, so I'd be safe. I know that. Would it really be such a hardship to just spend one night with me?"

It flashes in my mind: shedding my clothes in this tower, his mouth kissing every inch of my skin. I want his powerful body to move with mine. I want every piece of him. It would break my heart to give myself to someone for one night who clearly doesn't want this bond. But for Castletree, for the Enchanted Vale, I'd do it. Even if it would break all of me.

Heat blossoms between us as his gaze rakes over my body, and I wonder if his thoughts mirror my own. Then Kel moves, grabbing me and pulling me close to him. His stare is so intense, I think for a moment he's going to do it—rip my clothes off and have me here on this floor.

I'm yours, I'm yours, I'm yours.

His eyes squeeze shut, and he brings his lips to my ear. "Let me make something perfectly clear, Rosalina. I would rather fuck every man and woman in the Enchanted Vale before making love to you. And a thousand armies on my doorstep could not compel me to break this curse."

I push away from him, my heart shattering. The rejection feels like a physical blow, and tears sting the corners of my eyes. How can he be so callous? So cruel? My fists clench at my sides, and I take a deep breath, willing myself to be strong. "What did you want, Kel? Did you want me to stay in Orca Cove? Get married to someone else and have his babies? To forget all about you?"

If my words have any effect on him, they do not show on his face. "Yes. You shouldn't have returned."

"You'll never want me…"

He steps forward, and the whole tower seems to shake, the thorns trembling as he snarls, "I would see the Enchanted Vale in ashes and Castletree overtaken by briars before completing my bond with *you*."

"Fine," I say, my voice shaking. "I'll leave you to your curse." I turn on my heels and storm out of the tower, determined not to let him see me break.

20

ROSALINA

I storm through the halls of Castletree, knowing there's only one place that can make me feel better after Kel's words.

As I push open the doors of the library, I take in a deep breath, letting the crisp scent of Autumn fill my nose. It's the most beautiful place I've ever seen, the shelves like extensions of the tall trees that grow inside, their branches heavy with leaves that flutter down to crunch beneath my feet. Even the thorns that weave around the trees and snake over the shelves can't diminish its beauty.

Someone whips out from around a corner and smacks right into me. I fall to my ass, surrounded by books. My father is sprawled across from me in a similar fashion.

Of course, he would be here. I can't help but smile at our similarities, my anger drifting away. I'm glad he's already making himself at home. Tonight, I'm attending a private dinner with the princes to discuss a strategy for Autumn, so I'm glad Papa can keep himself busy.

"I see you found the library," I say, helping him gather the fallen books.

"Oh yes," Papa gleams. "Thought I'd bring these to my room for a bit of reading. That Marigold lady said she'd bring me some soup and a mug of hot cocoa. Can you believe that? The fae have cocoa!"

"It's delicious, Papa." As I help stack the books in his arms, I noticed he's gathered a vast array, everything from creature compendiums, to myths, maps, and stories.

"Is everything alright, Rose?" he asks softly.

"Just processing everything. I think I need some quiet time to browse the stacks."

"Well, you know where to find me. Besides," he casts a glance over his shoulder, "there's something here you should see."

My father leaves and I look around the library, noticing something that wasn't there before: a large wooden desk with a red mushroom-shaped chair. Behind the counter stands an empty shelf. It almost looks like…

Yes, there's a slot at the bottom of the desk that opens to a bin, and etched above it is the word: RETURNS. I step back, letting myself take it in. A smaller tree is bent over the desk and shelf, and a wooden sign hangs from one of its branches that reads: "Rosalina's Library."

Tears well in my eyes. How many times can a girl cry in one day?

"We made it," a soft voice says from behind me, "wishing that one day you'd return to us."

Farron steps out from behind one of the book stacks. Warmth blooms inside me, and something in my chest eases as I take him in. His auburn hair is a tangle, his eyes deep gold. A broad smile beams across his face, as if the sun has peeked out from behind a dark rain cloud.

"Farron!" I launch myself toward him in two steps, wrapping my arms around his shoulders.

He holds me close, face dipping into the crook of my neck. "Hey, Rosie."

I burrow myself deeply into his embrace. He's wearing a tunic of deep green and brown, embroidered with gold thread and adorned with acorns and leaves. His trousers are made of supple leather, and his boots are of the same deep green as his tunic. A cloak of russet and yellow swishes as we rock together.

"Rosie," he says, finally pulling away. "I'm so—"

"Don't." I place my hands over his lips. "Don't say sorry. None of this was your fault. Everything is okay." *We're together now.*

The flash of guilt in his eyes says he doesn't believe me, but he gently takes my hand from his mouth and places a soft kiss on my palm. "Do you like it?"

"Of course!" I run my fingers along the wood. With a plop, I test out the mushroom chair. "Wow, this is comfortable."

Farron gives a little laugh. "I remembered you telling me how you wanted to have your own library back home. So, it was just something I worked on. I asked the trees to move a bit and we created, well, this."

His thoughtfulness fills my heart, and it hurts to think of him here believing I had abandoned him. My mind still has such a hard time making sense of it. This kind and thoughtful Autumn prince who would never harm anyone ... and the beast he turns into at night.

A shiver runs through my body as I remember the dripping jaws, the brown matted fur. He hadn't recognized me at all.

"Day and Ezryn helped too," Farron continues. "Ezryn brought fresh flowers for your desk, but then he left the castle and they wilted. And Dayton made the sign."

I can tell Dayton's handiwork: the messy writing, the small holes in the wood filled with brightly colored sea glass that sparkle and reflect in the light.

Ezryn's flowers are dried in the vase on the desk but that doesn't make them any less beautiful. "Farron, this is amazing."

"I'm sure Kel would have helped too, but we didn't want to bother him," Farron mumbles awkwardly.

Something glitters on the far side of the returns box: a line of sparkling snowflakes etched into the wood. I pull out the box and see one book inside.

I recognize it immediately. It was the book I'd brought to Kel's room, the one I'd fallen asleep reading to him.

Carefully, I pick it up and a small slip of paper flutters out. In soft cursive, it reads:

Perhaps your books are not so boring. It was a clever move to freeze that annoying ranger in a block of ice at the end. Though I cannot fathom why the heroine would simply not use her fire to unfreeze him rather than getting into that silly battle with her brother.

Keldarion had read the book I left him? And wrote me a note. Had he expected me to return? Or were these words for a ghost?

"No." My eyes blaze with fury. A small thorn rises from the ground and spears the note to the desk. "He *was* here."

"Oh, uh, that's new." Farron looks nervously from me to the thorns, then murmurs, "I tried to keep up with the staff's book requests, but it was, uh," he lets out a sigh and runs a hand through his floppy hair, "it was harder than it looks."

"He was absolute shit," a smooth, cocky voice drawls from the corner. We both turn to see Dayton strolling toward us with a fluid grace that reminds me of a breeze on a summer's day. "Remember the time you gave Marigold that book—what was it called? Ah yes, *Aging Gracelessly: The Unseemly Behavior of a Fae Femme Fatale?* I thought that was the end for you."

I give a little giggle and jump up from the mushroom chair. I'm not sure Dayton will ever stop taking my breath away, with his sun-kissed skin, chiseled jaw, and piercing turquoise eyes. He wraps his arms around me. "Did you have a good sleep?"

"After you took such tender care of me, I slept like a lamb." His eyes flicker as he looks past me. I turn.

Farron stares at Dayton, eyes wavering, lip trembling. I look back to the Summer Prince, the scar over his eye still bright red, the gash peeking out from beneath his shirt. I remember seeing a scar over his back, too.

Are these all from Farron?

"You know," Dayton looks down at me, but I know his words are for Farron, "I was thinking of telling Ez not to get rid of this complete-ly." He runs a finger over the red mark across his eye. "It makes me look dashing. Don't you think, Rosie?"

I let out a laugh, trying to lighten the mood. "I'm not sure you need any more charm. Though it does suit you."

Ezryn probably could have already healed it, but he's been using so much of his magic on Lucas.

Farron says nothing. He's withdrawn deep into himself, arms crossed over his chest.

"Everything's sorted with your brothers. Got them confined to a chamber in the Autumn Wing," Dayton continues. "Your father's fitting in, eh, Blossom? Every time I see him, he's absolutely surrounded by staff. They're entranced by all his fascinating stories of the human world."

I can't help but grin. My father is a born storyteller, and I'm glad he's finding his place here.

"We've got a few hours before the big meeting, and I have the perfect idea." Dayton grabs my shoulder and reaches for Farron who dodges out of his grip. "You two are tense. And what better way to relax than with a dip in the hot springs?"

21

DAYTON

It was a fucking bad idea to go into the hot springs butt-ass naked. Not that I would've done it any other way. I just didn't expect Rosalina to show up looking like a goddess.

She'd run to her room before we walked down to the grotto. I can only assume Marigold and Astrid fixed her up perfectly for this occasion, those little scoundrels.

Rosalina's wearing a long black dress that wraps tightly around her arms before becoming almost sheer, with fabric crisscrossing over her full waist. It offers me a sight of what she has on underneath, or lack thereof. Only the swimming equivalent of a black bra and panties.

Beneath the translucent fabric, her breasts look so full. Her soft stomach and thighs yearn to be grabbed. Fuck, I'm so hard, it'll be clear the moment she gets close.

Right now, Rosalina stands at the sloping entrance of the hot springs, running her feet through the sand.

The water is crystal clear and glows with an ethereal light. The steam rises from the surface, carrying the scent of salt and citrus. I let out a contented sigh and sink deeper, feeling the tension in my muscles ease. It's peaceful here. The hot springs in Castletree have always been my retreat, and I'm more than happy to share it with these two.

My gaze drifts over to Farron, sitting beside the waterfall. Damn, I'm surprised a storm cloud hasn't formed above his head, he's so gloomy. I guess losing control of his beast, hurting me, having his stupid-ass brothers attempt to assassinate the Protector of the Realms, and learning his mommy went over his head to declare war on Winter is a lot to deal with.

But Rosie's back. Doesn't that make everything better?

Slowly, I wade over to him. Farron didn't even get in. Perched on the rocky rim, pants rolled up to his knees, he kicks his feet like a forlorn puppy.

He flinches away from me as I near, but I know it's not because he doesn't want my touch. He's afraid of hurting me again.

I turn back to our girl. "Coming in, Blossom?"

"Yeah," she says, then her dark brows shoot up, and she touches the moonstone rose pendant on her necklace. "I almost forgot. This is glued together, so I don't know how it'll hold up in the water."

"Got your own special locket now, eh?"

"Kind of. It's broken."

Farron quirks his head. "Bring it here. Maybe I can fix it."

"Always tinkering with something," I tease.

Rosalina walks along the edge of the hot springs and places her moonstone necklace into Farron's palm. He examines it for a moment before tucking it into his breast pocket.

Rosalina plops down beside him, letting her feet sink in the water. She tilts her head back and lets out a soft moan. "This feels so good."

I see my reaction mirrored on Farron. It's bloody dangerous for her to make those noises around us. Her eyes flutter open as she gazes at my body, and there's no way she can't perceive my hard length beneath the water.

"Sorry," I say, gesturing down at my uncontrollable cock. "It's been a while."

She eyes Farron and I. "You two haven't...?"

"It's hard to be with someone when they're too drunk to stand," Farron mutters.

And it's hard to fuck a ghost. Because that's what Farron had been after she left. He'd go to the library and open books, but he wasn't reading, wasn't researching. Sometimes at night, I'd creep up to the dungeon to watch the wolf thrash in its cell, because seeing its fury reminded me that at least there was one emotion left in him.

"Well, I'm glad to see you're not drunk now," Rosalina teases me.

"The only thing I'm drunk on is your beauty," I say. She flushes and Farron leans down, playfully splashing me.

"Hey." I wade closer, placing my lips to the bare skin of his knee. "You're beautiful, too."

A soft, surprised sound comes from the back of his throat, and desire floods me. Now that she's home, my cock aches for him. Aches for her, too. But I try to temper that desire. She's Kel's mate. Something I always suspected, but now we know for sure.

When I saw Rosalina in the library, I could tell she was troubled. I gently run a hand up her soft leg. She flushes but doesn't push me away. "Is everything okay?"

She bites her lip, as if deciding what to say to us. "Oh, yes. I mean, if okay means having your fated mate tell you that he'd rather fuck every single person in the Enchanted Vale over you, and that even the prospect of breaking the curse, of freeing his magic and realm, isn't enough to debase himself for one night to try."

I take a breath to let her words sink in, then anger boils in me so hot, I swear the water temperature rises. "What the fuck? Kel said that?"

"He wants nothing to do with me." She shrugs her shoulders. Her voice holds steady, but I can only imagine the hurt she's hiding inside.

"Kel..." Farron puts his hands behind his head. "He cares about you. I know he does. But sending you away, rejecting the mate bond ... It doesn't make any sense."

"Typical," I say. "Keldarion's always been like this. Secretive bastard. He doesn't trust any of us. Not even Ezryn. Not even his mate."

A curl has fallen loose from the bundle on Rosie's head. There are flowers pinned in her hair. Damn, if she isn't the most beautiful woman I've ever seen. So, what if she's human? That can't be why Kel doesn't want her. If she was my mate, I'd—

I stop myself. I won't permit myself to think like that. That's too dangerous a game. All I know is when or if I find my mate, they won't be able to compare to the two people sitting above me.

"And I have a secret of my own," Rosalina says. "One you must keep."

Farron and I exchange a look before I slide my fingers down her calf to her foot. "Prince's honor."

Her light brown eyes flick to the entrance of the hot springs, back to us. "Ezryn ... Ezryn kissed me!" She slaps her hands over her mouth, as if she can't believe she just admitted it.

"What?" Farron and I exclaim at the same time.

"Did you see his face?"

She shakes her head. "No, he was super dramatic. Like punched out a light then kissed me." Her voice quavers. "Then he just left."

"That's not like Ez at all," I muse, still in awe of her words. "How was it?"

"Magical." A dreamy expression crosses over her face before her eyes go wide. "You're not going to chop off his hands or anything, right?"

I chuckle. "No, Blossom. I only did that because you told the bastard no. If you'd wanted him, I would have endured it. Hated it but endured it."

She studies me carefully. "What about Ezryn kissing me? Do you ... do you hate that?"

I fall back into the water's warm embrace, searching myself for any hint of jealousy. When Rosie had sat with those fae in the Summer Realm, I'd been seething. I don't feel any of that emotion when I think of Ezryn kissing her.

Even the thought of Kel being her mate doesn't make me jealous. Envious of what they have, sure. Mad that he's not taking care of her the way a mate should, most definitely. But jealous? "Nope," I say finally. "In fact, it turns me on a little, thinking of that big metal lug finally getting some. I mean, *something* has got to fill his dark soul with joy, right?"

Farron's face flushes a soft pink. "Maybe it's because we've all been cursed here for so long. There's a special bond between the four of us. But with others, it's different. Dayton, when I saw you with that girl you brought back to Castletree—"

"Her name was..." I interrupt him, then pause. "What was her name?"

"Doesn't matter. I fucking hated it," Farron says, a sharp edge to his voice. "But when I saw you with Rosie, it was..." His breath becomes heavy, and he shifts. "It was beautiful."

Rosalina turns to Farron, eyes sparkling. "What do you think about Ezryn kissing me?"

"Honestly," he says, "if you liked it, then it makes me happy."

She seems pleased with our response and twirls a curl of hair around her finger. "Well, I don't think it's going to happen again. He stormed out of there pretty fast. Maybe I'm a bad kisser."

I grip her thigh. "Trust me, Blossom, you are *not* a bad kisser."

"Really?" Her smile turns devious. "You'll have to take me back to the Summer Realm again so I can practice with all those handsome fae."

"No," Farron and I say at the same time. I rise out of the water, pressing both hands firmly on her exposed legs, my body dripping with warm water.

She lets out a little sigh, biting her lip as her gaze drifts over me, my erect cock just below the surface.

"Here's the deal, Blossom." I tug her closer to the edge of the springs. "Kiss Ezryn to your heart's desire. I'd fucking die to watch you pressed against Farron."

Both let out the most adorable sound, but I just bring my wet lips to her ear. "I'll even allow you to kiss your mate if he ever pries the icicle out of his frosty ass."

She gives a half-hearted laugh.

I grab the back of her neck to make sure her gaze is on me, letting her know how serious I am. "But if anyone else touches you, including that asshole *ex*-fiancé upstairs, I'll take great pleasure in ending their life. Then I'll fuck you in their blood to remind you who you belong to."

The determination and intensity of my words surprise even myself. But Rosalina doesn't back away. A fire sparks in her gaze as she matches me. Letting out her own snarl, she says, "Day, you said kissing me was a *mistake*."

The pang of hurt in her voice stabs me deeper than any weapon. "And you don't think I've regretted that every single moment since?" I crush my lips against hers and drag her into the water.

22

ROSALINA

Warm water embraces me as Dayton pulls me down, his lips capturing mine.

If I thought kissing someone else after finding out I have a mate would feel wrong, I would have been mistaken twice over today. First, Ezryn's searing kiss, and now Dayton's bruising mouth, his tongue pushing between my teeth.

I moan, and when he tries to pull away, I don't let him. I don't need air, only him.

His hands are on my back, and he grinds hard against me.

Heat and desire swirl in my stomach. He's naked, he's *so* naked. I only caught glimpses of his body beneath the bubbling water, but I'm desperate to touch his cock.

Dayton's hands move lower, his fingers tracing my curves. I figure that's an invitation to do the same and run a hand along his broad chest, lowering until I grace his length.

It's massive and thick, and I can't help but grip it to see how it feels in my hand. Perfect. I rub his cock. He throws his head back, muscles in his neck straining.

"Fuck," he growls, voice deep and male. "Rosie."

A breathy gasp alerts me to Farron, so close to us. My hair has fallen loose, lying in wet strands around my head. He'd said seeing me and Dayton together was beautiful, and the look on his face confirms it: lips slightly parted in awe, eyes wide.

I'm frozen, caught between them, all three of us suspended in an intimate moment. It feels strange, but in a good way. *Where will this lead?*

Dayton chuckles deeply as he sees us looking at each other. "Come on in, Fare, the water's fine."

Dayton kisses me again, and I twine my arms around his muscular shoulders and wrap my legs around his waist. His iron-hard length presses against my throbbing core. He grunts under his breath, then rubs his cock against the thin fabric of my swimsuit.

I cry out as my whole body erupts with sensation. "Yes, Dayton."

"Call him by his full name," Farron says, voice low. His pupils are completely blown as he watches us.

"Your full name?" I gasp, and he doesn't stop grinding against me, powerful body moving so effortlessly in the water.

Farron crawls closer, a growing electricity on my skin at his nearness. As his fingers tuck my wet hair behind my ear, Dayton cups my breasts with his large hands, and I can't help but let out a mewling cry.

"Daytonales," Farron whispers, and his soft lips linger on the side of my cheek.

"Daytonales." I say the name like a prayer. "That suits you. Suits the Summer Realm."

"Hmm." Dayton slips a finger below the fabric of my swim bra, gliding over a nipple. "It's long, laborious. No one calls me that anymore."

"I like it," I gasp.

Farron moves away from me, and I miss his touch immediately.

"You know what I'd like?" Dayton smirks. "This to go." His hands reach the bottom of my sheer cover-up, and he moves to take it off.

"No," I say. That fabric is the only thing hiding the hideous scar on my wrist, the jagged letters that read *Lucas*. It's a story I'm not willing to share yet ... especially with him incapacitated upstairs. "It's too pretty to take off."

Dayton sticks out his bottom lip. "But what about these?"

His hands flicker over my swimwear. "Yes, yes."

"I was hoping you'd say that." He gathers me in his arms and pushes us away from the shoreline.

I realize we're deeper in the hot springs than I've ever been before. Dayton must notice my gaze because he whispers, "Hold your breath and open your eyes."

He dunks us beneath the warm depths. For a moment, it's only darkness until Dayton waves his hand and there's the familiar prickle of magic. The world shifts into a stunning array of pastel hues. The water is crystal clear, and the sand shimmers silver. Vibrant coral and seaweed grow along the hot spring's floor. It's as if I've been transported to another world. I can only imagine what the Summer Realm's ocean looks like.

But most magical of all is the fae male floating across from me, his golden hair flowing in the water. His smile is so genuine as he watches me take in this piece of his world.

Dayton's words come back to me: *Remind you who you belong to.* He'd told me I'd belonged to the princes of Castletree. I may be mated to Kel, but something about his statement feels so right. This is where I belong. And what I want more than anything right now is for him to do what he promised: take me, have me, show me I'm his. I want to give him my body.

His eyes widen as he takes me in, almost like he can sense my desire. He wraps me in his arms and kicks us to the surface. He lays me down on a smooth rock in the middle of the hot springs, taking care to keep a hand behind my head.

For one moment, we stare at each other. His tangled blond hair falls wildly around his face. We crash together, our kisses furious, and I raise my hips, desperate for any contact.

He moves away from me, then back again, like waves on the sand. His tongue finds mine as his hands make their way over my body. It feels like my skin is going to set on fire, consume us both.

Dayton raises himself up on his forearms. "You're so beautiful, Rosalina."

He removes the strapless black swim top and gently lifts my hips to slide off my bottoms.

"No destroying my underwear today?"

He gives a roguish smirk, playfully kissing the space between my ear and neck. "I do have a little self-control."

"Since when?" Farron laughs from the shoreline.

I tilt my head to look at him and realize this is the first time he's seen me like this. We've had plenty of moments, and I've always suspected he wanted me the same way I've wanted him. But I can't help but wonder: what does he think of me, all spread out here, naked and bare?

"Alright, pup," Dayton calls across the short expanse, "I'll show you how generous I can be. You take off your clothes, and get your tight little ass in the water, and I'll let you have the first taste."

Farron blinks rapidly, then stammers, "F-first taste?"

"Of our woman." Dayton lightly slaps a hand down on my thigh, then drags it up to cup between my legs.

The shock of his hand against my core is electric, and I let out a moan, grasping my sensitive breasts.

"She's so fucking wet," Dayton groans. My slickness coats his palm as he moves it back and forth against my entrance.

"Farron," I breathe, lifting my hips to grind against Dayton's hand.

Farron lets out a muffled noise and draws his knees up to his chest, almost as if he's in pain. "I'll just..." he mumbles, "I'll watch for now."

"Suit yourself," Dayton says and kneels between my legs. A series of featherlight kisses caress my skin, then his tongue laps at my entrance.

"Oh!" My hands grasp the smooth rock.

He laughs, sending vibrations through my core. He moves his hands to my hips and slowly slides two fingers inside me.

"Mmm," I moan. "I need more, Day."

Everything inside me tightens as he moves his fingers in and out of me, his tongue dancing around my clit. I arch my back, my toes curling as pleasure builds, cresting higher and higher until finally I let out a scream as my orgasm rolls through me.

I collapse onto the rock, panting and dazed, as Dayton pulls his fingers out.

"How was that to start?"

The breath is heavy in my throat. "To start?"

He kisses the inside of my thigh. "I'm never going to let you only come once."

My whole body shivers in anticipation as I rise on my arms to look down at him. But he just grins, then slides away from me, swimming toward Farron. He rests his elbows on the edge. "You have no idea how fucking good she tastes. Sweeter than nectar."

Farron stares down at the Summer Prince reverently.

"Taste her, Fare."

Farron's gasp is swallowed by Day's mouth as he heaves himself up and clasps Farron by the back of the neck. Their lips smash together. Farron's hair tousles and falls over Dayton's brow. I've always known it was so much more than hooking up between them. The proof is in the intense gaze on Dayton's face, the soft melting of Farron's features.

How could they not have been together while I was gone?

Dayton drops his lips to Farron's shoulder and growls, "Do you like that, pup?"

With a shaky hand, Farron brushes his lips. He tasted me. The thought ignites my core, and as our gazes meet, I can't refrain from letting my fingers drift lower, along my stomach, down to slip between my legs.

Farron lets out a choked sound. Dayton shakes his head, tsking. There's a splash of water, and two strands of pink seagrass burst out, tangling around my wrists, and forcing them above my head.

"I'm all for watching you do that," Dayton says, "but today, you're going to come when I say you're going to come. Understood, Blossom?"

I tug lightly on the grass restraining me, but my body has turned molten under his command. Dayton gives Farron a look, who is still staring at me as if stunned. Then Dayton dives in and before I know it, the Summer Prince is above me, naked and glistening.

"Are you going to fuck me?" I strain against the binds, eyes on his erect cock.

He swallows, and for a minute I think I see something akin to fear flash in his eyes. But he shakes his head, and that cocky grin returns. "Yes," he says. "But not today. When I have you, it will not be with any deadline for a stupid meeting."

A swirl of disappointment fills my belly, and I whine.

"Now, none of that." Dayton grins. "There is still plenty I plan to do to you today."

He trails kisses along my neck until he gets to my breast, bringing a large hand up to massage one while he plops the other into his mouth, sucking deeply.

I moan and tug against the restraints, desperately wanting to tangle my hands in his hair. "Oh, Day, I—"

He switches breasts, sucking harder and harder, like he'll never get his fill. Deep male groans vibrate in his chest, and he moves to massage my clit again. "Your pussy feels so good."

I gasp as his hand works me into frenzied pleasure. I'm so close, and all I want is to come. As I'm about to tip over the edge, Day pulls away.

A smirk plays on his lips, eyes alight with mischief.

"Remember, Blossom?" he teases. "You only get to come when I say."

Ecstasy pounds in my abdomen, and I gasp in the dense air. "You're so—"

But Dayton looks over his shoulder, golden hair knotted. "Are you getting in, Fare? She's so close. It might just end for me to watch you make her come, but I'm willing to risk it if you are."

Farron stares at us, then falls to his side again, letting out a tortured moan. "I can't. Just keep going. I'll watch."

I don't have time to question why he won't come in before Dayton lowers himself down between my legs, blowing warm air on my pussy. The sensation is maddening.

"Ready?"

"Stop teasing me."

"Then beg for it."

"You're so mean."

He pulls back. "Well then—"

"Dayton, please," I gasp. "Please, please, I need you. I'm yours."

He stills, then dives back toward me, mouth and tongue on my pussy, two fingers slipping inside. "Come for me, Blossom."

That's all it takes. With my hands still tied, pleasure rushes through me in waves, over and over again until I'm a quivering mess, my breath coming out in small pants.

Dayton unties the weeds from my wrists and pulls me up into his arms, pressing a kiss to my temple.

My vision is littered with stars, his kisses soft. But I know this isn't over, not when I can still feel his hard length beneath my legs. "I want to taste you now."

He stills. "Rosalina, you don't have to—"

"I want to ... If you want that."

"Seven realms, yes." He stands, and I settle between his legs. His cock bounces right in front of my face. It is *magnificent*.

I press my hands to his muscular thighs and suddenly feel a bit of embarrassment returning. "I'm sorry if it's not, uh, good or—"

Dayton fists my hair into a knot. "I don't think you could do this wrong if you tried."

Slowly, I part my lips and bring them close to his length.

"Start by tasting the tip," Farron calls over. "It drives him wild."

"Ah, now the pup speaks up," Dayton drawls. "Just in time to make me senseless."

Farron watches us with a wide gaze, muscles tense.

I do as he says, taking the tip of Dayton's cock between my lips.

"Now lick the length," Farron says.

I let my tongue drift along his shaft to the base.

Dayton groans, fist tightening in my hair.

"Now take him," Farron says, voice rich with desire.

I swallow all of Dayton's length into my mouth. His hands cup either side of my head, guiding me further down his cock and I swirl my tongue over him, moving faster and faster. I work him until he's panting, then I slow down a bit, pulling out to gasp in gulps of air.

The Summer Prince's face twists in pleasure, his muscular chest heaving. I look to Farron for approval.

Farron's dark brow raises. "That was good, but I think you can take him deeper."

There's a command in his voice I rarely hear from my sweet Autumn Prince, one that makes my spine tingle.

"I don't know," Dayton chuckles, "it's pretty big."

"She can do it," Farron assures.

A desperate need to please them both fills me, and I breathe deep before I take Dayton in my mouth again. I try to relax my throat as he pushes his cock deeper. My eyes water and I think I might gag, but I refuse. I want all of him.

"Good girl," Farron breathes. "And you too, Day. You're a good boy feeding our girl your big cock. Look how hungry she is for you."

"Fuck." Dayton stiffens in my mouth. "I'm going to—"

"Swallow him, Rosie," Farron commands.

Dayton's hips move at a frantic pace, and I moan with each pulse of his cock in my mouth as I desperately try to keep up.

He shudders, muscles tensing. I arch my back and moan. Holy stars, he tastes amazing. His cum coats my lips, and I lick it up, savoring every drop. There's so much, some of it spills from my mouth and trickles down my chin.

Farron bites his lip, eyes glassy and filled with desire. I know in this moment I've done something to please them both, and warmth blooms in my chest. Farron gives me a smile, a silent acknowledgement of my efforts.

"Let's go show our boy how good a girl you were," Dayton says, wrapping me in his embrace and swimming across the springs. Steam curls around Farron's body.

"You tasted her on my mouth, Fare." Dayton smirks. "Now taste me on her lips."

Dayton holds me up to Farron like an offering, his cum dripping from between my lips and down my chin.

Farron's pupils are blown. He swallows and the knot at his throat bobs. He lifts a trembling hand.

Where's the confident Autumn Prince from a moment ago?

"Decide, Farron," Dayton orders, one of his hands snaking up to deeply massage one of my breasts, the soft flesh escaping between his fingers. "Kiss her or don't."

How must I look to Farron, in his lover's arms, hair disheveled, cheeks flushed, and completely and utterly desperate for him?

Farron closes his eyes, auburn hair falling across his brow. Then in a flash he pulls back, landing in a heap against the slick stones. "I'm sorry, I can't."

"Your loss, Fare." Dayton gives a dissatisfied sigh, and the sharp sting of Farron's rejection is quickly replaced by Day's bruising kiss.

"I'm sorry," Farron says. "It's not that I don't want to. I'm already going to lose Day to his mate. One day, Kel's going to change his mind. And I can't lose you too, Rosie."

"Fuck Keldarion," Dayton growls in my ear. "Ignore the scared little pup. Focus on me."

His hand moves furiously on my aching pussy, not even giving me a moment to think about Farron's words. "You've done so much for me already, Dayton—"

"And I'm going to give you one more, okay? Give me one more."

Before I can say anything else, a cry tears from my throat as the heat builds, builds, builds.

He sits on the lower ledge of the hot spring, bringing me on his lap, his cock already hard again.

"This time you're going to scream," he snarls. "You're going to scream loud enough for your mate to hear you and realize what an idiot he is. For that fucking asshole to feel the pleasure he can't give you."

I squeeze my eyes shut, focusing only on Dayton's touch, and cry out in pleasure.

"Louder, Baby." He licks my neck, then bites down. Pain and pleasure. "Remember when you watched me and Fare?"

"Y-yes." I tilt my head back, barely able to comprehend anything beyond the bliss building inside me.

"He called your name when he came. Now when you come, you're going to look at him. Yell his name out."

Farron watches us so intently, it's as if nothing in the world could tear his gaze away from me.

Dayton's cock slides against my ass. His fingers move at a rapid pace, and when he pinches sharply and tugs on one of my nipples, I see stars. "Come for us."

That's it. I'm lost in his storm, waves of bliss flooding over me once more. I scream, my body trembling, my orgasm crashing over and over.

"Farron!" I cry out as I come undone, my inner walls clenching around Dayton's insistent fingers.

Farron's hands knot into fists and he slams them against the steamy surface of the hot springs. "Rosie. Day—"

"I fucking love the way you feel," Dayton rasps against my ear as I come back to myself. I collapse against the Summer Prince, feeling completely and totally satisfied. I wonder about Dayton's words. Did my screams reach Kel after all?

23

ROSALINA

My velvet shoes barely make a sound as I head toward the dining room, Dayton and Farron on either side of me.

After our experience in the hot springs, Farron helped Dayton and I wash our hair, then wrapped us in fluffy towels. It wasn't exactly the way I'd wanted his hands on my skin, but it was still comforting.

I tuck a loose braid behind my ear. Farron had weaved small plaits into mine and Dayton's hair before we left, explaining his mother taught him how. His voice had wavered as he spoke. I know he's worried about what's going on back home. But that's why we're meeting with the other princes now. To decide on a plan.

At least dinner is at a normal time with it being a full moon tonight—the one night of the month the princes and staff won't turn into beasts or animals.

I smooth down my skirts as we draw closer. Marigold and Astrid have gone all out for my first banquet back at Castletree. Farron and Dayton took great joy in helping them decide on the dress, as they lounged together on my bed. Finally, they'd decided on one from the Summer Realm.

It's made of the finest silk in a shade of soft ivory. The bodice is fitted, accentuating my curves, and adorned with delicate gold embroidery that glimmers in the light. A flowing skirt falls to the ground in layers, billowing as I walk. The neckline is low, revealing just enough skin to be alluring, but still leaving much to the imagination. Not that those two princes need imagination now.

I've got a light shawl overtop, not only to cover my arms, but because there's still a chill in the castle, the magic of the Winter Prince seeping everywhere.

Dayton grabs my arm before we enter the dining hall.

"Now, Blossom, you need to do something for me before we go in."

I raise a brow. "And that is?"

"Don't cower to him." Dayton fixes me with his turquoise gaze. "You're Keldarion's mate which means you're his equal. He's the one who told you he didn't want to be with you, so if he says anything about this afternoon, that's his own problem."

My whole body heats. "Wait, what? How would he know? Did someone tell him?"

Farron trails a hand through my hair. "Rosie, you've got Day's scent all over you. It's … intoxicating."

"Oh my gosh, I didn't think about that."

Dayton grips my chin. "Own it. He said he'd fuck everyone in the realm before you? Show him how desirable you are. Show him you're the one everyone wants, and he's the biggest fucking idiot in the whole Vale for not worshiping you as he should."

There's anger in Dayton's words, and his passion ignites inside me. I straighten my spine and laugh. "Maybe I'll fuck everyone in the Enchanted Vale before he has the chance."

I know instantly that was the wrong thing to say. Dayton and Farron each grab one of my arms.

"No, Rosalina," Farron growls, a flash of something feral in his eyes. He shakes his head, then sighs. "I thought you were going to be a good girl and listen to Dayton's rules."

Dayton's rules. Him, Farron, Ezryn, and that frosty jerk. I can't imagine wanting anyone beyond that. But … they're so easy to rile.

"I'm okay with that," I say, and they release me. I quickly bop Farron on the nose before turning to the door. "For now."

I throw open the doors of the dining hall.

I sense Keldarion is already here the moment I enter, his presence hitting me like a wave. But I don't look over at him, not yet. I keep my head high, my pace steady, kicking out my dress with each step as Astrid taught me.

I am the Lady of Castletree. I belong here as much as anyone.

At least, I think I do. My confidence falters for an instant, and I stumble over a partially protruding vine.

The dining hall is exactly how I remember, except most of it is covered in mounds of ice, including part of the table and the chair where I used to sit: the one opposite Keldarion.

What remains of the table is laden with delicious food. Ezryn sits in his usual seat with nothing in front of him. He doesn't look up at me.

The High Prince of Winter is slumped over, his elbows on the table, hands covering his face. As if he can feel my attention on him, his gaze rises.

I can't help the startled gasp that escapes my lips. He looks ... awful. Worse than he did this morning in High Tower. His hair is matted and wild, shading his eyes rimmed with red.

But I don't back away. He doesn't want me. Doesn't trust me. But I didn't return here only for him, and I know that with my whole heart.

Dayton and Farron move to the other side of the table. My regular seat is occupied. The easiest choice would be to sit next to Day and Fare, to hide behind them.

But Dayton was right. *I'm his equal.*

I walk past Ezryn and grab a chair, then drag it beside Kel at the head of the table. There's more than enough room.

A beat of silence passes, and I sense all their stupid, stunned gazes on me. I fall to my seat and snarl: "Well, are we going to eat?"

Dayton, of course, lets out a long chuckle. "I, for one, am positively famished." He begins to load his plate. There are platters of roasted mushrooms, steaming bowls of stew, and baskets overflowing with crusty bread. Fruits and vegetables of every hue fill the spaces in between. Farron awkwardly scoops up some glazed carrots and mashed potatoes.

I glance at Kel, expecting to see him glaring at Dayton. *Does he smell the salt and sea? The sunlight that seeped beneath my skin this afternoon?* But there's a strangely vacant expression on his face.

He doesn't deserve it, but my traitorous heart aches for him to let me in. Let me see behind this icy wall he's built.

"Guess I'll actually have to serve my own plate," I sigh and reach for the porcelain dish. A large hand clasps around my wrist.

"No," Keldarion says, voice gravelly.

Every line on his face is etched with tension, but there's something in his eyes, the briefest flash of softness that crumbles a tiny barrier in my walls. My whole focus narrows to the point of his hand on my skin, and it's like my body is still heated from the earlier encounter: a tightening in my stomach, a coil of tension that threatens to snap.

"Fine," I say. Let him *serve* me. Something in me trills at the notion.

While Keldarion moves around the table, filling my plate with delectable fae food, I carefully place my napkin on my lap and turn to the Spring Prince.

He very well could be a statue for how little he's said or moved.

"Good evening, Ezryn," I say, trying to muster all the confidence I don't feel. I will not let him know how much it stung that he walked out after kissing me. "I assume you had a pleasant day. Something very pressing must have required your attention."

"Couldn't have beat your earlier encounter." Dayton laughs as he leans close, grabbing some bread and winking at Ezryn.

Ezryn whirls to me, his fists tight at his side. I must be getting really good at reading his body language because everything about it screams betrayal.

He must realize I would tell Dayton. It's only polite to tell a fae prince that another fae prince kissed you after your mate rejected you, all before that first fae prince kisses you while his lover, another fae prince, watches. Ugh, my head whirls at the thought. My mouth opens and then closes, and I'm not sure what to say.

Mercifully, Keldarion drops a plate piled with food in front of me, and I murmur a quick thank you before digging in. I'm starving.

All of us, sans Ezryn, begin eating our meals. Marigold had assured me that Papa would be well taken care of while we have this private conference. I'm sure the staff are overjoyed they get to spend more time with him.

I wait for one of them to start this meeting. But none of them are doing a darned thing. "Argh!" I let out an aggravated sound, mouth full of mashed potatoes. No wonder nothing got done while I was away. "Okay, so we're obviously going to the Autumn Realm?"

Farron drops his fork, and it clatters against his plate. "W-what? No, we can't—"

"We have to act," I say. "Your brothers said your mother was preparing for war."

"Those two have always had wild minds," Kel says, sounding more like his old self now that we're down to business. "It might not be that serious. I've summoned Perth Quellos to the castle to see if he has any knowledge of this."

I stiffen at the mention of that name. Keldarion's royal vizier and current steward of the Winter Realm. Also, the fae man who called me a whore and told me I was distracting Keldarion—before Ezryn punched him.

Ez is looking at me now, and there's the slightest tilt of his head. The gesture feels like words. *I'll protect you.* No matter how awkward things have gotten between us, I don't think he'll ever let me be alone with the vizier again.

"Old Perth," Dayton drawls. "Haven't seen him since that lovely Solstice Ball. He's a slimy old bugger, that one. Kel, why haven't you kicked him out already and found a proper steward?"

Kel stiffens, and he growls low in his throat. "Quellos has served the Winter Realm as vizier for decades. My grandfather chose him for the role. My father trusted him. I never heeded my father's advice when he was alive, and that led—" Kel shakes his head. "By keeping Quellos as steward, I can at least honor my father's memory."

I shift awkwardly. Kel doesn't know how his steward treated me at the Solstice Ball. Though, I'm starting to understand why he trusts Perth. He's trying to honor the last High Ruler's wishes ... His father's wishes.

"Do you even know how those little rebellions in your realm are going, Kel?" Dayton continues. "Has Perth kept you updated on that?"

"Hard to be updated on anything when you're more beast than man," Ezryn says. The first thing he's said all night, and that anger I sensed earlier is back. Maybe it was never for me. His metallic gaze is fixed on Keldarion. Yeah, there's definitely some tension.

"Well, it's a good thing he's coming then," I say, placing one hand on Kel's arm and the other on Ezryn's. They don't stiffen under my touch like I expected.

The strain from the table dissolves a bit, and I try to guide my wayward princes back to the important matters. "I still think we should visit the Autumn Realm to see what's going on. Couldn't we go through the door here in Castletree?"

I'd opened it myself accidentally when Kel had shown me that it connects to the four realms.

"It's a possibility," Keldarion says.

"We can't go back." Farron taps nervously on the table. "At night—"

"We could use your necklaces to take us home to Castletree before each sunset," I suggest.

Ezryn sighs. "The lockets work more for emergencies. They wouldn't be feasible to use long-term, especially if we stray from Castletree. Our magic is already limited as it is, but the longer we're away from here, the harder it will be to activate the portals."

"Okay, what about a day trip?"

"There's no way we'll be able to sort this out in a day. Then my parents will question why I'm leaving and," Farron shakes his head back and forth, "what if they ask me to stay?"

"We could ask to reside in the Ember Wing," Dayton says. "It's distanced from the main keep."

"We could stretch the truth and say you need to commune with your magic at night." I look up, thinking. "Or some other excuse for why you'd be unavailable."

"That's not a horrible idea," Ezryn offers.

"No." Farron stands. "What will you do with the wolf? I can't very well go to Keep Oakheart's dungeon and lock myself up. And it's irrelevant. Day or night, the beast doesn't care." A tear falls down his cheek. "Look what I did to Dayton!"

We're silent, and my heart mourns for him. So trapped he can't even go back to protect his realm.

"You're the High Prince of Autumn, Farron," I tell him, feeling like he needs the words to be spoken aloud. "Your people need you. We have to figure out a way."

"There isn't one, Rosie."

Slowly, the door creaks open, and Astrid stands there, her face paler than usual.

"We're in the middle of a meeting," Kel says. "What is it?"

Her red eyes flick from me to Kel. "There's someone here … Someone who says they've been invited to dinner."

"Perth shouldn't have arrived yet," Keldarion says, waving a dismissive hand. "I certainly haven't invited anyone."

No, a smooth voice purrs in my mind, *but you did.*

My heart races. "It's Caspian."

24

ROSALINA

T he Prince of Thorns is at Castletree.

Kel stands up so fast his chair clatters to the ground. Ice grows from beneath his feet, a sheet cracking along the floor. "What is *he* doing here?"

A little peep escapes me as a memory returns.

"What?" Keldarion snarls.

I throw my burning face into my palms. "When we were dancing at the Winter Solstice Ball, I jokingly invited him." Peering between my fingers, I gaze upon three stunned faces and my awkward reflection in Ezryn's helmet. "But it's not a big deal. I'll tell him his invitation is rescinded after he threw his tantrum and destroyed the entire ballroom with his thorns."

I jump up before any of them can stop me and rush out of the dining hall. Unsurprisingly, I'm followed by a 6'5 frosty giant. As I scurry past Astrid, I whisper an apology. The poor thing, I can only imagine how traumatizing it would be to hear a knock on the door and see the bloody Prince of Thorns standing there.

I march into the entrance hall, ready to tell Caspian to go to hell, but stagger to a stop. I find myself unable to draw in a full breath as I look upon him, radiant and otherworldly in his beauty.

He's really gone all out for this dinner.

The Prince of Thorns is resplendent in his formal attire. A rich maroon shirt emphasizes the purple flecks in his dark, alluring eyes. His toned forearms are on display with sleeves rolled up. The fitted black trousers perfectly hug his legs, while a matching waistcoat adorned with shining buttons completes the ensemble. A cloak of shadows, black as night, drapes over his broad shoulders, adding a hint of magic to his already striking appearance.

A half smile curves his full lips, while his dark hair has been slicked back, except for a single piece that falls over his brow.

Surprisingly, Kel hasn't launched into a tirade yet. I turn to see his stunned expression mirrors my own.

I guess it's not every day you see your arch enemy standing in your entrance hall expecting dinner. They have some sort of history. A betrayal. My gaze drifts to Kel's wrist. He has a bargain with Caspian, one he refuses to tell me about.

"Well," Caspian's dark eyes roam over us, "if it isn't my two favorite people in all the Vale."

"You're not welcome here," Kel finally speaks, stepping in front of me.

Caspian picks an invisible piece of lint from his shirt, positively unbothered. "Really, Kel? After your mate was so kind to invite me?"

So, he knows I'm Kel's mate. "That was before you decided to spread your thorns in the Winter Realm," I say.

"Hmm." Caspian smirks. "I thought you liked my thorns, Princess."

Two small vines slither up from the ground and twine around my ankles. *Pleasure and pain, remember?* His voice echoes in my mind.

I remember the day he watched me pleasure myself in the castle gardens. Rage sweeps through me, and I free myself from the briars.

It won't be enough to ask him to leave. He's too powerful. He's literally got the entire castle under his wraps. And the princes' magic is weak because of it, while his own remains unbridled. Perhaps even stronger if he truly is sucking the magic from Castletree. Keldarion can puff his chest all he wants, but the only way Caspian leaves here is if he wants to. "Tell me why you came."

"Is it so hard to believe I want to eat dinner with you lovely fae?"

"Yes," Keldarion and I say at the same time.

"Stars." Caspian holds his hands up in a peaceful gesture. "Fine. I heard you have an impossible problem. And I love to figure out the impossible."

"Farron?" I breathe.

Caspian reaches toward me, almost as if to touch my cheek, before dropping his hand. "Come now, loves," he purrs. "I can hardly discuss details on an empty stomach."

I've had my fair share of awkward dinners at this dining table. And I expected one with the Prince of Thorns to be the most awkward of all.

Except it's not.

Not in the slightest.

Were the three fae princes surprised when Keldarion and I walked in with Caspian at our side? Indeed.

The vacant seat beside Farron and the ice wall didn't please him, so he dragged the chair all the way around the table and pushed it between Keldarion and me, so now I'm in the middle of the Prince of Thorns and Ezryn.

But that was it, the only awkward thing. Because now, the wine is flowing, plates are empty and … everyone is laughing. Even Keldarion. And the Prince of Thorns has the goddamn cockiest shit-eating grin on his beautiful face.

I pop my fifth jelly tart into my mouth, waving away the wine Dayton offers me. Don't these idiots realize the Prince of Thorns is here and we need to be on high alert? But they're all so invested in some story he brought up. A memory of a lake by a place called the Prismatic Palace.

"I bloody knew it was you who put the frogs in Tilla's bed," Dayton laughs, his cheeks flushed from the wine.

Caspian just tilts his cup.

Farron clutches his belly and wheezes. "I remember asking Day if a rooster got loose in the palace. That's what her scream sounded like."

"Who is Tilla again?" I ask, losing count of all the names they've mentioned.

Caspian wipes a crumb off my cheek with a napkin. "Darling, swallow before you ask questions. No one can understand you with a mouth full of pastry."

I meet his gaze, angrily swallowing. "Who. Is. Tilla?"

"Oh, *Tilla*." Dayton draws out her name. "She was Kel's old flame. Long black hair, huge—"

"I don't want to hear it!" I snarl, fire flashing inside me like a match lit.

"Huge *armor*." Dayton slumps down in his chair. "She'd wear steel even over her dresses. She's from the Spring Realm, after all."

My eyes flick to Ezryn. At least he's still on my side, acting his usual rigid self. Though I can't see, I can feel his constant glare at Caspian.

"Why are they all acting like he's some long-lost friend?" I whisper, leaning closer to Ezryn. "He's the bloody Prince of Thorns."

Ezryn gives a long sigh, and whispers back, "Because in a way, he is a long-lost friend. There was a time the five of us spent many nights like this together." Ezryn hesitates, and I spy his fists tightening under the table. "And now we have no choice but to play this twisted game of pretend. With our magic so weakened, we cannot evict him from the castle. With his power unbound, challenging him to a fight would be unwise."

I'd had the same thought earlier; I just didn't think playing pretend with the Prince of Thorns would be so easy for the Princes of Castletree. Especially Kel.

"Ezryn." Caspian leans on the table, twisting his body to us. "Do you remember? I think your father came from Florendel to join us for a day, didn't he?"

"Yes," Ezryn says stiffly. "It was the first time he left Keep Hammergarden after my mother's passing."

A silence falls over the table. What's Caspian's game with this? If he's trying to win Ez over, he just made him more uncomfortable.

"There was one night," Caspian looks up as if striving to recall, "you two went out into the forest, and when we looked out, you were both surrounded by all manner of creatures."

Ezryn emits a soft sigh. "We went for a walk in the moonlight and we came upon a stag with a broken leg. As fierce as my father's reputation, he took pity on the animal. We knelt beside the poor beast and worked together to set its leg."

"With magic?" Caspian leans in, dark eyes wide.

Ezryn gives a breathy laugh, and it's like I can feel a weight being lifted off his shoulders. "My father was never much of a magic user, but Mother had taught him a few things. She'd taught me, as well. Our magic entwined. I hadn't thought I'd ever wield magic again after my mother's passing, but my father's presence gave me strength. Many creatures of the wood came to watch us work. It almost felt as if —" He shakes his head. "Almost felt as if my mother was there with us."

My heart lifts at the happiness in his voice. Okay, so maybe Caspian's story isn't so bad. "What were you all doing there?"

"It was a celebration of the Spring Equinox, a small gathering for the High Rulers,"Farron explains. "Ezryn and I had just been crowned. Kel had yet to take the rule but came in his father's stead."

"You brought Dayton as your special guest." Caspian gestures to the Autumn and Summer Prince.

Farron flushes, but Dayton throws an arm around him. "You were so nervous to ask me." He smiles. "But Damocles was happy I was there. Made me go berry picking with him."

Damocles. The name makes me pause. I overheard it in the Summer Realm. If Dayton didn't attend as High Prince, it meant there was another High Ruler of Summer during that time. Caspian's words from the ball play in my mind: *The drunkard who let his brothers go off to battle alone.*

But the memory doesn't seem to haunt Dayton. It energizes him.

"Hey, it was a better choice than Tilla," Farron mumbles.

ELIZABETH HELEN

All four of them collectively groan. I'm almost inclined to join in. Dayton had told me Kel had a former great love. Was it this Spring Realm woman? Is that why they all hate her?

And if this was a retreat for the High Rulers, why was Caspian there? It doesn't sound like he was their enemy at that point.

But something about recollecting this time has allowed everyone to unwind. Even Kel has lowered his guard as he joins in the complaints about Tilla.

What is Caspian's scheme here?

The easiest way to gain favor with people is to hate someone together. Caspian's words float through my head even as his lips tell another story.

How is he doing this? Dark magic from the Below? I try to concentrate on the words in my head and push them back. *Doesn't seem like a great way to forge lasting relationships.*

Oh, I don't know, Princess. See how united your four princes have grown against me.

"Tilla was pretty though," Caspian says out loud, and I'm drawn back to the conversation. "But her hair didn't shine like polished mahogany in the sun."

Five heads turn to me.

"No." Kel's voice is low, almost gravelly.

"She also didn't have the annoying habit of twirling her hair around her finger when she's thinking," Caspian continues, and I feel a hand on my thigh.

All the men at the table are watching me.

"Or," Caspian's fingers glide against the thin fabric, and the muscles in my core tighten involuntarily, "have eyes like a golden sunset."

The breath catches in my throat. I refuse to be charmed by him. I'm not some idiot fae prince. I slap him away, but when I look down, I see his hand isn't just on my thigh. His other hand is pressed on Keldarion's leg.

Kel's gaze is entirely on me. Does he even notice?

Something snaps inside me. Fire bursts in my chest, and I slide my chair back, screaming: "Get your hand off my mate!"

128

The thorns on the floor burst up, curling around Caspian's chair, and whip him into the wall.

The other four princes all stand and gape at me. Caspian picks himself up and gives a small laugh. "Good show, Rosalina. It seems that mate bond of yours is really heating up."

The breath is heavy in my throat and all I can do is glare. Keldarion lunges at him, grabbing him by the collar. "Is this your doing? Did you give her this power?"

The Prince of Thorns rolls his eyes. "Oh yes, I gave my greatest enemy's mate the power to manipulate my thorns." He slithers out of his grip gracefully. "Of course not."

"How is this possible?" Kel stares at me.

"I told you I could control the thorns." I redirect my glare to my mate. "You didn't believe me."

"You couldn't possibly think the mate of the High Prince of Winter was only a mere human. She's got power bubbling beneath the surface. All of you are too distracted to see it."

"Does Sira know?" Kel growls.

Caspian's face turns serious. "No. I have to have some secrets. And if you want to keep it that way, Kel, you better behave."

"Then you've lost, Caspian." I turn to him. "I'll remove the thorns from Castletree."

He tilts his head. "Rip them out. Burn them. Ask them nicely to retreat. Be my guest, Princess. But if you want this tree to remain standing, you'll leave them where they are."

"So you can keep siphoning the magic?" Dayton asks.

As if to test his theory, I concentrate on a cluster of thorns by the dining room window. My awareness spreads, traveling through the briars like a deep breath. I will the thorns to retract. It's as though I can sense their resistance at first, not in words so much as a feeling. When I used the thorns to help the roses in High Tower and to save Kel's life, they'd been eager to obey my command.

"Come on," I whisper.

Reluctantly, the thorns spiral downward, revealing the dining room's wallpaper and a bright window. Immediately, the glass caves in on itself, shattering. The wall crumbles, stones and bark crashing to the earth.

"Rosalina!" Ezryn grabs me around the waist. He tugs me away, even though the debris is across the room.

I release my control on the thorns, and Caspian clicks his tongue. With a wave of his hand, cords of new vines spring up, threading between the cracks on the wall.

The same thing happened when Kel ripped them out. Somehow, Caspian's interwoven his enchantment with that of Castletree. I don't feel any siphoning, as Dayton put it. But perhaps I still need to work on this connection, this magic deep inside.

"Told you so." Caspian raises a dark brow but then his gaze shifts. "Now, as charming as it has been catching up, I did come here for a reason. Your impossible problem, Farron."

Farron shakes his head. "There's nothing I could possibly want from you."

"This isn't about want, Autumn Princeling." Caspian strides toward him, his black cape curling like smoke. "It's deeper than that. More insistent. A craving. You don't want what I have. You *need* it."

"What are you talking about?" Farron breathes.

Caspian stands in front of him, lips parted as he smiles deviously. "Don't you see? I'm here to offer you a bargain."

25

FARRON

I s this how Keldarion felt all those years ago, trapped amidst the
cosmos of Caspian's eyes?

How easily he had charmed us back then. Not just Kel, but
everyone who spoke to him. Everyone denied it because of his connection to the Below, but during that time, the staff blushed at his very
mention and the nobles longed for a scrap of conversation.

And I knew better than to get swept up in his cosmic storm.

I know better now.

And yet...

"What bargain?" I ask.

Kel crosses the room in a flash, snatching Caspian up by his lapels
and slamming him into the table. Plates and cups clatter to the floor.
"Don't you dare do this to him."

"My goodness," Caspian practically purrs. A serpentine smile
slithers up his face as he stares at Kel. "At least let me finish dinner
first."

I touch Kel's shoulder. He jolts, expression rabid with anger. "I
want to hear him out," I say.

Kel's chest shudders with his breath. He shoves Caspian to the side and turns away. The Prince of Thorns gives me a wide-eyed smirk as if we share some private joke about Kel's temper.

"Spit out your bargain so I can reject it," I snap. The others cluster around me until we're all staring at the Prince of Thorns.

Caspian rights himself, smoothing his jacket. "Let me lay out the facts, Farron. Your realm is on the brink of war, and Keldarion is to blame. Despite my delight in seeing Kel in as much misery as possible, I can't stand to see the four of you knocking your heads together and nary being able to come up with a thought."

"Hey, I'm here too," Rosie snaps, crossing her arms.

"Apologies." Caspian smiles. "Trust me, I used to be the little mascot to this group of empty-headed princelings, just as you are now. The stupidity is, unfortunately, contagious."

Rosalina blinks, unsure if she's been insulted or not. But before she can retort, Caspian strides up to me and straightens my collar. "You say there's no way to help your realm as you are now. Let me show you, Farron, that sometimes monsters are the best heroes."

He leans in close, pulling hard on my jacket, until his lips are right by my ear. His breath is hot on my skin, causing a rush of warmth up my neck and to my cheeks. "Because we already know that heroes are the best monsters, aren't they? The other princes have shown us that. You're not like them. You can still be saved. And maybe then," his dark eyes flick to Rosalina, "the coward could finally deserve a queen."

He pulls back and grins so beautifully and so wickedly, it's like a crack of lightning.

"I don't like this," Dayton grumbles. "He shouldn't be here."

"What are the terms of your bargain?" I ask.

Everyone shouts out cries of protest, but I say louder, harsher: "What are the terms of your bargain?"

Perhaps it's my imagination, but the room seems to darken, the candles flickering on the table. My vision tunnels until all I can see is Caspian, silhouetted by his thorns. "The bargain is so, Farron, High Prince of Autumn." His voice is a hypnotic melody, wrapping around me in echoes and whispers. "I will conjure a spell on you, one of thorn and shackles, that will confine your beast. Though you will still turn each night, this spell will ensure you remain … under control."

"I'll continue to shift?" I ask.

"Yes, but you will not have to worry about running through the halls as a mad beast or accidentally hurting someone you love." Caspian gives a pointed look down at Rosalina's leg, then up to Dayton's face. "Until the bargain is broken, of course."

"I *really* don't like this," Dayton says. "Come on, Ez, let's kick him out of here—"

"Farron is High Prince of Autumn," Ezryn says, voice a low timbre. "It is his decision alone to do what is best for his realm."

"What?" Dayton laces his hands through his hair. "Someone back me up. Kel?"

But Keldarion stands dazed, staring at Caspian with a mix of disgust and reverence.

If this bargain works, I think, *I could return to Autumn without fear of hurting my family or my people. I could remain hidden at night and not worry about breaking out or losing control of myself during the day. I might be able to be the High Prince for once.*

"If this is a bargain," Rosalina says, "what do you want in return?"

Caspian throws a casual arm around her shoulders. "In exchange, I would like you all to attend my birthday party."

Now it's my turn to join the collective gasp.

Dayton slams his foot down. "Is this some sick joke? Why the fuck would you want us there?"

"To trap us in the Below." Ezryn prowls toward him. "We are not fools, Caspian."

"No, but you're certainly paranoid," Caspian says without missing a beat. "You know I love a good festivity. I'm hosting a grand celebration for my Revelry Day in two full moons' time down in the pleasure-yard of Cryptgarden. I simply want the satisfaction of forcing you there." He touches his chest. "Trust me."

Keldarion walks over and yanks Caspian's hand off Rosalina. "Your birthday isn't on the full moon."

A flush seems to appear on Caspian's cheeks. "Well, that's when I'm hosting my party."

"We can't go to the Below," I say. "Our magic has no connection there."

Caspian clicks his tongue and pulls a tiny seed out of his front pocket. He flicks it to me, and I fumble, barely catching it. The small, purple oval is smooth to the touch.

"Plant this and a portal shall sprout for you and remain open for twelve hours. I recommend somewhere where no poor souls will accidentally come across it. It grows best in soil touched by tragedy." Caspian raises a brow. "Perhaps your old library would do."

Shame and anger flow through me, and I hold the seed between my fingers, ready to crush it.

I can't make a deal with Caspian. He betrayed Kel. He's sapping the magic from Castletree. He's a villain.

And he's the only way I'll ever be able to save my home and make sure what happened to the old library never happens again.

"This bargain includes everyone." I take turns staring each of my family members in the eye. "Will you come to Cryptgarden with me?"

Ezryn grinds his fists together. "It doesn't make sense. Why would the traitor want us there?"

Caspian opens his mouth to respond, but Rosalina interrupts him, giving him a dead-pan stare. "I think it's because he doesn't have any real friends." She takes my hand. "Trust your heart, Farron. If this is what you need to do for your people, I'll stand beside you." Then she flings a nasty look over her shoulder. "Even if it means attending a boring birthday party."

"Oh, trust me, Flower," Caspian purrs. "My parties are anything but boring."

Dayton looks up at the ceiling and gives an audible exhale. "Same as Rosie. I'm with you, Fare." He storms over to Caspian and pokes his chest. "But if anything seems fishy, I'll use that seed to go straight to the Below and cut off your pretty head."

Caspian rubs his chest. "Dayton, dear, I could teach you a thing or two about pretty head."

Now, it's Dayton's turn to blush.

Rosalina turns to Kel and Ezryn. "What about you two?" I ask.

Kel's gaze is a hailstorm driving into me. "Are you sure about this, Farron?"

I'm not sure about anything except that I can't do this alone. "Yes. I'm sure."

Kel's eyes close and his face softens in an expression akin to grief. He flicks one eye open and looks toward Ezryn. "I'm not going without you." His voice lowers a pitch. "I made that mistake last time."

Moment after moment passes as Ezryn stands eerily still. And then he says, "If this is the will of the High Prince of Autumn, then I will stand with you."

The air feels thick with anticipation, and I stumble as Caspian drags me away from the others. Rosalina reaches for me, and Dayton entwines his fingers with hers.

Caspian holds out his hand and I stare at it, knowing the fate of my realm lies in a deal with darkness incarnate. "Do we have a bargain?" he asks.

I pocket the seed, then take his hand. A cold wind rushes up from our connection, blowing my hair back as the bargain's magic springs into existence. "We have a bargain," I say.

Caspian throws his head back and laughs, the dark sound coming from every corner of the room. "I always knew I'd get my hands on you sometime," he drawls. In a flash, he grabs my throat.

Dayton steps forward but I wave him back, holding steady. Caspian plucks two thin thorns from one of the brambles on the floor. They wriggle out, one lacing around my neck like a choker, the other doing the same around his.

When he pulls away, I claw at the binding. The sharp barbs poke just light enough not to break through my skin, but tight enough I can't rip it off.

"I thought all bargains were bracelets," Rosalina says softly from the side.

"Sometimes," Kel responds. "Bargains are bindings, so it can be anything circular."

"But with you five geniuses, I don't think it will take you too long to figure out this little frost debacle," Caspian says mockingly. "I'm sure our bargain will be over before you know it."

26

ROSALINA

Dayton holds my hand so tight; I'm surprised my fingers aren't broken. He clenches his jaw, and a bead of sweat runs down his brow. *He hates this.*

But there's one person who hates it more. Keldarion looks in control on the outside, unfazed. But I can feel the caged beast of his rage blooming in my veins.

Farron staggers away from Caspian, pawing at the choker of thorns.

"Fare," Dayton chokes. He takes Farron into his arms, both of them shaking.

I ache to comfort him but the best I can do is caress his disheveled hair. "Are you alright?" I ask.

"Yeah, just dizzy."

"Don't worry," Caspian says. "That's a common side effect of staring into my eyes."

Both Dayton and I fix the Prince of Thorns with matching glares. A part of me hates that Farron made a deal with Caspian, but I understand. What choice did he have? He must take control of the Autumn Realm, but how can he do that if he's in constant fear of his beast breaking free and wreaking havoc?

I know what it feels like to make a deal with a beast to save the ones you love. It's what drove me to bargain with Keldarion when I was first imprisoned in Castletree.

What fear did Kel have when he made his own deal with the Prince of Thorns? Keldarion turns to Caspian and snarls, "You're done here." Then he storms to the door. "Perth will be here soon. I will await him in the entrance hall. Ezryn, make sure Caspian leaves."

As soon as Kel's gone, Ezryn grips Caspian's arm. "You heard him. Dinner is over. It's time to go."

Caspian slowly tears his eyes from the doorway to Ezryn, gaze glassy as if lost in thought. "What?"

"Return Below, Caspian. It would be unfortunate for Keldarion if Perth knew you were here," Ezryn says. He's so much taller and broader than Caspian, but the Prince of Thorns doesn't seem intimidated at all.

"Haven't you filled your chaos quota for today?" Dayton sneers, sitting back down at the table. Farron's head slumps on his shoulder.

"Fine, I'm leaving." Caspian dusts his shoulder where Ezryn grabbed him. "But before I go, might we have one game of Moonlight Mastery?"

A thicket of thorns rises from the ground and unfolds like a blooming flower. In the middle is a small purple box.

"If I recall," Caspian says, "you, High Prince of Spring, lost our last match." He plucks a scroll from the purple box and unfurls it.

I squint at the scroll. It's divided into three sections by a large T, with an *E* and a *C* above each column. Below the horizontal line is a series of tallies. A scorecard?

Ezryn looks between the box, to the door, and back at the box. I sense an incredible internal debate going on within him.

Caspian begins to roll up the scroll. "I mean, if you don't think you can win—"

"One game," Ezryn snaps. "Then you go."

"Perfect." Caspian sets down the box.

I drift to the other side of the table, and Dayton snakes an arm around my waist, gently pulling me to his lap. The movement is so fluid and comforting, it warms my heart.

"The game is Moonlight Mastery," Farron explains, seeming to have recovered though his voice is still raspy. "Ez and Cas have had a bitter rivalry for years."

Cas. That's the first I've ever heard him called that. The princes know Caspian much more intimately than I realized. And here he is, playing a game with them while his thorns throttle our home.

Can you both hate and love something? Someone?

As I watch the Prince of Thorns slowly remove the pieces from the game box, I cannot tell if he has a nefarious reason for delaying his departure or if he's just … lonely. All he wanted in exchange for the bargain was for us to attend his birthday party.

The game set is beautiful: a circular board made of polished white stone, with small orbs in various colors. "The raised ring around the edges prevents the pieces from falling off," Farron says. "The tokens each correspond to a different element in nature, such as fire, water, air, and earth."

"How do you play?" I ask, hoping the conversation will distract Farron from overthinking the bargain.

"The objective is to use strategy and manipulation to control the paths of light and shadow that crisscross the board," he says. "Players take turns placing their pieces and using their abilities to obscure or illuminate certain areas of the board. The goal is to trap your opponent in a ring of shadow or encircle your own pieces in light."

I look over at Ezryn and Caspian, both beginning to set up their pieces with great intensity. "Does the winner get a prize or something?"

"I think they may have made some ridiculous bet back when this all started," Dayton says with a hint of amusement. "But it's more about the bragging rights now. Which is quite valuable to those two."

The game begins, and I find myself entranced as I watch the princes battle it out. Ezryn moves with quiet concentration, while Caspian feigns disinterest before interchanging his pieces in a chaotic fashion. Dayton and Farron are engrossed, each offering Ezryn advice, most of which only frustrates him. He gives angry shushes without looking away from the board.

I wish I could just settle into the warmth of Dayton's embrace and enjoy the evening, but there's a quiet tugging in my chest. An unsettledness.

Keldarion is suffering.

I slip off Dayton's lap. "I'm going to check on Kel," I whisper.

Ezryn straightens and watches as I pass. "I'll come back as soon as the vizier arrives," I say. "Promise."

He doesn't like it, but he trusts me. He nods and returns to the game. I leave the dining hall and make my way to the entrance of Castletree.

KELDARION STANDS in the entrance hall, one hand against a pillar, silhouetted by thorns and ice.

"Kel?"

"Go enjoy your evening, Rosalina," he says without turning. "Tomorrow, we travel to the Autumn Realm, and I suspect there will be little rest there."

I move in front of him. "I can't rest. There's a storm inside my chest that cannot be quelled."

He grips one of the thorns. "Your bond has awakened. With us being so close, it's strengthening."

A defiant part of my heart leaps at that. He cannot deny what we have. But also … Do I want to be with someone only because of a mystical connection and not because they truly care for me?

"Tell me what's wrong," I plead.

Keldarion shifts his gaze around the room. Perth Quellos hasn't arrived yet. When he does, he'll come through the door. Unless things have changed, he's the only one allowed in or out of Castletree. Whereas the large mirror by the entrance can take the princes anywhere, the door is enchanted to open to distinct points in each of the realms.

"It seems every day there is another mountain," he grumbles, pushing away from the wall. "Rebellions in my realm, frost in Autumn, Farron making a bargain, and you able to control the thorns, a power *he* has that belongs to no other."

"You will speak to Perth today of the rebellions and the frost. Tomorrow, we depart to Autumn to set things right. Farron has made his choice and be thankful the price is one we can pay together. We are more powerful united. As for the thorns, this is a good thing. If I manage to understand them, then I might be able to use that to aid Castletree."

He gapes at me for a moment, but that coil of frustration, anger— something else—only grows stronger.

"Is that all?" I ask when he doesn't reply.

"Leave," he tells me and begins pacing up and down the entrance hall.

I storm, or rather skate a little on the frosted floor, before sliding and catching myself on one of the side tables. "Hey," I snarl. "You can tell Caspian to leave all you want, but this is my home."

His gaze darkens. "Do you really have no comprehension of the agony your presence brings me?"

Now, I'm gaping. "What have I ever done but try to help you?"

"Go back to the others."

I still, realization seeping into my bones. "You can smell him."

"I *felt* you." He whirls, hair a tangle of matted white waves. His voice lowers to a primal growl. "All three times."

I almost cower. But I recall Dayton's words and hold my chin high. "I'm surprised you remember what that feels like. What has it been? Twenty-five years?"

A shocked expression rolls over his features. Autumn may be preparing for war on the Winter Realm, but their prince started one with me the moment he told me he'd rather watch the world burn than accept our bond.

I will not let the Enchanted Vale fall or the other princes suffer for this man's ego.

A husky growl comes out of his throat, "You are the most infuriating creature I have ever encountered."

I swish past him, my ivory skirts billowing. "It can hardly bother you that much, Kel. Farron informed me that a mate bond can drive a person into an uncontrollable jealous rage."

"Is that why you nearly impaled Caspian on his own thorns?"

"I don't like people touching what's mi—" I bite my tongue. Kel's not mine. He's made that clear. "That was a little crazy."

"On the contrary, that was the best thing I've seen in ages."

My body trills at the scrap of approval from him. *Ugh.* Is this the mate bond or my own traitorous heart?

"You weren't bothered by Dayton and me..." I say, a hint of awkwardness seeping out. "We messed around, but we didn't sleep together or anything."

I know Keldarion doesn't deserve an explanation, but despite him rejecting our mate bond, he's a part of my life. I need to be honest with him.

Keldarion places a large hand on the end table, gripping tightly. "Perhaps my bond is as broken as my heart. Many emotions plagued me as your feelings collided with mine, but in the end ... There is only contentment in me that you were satisfied."

A wave of disbelief washes over me as I struggle to make sense of the situation. "That is not the answer I expected. I didn't see you as the type to allow your mate to be with anyone else. Even if you want nothing to do with me."

He gazes at me for a second, then shakes his head. "I could kick Dayton's ass if it would make you feel better?"

"No."

There's silence and then Keldarion grumbles, "Dayton's not *anyone else.*"

I grab his arm. "Farron has a theory. He thinks the reason he and Day don't experience jealousy is because there's a connection between the princes. Maybe from the curse, or maybe from living in Castletree all together."

"Farron and his theories." Kel quirks his head, studying me in a new light. "I know about you and Dayton, and Farron couldn't be subtle about his affection for you if he tried. Did something happen between you and Ezryn?"

Shit, I'm officially the worst secret keeper in all of Castletree. A flush blooms over my cheeks. It wasn't like Ezryn told me to keep it secret before he rushed out of there. "He might have kissed me."

"His helmet?"

"Did a whole light smashing, complete darkness thing," I explain. "I didn't see his face."

Keldarion seems to consider this for a moment, running a hand through his long hair. I know I've sensed tension between the two of them lately, and I don't want to worsen it. But he says, "It makes sense."

Maybe Farron's scientific methods are rubbing off on me, or maybe it's my need to figure out this new magical thing inside me, but I want to test Farron's theory.

"So, if the whole jealousy thing doesn't affect you," I say, "I should go down to the Summer Realm and visit one of those naked orgy rooms Dayton told me about—"

Keldarion is on me in an instant. He grabs me around the waist and lifts me to the small end table. His arms create a cage around my body, his breath a warm growl by my ear. "You will do no such thing."

I reach for him, desperate for this show of affection. My dress snags on the thorns, a chill rushing over my shoulders. But his chest is comforting as it presses against mine. "I guess your bond isn't entirely broken."

He looks down as I spread my legs to wrap around his waist. "So it would seem."

"Dayton told me that if I was with someone other than the princes of Castletree, he'd kill them and take me in their blood."

At those words, Keldarion pulls me tighter against him, and I can feel all of his hard body. "Not every word out of his mouth is complete idiocy."

I nearly melt into his touch, my mind muddled with his closeness. "Would you do the same?"

He cups my face. "What wouldn't I do for you?"

"Would you let me love you?"

He stills, and I come roaring back to reality. The reality where Keldarion hates me, and these small glimpses of affection fade like a dream.

He shakes his head and begins to step away.

But I scramble forward, more of my flowing dress catching and ripping on the thorns. I snatch Keldarion's shirt, hauling him closer, still seated on the tiny table. "Why do you do this, Kel? It's cruel. I'm so sick of trying to make sense of you."

"Fulfill your desires with the other princes, Rose. This fate is not in the stars for us."

"But you're my *mate*." I tug his face down to mine until we're nose to nose. "Our bond could break the curse."

His gaze trails down my body. I realize the gauzy dress has torn, loosening the fabric around my chest, the upper curve of my breasts on full display. His calloused hand runs over the delicate skin. A wave of molten desire courses through me. I drive my hips forward, feeling his steel pleasure waiting.

His thumb presses in the soft flesh, exploring, and a male groan emits from his throat. The mere sound of it causes wetness to pool between my legs. "Kiss me, Kel," I whisper, arching my neck, "or I will die of it."

Roughly, he grips the back of my neck with one hand and my arm with the other. My eyes flutter closed.

But the kiss doesn't come. I blink my eyes open to see Keldarion completely still.

"Kel?"

His grip on my arm tightens, his whole body vibrating. Something feral flashes in his gaze as he growls, "Who did this to you?"

27

ROSALINA

My blood turns to ice. I try to yank my arm away, but it's too late. My ripped dress has revealed the scar on my wrist. One I've been trying to hide for my entire adult life.

"Lucas," Keldarion reads, the word laced with pure venom. "That *boy* who pulled you from the frozen lake? The one you loved?"

Desperately, I slap my palm over my wrist to conceal the scar. A desperate sob bubbles in my chest, and my true fear bursts out. "You must be so ashamed to have a mate who allowed someone to do this to her."

I'm not sure how many of my words are coherent and how much is a garbled mess, but Keldarion instantly pulls me against him. "No, Rose. Do not say such things. My anger arises because I was not there to protect you."

I wipe my eyes. "It was a long time ago."

"Tell me, when I sent you back, was that man there? Did he harm you?"

Lucas's hands on my skin. The flash of the knife. If the others hadn't shown up... "No." I shake my head vehemently. "I told him to leave me alone."

Gently, Kel caresses my face. In the strangest show of intimacy, he places a soft kiss on the side of my cheek before striding toward the giant mirror beside the door.

"Where are you going?"

"To your home," he says simply.

"Why?"

"To find this Lucas." Keldarion's eyes blaze, reminding me that my mate is no mere man. He's a fae prince, one of immense power. "And when I do, he will beg me for the mercy of death."

My breath catches in my throat. He doesn't know Lucas is here in the castle. The others must not have told him.

I rush up to Kel and wrap my arms around his waist. "There's nothing for me in that world anymore. My life is here in Castletree."

He grips my chin gently. "I see that now, Rosalina. I do not intend to send you away again. The other princes have proven they can protect and care for you, even if I cannot. This is the safest place for you, but I will not rest until that man—"

A cold gust of wind blows into the entrance hall as the door opens.

Perth Quellos, Keldarion's vizier, enters. His slender face is bereft of hair, scalp smooth and gleaming like polished marble. His complexion is pallid, with a faint bluish hue that brings to mind the chill of a winter's night.

Feral anger floods me as I look upon the steward of the Winter Realm. As if feeling my emotions, Kel's grip on me tightens.

"Ahem." The vizier clears his throat. His lips are tinted blue as if he has savored a bounty of ripe berries. "I have come at your request, sire."

"Apologies, but a more pressing matter has arisen," Keldarion says.

"More pressing than the ravings of the Autumn Realm?" Perth asks. "You seemed quite urgent in your summons."

It *is* urgent. I grip Keldarion on either side of his face and make him look at me until his breathing steadies. "This can wait. The meeting with your vizier is important, Kel. For Farron."

He fixes me with a steely gaze, then straightens. "This isn't over,

Rosalina." Then he unlaces his jerkin and slips it off, revealing a tight black shirt. He drapes the fabric over me, covering my slightly torn dress and the scar on my wrist.

Does he realize now why I always wear long sleeves?

"Are you sure you're alright?" Keldarion asks, keeping his attention solely on me as Perth sways from foot to foot impatiently.

"I'm okay."

"Stay with the others until I return," Keldarion commands before turning to Perth. "Come, let us retire to the council room. The staff recently cleaned it up."

Perth nods, then slithers past me. "A pleasure as always, Lady of Castletree." The title Ezryn dubbed me after he threw Perth across the gardens.

I narrow my gaze. There's something odd about him today. He wears his typical white cloak with a geometric blue pattern. But atop his bald head lies a silver crown adorned with a large gem. I've never seen that shade of green before, almost phantasmal.

I release a breath as Keldarion vanishes up the stairs and into the council room with Perth. The weight of the vizier's presence lifts from the room, and the air seems to stir with newfound ease. I rub my wrist, touching the scar. He saw. Kel saw my scar ... and he didn't call me a coward, or feel disgust, or think that I'm a pathetic little girl who let someone hurt her so deeply. No, there was only rage in his eyes. A deep protectiveness. Seeing him like that ... *He cares for me in his own strange way.*

But he was ready to go off and murder Lucas. As much as I don't believe Lucas deserves any compassion, I can't be responsible for his death. I might be able to stop Keldarion from going to the human world, but if he finds out Lucas is in this castle, it's game over.

I have to get Lucas home. Tonight.

Slowly, I turn to the large mirror beside the door. Tall, stretching almost to the floor, its golden frame is adorned with delicate inlaid roses that seem to bloom before my very eyes. The glass looks clouded and aged.

Castletree has helped me before by opening the bars in my cell and leading me to High Tower. Would it help me use the mirror like the princes can?

I was able to use the necklace to contact Ezryn and; I can control the thorns.

Something simmers in me below the surface.

I've seen Farron send someone through. Dayton and I used it to travel to the Summer Realm. If this was how the princes came to Orca Cove, surely, I can use it to get Lucas home.

Taking a steadying breath, I touch the glass. The mirror ripples, waves of metal water. "Show me Orca Cove," I whisper.

The glass shimmers with pearlescent light and I see it: the willow tree, the road, Orca Cove's new gift shop.

It works.

It works!

As soon as I pull my hand away, the mirror turns back to normal. I can activate it again when I get Lucas here.

I've got time. Keldarion should be in that meeting for a while. I peer into the dining room as I pass. They're still playing Moonlight Mastery, and it sounds like it's getting heated. Farron and Dayton lean over Ezryn as he ponders a move. Meanwhile, Caspian tilts back in his chair, grinning like the Cheshire Cat.

I suppose I could ask for their help with Lucas, but if they somehow discovered my scar, they're likely to fly into a murderous rage. Plus, I know there's already tension with Kel and I don't want to add to it by getting them to do something behind his back. Papa would assist, but I don't have time to search the whole castle to find him.

I can do this myself. A quick trip to the mirror and goodbye Lucas. See you never.

The healing chamber is silent. I creep over to where Lucas sleeps. He's still not fully healed, but he's a lot better than yesterday with his guts no longer hanging out.

I shake him, but he doesn't even stir. Ezryn must have put him into a deep sleep. Blowing a tuft of hair out of my face, I rush to the pantry and quickly scan all the beautifully labeled jars.

"A-ha!" Smelling salts. I pop the cork and stick them right under Lucas's nose. He blinks awake, and I place my palm over his mouth. "If you want to live, you'll be quiet."

He shakes his head, strands of red hair falling in his face, voice groggy. "Rosalina? W-where am I..."

Okay, this is good. As long as he can walk, I don't need him to be too coherent.

"Come on." I lace my arm under his and help him out of bed. My whole body feels sick at his touch, but I try to push my emotions down so Kel doesn't feel it.

Lucas stands on shaking legs, groaning. He's dressed in nothing but a simple beige tunic and loose pants. "We're in the castle of the fae," I explain, "and I'm taking you home. That's all you need to know."

A groggy moan is his only reply.

Carefully, I peer both ways. The halls are empty. Being the full moon, most of the staff are spending the night celebrating and partying together. A small blessing.

We move slowly, Lucas leaning heavily on me and groaning about his sore legs.

My heart hammers as we make it to the entrance hall. Lucas's eyes flick every which way. "These thorns..." he mumbles, more coherent by the second. "Like when we went through the rosebush."

"Don't talk," I hiss.

He seems fine to obey me for now. Unease quivers in my stomach. What about when his fatigue wears off? Before he'd been attacked, he'd been trying to carve a ring into my finger.

As we pass the dining room, the voices of my fae princes drift out, comforting and warm. Every instinct in me wants to call out for them, beg them to protect me from the monster currently leaning on me.

But only a few more steps, and Lucas will be out of my life forever. He won't have power over me again. Then I can return and help Ezryn with his game, embrace Day and Fare while watching Caspian's strange but beautiful smile—Wait, no, not that.

My thoughts draw back to the present as we reach the mirror. No one is around; we're in the clear.

I place my hand on the glass pane. But it doesn't change at all. "Show me Orca Cove," I demand, pressing my fingers against the glass.

All that gazes back at me is my reflection and Lucas slumped on my shoulder.

"You really are fucking crazy," he says. "That's a mirror."

Steps sound from above the stairs, a murmur of voices.

"This mirror is the only thing that will save your life," I whisper. I slam my palm hard against the pane. "Show me Orca Cove."

"As I said before, sire," Perth Quellos's voice drifts down to us, "we did notice a strange frost along the border but did not realize it was dangerous. My summons to you have gone unanswered, and we've received no word from Princess Niamh."

Kel's voice booms in response: "Send the Kryodian Riders to investigate. Our finest legion will surely be able to get to the bottom of this from Winter's side."

No, no, no. If this mirror doesn't work, Keldarion is going to *kill* Lucas. "Please." The gilded edges gleam like the castle is listening. But the mirror does not open for me again.

"Rosalina," a stern voice says from behind me.

Keldarion is here.

"Don't tell him your name," I whisper to Lucas as we turn. "And don't be a dick."

Lucas grunts in acknowledgment. He's still got his arm slung around me. And yep, the mate bond must be perfectly functional because the fury on Kel's face is clear. He storms down the stairs, leaving Perth Quellos scampering behind him. "Who is this?"

It's on the tip of my tongue: *Oh, the injured human Ezryn healed. I'm just sending him home.*

But before I can say anything, Lucas straightens. "I don't know who the fuck you are. I'm Lucas Poussin, and this is *my* fiancé."

I swear even Castletree takes a breath. I inhale, and Kel stills. Then all fury explodes. A blizzard thrashes down the hall, hail and snow rising around the Prince of Winter as he storms toward us and snarls, "Get your hands off my mate."

28

ROSALINA

I thought I'd witnessed Keldarion's wrath before—when Farron attempted to eat me, when Caspian crashed the ball, or even when I dared to enter High Tower. Yet, what I behold now is unlike any of that.

It's in the unyielding set of his jaw, the controlled gait of his stride. A palpable fury that crackles the surrounding air. A rage so intense that each flake of snow and ice-tipped breeze falls into his command.

Maybe I should be afraid. But it's like every part of my body wants to run to him.

Lucas springs his hands off me and stumbles to the door, tugging on it. But of course, it doesn't open for him. "What the fuck, Rosalina?" Terror radiates through his words. "Where are we, you crazy bitch?"

"Kel, wait." I hold up my hands. "I can explain."

Keldarion ignores me. Behind us, Perth Quellos watches with a calculating gaze. Another fear bursts to life in my chest. Keldarion usually has complete control over his wolf, and it is a full moon. But what if it breaks free? The last thing we need is that foul vizier seeing the truth of his curse.

"Ez!" I call. "Day! Farron!" I'm going to need their help if I want to stop a murder and Kel's wolf from breaking free.

In an instant, the three princes rush from the dining hall. Caspian must have left, which is for the best, because it wouldn't do for Perth to see him either.

Dayton pulls me against his chest, and Farron grabs my trembling hands. Ezryn stands in front of the three of us, surveying the situation, every step charged with dominance.

"I was trying to send Lucas home," I say, "but the mirror wouldn't work, and then Kel came down and—"

"Kel," Ezryn says, "what is going on? This man is my patient, under Rosalina's request."

Keldarion only gives the briefest grunt of acknowledgement. He stands over Lucas, who has slunk down, trembling in front of the door. I've never seen him like this, cowering like the animals he hunts.

Keldarion's voice rumbles low and dangerous. "This man has committed an unforgivable crime. Death would be a mercy he does not deserve."

Lucas looses a string of unintelligible curses. He whips his head back and forth, but I already know there's no escape for him.

Dayton rubs my shoulders in a comforting gesture. "What's going on, Blossom?"

Fresh tears spill down my cheeks. Farron takes hold of my face with a tender touch, his eyes full of empathy. "Rosie, we're here for you. You can tell us anything."

I shake my head, breaking free of his grip. "You're going to be so ashamed of me."

Ezryn turns around at my words, all three of them protectively encircling me. "You have seen our pasts laid bare before you," Ezryn says, "yet you returned to us."

Farron holds me with his amber gaze. "There is nothing you could tell us that would have us turn away from you."

"Nothing," Dayton agrees.

My fingers tighten around my wrist. "Lucas left many scars on me. But this is the only one that can be seen."

I raise the sleeve of Keldarion's tunic, revealing this most wretched scar, the jagged lines of *LUCAS* written on my skin.

As the three princes stare at my greatest shame, I feel their rage rise like wildfire.

Ezryn reaches for me, holding my arm in his shaking gloved hand. I catch my reflection in the black T of his visor. There is fear in my face, but something emerges between my quivering lips, my watery eyes.

Anger.

At myself for feeling so afraid for so long. At Lucas, for making me feel that way.

They don't say words, but Dayton pulls me tighter against his chest, and Farron closes in on my other side. Ez turns, still blocking us in.

"Protector of the Realms," Ezryn's voice rumbles with a foreboding intensity, evoking the sound of a gathering storm. "I stand with you."

"I stand with you," Dayton growls deeply.

Farron takes a deep breath, something flashing in his eyes, but it seems to quell when he gazes upon Keldarion. "I stand with you."

They will not stop this.

Darkness curls in my chest. Is it Keldarion's rage?

No.

It's my own.

"Good," Keldarion snarls, his grip tightening around the collar of Lucas's shirt before he flings him across the room. With a sickening thud, Lucas crashes into a pillar adorned with vicious briars, shredding his flesh on the razor-sharp thorns. As he crumples to the ground, his agonized cry fills the chamber. He tries to rise, coughing up blood, but Keldarion gets there first, delivering a swift kick to Lucas's gut as he rolls on his back.

The other princes still surround me, their bodies radiating with anticipation, content to watch until the Protector of the Realms calls on them.

Keldarion kneels beside Lucas, his white hair falling in disarray. The cords of his muscular arms bulge as he leans forward, resting them on his knees. "Tell me, which hand do you use to hold your knife?"

Lucas's eyes widen and he mumbles incoherently. Keldarion grabs his wrist, then pushes it back. A horrible snap echoes through the chamber, followed by Lucas's garbled scream.

"You know what?" Keldarion says plainly. "I've decided I don't care." He stands, then slams his boot down on Lucas's other hand with a sharp crunch.

A whine like the keening of a dying animal emits from Lucas as he writhes on the floor. Kel has broken both his hands. Even if he heals, he'll never hold his gun or his knife the same way.

Keldarion looks down at him in disgust. "You will regret the day you ever laid hands on her."

He grabs Lucas by his torn shirt and lifts him. The boy I had once considered marrying goes limp as a ragdoll. Keldarion slams him against the pillar. Ice grows and encases him up to the waist. His arms hang at his side, head lulling on his chest.

Kel flexes his fingers, and a jagged knife of ice grows in his hand. "I will not debase the Lady of Castletree's name by carving it into your wretched flesh. But I'll carve mine, so you know who brought you to your end."

Lucas howls, "I'm going to fucking kill you."

"I won't stop at your flesh." Animalistic fury etches its way into Keldarion's words as he drags the knife along Lucas's collarbone. "I will peel back your skin, rip apart your muscles, and carve into your very bones."

A choked sob escapes Lucas's mouth, stringy strands of red hair sticking to his sweat-laced brow. A wintry numbness crawls up my body as I watch the scene play out.

"But the first cut does not belong to me." Keldarion lowers the knife and turns to us. "Your blood belongs to my mate, the Lady of Castletree."

Kel's gaze turns from fury to reverent as he looks at me, the ice knife outstretched.

Ezryn steps aside, inclining his head. Dayton releases his grip on my shoulder, whispering, "Make him pay."

"He doesn't deserve mercy," Farron says.

I walk toward Keldarion and take the knife in my hands. The chill of it shivers through me and ignites my blood. An absolutely devastating smile crawls across Kel's face as he looks down at me. "Vengeance is in your hands, my Rose."

I prowl closer to Lucas and his eyes widen. "Get me out of here. There's the monster, Rosalina!"

"Shut the fuck up or it'll be me ripping your guts out this time," Dayton calls to him, putting his arm around Farron. "But you're lucky I don't want to deny my girl the satisfaction."

Farron hardly seems bothered by Lucas's words. There are no signs of the wolf. His gaze is fixed on me, and he nods encouragingly.

"Your girl?" Lucas looks delirious. The pain is getting to him. "You some kind of whore, Pumpkin?"

A collective growl emits from the princes, but none of them step in front of me as I slowly walk before Lucas.

"These are the Princes of Castletree, and you will address them with the respect they deserve," I say, voice dripping with venom. "As for me," I continue, taking a step closer to Lucas until we're practically nose to nose. "I am not anyone's whore or your pumpkin. I am Rosalina O'Connell, the Lady of Castletree, and you will show *me* the respect *I* deserve."

Lucas's delirious expression turns to one of fear as he realizes the gravity of his mistake.

"Rosalina, w-wait," he says. "I-I saved your life."

"No, you didn't. You stole it. The day you pulled me from the ice, you snatched my life, held it hostage, and made me believe the only way I could glimpse it was in the flash of your smile. And yet, I was still drowning, like you never rescued me at all."

"I-I—" Lucas flounders.

"I'm not afraid of you anymore." An angry fire blazes in my chest, and my skin feels too hot. "And I don't owe you anything."

Every painful moment flashes before me. He left his mark on my body with the hunting knife that night, but that wasn't the only time. His poisonous words were as sharp as any blade, and his actions, the manipulation, dug just as deep beneath my skin.

I grab his arm, his broken fingers turning purple.

"Thief," I breathe. "That's what I'm going to write. For everything you took from me."

It won't bring back the years of my life he stole. It's impossible for me to save the girl he hurt, but still, his screams will sound sweet. I know the blade my mate made for me will be sharp. I raise my knife and drive it down.

Someone jumps between me and Lucas, holding my arm.

"I'm sorry, Princess," Caspian says, wild black hair falling in his face. "I can't let you do that."

29

ROSALINA

My heart careens in my chest, fingers trembling on the ice knife. Why is Caspian here? Why does he care about Lucas? His hand is firm on my arm, his eyes a swirling constellation of stars.

A shadow looms over us. "You will not deny my mate her vengeance."

The stars turn dark, and Caspian shoots a venomous glare at Keldarion. "Carving into a man's flesh? This is madness."

"Move," Keldarion growls. "You well know I slipped off the edge of madness years ago."

"Oh, Kel, of course I do." Caspian's lip curls, but then he looks to me, and there's a strange softness in his gaze. "But she hasn't. Don't let her fall into the darkness as we have."

Something in his words clears the anger from my mind. The ice knife falls from my grasp, and I stumble away from them. What was I going to do? Carve into Lucas's flesh as he writhed helpless below me? He doesn't deserve my mercy, I know that. But taking his own cruelty and returning it to him … That's not me.

"This man deserves death," Keldarion says.

Caspian straightens, putting a reassuring hand on the Winter Prince's chest. "I agree."

At Caspian's arrival, the three other princes have closed in around us. Peering out from behind a pillar, Perth Quellos observes us with his bird-like stare.

He cannot be pleased to see the Prince of Thorns here.

Caspian drags his fingers down Kel's chest before turning to me. "Let me take this monster down to the Below," he says. "I will give you the vengeance you deserve, Rosalina. There are ways to break a soul in those chasms with nightmares you cannot possibly imagine. I will make sure he suffers every single one of them before I release him to oblivion."

My heart thumps in my breast, the only sound besides Lucas's whimpering. Even the other princes aren't speaking, instead watching Caspian watch me. "Trust me." Caspian grabs my hands, and something in me relaxes at his touch. The angry fire quiets, not dimming but settling to a comforting glow. "Princess, you need not tarnish your soul to know justice has been served. Lay that burden upon my shoulders. Let me be your darkness."

This isn't a bargain or a deal. I'm not sure why, but there's something about the fierceness in his expression that makes me think, at least in this, I can trust the Prince of Thorns. "Caspian—"

"Trust you?" A soft voice slinks between us as Perth Quellos steps forward. "Wasn't that what brought Winter to its knees all those years ago?"

"Ah, Perth," Caspian says smoothly. "Trust me, it takes a lot of determination and just the right amount of begging to bring Winter to his knees."

"Enough," Keldarion snaps, snatching the arm of his advisor. "You will leave while we settle this matter."

"What matter could bring the Prince of Thorns into your company again, High Prince of Winter?" Perth's voice is slick as an icicle. "After I worked so hard to quell those rebellions that arose from your little Solstice Ball?"

"I invited the Prince of Thorns," I say. "I wanted to attempt a diplomatic approach to our thorny problem."

"Ahh yes, the human." Perth takes a step toward me, but Ezryn moves quicker, blocking his path. Perth hesitates, no doubt remembering the treatment Ezryn gave him last time we were together. "Did I hear that right, sire? Your mate, is she?"

Keldarion heaves in a breath. "That is correct."

"Most interesting," he says. "Any more secrets I should know of here in Castletree?"

Yeah, one giant slobbery wolf problem. Or rather, *four* giant slobbery wolf problems.

"Look, it's great we're catching up," Dayton says, "but this guy's moans are really getting on my nerves. Can we just let Cas take him already?"

"Gladly," Caspian says, shadows curling around his boots.

"I may have an alternative to murder," Perth says, steepling his fingers. "There is an entrance to the human world in the Winter Realm. Allow me to fix his hands and I'll send him on his way."

"He deserves—" Keldarion roars.

"Death," Perth says. "Yes, so you've said. But is this not your mate's decision?"

Kel grits his teeth, then turns to me. "That it is."

I look to my princes; I know their choice. Give Lucas to Caspian and let him face every nightmare of the Below. Or I could simply ask them to end him quickly. Maybe we could throw Lucas through the mirror to Castletree, but I'm not sure Perth knows about it. Perhaps it's another of Castletree's secrets.

The decision lays heavy on me, but I'm done giving Lucas everything I have. If he's to die, his death won't be from my hands. And though Perth may be a cruel man, Kel trusts him. After the vizier takes Lucas away, I'll never have to think about him ever again.

"Take him away," I tell Perth Quellos, trying to emulate some command in my voice.

"Rosalina, no—" Caspian snarls. "You can't let him live."

"My decision is final," I say, stepping away from the princes. But when I look at Lucas, there's no gratitude in his expression, only a vacant stare.

Keldarion's lip curls into a snarl, and he thrusts his hand forward in a sweeping gesture. A surge of power ripples through the air. The ice binding Lucas to the pillar shatters like brittle glass. With a gasp, Lucas tumbles to the ground, his limbs shaking as he struggles to sit up. Keldarion towers over him, eyes blazing with an icy fire. "If I ever see you again, I will not show you the mercy my mate has granted."

Perth kneels beside Lucas, tsking. He waves a gnarled hand, his jeweled crown emitting a strange greenish glow, and slowly Lucas's fingers snap back into place. "Very well. Come with me, human."

"Learned some new tricks since I last saw you, Quellos?" Kel mutters.

"We can't all wield a Blessing. Some of us must study our way to higher power," Perth retorts, walking to the door.

Dayton stomps over and switches the handle to the emblem of the snowflake. It opens with a creak, and a gust of bitter wind flits in.

Lucas stumbles unsteadily to his feet and hobbles after Perth. He pauses beside me.

"Goodbye, Lucas," I say, lifting my chin defiantly.

He gives a half-laugh, half- sigh. "You know, I had this dream once. I'd fallen asleep after gutting a deer. I dreamt I was fucking you. While you were screaming, I took my knife and sliced your skin. And I removed each of your organs until I got to your heart and squeezed it."

A frigid terror grips my body as a twisted smile creeps over Lucas's face. "I thought of it many times after that, when you were beneath me." Sickening glee fills his voice. "I don't think I'll survive this. Not really. But at least I'll take you with me."

With a swift motion, Lucas raises his arm, revealing the ice knife glittering in his hand. He must have picked it up. He brings it down toward my chest.

Time seems to still. All the princes lurch toward me. Thorns explode around Caspian. Ezryn grips my waist and pulls me back, but

161

he's too slow. The blade nicks my arm, and my blood sprays over the ground.

Each drop falls onto the icy floor, loud as a sonic boom.

I look up to see the wild frost blue eyes of Keldarion before he changes. His skin shifts, fur and claws breaking free as a giant white wolf emerges. It lunges toward us, tackling Lucas.

Lucas doesn't have time to scream before Kel's claws slice down his middle. Blood gushes up, staining Kel's white fur. Massive jaws clamp down on Lucas's head, teeth piercing the skull with a crunch. Sinew is ripped from bone, Lucas's head barely clinging to his shoulder. With his jaws fastened around the torso, Kel shakes the limp, lifeless body and throws it through the door into the Winter Realm.

Ezryn holds me against his metallic frame, tight as a vice grip. Dayton's sheltering Farron, who is curled into a ball, shivering. "She's safe," Dayton says over and over to him. "He's dead. Kel killed him. We don't need your wolf now. She's safe. She's safe. Kel protected us."

Perth has collapsed by the door, shaking. Keldarion walks over to him, maw dripping with blood.

"Now you know, Vizier, that not only is Castletree dying," Keldarion growls, "we princes are cursed. Return to the Winter Realm and throw that scum's remains in the deepest pits of the Frosted Wastes. Do not disappoint me in your duties."

30

KELDARION

My wet hair falls over my shoulders as I make my way up from the hot springs. I'm finally cleansed of that monster's blood.

I don't regret it, even though Quellos saw my truth. This will be the utmost test of his loyalty. His claims of uncertainty about the frost seemed sincere, and it's very likely I missed his summons while I was deep in the cold depression of my wolf. But will he send patrols to the border as I commanded now that he knows a beast rules his realm? Surely, after all his years of loyal service to my family, he will find forgiveness for a beast.

Besides, I ordered him to have the Kryodian Riders investigate the situation. They are Winter's elite squadron of mounted warriors, honed by years of rigorous training and harmoniously bonded with their steeds. I must have faith in the strength left in Winter.

Even the hot springs could not chase the weariness from my body. Dayton had stayed on the edge of the grotto, not giving me a moment's peace. He was most likely bored since Farron had retired early, drained from the bargain. Ezryn had muttered something about guarding the grounds, voice shaky with rage.

And Caspian disappeared into his thorns.

"Excuse me, Master, move that firm ass." I leap to the side as a woman with a large tray comes racing by. "Got to get this out while it's hot."

"Marigold?" I grumble before silently following her.

She disappears into Rosalina's chambers. Laughter cascades from within. I stop at the entrance and peer through the crack in the door.

The room overflows with staff, all the friends Rosalina has made here. Marigold unloads the tray filled with cookies and hot chocolate. Rose grabs a mug and takes a sip, and Astrid giggles as she wipes whipped cream off Rosalina's face.

On her couch, Paavak and Mandaria lounge with a tall stack of books. Flavia holds up outfit considerations for the Autumn Realm. Rosalina has a beautiful smile on her face. Despite the trials of earlier, she is still safe and happy here.

Her smile is mirrored tenfold in those around her. She brings light to the staff. I thought I had been doing the right thing sending her to the human world. But I had only brought her closer to a monster.

No, she must remain here. A new comfort settles in me. I saw firsthand today how my brothers would protect her with their lives. I feel the strange semblance of my own smile as I click Rosalina's door shut and continue to my quarters.

Inside, I cross the icy expanse to my wardrobe. Reaching behind my back, I tug off my shirt, tossing it into a bin, then begin to undo the laces of my pants.

"Well, aren't we eager?" a dangerously smooth voice says.

I whirl. There he is, lounging on my bed as if he belongs there.

"I told you to leave."

Caspian raises up on the back of his arms, a frown on his lips. "Before dessert?"

"Get out," I snarl, storming toward him.

"You smell delicious with all that wretch's blood off you." Caspian tilts his head back, black hair falling over his shoulder. He's removed his jacket, now wearing only a simple shirt and trousers, the laces loose. "I wanted the honor of torturing him before he met his end."

"It was Rosalina's choice."

"And your advisor's fault," Caspian says. "She longed to let me."

"What are you doing here?" I lean against one of the bedposts. "You made your bargain."

"But I haven't gotten what I want." His gaze is a brand. "Only you can give me that, Kel."

My hand instinctively goes to my wrist, rubbing the bargain frosted thorn bracelet. "I'll never give in."

"Then you'll never break your curse."

"Isn't that exactly what you want?" I turn away from him and walk to the fireplace. It hasn't been lit in so long.

He looses a long, deep sigh. "Like that dim mind of yours could possibly comprehend what I want."

I stack the logs, then grab a match and light the fire. Flames spurt up, filling the room with warmth. When I stand up, he's still lying there. His arms are stretched high above his head, lifting his shirt to reveal his sharp hip bones.

"You were right," I say.

He sits up in a whirl, a surprised, genuine smile on his face.

But I should know by now, nothing about him is genuine.

"What did you say, Keldarion?"

"That you were right." I close the distance between us. "Rosalina did not need to awaken that darkness in her heart. At least not for this."

"Oh, I love when you talk to me this way." Caspian kneels on the edge of the bed, narrowing his dark gaze.

"You don't hate her."

"I could sneak some frogs into her bed if it would make you feel better. But I think she'd assume they were cursed staff and befriend them."

I can't help but laugh at the thought, and when I glance back down at Caspian, he's giving me a peculiar look. "Maybe that icy heart of yours can be pierced."

He's being strange tonight. There's a softness to him I haven't seen in years. Though I know it's an act, I can't stop myself from asking the very question plaguing me. "What would you do if she came to you?"

He considers for a moment, then trails a hand along my torso before rising on his knees, his face almost parallel to mine. "Does it matter what I say, Prince? I could tell you what you want to hear. Or I could say your worst fear, that I'd seduce her until she begged me to fuck her into sweet oblivion."

A rough growl emits from my throat, and my fists clench to resist the urge to throttle him. He gives a little sigh, then rests his arms over my shoulder. "It doesn't matter what I say, you won't believe me. And it won't change your self-imposed celibate streak, will it now?"

I clench my teeth together. "You are infuriating."

He chuckles, a hand drawing down my stomach again as he purrs, "Though, this isn't the reaction I suspected you'd have. We could always—"

He stills completely before his hands begin to shake, eyes widening. His body spasms and convulses. An explosion of black sludge shoots from his mouth and onto my bare chest.

"Caspian!" I grab his shoulders, but he scrambles away, clutching the sheets of my bed. He heaves again as another deluge of blackness spills from his lips. His eyes water with darkness, sludge dripping from his nose.

After a heartbeat, he falls back, holding his stomach, body still trembling.

"Sorry," he wheezes, voice hoarse. "I know you probably had these cleaned for the full moon."

"How long have you been on the surface?"

"Only for dinner." He shrugs.

"It used to take at least a month."

He turns to me slowly, and there's such sadness in his expression. Watery black tears mar his face. "It's hard to help yourself when most of your power is going elsewhere."

Now I notice the shuddering thorns. Bits of stone crumble to the ground. I should have considered it before: the Briar beyond, the countless twines around Castletree. How much magic is it taking from him?

Caspian is powerful, something I've always known. But no one is infinite.

Anger rushes within me, and I grab his shirt, not caring as his hands smear darkness over my arms. "Tell me why you're doing this. Why corrupt a castle you'll never be able to live in? Is it all for *her*? For Sira?"

He weakly smacks my cheek. "Never say never, my dear Kel. Even you don't know all the magic of the world. Why, all those years ago, did you ever imagine such a power to curse you?"

"You are mad." He's still trembling. He's so weak. I could ... I could kill him right now. Or I could trap him here and let death come for him on swift wings. But I only snarl, "Go back to the Below, Cas."

He gives me a sad smile, then his head lolls forward, collapsing onto my shoulder as briars rise around him. "See you in two moons. If you want to send me an early present, I won't complain." The last of him to disappear is his hand touching my wrist, fingers tracing the bracelet that binds us. .

He disappears, and I am alone, my sheets and body stained with darkness.

I should have killed him and freed myself. Then I could finally break the curse.

I'd told Rosalina I'd let the entire Enchanted Vale turn to ash for her. But what I can never admit is that I started the fire for him.

PART THREE
AUTUMN'S GOLD

31

ROSALINA

My boots crunch on fallen leaves as we make our way down the winding path in the Autumn Realm.

"I can't wait to see the capital city of Coppershire," my father says, walking beside me. "Those twins have been telling me all about it."

I smile. Papa spent all last night chatting with Farron's little brothers. Apparently, they snuck out and joined the staff in celebrating the full moon.

Our party set out at dawn, using the mirror in the entrance hall to travel just outside the capital. We decided it would be best to arrive officially as an embassy, rather than surprising the fae royals by reopening the door from Castletree and appearing directly in the keep.

We opted for a minimal group: the princes, Papa, Farron's brothers, Astrid, Marigold, and me. We don't need much, as Farron assured us the Autumn Realm would have everything we require. I brought my trusty pack, anyway, filled with my treasures: the necklace Kel gave me, the plush lion Dayton bought me in the Summer Realm, and my crown of thorns.

I'm not sure why I brought the last one. Maybe it won't feel like home in the Autumn Realm without some thorns.

"Nothing out of the ordinary yet." Papa smiles.

"No," I agree. "This is beautiful."

Chestnut trees line the trail, growing so close together they almost form a tunnel. Red, orange, and yellow leaves fall like rain, mirroring the sky's fiery sunrise. Lingering blue mist wraps around our ankles. I inhale deeply, loving the crisp air and scent of wood smoke and apples that float on the soft breeze.

At the front of our party, Keldarion walks beside Ezryn, their sharp eyes scanning the path ahead. Behind them is Dayton, carrying both his and Farron's packs. He chats animatedly with Marigold, Astrid, and the twins.

Astrid and Marigold look hilarious. After they cleaned up the Orca Cove hoodies that came back with us from the human world, they took a shining to them. Now, they're both decked out in the vibrant hoodies, repping my small town.

Drifting behind, Farron kicks his feet through the crunchy leaves. Every so often, he pulls down his scarf to touch the thorn collar around his neck. I tried to talk to him before we left, but I get the sense he wants to be alone with his thoughts. I need to give him that space.

"Staying in the Autumn Realm won't only help the princes' cause," my father continues. "Exploring their world could be the best chance at finding information about your mother. Now, if Coppershire has a library anything like Castletree's, we'll be in for wonders galore."

My heart warms as I look at my father. He'll never stop learning, never stop trying to find her. But I admire that he can still take pleasure in the journey. Plus, he looks dashing in the fae clothes Marigold suited him with. He's trying so hard to fit in.

I dressed practically for our travels today, wearing fitted black trousers and an emerald tunic. The neckline is embroidered with autumn foliage in a cascading pattern, as if caught in a breeze. Brown boots hug tight to my calves. My deep burgundy cloak completes my ensemble. The oversized hood cocoons me in its warmth as we make our way through the woods. I've swept my chestnut waves back with a simple golden clip, leaving a few loose tendrils down to frame my face.

I felt lighter getting dressed this morning.

He's gone. Lucas is truly gone. Last night had been horrific, but I feel a sense of closure. My princes protected me. Hell, even the Prince of Thorns protected me.

I can only hope Perth Quellos can help the Winter Realm from his side. I still don't like him and I'm anxious that he knows Keldarion's secret, but he's served the royal family for generations. Surely now that we're all working together, we can see this through.

"I know you took care of that dreadful man—"

I tear myself from my thoughts and look up to see Keldarion has fallen into step beside us, and he's conversing with my father. Besides a few brief exchanges, the last time these two spoke was when Kel threw my dad in the dungeon.

"His departure from this world was a great mercy," Papa continues. "And you may be so-called 'mates' with my daughter, but that does not mean you have my approval. Not that Rosalina requires such a thing, but she deserves—"

Keldarion fixes his icy gaze on my father. I expect him to spout something about never wanting me even if I was the last woman in the Enchanted Vale, but he just says, "I will not let harm come to her again. Anyone who hurts her will earn a similar fate."

Papa gives a curt nod, no doubt proud of himself for talking to the High Prince of Winter. I know he's trying to take a more active role in my life now, and I appreciate the gesture.

"So," I slide between them, eager to change the subject, "do you think Papa and I will stand out in Coppershire with our round ears?"

"Doubtful," Keldarion says. "The realms are quite accommodating to wayward humans."

"Besides the ones that wander into Castletree," I chide.

Cries of excitement sound from up ahead. Dayton turns around, winking. "We're almost there."

As I round the bend, the trees give way to a breathtaking sight—a magnificent fae city nestled in the valley below.

The buildings are adorned with ivy and wreaths of orange and red leaves. In the distance, a castle towers over the city. It's Castletree, except its branches flutter with fall leaves. I know it's only an illusion: though the Queen's magic makes Castletree appear in all four realms, there's only one true physical location in the Briar.

But the keep at the base of Castletree is real ... and it's huge. Towering spires stretch upward, with walls made of shimmering bronze and gold.

The sounds of laughter and music drift up to us as we draw closer. I slow until I fall into step beside Farron. He looks down at me, a soft smile on his face. "You look beautiful today, Rosie. Like you're ready for a proper adventure."

"This is an adventure, Farron." I take his hand. "One we're going on together."

He gives a brief nod, the chilly breeze blowing the loose brown hair back from his brow. "I suppose."

"I'm so excited to see where you grew up," I say, trying to stay positive. There have been no signs of a frost yet.

We approach a large stone wall that surrounds the entire city. The gates are made of gold, designed with intricate carvings of leaves, acorns, and fae creatures.

"We're here," Farron says, straightening a little, the hint of a smile on his face. "Coppershire."

The great gates swing open, and a host of mounted soldiers storm out. Hooves thunder as they form a perimeter around our group. We huddle close together, Keldarion pressing me tightly against his side.

"What is the meaning of this, Farron?" he growls.

"I-I don't know!" Farron stammers.

The guards of the Autumn Realm are dressed in ornate armor atop their long, flowing orange robes thatthat they've belted with braided rope. The fabric seems to be made from woven leaves and petals, which rustle softly as they move. Each carries a weapon crafted from the forest itself: a bow of twigs and vines, or a spear adorned with foliage and berries.

Why are they surrounding us like we're the enemy?

Two guards pull Billy and Dom from our circle, despite their complaints.

Another soldier steps forward. He removes his golden helmet, and Farron lets out a sigh. "Captain, what's going on?"

The captain frowns. "You are all under arrest for fraternizing with the High Prince of Winter."

Keldarion stiffens beside me. "What?"

Farron looks at the tight circle of guards. His lip trembles. "But I'm, uh, I'm your High Prince. I would very much appreciate it if you stood down."

Dayton gives a frustrated sigh. "Fare, command, don't ask."

The guards don't shift.

"We do not answer to you," the captain says.

Farron opens his mouth, closes it.

"Do something, Farron," I whisper. "You're their High Prince."

He swallows, straightens, clears his throat, says nothing.

Keldarion growls, "If you traitorous lot do not answer to your High Prince, then who do you answer to?"

"They answer to me."

My lips part as a fae woman walks through the line of soldiers. She stands tall in an elegant dress, her long dark hair flecked with strands of silver and braided down her back.

The guards bow their heads and the captain mutters, "Princess."

But Farron gapes at her, his face shattered with pain as he whispers, "Mother?"

32

FARRON

So, this is how the High Prince of Autumn returns to his realm. In chains.

I pull against my bonds despite knowing they're unbreakable. The metal was mined from Spring, received in exchange for our bountiful lumber, and then forged in fire milked from the dragon-mouth plant. I doubt even Keldarion could find a way out of this steel.

We are marched through Keep Oakheart and into the war room, then forced upon our knees, hands cuffed behind our backs. Our chains are connected, binding us in a row: me, Kel, Ez, Dayton, Rosalina, George, Astrid, and Marigold. Dom and Billy hover nervously nearby, not happy with the situation but unwilling to stand against our mother.

Perhaps cowardice runs in the family.

I've hardly been in the war council room, even after I took the mantle of High Prince. It's an imposing chamber, the furniture all built of dark, polished wood. Ornate tapestries hang by the enormous windows, depicting scenes of great battles fought on the back of the legendary Storm Rams, a mystical vanguard that was said to have long disappeared into the Emberwood.

I take a deep breath, trying to steady my racing heart. Looking over, I see Dayton's piercing blue eyes. His face is twisted in worry. "You're okay, Fare," he whispers.

I have to be. If the wolf gets the best of me here, in a room with those I love most...

The bargain. The thought sends a searing pain through my neck. Caspian has sworn his magic can control my beast. *I can't believe I've resorted to trusting the star-damned Prince of Thorns.*

I breathe in shakily and survey my friends. Kel somehow manages to look imposing, even on his knees. He stares up, ice chip eyes unblinking, mouth so natural in a frown. Ezryn's still, save his hands. He's pulled off his gloves and is slowly running his fingers over what metal he can touch. Does he recognize this steel?

Dayton starts yanking on his chains. "You should know better than to contain me, Niamh," he snarls, using my mother's first name.

"Dayton," I warn.

But my mother says nothing. She stands behind the massive oaken table, its surface inlaid with intricate carvings of towering trees. I remember being a boy and sitting on her lap, trailing my fingers over the designs. She's staring at Rosalina.

Out of all of us, she is the stillest. She holds her chin high, deep breaths making her chest rise and fall. Fear flickers in her gaze, but there's strength there, too. I close my eyes. *If you can be strong, so can I.*

Strangely enough, George seems delighted by the whole ordeal. His head swivels around like an owl, and he keeps asking the guards what the sigil—a golden emblazoned ram with a crown of red and orange leaves—on their breast plate means. They all ignore him.

Astrid trembles. Marigold is mercifully silent—for once.

"Mother," I say. "Please, let me explain."

Slowly, she sweeps her gaze from Rosalina to me. Her golden eyes flicker like a breeze through a wheat field. "Where were you to explain," she says, "when our villages fell to the frost? Where were you to explain when the refugees showed up at Coppershire and we had no food to give them because our crops have failed?" Her body shakes, voice growing raspy. "Where were you to explain when I traveled to the border with a host and watched them fall one by one to the frost and I could do nothing because I'd passed along Autumn's Blessing to someone who took the power and hid?"

"I-I..." Words start and stop in my throat. Mother's statements rain upon me like a volley of arrows, each one penetrating deeper. But there is nothing to say to defend myself. No defense I deserve. My body weakens, and I stay upright only because I'm bound to Kel.

My mother sighs deeply. "I should force you to pass the Blessing back to me right now."

"Excuse me," Rosalina says, her voice soft. "I'm sorry about this frost. And about your crops. And your people. I truly am. But you have no idea what Farron's been through. What he's accomplished."

"Rosalina," I croak. "Don't."

I don't want her protection. I don't deserve it. What have I accomplished? We have nothing to show for our work. The only one of us who has any chance of breaking the curse refuses to do so. I have no conclusions, no progress. I've lost control of my realm. Worse than that, I've lost my mother's love.

My mother walks out from behind the table and stands over Rosalina. She looks just as she did when she was High Princess: her dark hair mixed with silver and tied in a tight braid, a gown of brass chain-link with a tartan sheath, and a golden sword holstered to her side. She was the finest leader the Autumn Realm had ever known.

She'd willingly passed the title to me, her eldest son.

There's a great bumbling sound as the guards are pushed aside and then an absolutely enormous man blunders into the room.

"Fare-Fare!" he cries and grabs me around the shoulders, squeezing and lifting me all at once. The force of the movement yanks Kel and the rest of them along, and I'm suffocated by his immense red beard.

"Father," I try to say against all the hair. He smells like my childhood: bonfires on crisp nights, mulled cider, and stag.

"Paddy," my mother warns.

My father Padraig slowly lowers me, looking sheepish. "Niamh, is this really necessary? You've got our boy in chains. He's not a threat to anyone!"

I know my father is standing up for me, but it stings anyway.

"Look who he's chained to," Mother says. "Farron has been consorting with High Prince Keldarion. I will have no traitors in my midst, even if they are of my blood."

"Even if they possess Autumn's Blessing?" Dayton snarls. "Hi, Paddy. Great to see you."

"Daytonales!" My father walks over and ruffles Dayton's hair. "Fit as ever, boy."

Marigold gives a deep sigh. "Now there's a man if I ever did see one."

Mother looks like she may burst into flames, the way the hooves of the Storm Rams did in legend. "Paddy, if you do not stop fraternizing with my prisoners, I will have you removed."

"Enough of this," Keldarion growls. He rises to his feet, tugging all of us with him. The guards shoot forward, spears drawn, but my mother waves them down. "Princess Niamh, please trust me when I say I have nothing to do with—"

"Trust you? Trust you?" She stalks forward. Though she's far shorter than Keldarion, her presence towers above him. "The only reason our realm still stands is because we *didn't* trust you. You nearly destroyed Winter all those years ago, and you would have brought all the realms with you. 'Trust me', he says. Does the High Prince of Winter think I'm a fool? Word has spread of your Winter Solstice Ball. You've aligned yourself with the Below again."

"Caspian was not bidden in my realm," Keldarion says. "I will never make that mistake again."

Pain burns along my neck. Keldarion might not, but I have.

Mother moves in a flash, pulling a bronze dagger from her sleeve, holding it right beneath Keldarion's chin. "I shouldn't give you the chance."

"Not so quick, Princess," Dayton says, a darkness to his words. "You don't want to make trouble with the High Princes when there is none. Remember who is a ward of Summer."

Fear flashes in my chest at the threat, and I turn to Dayton with wide eyes.

"You dare threaten my daughter, Daytonales?" Mother whispers.

Word came to Castletree two years ago that my sister Eleanor, the youngest of us four, had chosen to be a ward in the Summer Realm.

"With all due respect, my lady," Dayton says, his voice pure silk, "you're the one with a knife to the neck of my brother."

Kel flicks his gaze at Dayton and there's a flash of respect between the two of them, a rare gift from Keldarion.

Mother's lip twitches and she snags Dayton's chin, looking down at him with repulsion. "Last I checked, Daytonales, you had no more brothers."

A knot forms in the pit of my stomach as I try to comprehend the cruelty of her words.

Dayton stares up at her blankly. She drops his chin and staggers back to the desk. "Look at you four. High Princes of the realms, indeed. Autumn and Winter are on the brink of war. Summer's being run by a child. And no word has come in or out of Spring in months." She looks back. "The Queen left High Rulers for a reason. To keep the people safe. And you lot have all but turned your backs on us."

A heavy silence permeates the room, and I hang my head in shame. She's right. Just as the Enchantress was long ago.

"What if we can fix it?" Rosalina pipes up. "What if we can figure out what's causing the frost and stop it? Would you call off the war against Winter?"

Mother raises a brow. "Who is this human?"

I stare at Rosalina, her shining eyes, the resolute set of her jaw. "She's the Lady of Castletree," I say. "And she's going to help us stop this frost."

Mother strides over to her and takes Rosalina's chin in her hand, moving her head back and forth. "You look familiar. Have we met before?"

Rosalina gives a nervous laugh. "I think I would have remembered you."

"Hmph." Mother walks behind Rosalina, trailing a hand through her long dark hair, running a finger over her round ears.

"I know you don't trust us," Rosalina says. "Any of us. Why should you? Your people are dying. You're scared. But I promise, Keldarion did not cause this frost. And Farron will do anything for his people. No one else needs to die. Let us show you what strength remains in the people of Castletree."

My father laughs from the corner of the room. "The human's got spunk. What say you, Niamh?"

Mother holds up her bronze dagger, pointing it at Rosalina's back. I intake a sharp breath, my blood growing hot. Then Mother uses it to click open the chains. She goes down the line, releasing each of us in turn.

"At the rate the frost is moving, it will arrive at Coppershire in about two months' time," she says. "Fix it before it reaches the capital. And if not," she holds Keldarion's gaze, "Autumn will march on Winter."

33

ROSALINA

How is it that in the Enchanted Vale I'm always going from being a prisoner one moment to being given the most exquisite chambers one could imagine the next?

"Look over here!" Astrid cries, flinging herself into a velvet armchair and wrapping herself in a huge chunky knit blanket. "Perfect place for reading, don't you think, Rosie?"

"Is it ever!" I squeeze myself into the chair beside her.

Our party has been given our own personal chamber with a shared living space that deviates to private rooms. The main room is massive, the centerpiece being an open fireplace that crackles merrily, surrounded by all sorts of seating, from plush chairs to flouncy pillows strewn about in every autumnal hue.

A nearby table is laden with plump apples and pears, warm spiced cider, and a tray of flaky pumpkin pastries that still steam with their delicious aroma. Marigold stuffs one in her mouth. "Not as good as the ones back home."

Papa stands at the door leading to the hallway, arguing with Dominic and Billagin. The twins were instructed to set us up with our quarters. "No, no, no, pumpkin spice has been recorded in human history since 1675," Papa says. "The blend is simple: nutmeg, cinna-mon, cloves, pepper—"

"You've got it all wrong, old man," Dominic chides. "A fae alchemist made it by accident."

"He was trying to enchant some pumpkin seeds into growing into objects other than pumpkins, but he came up with that instead," Billy continues. "We've been using it in cooking for centuries. 'Course, once a fae brought it to the humans, well, then they made their own version. Nowhere near as good as ours."

"I simply don't believe it," Papa says.

Dom bumps him on the shoulder. "Come to the kitchen. We'll show you."

Papa's face lights up and the three run off like schoolboys. He seems so full of life.

But isn't that what the Vale had done for me too? Brought me back to life?

The princes are milling about, claiming rooms and talking in quiet voices. I observe the matter-of-factness between Kel and Ezryn as they solidify plans to keep Farron safe tonight. *Something happened between those two.*

I lean my head on Astrid's shoulder and try to take a peaceful moment. Large, arched windows offer a stunning view of the land-scape outside: a riot of reds and golds from the massive trees that stand beyond the keep. We've been given a chance to clear Keldarion's name and save the Autumn Realm. Together, we can do this. Farron can do this.

Farron. Where is he? "I'll be right back," I murmur to Astrid. I peer into a couple of the bedrooms, but don't see him anywhere.

I push open the door to the corridor. He's standing about halfway down the hallway, gazing up at a tapestry. I drift over and stand shoul-der-to-shoulder with him.

It's not hard to tell the tapestry is of his family. There's his mother in the middle, dark-haired and regal, though she's depicted softer here than when I met her. His father, smiling and joyful. Two identical young boys in the distance, each riding a stag. Standing beside the large tree in the foreground is an adolescent girl. *That must be Eleanor.*

And right beside his mother is Farron: younger, but unmistakably him. Somehow, the tapestry manages to capture the curiosity in his gaze. I run my fingers over his shape. "You look really happy here."

"For so long, it felt like nothing in my life ever changed. Like I was stuck reliving the same day over and over." Farron's voice is raspy, unsure. "And now I've woken up and realized that it was only me who was stuck. The world's moved on. I can't keep up."

I lace my fingers through his.

"They're so different," he whispers, eyes still on the tapestry. "My brothers have become fighters. My mother can barely look at me. She was always so gentle with me. We used to take long carriage rides together, pass books back and forth. Now she's waging war. And she can't even *look at me.*"

"Fear changes people. She's scared, Farron."

"If she had Autumn's Blessing, she could have already stopped this. But Autumn's stuck with me. I can't even remember the last time someone took back the Blessing."

"It's not all up to you." I squeeze his hand. "We're here with you. Kel, Ez, Dayton. Me. We're here with you, Farron."

"But isn't that worse?" Tears well in his eyes, and he hastily wipes them away. "We have to break the curse. And they're here *for me.* What about finding their mates? Saving themselves?"

"We have time." Gently, I touch the side of his face and turn him away from the tapestry. "We're going to struggle to break this curse if the realms are at war. I know it's difficult to see, but you matter so much to them. Take strength from their love, Farron." My breath catches in my throat. "Take strength from me."

He stares down at me; eyes shining and mouth a half-opened question.

"I'm with you," I say. "There and back. I'm with you."

"I'm with you," he repeats. "The whole way."

I lace my arms around his neck, pulling him against me as if it could keep him safe. His embrace envelops me as he nuzzles into the curve of my neck.

If only you saw yourself how I see you.

"You have no idea how much I missed you," he says.

"I can feel your heartbeat," I whisper. It's rapid and strong and I never want to tear myself away. *I love this heart.*

"Rosie?"

"Yes, Fare?"

"I think you're the best friend I've ever had."

I draw back slightly to study him, to map the contours of his face. My heart blooms like the sun from beyond the gray clouds. "I *know* you're the best friend I've ever had."

He leans his forehead against mine. "I guess we should get back to the others."

"Yeah." A window at the end of the hallway filters in red-orange dusk. "It's almost night."

Time to see if making a bargain with the devil was worth it.

34

ROSALINA

I've never seen a sunset like this. The sky's blistering red and orange, rays of light gleaming off the rooftops of Coppershire. Standing on the balcony outside of my private room, the capital city of the Autumn Realm stretches before me, bathed in crimson light.

Growing up in Orca Cove, it seemed like everyone around me was constantly exploring, wandering. Papa had hit one hundred countries before I was fifteen. Lucas's family took fancy vacations every summer to Mexico or Europe. Even some of my school friends went to university abroad. The only traveling I ever did was in my stories, but that felt like enough.

Now, staring down at the bustling city, the buildings a mix of brick, lumber, and shimmering gems, I wish I could sprint from the castle and lose myself in the markets and alleyways. For once, the whole world feels ahead of me.

But as much as I want to revel in that thought, my gaze drifts higher, beyond the city and the fields and forests that border Coppershire. Over the orange-baked hills, a glimmer of white-blue shines on the edge of the horizon. The frost.

I rub my arms. I'd tried to put on a brave face for Farron, but I'm scared, too. *I just got this world back. I can't lose it.*

The men are preparing Farron's room as best they can, in case Caspian's bargain is bullshit. But somehow, I know it will work. There was something about Caspian that seemed ... sincere.

You're a fool like them, Rosalina, I chide myself.

I should go back inside and check on everyone. But I can't tear myself away from this sunset, the apple-scented breeze that makes my white sleeves billow like wings.

Metal clinks behind me. I turn to see Ezryn leaning against the doorway. Somehow, I get the feeling he's been there for a while and only shifted so that his armor would alert me to his presence.

"Hi," I say softly.

He doesn't reply but moves to rest against the balcony railing beside me, staring out at the horizon. The sun gleams off his armor in a way that makes me think of legends of Sir Lancelot riding into battle.

"How are you doing?" he asks slowly, almost as if he had to think about those words for a long time.

My stomach twists nervously. I haven't really had a chance to talk to him since our kiss in the pantry where he'd walked out, leaving me stunned. My fingers trail over the railing, and I try to forget how good they felt tangled in his thick hair.

"I'm okay," I answer. "I'm pretty used to being imprisoned by faeries, you know."

He snorts. "At least you didn't have to spend a night in the dungeon this time."

"True." The wind catches my long hair and sends it tumbling across my face. I stare at him through the waves. His shoulders are slumped, body heavy. "Are you okay?"

Why do I get the impression no one ever asks him that?

"Princess Niamh mentioned she sent word to Spring but never heard back. My father is the steward there. It borders Winter on the other side." His dark cape flutters in the wind. "My father's been sick for a long time."

I place a hand on his arm. "Do you want to go to him?"

He shakes his head, little *tings* ringing in the air. "Farron and Kel need me right now. Besides, Spring would send word if something were wrong, I'm sure." He reaches into his chest plate and pulls out a piece of parchment. It's filled with the same beautiful handwriting I saw on the jars in the healing pantry. "But I'm writing to Father to be certain."

I notice now he's not wearing his leather gloves, his large, tanned hands delicately running over the paper. My breath quickens as I remember their firmness on my waist, the strength as he pushed me back into the shelves.

With quick and elegant movements, Ezryn folds the parchment over and over again, then holds it up in his palm.

"A bird!" I gasp. "That's magnificent. I was never good at origami. Mine always came out looking like someone sat on it."

He quirks his head in the way I've now learned means he's smiling. *If he ever takes off his helmet in the dark again, I'll ask him to smile. I'll feel it with my fingers, memorize how far up his face it goes.*

He cups the little paper bird in his hands, palms sparkling with green light. He brings it up to his helm and murmurs in a language I don't understand. The bird springs up, flapping its parchment wings, and leaps off into the breeze.

I gasp, then clap my hands. "Ez! That's incredible."

"It's not very hard. A little trick my mother taught Kai and me."

"Kai?"

"Yes. Kairyn," he murmurs. "My little brother."

I twirl a piece of hair around my finger, trying to recall the name of the capital city of Spring. Marigold has mentioned it in plenty of stories about her life before Castletree. "Does he live in Florendel with your father?"

Ezryn stiffens. "No. He resides in a monastery outside of the city. I haven't seen him in a very long time."

Before I can ask more, Ezryn sighs. "I don't want to think about Kairyn right now. I came because I wanted to ask you something."

Heat springs to my cheeks. "What is it?"

Ezryn turns to face me. When we're chest to chest like this, I remember how huge he is, how tall and broad in his armor.

He delicately takes my left hand. His calloused thumb trails over my skin to the wrist bone. I become conscious he's drifting his fingers toward my forearm, and try to jerk back, but he holds me firmly.

With his other hand, he touches the cuff of my sleeve, then stares at me. My breath catches, eyes lost in the dark visor within his helm. He's asking my permission to look at what I've kept covered for years, at what I can barely look at myself.

I nod.

He pushes my sleeve up, revealing the ugly scar, the raised, jagged lines spelling my abuser's name.

A thought rushes at me unbidden: *I'm glad Kel killed him.*

Ezryn places a featherlight touch over the scar. "I can heal this for you. If you want me to."

"It's so old. Can you really do that?"

He nods. "Spring's Blessing is strongest in renewal. If you want a fresh start, I ... I can help."

I run my hands over each letter. Tears well in my eyes because that's exactly what I want. A fresh start.

"Yes, Ezryn," I say, voice catching. "I would like that very much."

He nods again, more boyishly this time. I straighten my arm for him, cringing a little at how on display the mark is. I'd never allowed anyone to see it. "Do you need to get anything? Herbs or something?" I ask, remembering how last time he healed me, he'd used a combination of leaves and his own spit.

"No," he murmurs and holds my arm with one hand and places the index and middle finger of the other on the *S*. "This time, the magic comes from within."

My heart hammers in my chest as he bends over, helmet's gaze intense upon my forearm. An emerald glow ignites on the tips of his fingers and streams down into the raised skin. A tingling sensation, like the taste of peppermint gum, follows each stroke.

My eyes widen in disbelief. The letters are disappearing. But Lucas's voice rings in my head: *She'll always come back to me.*

"Do you believe people can change?" I ask softly.

Ezryn glances up. "What do you mean?"

"The person we were a decade ago or a year ago or even yesterday ... Are we stuck being that person forever?"

Ezryn is silent for a long moment, and I start to think he's regretting offering to help me. But then as he moves his fingers over the A, he says, "As children, my brother and I would often play in the woods near our castle. He'd be off running and catching frogs, but I'd find myself sitting on stumps. Taking in the life encircling me."

I blink softly as I watch him work, lost in the mesmerizing softness of his touch and his voice.

"In Spring, we're taught rebirth is all around us," he continues. "The seed becomes a sprout, becomes a flower. The egg becomes the bird, which dies and becomes the dirt that houses the worm that feeds the bird. The deer feeds the cougar, which then lays to rest upon the grass, which in turn, feeds the deer. And the stumps that I would sit on ... There were rings and rings and rings, more than I could count. Ages upon ages of growing. It may all begin somewhere, but it changes, dies, renews."

I hear the rasp in his voice and wonder what memories belong to him alone in those woods.

His fingers tingle over the C. "We are all a part of the cycle. And though the seed may always be a part of us, nothing stays the same." He pauses, helmet downcast. "Nothing stays."

"So, that person may always be a part of us," I whisper, "but we don't have to hold on to them."

"Does the river hold itself back from running?"

"It's sometimes hard to let go of that person," I utter softly. "The one we used to be."

"I'm still trying," he says, then pauses for a long moment. "And I hope you know, Rosalina, he was the monster. It wasn't your fault."

"I know. Deep within me, I know." I look down at my forearm. Half the name is gone, replaced by red flesh, raw and new.

I forgive you, I think. Not to Lucas. But to myself, the younger me. The one who didn't know how to leave. Who didn't know how beautiful the world truly was and didn't think she deserved what beauty she could find. *I forgive you, and I can let you go.*

The moment passes in comfortable silence, the setting sun bathing us in its last warmth. And as Ezryn's light illuminates the *L*, coaxing new skin to heal the old, I think, *I hope you can forgive yourself, too.*

Ezryn holds up my arm, examining it in the crimson sunset. "All done."

There are so many things I want to say to him, so much emotion right on the tip of my tongue. But all I manage is, "I can finally wear those short-sleeved dresses Marigold loves."

He tilts his head, then turns toward the door.

As he's about to step inside, I call out, "Ez?"

He stops but doesn't turn around.

"Why did you leave? After you kissed me?"

"Rosalina..."

Heat trills through me. I run my hand over the raw skin of my forearm, a choking sensation in my chest. He gave me something I can never thank him for, and he's going to walk away.

"I've seen you do this with Kel," I say, voice breaking. "One minute you're present, every piece of you bright and available. And the next ... You're gone. Sometimes literally, out running around the Briar or whatever you do. But sometimes you can be right in front of me, and it feels like if I reached out and touched you, you'd disappear."

"Rosalina," he says lowly, "you don't know who I am. What I've done."

"Then let me in," I whisper. "Plant your roots in me, Ez. I'll keep you safe."

He turns, body rigid. "We can't do this." But he's stepping toward me.

"Why not?" My words are a breath, carried away in the bracing wind. I back up as he stalks closer, bumping against the railing. My heart hammers like a cornered rabbit.

He shoots an arm out on one side of me, seizing the rail. "Because I'm dangerous."

"I'm not afraid of you."

He's so close, I have to arch my back over the railing to avoid being pressed against him. There's something inhuman about the way the helmet glowers down at me, his body made of steel. Electricity nips through my core, a desire to push that steel until it snaps.

He captures a loose strand of my hair and curls it around his finger. "You're tempting the fates." His head lowers to the crook of my neck, and I catch a glimpse of his skin between the armored collar and the helm. I inhale, taking in his familiar scent of leather, iris, and cedarwood. "And yet," he murmurs. "I find myself doing the same."

His other hand slams down on my opposite side, fully caging me in. I brace myself on the railing and breathe out, my bust pushing against his huge chest. The cold armor of his breastplate sends a shiver through the thin fabric of my blouse.

"You know," I murmur, "I'm Kel's mate."

"Obviously." His body pushes harder against mine.

"And Dayton and I like to fool around."

His voice is a dusky growl. "I know that, too."

"And Farron and I … Well, Farron is special to me. Very special." Little gasps escape between my words.

"Why are you telling me this, Rosalina?"

My mouth falls to that gap between his armor and his helmet. "In case you kiss me again, I want you to know those facts. I've told them you kissed me. And they don't care. Dayton and Fare said they liked it, actually—"

His knee jams in between my legs, wedging them apart. "But did *you* like that I kissed you?"

I gasp, the feeling of his huge, hard leg in between mine filling me with pressure. My lips linger on that precious gap of skin. "Very much so."

He sighs, as if in resignation. Then he grinds his leg into me. I let out a small whimper, hands lacing around his neck.

As if aware of how weak he's made me, Ezryn embraces me. I grasp the edges of his armor, wanting nothing between us.

His hands grip my hips and I melt against him, wondering if his touch will consume me whole. He dips his head to the space between my breasts and lets out a growl. "Sometimes I hate this fucking thing."

"W-what?" I shake my head, trying to remember what words are.

"The helmet. I want your perfect—" His words turn into a feral snarl.

My breathing grows labored, and I press myself down harder on his knee. Electric pleasure rushes through me, and his name is on my lips. "Ez—"

"Hello?" a voice calls from inside the bedroom. "Rosie? Ez?"

Immediately, we spring away from each other, and I'm left panting and on the edge of madness.

"Where are you?" Dayton's voice calls. "It's almost nightfall. We need to make sure pretty boy Caspian's spell works on Fare!"

"C-coming!" I call.

Ezryn cups my chin. "Next time," he growls, "you will be."

Then his cape snaps in the wind as he turns away from me.

35

EZRYN

Rosalina's long hair swishes behind her as she leaves the dusk-swept balcony and enters the bedroom. Dayton's waiting there with his usual shit-eating grin. He sweeps an arm around her as they walk back into the living space, but not before looking over his shoulder and giving me an exaggerated wink.

Stars Above and bones Below. My weight shifts forward until my helmet *clunks* against the doorframe. I can't do this to myself. I can't do this to her.

Since I inherited Spring's Blessing, I've known getting close to people is dangerous. In a selfish way, the curse allowed me an excuse not to engage with the outside world. I'd check in on Spring occasionally, fulfill my needs with women who wanted as little commitment with me as I wanted with them, and then return to Castletree. To the only three people in the world I am unafraid of hurting.

I bang my head against the wall. Stupid. *Clunk.* Stupid. *Clunk.* Stupid. There are more reasons to stay away from Rosalina than there are stars in the sky. She's a human, with a lifespan so much shorter than that of a fae. She's Kel's star-damned mate. I need to find my *own* mate to break my curse.

You'll hurt her, a familiar voice breathes in my mind. A voice that comes from the darkest core of me, one made from memories. *And your brothers—your new brothers—will never forgive you. Just like I haven't.*

"Get out of my head, Kairyn," I growl under my breath. I know it's only my imagination. Kairyn is gone, banished. Yet, it's like he's taken up resident in my mind, whispering truths I've long buried.

I shake my head to rid myself of his memory and instead concentrate on the fading sun. Even through my darkly tinted visor, the bursting rays burn my eyes. This would all be so much easier if she wasn't like the literal sun itself, tenacious and warm. An unbidden smile creeps up my face as I think of her sitting in that armchair with Astrid earlier, or the light in her father's eyes whenever she enters a room. *She makes everyone feel important.* Like the sun coaxing a seed to sprout through frost-covered ground, Rosalina brings out the best in those around her.

I give my head a firm shake. The sun has nearly dipped beneath the horizon, and the others need me.

I walk into the shared living space. Five bedrooms are connected to the central room, one for each of the princes and one for Rosalina. Marigold and Astrid are sharing a room on a lower level, and George has his own space down the hall.

If it was up to me, Rosalina would be far away from Farron's first transformation while testing Caspian's spell, but she would have none of it.

Kel, Dayton, and Rosalina stand in the doorway to Farron's room. Farron paces beside the bed. The curtains are drawn, so I can't tell exactly when night will fall, but I can feel it. My wolf rising within me. It's close.

I approach Kel and ask, "Are we prepared?"

"I put a sealing enchantment on the main door to this whole chamber. No one's coming in here unless I say so."

At least we won't have to worry about any poor Autumn staff wandering in and discovering four hideous beasts in the middle of the night. I quirk my head toward Farron. "How is he?"

"Agitated," Kel mumbles.

"If things don't go according to plan with Caspian's spell, he'll be hard to subdue."

Kel's gaze pierces into the room. "Caspian's bargain will work."

I sigh. Kel and I are talking, but only about important matters. There's a distance between us, one I haven't felt since our argument during the War of Thorns. *And that took me scaling an entire mountain and Kel almost losing a hand for us to move past it.*

But Kel isn't my priority right now. I push past him into the room.

"Careful, Ez," Dayton warns. "It's going to happen any minute."

I ignore him and approach Farron. He's sitting now, back pressed against the side of his bed, staring at the wall. I squat down and place my hand on his neck, just above the thorn collar.

"Your heart's going too fast," I say.

Farron's chest rises and falls, and it's like he can't figure out where to focus. His golden eyes race back and forth.

"Look at me, Farron." I place my other hand on the side of his face.

He does, and I see his fear. His shame. It is a look I know too well, if only because it was the same expression looking at me in the mirror many years ago.

His mother threatened to take back the Blessing—an act not done in recent history of the Vale. The magic is only intended to move forward. I know it is an empty threat, for an attempt to retake the magic could kill them both.

"What if I've ruined everything, Ez?" Farron asks, voice breaking. "What if Caspian's done something terrible to me?"

"Then we put it back together," I tell him. "All of us."

He closes his eyes and tears squeeze out, running down his face and over my hands. "I don't want to hurt people anymore."

My chest tightens, and I roughly brush his tears away with my thumb. "I'm right here, Farron. We're staying here with you, alright? I swear, I won't let you hurt anyone."

He brings his hand up over mine. "Promise me something, Ez?"

"What?"

"If it doesn't work," his gaze is so intense, piercing into me, "then you'll kill me. You'll do it, won't you, Ez? I need you to promise."

I recoil, horrified, but Farron holds me tighter and pleads, "Please, Ez."

"I … promise. Now breathe with me." I place his hand on my chest so he can feel the rise and fall of my breath. In and out, we breathe. I am steady for him, a mountain to his gale. But the tempest claws within me. *I have made a promise I cannot keep.*

We take another deep breath in and out, and his pulse slows beneath my fingertips. "I think it's about to happen, Ez."

"I know." I pull him toward me. Then I raise the barest edge of my helmet, just enough so I can kiss the top of his forehead. "I'm with you, little brother."

"You need to leave," he says, voice deep and guttural.

I stand, armor trembling with the movement, and back up to the others. Kel and Dayton have stripped down to their flesh to avoid destroying their clothes, but Rosalina's not looking at them. She's fixated on Farron.

I quickly shed my armor except for my helmet, which my snout pushes off during the turn. Then I stare out the big window in the living area. The sun dips below the horizon.

Energy crackles through my body as my bones snap, grow, rearrange. At first, the shift made me nauseous from the mere thought of my body mutating, but now each change feels natural. The line between the man and the wolf grows thinner with each turn.

A growl surges up my throat, but I contain it. There must not be any suspicious noises or hints of the curse. I can only imagine what Princess Niamh would do if she knew of our true nature.

Kel's frozen beast stands in the entranceway to Farron's room, but Dayton's shape, dripping briny water, shoves forward to look. Then Rosalina squeezes between both of them.

Farron's body is still changing. The man's back arches unnaturally, his legs furry and crooked like that of a wolf. Long canines erupt from his mouth, and his eyes glow with golden hunger. Then the wolf erupts from him, the beast of rotten leaves and burnt brush.

It's not working, I think. *Caspian tricked us. Farron will be lost, and I'll have to—*

The thorn collar erupts from around Farron's neck. It grows like a thicket, winding around his legs, his body, even his muzzle, then sinking thorns deep within the floor. The wolf remains still, only its golden eyes flitting this way and that.

"He's trapped," Kel growls.

I creep past them, stepping into the room. Tentatively, I sniff the thorns. Every inch of Farron is covered, except for his eyes and a bit of his nose. His wails and thrashing usually fill the night. But now, all I hear is the rapid in and out of his breath through his nostrils.

"He's not getting out," I say. "It worked."

Rosalina rushes forward, but Kel snags the back of her shirt with his teeth. "He's still dangerous, Rose," he mutters through fabric. "We haven't seen enough yet."

"He's scared," she cries, ripping free. "Can't you see it? He's terrified." She turns to Farron, hand outstretched for the tip of his snout visible through the thorns. "He's in there, all alone—"

Kel bursts in front of her, nudging her hard in the belly with his snout. "*Out.*"

Rosalina looks like she's going to snap back, but I bump against her. "We're only going to rouse him by being here. Let's shut the door and let him rest."

She wrinkles her nose, battling her tears, but nods. We leave the bedchamber and Rosalina clicks the door shut.

Dayton's sitting there on his haunches, a fluffy pillow in his mouth, tail wagging. Rosalina strokes an affectionate hand over his ears. "You look like a golden retriever with a frisbee."

Dayton spits the gob-covered pillow out on the floor. "Maybe we can't be in there with him. But I can be right here." He lays down, snout peering under the door. "I'll always stay."

The idea lights Rosalina up, and a smile forms on her tear-streaked cheeks. She runs to the firepit in the center of the room and starts gathering up all the pillows she can.

"What are you doing?" Kel asks.

She positions the pillows right by the door, tucking some under Dayton's paws. Then she rushes back to grab the blankets off the couch. "Dayton's right." She touches the door. "Somehow, Farron will know we're right here with him."

I raise a wolfy brow as I watch Rosalina and Dayton create a nest of pillows and blankets. *They're a good team,* I think. *Both determined to see the light in even the darkest situations.* My chest warms at how Dayton makes Rosalina smile. *I hope he can see how happy he makes her.*

As they're debating what would be better to sleep on, piled blankets or piled pillows, Kel gives an exasperated sigh. He yanks the cushions off the couch. "These are best," he says through gritted teeth.

"Here's a lesson, Rosie," Dayton says, his wolf's smile strangely similar to the man's. "The best way to get Keldarion to do something you want is to do it wrong. He'll be sure to correct you."

Keldarion stands in the middle of the nest—a giant creation of fluffy blankets and plush pillows—and turns in a circle, then turns the other way. Then he plops down. "If I'm going to sleep here, it might as well be comfortable."

Rosalina gives the softest smile and somehow, she's shining brighter than before.

Dayton gets into the nest beside Kel. "Big strong protector has to watch out for us?"

Kel cracks an eye open. "Yes."

Dayton laughs, and I notice his fur isn't damp anymore. In fact, I don't even see the usual strands of rotten seaweed that wind through his fur.

Rosalina dives into the middle of the nest. She'd ran into her bedroom and changed into a light pink nightdress.

Warmth spreads through me. *Short sleeves.*

Dayton crawls beside her and tugs the blankets over her body with his mouth. I sit awkwardly to the side, watching them. Keldarion's curled in a tight ball, but Dayton lays his snout on the white wolf's haunches. Rosalina curls between them, nearly engulfed in white and gold fur.

I walk quickly toward my bedroom, alone.

"Ez?" Rosalina calls. "Are you coming?"

An uneasy beat passes in my chest. *You deserve to be alone,* the voice that sounds like Kairyn whispers in my head.

"Hurry up," Dayton says sleepily. "You're the last one in so you're the foot warmer."

I squeeze my eyes closed. *Shut up. Shut up. Shut up,* I say to the voice in my head. *This is my family.*

Each step feels cautious as I approach the plush nest and step a foot in. Slowly, I lay the front of my body over Rosalina's legs. Her eyes are closed, but she smiles and reaches down, scratching between my ears.

It feels … nice.

"Goodnight, everyone," Rosalina whispers sleepily. "Goodnight, Farron."

As I drift into oblivion, I hope he knows we're right outside. His family, waiting for him to return to us.

I WAKE BEFORE DAWN. I'm so … warm. I know I must return to my own chamber before the sun rises, so I'll transform in private and have access to my helmet. But I don't want to get up.

Forcing myself up to my feet, I look at the strange nest we created last night. Dayton's sleeping on his back, all four paws in the air, and a huge glob of drool running out of his mouth. *Rosalina is right. He does look like a golden retriever.*

And Kel…

Kel is a man, his naked form wrapped in Rosalina's arms. They're fast asleep, but Kel's face is soft, reminding me of my friend from years past. A boy who had no knowledge of the trials of manhood.

He may not have accepted the mate bond yet, but there is still magic here. Proof the Enchantress's curse can be broken.

Proof that Rosalina's touch is magic.

I press my ear to the door, and thankfully only hear rhythmic breathing. Hopefully, Farron found rest, despite the chains of curse and thorn.

I creep from the nest to my room, careful not to wake anyone. I take one look back at Kel in Rosalina's arms and a pang of sorrow tightens in my chest.

You deserve to let yourself be loved by her, Kel, I think.

I only wish I could be so lucky.

36

DAYTON

I love Autumn: the bright calamity of colors, the warm hearths crackling inside the keep. The first time I visited as a child, it felt like the chill breeze whispered secrets and stories of the forest and ancient fae. It's so different from the Summer Realm, with its vast ocean horizons and open buildings. Something about Autumn is cozy, familiar, inviting.

Like Farron.

My gaze rests on the High Prince of Autumn perched on his great elk, Thrand. He adjusts the collar of his deep red tunic. It's paired with fitted black trousers and knee-high brown boots. Over his tunic, he dons a leather jerkin with golden clasps that taper to his slim waist. His wild mane of auburn hair flutters in the breeze, a stray strand framing his jaw.

Damn, I want to kiss him.

Rosalina trots her horse up beside him, a beautiful white mare named Amalthea. Except the horse decides she'd rather graze on the grass.

"Come on, Thea," she chides. "You just had a snack."

I can't help but chuckle and trot closer to grab her horse's reins and direct us to Farron. It's been a week since we've arrived in

Autumn, and I took it upon myself to show Rosie the ropes of horse-back riding.

She was a quick learner, charming the horses as easily as she did all of Castletree. She's mostly able to ride on her own now, with a well-trained horse on even terrain. I do miss our first lessons, with her soft body pressed against mine on the same mount. Or the time we lost focus and were almost found by a pair of guards with her top off and my hands beneath her waistband ... It's not my fault she screams so loud when she comes—a sound I'll never tire of.

"Thanks, Day." She smiles across at me, a pink blush to her cheeks. Her long brown hair is tied in a high ponytail, clasped with a golden circlet. Fuck, I want to wrap her hair around my hand and pull back, exposing her throat, so I can bite and lick my way up to her lips. She wears a form-fitting top that hugs tight to her full breasts. Some laces are undone, leaving a tantalizing hint of cleavage. A sweeping cloak crafted from dark red velvet drapes over her shoulders and hangs off the back of her horse.

She suits the Autumn Realm too.

"I'll get the hang of this eventually." She flushes.

"Everything alright?" Ezryn calls from up ahead. He's beside Kel, both also on horseback.

"We're coming!" She looks to me and Farron. "Race you!"

She kicks the side of her horse, and Amalthea begins an awkward canter. Farron bursts into a laugh, the sound musical and charming—one I haven't heard in a while.

"Come on, pup." We urge our mounts into a run.

As we crest the hill, I'm stilled by the beauty of Farron's realm. The rolling hills shine with purple heather. A stream snakes through the valley resembling a ribbon of silver. Below us lies the sprawling Emberwood Forest, a chrysanthemum field, and beyond that, a cluster of ancient ruins.

"It's beautiful," Rosalina sighs.

"Excluding that nasty frost," I say, not able to resist pointing out the obvious. A white-blue shine clings to the trees, flowers, and ruins. "Sorry, Kel, but I don't think your touch suits this realm."

"This isn't me," he growls.

We spent the first week here preparing and gathering intel from Autumn. Niamh seems more at peace having Keldarion where she can see him, but I know her ferocity. If we don't discover the true source of this frost, she will attack Winter.

Kel's sour-faced vizier has sent barren reports, noting the creeping frost along the border of Winter and Autumn, but no discovery or theories of its origins. We need to understand how it's spreading if we're to have any chance of stopping it.

Today is our first venture into Autumn's wild realmlands. Surely, there are answers here.

"What are those stones between the flowers?" Rosalina asks, looking into the field of orange and yellow chrysanthemums.

An awkward silence fills the group before Farron clears his throat. "They are grave markers. This was a battlefield during the War of Thorns."

Rosalina shifts to look at him.

"Autumn forces marched from Coppershire to confront a legion from the Below that sallied out from the Winter Realm. However, during the conflict, there was a horrible mudslide, and it engulfed both the armies. We normally burn our dead, but they were too deep. We planted these flowers atop the site and used markers to remember the names."

Rosalina's brow furrows. "Why would forces from the Below march from the Winter Realm?"

Because Keldarion is the biggest fucking idiot to ever rule, and he was dangling from the side of a mountain at the time. Tension feels palpable in the air, and I cast a steely gaze at the High Prince of Winter. *When are you going to tell her?* But there's a part of me that doesn't want her to know. What if she leaves him? *What if she leaves us?*

"Are you a princess?" a small voice asks, interrupting the silence.

My horse gives a whinny of surprise as a child approaches, staring up at Rosalina. His eyes are the bright blue of a robin's egg, and he hasn't grown into his ears, which look two times too big for his face.

Tawny hair peeks out from his hat, an oversized mushroom cap, red with spots.

"I'm not a princess." Rosalina laughs and awkwardly tries to clamber off her horse.

Before she struggles too much, Farron quickly dismounts, and lifts her to the ground. She mouths a silent thank you before they both approach the boy.

"Well, you look like a princess," he says.

There's a soft woof, and a brown and white dog bounds out from behind him. Rosalina gives a squeal of delight as the dog licks her hand. It's short with stocky legs, long droopy ears nearly touching the ground, and an adorably wrinkled forehead.

"There's no village close by," Farron says, considering the boy. "What are you doing out here?"

The boy points a confident thumb at his chest. "I'm mushroom hunting. Name's Flicker, by the way. My old patch got the frost, so me and Koop been looking for a new one. My little sis has a bad cough, and only the luminesce mushrooms help it." He stops and narrows his eyes, then a bright grin lights his face. "Hey! You're the prince, right? Here to stop the frost?"

Farron flushes. "I, uh, we're—"

"We're on an adventure," Rosie says, giving Koop the best belly rub of his life. "We're searching for a way to end the frost. Have you seen much of it around here?"

"Yeah, it's really bad in the forest and down at the Shrine of Nymphia." He nods to the ruins down the hill.

"I guess that's where we should start looking." Rosalina straightens. "Thank you so much for your help."

A bright grin flashes across Flicker's face. "You said you weren't a princess, but you will be once you two get married, right?"

Rosie and Farron both flush the most adorable shade of pink, and I lean forward on my horse, a laugh booming from my chest. Rosalina only smiles and pats Flicker's head.

Ezryn jumps down from his horse. Usually, a giant in armor would startle someone, but Flicker tilts his chin way up, and Koop sniffs Ezryn's boots curiously.

Ezryn grabs a small paper package from his horse's saddlebag and kneels in front of the boy. "This is an herbal tea. It may help soothe your sister's cough. Let it steep in boiling water, then bring it to a simmer. You can add some maple syrup to sweeten it."

The boy's eyes gleam as he thanks the Spring Prince, then trots down the hill toward the Emberwood.

"Be careful," Farron calls after him. "Stay away from the frost."

"Will do, Prince," Flicker beams. "And thank you for fixing it."

Farron's gaze falls at the boy's words, "If only it were that easy."

I'M PRETTY SURE this is the thirteenth mushroom Farron has described to me, no doubt inspired by that little mushroom boy.

Our party split up to save time. Fare and I are checking out the ruins, and the others are heading to the edge of the forest. We've left our mounts at the top of the hill and descended on foot down the rocky gully to the ruins.

"Actually," Farron says, sliding nimbly over a rock, "there are over 75,000 different species of mushrooms in the Autumn Realm alone. We have the largest variety here, but there are a few types specific to the other realms. There's a particular strain of marine fungi that only grows in the ocean of Summer."

"I didn't know." I spin around, giving him a wide grin. "Is that one poisonous too?"

"Yes, but you can negate the poison with a little lemon juice and..." He trails off, then knits a hand through his hair. "I've been talking about mushrooms for a long time, haven't I?"

"Yes, but now I'm dying for that portabello stew you mentioned." I throw an arm over his shoulder and bring my lips to his ear. "I love when you talk shroomy to me."

He laughs, a sound I haven't heard enough of lately. So what if

Farron's stories have a tendency to go on from time to time? I don't care. As long as I'm the one he's talking to.

Farron's laugh dies as we approach the ruins, and he sighs. "Even Nymphia couldn't stop the frost."

Crumbling ruins spread across the field. Moss and vines crawl over long-fallen statues and pillars. This was once a place of worship, but now only a circular broken staircase leads to a fallen tower.

Worse than the passage of time is the frost. It covers everything with a pale-blue gleam.

"Poor Nym." I follow Farron to inspect the worst of the frost. "I suppose you know all about her too?"

"I do," he says. His hand dangles loose at his side, and I almost grab it. "She was the first High Ruler of Autumn and said to be a great friend of Queen Aurelia."

"Ahh, yes," I say. "Our lost Queen. Would be nice to have her help right about now."

"You don't think she's ever coming back, do you?"

"I don't know, Fare." I run a hand through my hair. "Five hundred years is a long time to be gone. What do you think?"

"I think she's out there," he says softly. "Only because Castletree is still standing. It was her magic that created it. I think … I think we'd feel it if she were truly gone."

We lap the ruins twice, investigating the ice, but there seems to be no source. This trail only leads to the nearby creek. Frustration lines Farron's face.

Desperately, I search the ruins again, my gaze landing on the tower. Despite the collapsed walls, I'm sure we can still make it to the top.

"Come on." I grab his arm. "We can see for forever up there. Might find a clue."

We ascend the spiraling staircase. Despite its decay, the tower still holds a haunting beauty. The sun shines in through the broken windows, casting the stone in a golden light. As we climb higher, Farron's hand slips into mine, our fingers intertwining. I wonder how this tower would have looked in its prime, with its walls gleaming and halls filled with the laughter of fae nobles. Did the Queen herself visit here?

As we reach the top of the tower, we step out onto the remains of a circular room. The roof has long since rotted away, giving us an unobstructed view of the Autumn Realm.

It is magnificent. But nothing is so enchanting as the man beside me.

He leans on the collapsed wall, his auburn strands dancing in the wind. He really belongs here.

If only he could see it. "Fare."

He looks up at me, blinking. I cup his cheeks and pull him into a kiss.

A soft, surprised sound comes from the back of his throat. For a moment, the ruins fade away, and all that exists is the warmth and softness of Farron's lips against mine.

A smile plays at the corners of his mouth. "It's been a while since you kissed me."

"Too long. But for the record, my mouth is available for you anytime. My body, too."

He sighs deeply, and my cock hardens at the sound. Gently, I kiss along his jaw, breathing in the scent of his skin. My hands drift through his soft hair and down his neck, but something cuts my finger.

Farron lets out a sigh and adjusts his shirt over the thorn collar. "Sorry."

"I fucking hate that thing," I growl.

"And you think I like it? But I'm grateful for Caspian in a way. There's a peace knowing if I turn, this *thing* will take over, day or night. I don't want that beast to hurt anyone anymore. I don't want to hurt *you* anymore."

There are scars all over my body from Farron's beast, like the three jagged lines down my back from our first year being cursed. Ez can heal the injuries, but the scars remain. A mark inflicted by a cursed beast is a hard thing to get rid of, even with Spring's Blessing. Most recently added to the collection is the one down my chest and the other across my eye. But the biggest scar he left was not from the beast, but the man. One right into my heart.

I think he broke it. Broke it so badly I don't ever want to find my mate, even if it means never breaking my fucking curse. A sick, twisted part of me would rather stay a beast forever than give him up.

And Rosalina ... I need her, too. That became obvious when she left us. *We* need her.

"You've got a strange look on your face, Day," Farron says tentatively.

I comb my fingers through my hair, attempting to recall what he said. "It's hard seeing you tangled up in those thorns."

"It's my wolf, not me."

"But you're in there, just like the beast is in you now."

I touch his jaw, unable to take my gaze off the thorns. I hated the way Caspian looked at him when they made the bargain, like he'd been offered the most delicious spread of food, and Farron was the main course.

"A beast for a ruler," Farron mutters. "No wonder my people have no faith in me."

"You just need to show them who you are."

"What?"

"The High Prince of Autumn has returned," I say, voice rising. "Remind them who you are."

"It shouldn't be me," he says. "What are you doing?"

"Bending the knee for the High Prince of Autumn." I lower to the stone.

"There isn't a High Prince of Autumn. At least the people don't think so."

"Well, I see one." I undo the laces of his pants. "He's tall and handsome and smart. And deserves to be worshipped ... passionately."

"Day," he whispers as I slide his pants down. His hard cock bounces up to his stomach. "Here? What if someone sees?"

"There's no one around." I press my lips to his inner thigh. "Let me do this for you."

He grips the stone wall, scanning the surroundings.

"See anyone?" I ask, dragging my tongue along his soft skin.

"No, but—" He cuts off in a long sigh as I take his cock in my mouth.

The feeling is exquisite. My hands slip beneath his tunic to touch his skin. His hips jerk, thrusting into my mouth.

He brings his hands to my hair. "Daytonales…"

I keep going, taking him deep, swirling my tongue up his steel length, drawing out his pleasure until his whole body quakes.

"W-wait," he stammers, pulling my head back.

"What?"

"I, well, I want to come with you. If you want…"

I grip his thighs hard enough to bruise. "High Princes don't ask. Tell me what you want."

He bites his lip. "I want to come as you fuck me."

"There you go." I laugh, smacking his bare ass. "I can promise you that, love. But remember what I told Rosalina in the hot springs? I don't let those I care about come only once. First, you're going to come in my mouth, then you'll take my cock like a good boy. Deal?"

"Yes." He smiles down at me, looking so damned beautiful with the golden sky swirling behind him.

"Now picture our girl bouncing up and down on my lap, screaming your name as I worship your beautiful cock."

Fast, that's how I take him, one hand on his waist, as his hips thrust into my mouth, again and again and again. When his fingers grip my hair tight, and his body shudders, I know he's close.

"Fucking give it to me," I release him quick enough to whisper before placing my lips around him again.

He moans, thrusting his hips once more, and then he's coming, spilling his delicious pleasure onto my tongue. I swallow it all down, and he collapses into my arms, panting.

Farron brings his mouth to mine, and I part my lips, knowing he's tasting himself on me. When we're together in this way, my soul feels ablaze.

"You're not fucking done, pup," I remind him.

He gives me a devious smirk, one that shows me he craves me just as much as I do him. His hand slides down my chest.

"I could just leave you like this," he teases, massaging my bulging pants.

"No," I murmur huskily, "because this hard cock is going to fuck you raw, right here out in the open as you look over this land and know that it belongs to you. That *I* belong to you."

"But—" he begins. I cut him off with a kiss, hauling us both up. I grasp at his shirt, pulling it up over his head to reveal his bare chest.

"What if someone shows up?" Farron stammers, flushing. His nipples harden in the chill air, and I can't help but tug on one. He grimaces, swearing.

"There's no one around." I force him to bend over the low wall. "See for yourself."

The realmlands spread before us, but I've got the most beautiful part of Autumn by my side.

"Suck." I shove my fingers into his mouth. A shiver runs through my entire body as his tongue swirls around my skin, the soft sounds of his pleasure.

I prepare him quickly. "How long has it been?"

"What?"

"Since we fucked?"

A slight frown appears on his face. "Before Rosie left."

"No wonder I want you so badly," I growl.

When I feel he's ready, I gently place my cock at his entrance, then push inside. Our joint moans are proof of how much we both need this. I rock my hips forward, feeling him clench around me every time our bodies connect.

I press Farron harder against the wall, using it as leverage as I take him deeper. His breathing quickens.

"You're hard again." I smirk, satisfaction rippling through me as I gaze at his perfect cock.

"Always for you." He sighs. "Always, Day."

Something painful clenches in my chest. I feel completely alive in these moments with him, and I let that energy pour through me as I thrust faster. His moans become louder and more desperate. His body moves in sync with mine, so fucking perfect out here in the open. Perfect except for the thorns around his neck.

"I told you I hated the collar," I rumble. "But I hated the way he looked at you more."

"Caspian?" Farron's fingers dig into the stone.

"Like he owned you, like you were *his*."

Farron tilts his head back as I drive in hard. "Yes, deeper, *please*."

I'm more than happy to give him what he wants, adjusting my angle to hit every inch of him. "But you're not his. You're mine."

He moans at my words, and I think that might be drool dripping down his chin.

"Say it," I demand, slowing my pace to firm, languishing strokes.

"I'm yours," he bites out, saying the words like a mantra with each thrust of my cock. "I'm yours, I'm yours, I'm yours."

I grip his steel length. "And I'm pretty sure we're both *hers*."

A low mewl sounds from his throat as his whole body stiffens and his release sputters out, coating my palm.

I groan, feeling my cock spasm, so relieved to have claimed him. "Farron, I—"

White hot pleasure flashes, and everything releases into him, ecstasy rippling through me in waves. Pure fucking bliss.

Farron's body relaxes as we both come down from our high, falling in a tangle of limbs to the stone floor.

His face is flushed and his eyes bright, and for a stupid idiotic moment, I think he's going to tell me something he never has before. But he just shakes his head. "They'll be mad if they find out we got distracted."

"Hey." I tug him against me. "It's hard work to remind you of your perfection."

We kiss until there's no air left in our lungs, then slowly dress and make our way down the tower to clean up in the cool stream.

As I finish lacing my pants, ice crystallizes along the water.

"Hey, Fare," I say. "Something strange is happening to the stream."

I pull away just as the water below solidifies into pale-blue ice.

Our gazes track upstream, where the frost first emerged. Everything past the chrysanthemum field all the way to the forest is completely frozen.

Rosie, Ez, and Kel wander out from the south end of the Emberwood, thankfully away from the water. But to the north...

There's a creature, a staggering being of white-blue skin. It's too far away to make out the details, but the frost trails in its wake.

It's heading toward two smaller silhouettes walking on the edge of the trees: a little boy and a dog.

"Flicker and Koop," I breathe.

Farron's brows shoot up and he trembles. Then he shakes his head and takes off in a run. "We have to help them."

"I stand with you, High Prince," I say, running after him. "Always."

37

FARRON

Dayton and I run alongside the frozen stream, my feet nearly tumbling out from beneath me.

"Kel! Ezryn!" Dayton booms. "Rose!" They turn to us. "This way!"

They run to us, and we meet along the edge of the forest. My words are ragged in my throat. "It's Flicker. He's in danger."

Rosalina covers her mouth and gasps. "Oh no."

Then we're off again. "There!" I point near the maple trees. Flicker's small body writhes against the frost that covers his feet, trapping him to the ground. Ice captures Koop's small legs, and he howls miserably.

Ezryn is fastest, not even stopping to assess the situation. Ezryn leaps on the frozen stream, using the slick surface to slide toward them. He vaults onto the brown grass and runs to the boy.

"Ez!" I call. "Watch out!"

Ez turns just in time to raise his sword against the stumbling pale-blue creature.

I'd hoped it had been a hallucination, a trick of the sun beaming off the growing frost. But I realize with sickening fear, this thing is real.

A walking corpse made entirely of ice, frost, and bone. Its body is a crystalline structure, glinting under Autumn's cold sunlight. With empty sockets for eyes, its mouth hangs open in a silent scream. Each movement is jerky and unnatural from the frozen solid limbs.

The temperature seems to lower, and I shiver uncontrollably. This thing is not alive—not in any way that I understand. It's a creature of winter, a being of frost and snow and cold.

Holding tight to Ezryn's blade, the wraith pushes against him, and he slips in the grass. Then a glacial frost grows over the sword, emitting from the corpse's touch. Ezryn's entire blade cracks, then shatters.

"Ezryn!" Rosalina screams. He leaps back, disbelief evident as his helm tilts down at the shards of his blade.

"Fuck this." Dayton sprints ahead of us. "Blades are a no-go, eh, ice-bones? How do you feel about magic?" He throws his hands forward and a gale bursts from him, a wind of salt and storm, summoned straight from Summer's Blessing.

The frozen corpse screeches, a sound like cracking ice. Holes tear through its flesh, revealing moon-white bone. Dayton grunts, continuing the wind, but smiles as more and more frozen skin peels away from the creature.

I hold my breath. *It's working. He's got it.*

The wraith falls.

Kel and I catch up, and Rosie runs to Flicker. She touches his head, his hands, asking if he's okay.

It's all right, I tell myself. *It's dead now.*

Ezryn slaps Dayton on the shoulder, but Dayton doesn't respond. He stares straight at the corpse, eyes all too serious. "Wait..."

The creature spasms and jerks. Then it rises. The holes Dayton ripped through its body... They're knitting together, frost filling the gaps. The wraith tilts its head, then charges.

I leap to stand in front of Rosie and Flicker while Ez, Day, and Kel trap the creature in a semicircle. The ice making up its form is mottled with dark veins, like frozen blood vessels. Its joints rattle with each movement as if it's about to fall apart. And yet, it keeps moving forward, milky eyes darting between each prince.

"I'm going to get you out of here," Rosalina says. She grabs the small dagger we'd given her before our journey today and starts chipping away at the ice trapping the boy's feet.

Flicker's face is knotted up with courage, but his nose is bright red. "I'm ... I'm real cold." Koop lets out a mournful howl, half his body now covered in ice.

I stumble away from them. My heart races. I need to help, but what can I do?

Keldarion paces before the wraith. It grabs for him, mouth agape in hunger, but he dodges easily. "You are no creature of Winter," he growls. He bends his knees, then surges upward, arms reaching for the sky. "You're a monstrosity!"

Huge ice spikes shoot up from the ground, impaling the creature through its legs and chest. The wraith lurches and a gurgling squeal fills the valley. Then its head jerks, eyes like twin points of frozen lights. The ice spikes creak and groan ... and merge with the being. It grows, as if enveloping the magic, Kel's ice making the creature bigger, taller.

"I think you fed it," Dayton says.

Ez grabs Dayton and Kel by their tunics. "Get down!"

The ice monster erupts, shooting daggers of frost. The princes barely leap out of the way before the creature is on them again.

Oh no, oh no, oh no. I grip my hair. I have to do something. But if Kel can't even stop this thing, what good am I?

Rosalina gives a frantic look at the fight, then jams her dagger harder against the ice crawling up Flicker's chest. "Koop!" he cries, fingers straining for his dog.

Koop's big, sad eyes stare up at his owner before the ice covers him completely. He's frozen, mouth trapped in a sorrowful howl.

Now, Flicker's crying in earnest, the ice nearly overtaking his arms. Rosalina swears and tries to pry her dagger into the growing frost. Her dagger snaps, the tip shattering. "No." She stumbles back. "No, no, no." She's using her fingernails now, scraping at Flicker's frozen body.

I can barely breathe; my heart is racing so fast. The abomination has Ezryn in its hands. Frost crawls over his armor. Kel roars, ramming his sword into the creature's colossal ice leg, but it gets stuck and is yanked from his grip. It throws Ez straight into Dayton and Kel, and they roll one over another before landing in a pile.

This is what's killing my home. It's going to freeze my friends first, then take Coppershire. My family ... And Rosie. Rosie's here.

The abomination stretches a frozen claw over the princes, who stare up in horror.

But I can't let them do this alone.

There's a well within me, a reserve of power in the deep darkness of my spirit. A well that needs only a spark to ignite.

My friends, my family, Rosalina ... They are that spark.

I focus all my energy on the abomination. Heat spreads through my chest, growing outward, lacing through my veins and swelling at the tips of my fingers. Flames erupt from my hands.

A torrent of fire hits the creature, each burst striking like an explosion. The wraith staggers, struggling to maintain its footing on the slick ice beneath it. But I don't give it a chance, pouring every reserve I have into the attack.

Its frozen flesh begins to melt and crack. A roar explodes out of me, and flames engulf the corpse. The ice dissipates, and all that is left is charred bone.

I slump to my knees, breathless. Kel, Ez, and Dayton rush over. They pat my shoulders, touch my face.

"Good work, kid," Keldarion murmurs. "We were in a tight spot."

"You been holding back on me, Fare?" Dayton smirks.

I try to smile at him, but I feel like I've just walked through an inferno.

Our moment is broken by Rosalina's scream: "Help! Quickly!"

We all rush to her. She clutches Flicker's face; his body is like an ice sculpture, hands frozen as they reach for Koop. Only his face is untouched, but the frost is moving quickly, crawling over his skin.

"I want to go home," he whimpers. "I want Koop."

Rosalina laces her fingers through the little boy's hair and turns to us. "Help him."

I feel it: everyone's eyes on me.

"High Prince of Autumn," Ezryn says lowly, "your people need you."

I sink to my knees beside Rosalina and place my hands on Flicker's face. His eyes are desperate, pleading.

That well within me is still there, burning brighter than I've ever felt it before. But I can't very well firebolt this child like I did the ice abomination.

I close my eyes, seeking within myself. I think of my mother, who she was as High Princess. *Everything you need is inside of you already, Farron,* she'd told me when she passed the title down to me. *But you must be brave enough to claim it.*

Warmth drifts through my body, but this time it's not an inferno. It's the glow of the bonfires we hold at night, the steaming mugs of mulled cider shared with friends, the coals of a bushfire that has cleared the forest of debris and made way for regeneration.

My hands dance with orange light, and I trail it over Flicker, chasing away the frost. The ice retreats and melts down his body. With a crack, his arms are free, and he gives them a big shake before hugging himself.

"Keep doing whatever you're doing," Dayton says. "It's working."

Sweat drips down my forehead, but I hold that reserve in my chest, keeping the warmth of Autumn close to me. The Fool's Summer, we sometimes get where the sun's rays burn too hot; the crackling hearths in the great halls where we hold festivals; the looks of love shared over a bountiful harvest. I hold it close to me, then it flows to him.

Flicker falls forward, feet finally free of the frost. I catch him in my arms, and he holds me tight around the neck. "You saved me, High Prince."

"I ... I suppose I did."

Still, he sniffles. "Koop?"

I shuffle over to the dog trapped in this frozen tomb. *Is the Blessing of Autumn enough to save those we thought lost?*

Orange light glitters off the ice as I summon the magic once more. My friends don't make a sound, all of them holding their breath.

A howl fills the valley as Koop shakes melted ice from his coat and runs to Flicker. The boy grabs his dog, and they collapse to the ground, laughing.

I fall.

"You did it!" Rosalina wraps me in her arms until she falls to the ground, too. "Oh, Farron, I knew you could."

Kel raises a brow. "We might have a fighting chance yet."

"I don't know." I touch my chest. "My own well of magic feels so small. I don't think I could do much more than that."

"If only Caspian wasn't sucking all the magic from Castletree," Ezryn growls.

"At least we know how to kill them," Rosalina says perkily. She still has her arms all over me and I pull her close, breathing her in. "I bet we could figure something out. Maybe there's a way to channel your magic."

"That's a good idea," I say. "Autumn has many old spell books. I wonder if one of them contains—"

"Hey, I hate to break up the party," Dayton calls. He's standing up at the top of the hill away from the wood. "But you should get up here."

We all exchange a look, then run up the hill, joining Dayton at the very peak.

"Oh my god," Rosalina breathes.

"Yeah," Dayton says. "I think we're going to need some more fire power. And fast."

At the very edge of the horizon, a shambling line of glinting white hobbles over the rolling hills.

An entire herd of frozen corpses, bringing the deathfrost with them.

38

EZRYN

I inhale deeply and swing my arms, taking in the comforting sounds of metal against metal, grunting soldiers, and the smell of sweat and steel. I haven't trained with other warriors in years, and I've forgotten how good it feels.

As High Prince of Spring, I've practiced with some of the greatest warriors in the Vale, but the fae men and women in the Autumn troops are a force to be reckoned with. A crisp wind wisps past the slight bit of bare skin between my helm and the loose black tunic I'm wearing. The open-air training grounds in Keep Oakheart are well-kept but harsh. The ground is hard, reddish-brown rock, and a wrong fall could crack a fae's skull.

Dayton and Kel are at my side, along with Farron's little brothers, Dominic and Billagin, and a handful of specialized magefighters selected from the army. There's an excited buzz in the air, and even I find myself unable to stand still.

It's been two weeks since our discovery of the winter wraiths. After our report, Princess Niamh sent out scouting parties to patrol the villages and dispatch the wandering wraiths. But no matter how many we kill, more keep coming. We haven't figured out where these wraiths are coming from: they're all over the Autumn realmlands. And

Niamh still isn't convinced Keldarion doesn't have something to do with it.

Tomorrow, Farron begins daily expeditions to visit the villages destroyed by frost. The hope is he can unfreeze the villagers the same way he did the boy and dog two weeks ago. And in his absence, we must be prepared to protect Coppershire with our greatest weapon.

Fire.

So far, regular soldiers have been successful at killing the monstrosities by using torches and oil-coated swords and arrows. But fire magic is in the blood of the Autumn fae.

And none wield it quite so powerfully as the holder of Autumn's Blessing.

"Is he even going to show up?" Kel asks, crossing his arms. "I can figure it out myself."

Dayton claps him on the back. "Give him a chance. You know how he gets about public speaking."

Those who are gathered in the training grounds today are here to learn from Farron. Most of the magefighters from Autumn can already cast some innate form of fire, but hopefully Farron's lessons will teach them to wield it with deadly purpose.

The High Rulers have always had the ability to create all the elements in one sense or another, though certain skills lie dormant. I know the three of us have never wielded flame in the way Farron has. Dayton and Kel are here to learn how to do it.

I'm here to watch.

Boisterous laughter and grunts sound from the corner of the training ground. Farron's father, Padraig, has been mentoring George in the ways of the sword. There's a playful air to their sparring as the two large men clash wooden blades against one another. *Rosalina's a lot like her father*, I think. *Adaptable. Resilient.*

Speaking of Rosalina … I hear her in the doorway leading into the grounds, voice tinged with that distinctive stubborn tone she occasionally gets. She's pushing Farron hard, urging him inside. When he's too far out and everyone turns to see him, Rosalina gives a satis-

ELIZABETH HELEN

fied smirk and disappears, leaving Farron standing sheepishly in the forefront.

"Oh, uh, hello. T-thank you for coming for training. I'm here to, uh, teach you."

Pained silence follows before Dayton bellows, "Hail the High Prince! Bestow your great knowledge upon us, my liege." He bows low with that signature shit-eating grin. Kel shakes his head.

Stars, this is painful. Farron looks like he might throw up.

Minutes pass of excruciatingly confusing instruction as Farron attempts to lead the group through the act of firecrafting. I've stepped aside, leaning against a wall in the shade and staring at the whole mess.

The magefighters are only half paying attention, some of them looking bored out of their skulls, others distracted, and some snickering to one another as Farron fumbles a fireball and accidentally sets his tunic on fire. Kel douses it with an irritated flurry of snow. Dayton looks like he's napping with his eyes open and only jerks himself awake when Kel shoots a cold blast of wind across his face. Dom and Billy have wandered off, finding more joy in spitting seeds at Paddy and George.

"Are you sure you're qualified to train us?" A magefighter calls.

Farron looks struck, and the flame he holds on his finger dies.

I can't watch this anymore. I straighten, ready to rough up these damn soldiers until they learn respect—

"Psst!"

I jerk my head up to see Rosalina looking down at me from the ramparts above the training grounds. She is beautiful, her long dark hair tumbling down toward me. I have a vision of ascending the wall to get to her, but quickly suppress such madness.

"Ez, you've got to help him," she whispers.

"I know. I'm on my way to relieve that, little shit, mage of his teeth."

"No, no, no." She shakes her head exaggeratedly, making her corset-bound bosom bounce. Now, I'm *really* thinking of ascending

222

this wall. "You must help him do it. He has to be the one to earn their respect."

I tilt my head back in exasperation. That is so much harder than knocking the asshole's teeth out myself. But she has a point.

"I'll see what I can do," I say.

I storm over to Farron and grab him by his shirt collar.

"What—" Farron starts, but I drag him over to the shadowed archway leading out of the training grounds.

"Farron—"

"I know what you're going to say, Ez," he interrupts. "I have to take control. I'm the High Prince. How can I lead my people if I can't even lead a training group? Look at them! How am I supposed to teach Kel anything? He's the Protector of the Realms. And I'm..."

I pat his shoulder. "Actually, I was going to tell you that you should try letting go of control."

He raises a dark eyebrow.

"Kel, Dayton, and I know better than anyone what you've lived through. Use it to your advantage." My hand drifts to his chest. "There is a fighter in you. Do not fear him. Welcome him."

Farron shakes his head and pulls down his tunic, revealing the thin barbed choker around his neck. His skin is raw and torn beneath the spines. "I've done everything I can to keep that thing at bay. I'm not about to welcome him in now."

"I know you see him only as a vicious beast, but remember ... He keeps you alive. He protects you in moments of danger." I turn to look at Rosalina, leaning over the railing. "He protects those you care about as well. Channel that instinct. And above all else, trust yourself."

Farron sinks lower against the wall. "Come on, Ez. Even you know I shouldn't have been given the rule."

I shake my head. For being so intelligent, the young man has so much wisdom to learn. How can he look at Kel and Dayton and me as rightful rulers when we all came into our thrones covered in blood?

"You were chosen to be High Prince for a reason. The fact that you're here, fighting for your people, shows that you have the courage and determination to lead." I grip him on the back of his head. "Do not let anyone tell you otherwise."

Farron lets loose a sigh, then straightens. "Do I have to believe you?"

"No, but you should trust me."

He intakes a deep breath and marches out into the training grounds.

I lean against the archway. Rosalina gives me a big smile. Always the optimist.

But ... maybe something I said took hold. Farron leaps up onto the wooden hurdle.

He points two fingers into the air, releasing a massive blast of fire. It cracks and plumes, and all in attendance turn to face him.

"Line up," Farron calls. "We begin training now. Nobody departs the grounds until I'm satisfied. Understood?"

Kel and Dayton stand to attention. But one of the magefighters rests against a dummy. "Can't you get High Princess Niamh to train us?"

A beat of silence passes, and I hold myself back from thundering over to the bastard and taking out his tongue. *No. He must do it.*

Farron leaps down and strides over to the warrior, and there's something in his gait that makes the hair on the back of my neck rise. The magefighter crosses his arms and smirks.

"Have you seen what we're facing out there, soldier? Have you looked into the eyes of a winter wraith and felt the frost creep over your bones?" Farron asks cooly.

"No," the soldier says. "But I'm sure I could—" Then he looks down, and fear floods his expression. "W-what are you doing to me?"

An icy frost creeps over the soldier's boots, inching up his legs. This is a familiar crystal white, different from the frost in the fields. I smirk, noticing Kel seems entirely too interested in a wooden sword.

Farron gives a dark frown as his eyes trace the frost's path up the man's shaking body. "This cold will claim your home; your family turned to frozen monuments; your very blood becoming ice. And the only way to stop it—" He slams his palm into the man's chest. His skin radiates with an orange flame. "—is to embrace your inner fire. *I am your High Prince, and you will learn from me, or you will be lost to the frozen abyss.*"

The frost melts away under Farron's fire, and he turns, leaving the soldier a shivering mess.

Up on the ramparts, Rosalina looks at me and winks.

THE NEXT FEW hours pass quickly as the soldiers listen with rapt attention to Farron's instruction. Even Dom and Billy have shaped up, staring a little doe-eyed at their big brother.

Kel and Dayton are the best students of all. In fact, I think their competitive spirits have assisted them, both eager to produce a bigger and hotter flame than the other. Keldarion's flashes a brilliant sapphire blue as he spirals fireball after fireball at the rock wall, while Dayton juggles several turquoise flames and yells for everyone to watch him.

Farron walks over to me. Once I saw he had everything under control, I went about my own training with sword and dagger.

"So, who do you think is going to need burn healing first?" He smirks toward Kel and Dayton.

"Oh, definitely Dayton. If someone doesn't praise him for his performance, he'll start juggling heads."

Farron chuckles, but then his expression turns serious. "Why didn't you join in the training?"

I hold my weapon up. After the wraith destroyed my sword, Paddy gifted me his old longsword, a gorgeous blade the color of brass. While no weapon could compare to a sword made by Spring, I have to admire the fine craftsmanship of Paddy's. "Don't worry about me, Fare. I'll coat the Windscythe with oil and be twice as deadly as any magic user."

Farron holds me in his golden gaze. "Ezryn … Are you afraid?"

I stifle a laugh. "I don't like new magic. You know that."

Quickly, I swing my sword hard at the dummy, embedding the

blade in the wood. I need to fill my head with action, with thoughts. Otherwise, *he'll* start talking.

"Ezryn," Farron says and puts a hand on my arm.

I shudder as memories pass in my mind. The beautiful green dress, so soft compared to the harshness of her metal helm. The sound of blood rattling through lungs. Weeping willow trees drenched in red.

Farron takes my hand and smiles up at me. There's something so strong within the softness. "You're always telling me I don't have to do this on my own. Neither do you."

A tremble shudders up my body. Because I want to believe Farron. I want him to train me like he has the others.

But all I can picture is him lying on the ground beneath me, a charred and bloody corpse, as Kairyn whispers, *"You killed him, too."*

39

ROSALINA

o not be afraid of the fire within. My father's words replay in my mind. Today marks one month since we've arrived in the Autumn Realm, and it feels like there's been nothing but fear.

I walk behind Dayton and Farron as we investigate the Emberwood for any signs of the winter wraiths. The brilliant glade's trees bristle with berries. Some still shine bright orange, while others glitter with frost.

Farron and I have spent the last couple of weeks riding out to villages frozen by the wraiths. My heart flutters as I think of Farron thawing the homes people thought were lost, his touch both gentle and powerful. But word keeps coming that as soon as we free one village, another falls. Kel, Ezryn, and Dayton aren't making much progress either. The frost is spreading faster than we can contain it. And the closer it gets to Coppershire, the more on edge Princess Niamh becomes.

It's been so busy, the five of us haven't all been in the same place at the same time, except at night. All the princes have taken turns returning to Castletree. Farron explained the relationship between the castle and the princes is symbiotic; their magic is enriched by the castle, as their own presence strengthens the castle's magic.

Today, we returned to the first place we saw a winter wraith in hopes there's a trail, some clue of their origin that we missed before. Ezryn and Keldarion took the northside of the forest, but I've decided to stick with Farron and Dayton for now.

The ground below my feet is soft and squishy, wet earth and rotting leaves. Though sunlight shines in through gaps in the branches, the forest is so dark, it appears almost night.

Dayton throws an arm over my shoulders, tearing me from my thoughts. "So, how come you decided to stick with us? Mommy and Daddy too serious for you?"

I roll my eyes but laugh. "Maybe I thought they were more capable than you two."

Dayton waggles his eyebrows at Farron. "We did get distracted last time we were here."

Farron's cheeks redden. "I have no idea what you're talking about."

Something electric shoots between them. "What are you two hiding?"

"Nothing," Farron says. "Dayton's just being an idiot, like usual."

"Oh, come on." Dayton spreads his arms out. "You didn't call me an idiot in the ruins."

Yes, I can see it in the hungry glint in Dayton's gaze, the quirk of a smile on Farron's lips. "Oh my god. You two totally did it last time."

Farron blows out a breath, but Dayton laughs. "Don't rat us out to the bosses. I'm sure you three had a great time."

"Kel and Ez spent an hour debating a slimy pattern of ice on a rock until we realized it was snail goo," I say. "Sounds like being with your crew would have been a lot more fun."

Something feral flashes in Dayton's gaze, his pupils darkening. Dayton moves so quick that I barely have time to register what he's doing. He shoves Farron against a tree and pushes me toward him, caging us both with his arms.

"Dayton!" I cry out, but it comes out more of a breathy moan as he presses his hips into me, squeezing me between them.

"Day." Farron tries to squirm away, but it just makes his body rub against mine.

"Neither of you are moving," Dayton says, the muscles in his arms straining. "Not until Fare tells you who he was thinking about."

"Come on." Farron twists a hand free and grips Dayton's arm.

"It wasn't that long ago, Fare," Dayton says. "Who were you thinking about as I swallowed your cum?"

I feel the reaction of their bodies on either side of me.

"Kel and Ez are close," Farron says, but he's stopped trying to get out of the hold. Instead, there's now a desperate whine to his voice.

"Then you better get talking." Dayton follows his words with a quick thrust, pressing his cock against my thin leggings. The movement pushes me into Farron, and my head tilts to his shoulder.

It feels so right to be caged in by these two tall fae males. A mixture of pure safety and unhinged desire floods through me.

Farron's breath is warm against my cheeks, and my eyes flutter closed. "Tell me."

"You, naturally," he says.

Dayton lets out a purely male groan. "How did you like it, pup, being so exposed out in the open, fucked with the wind on your skin?"

"You know I fucking loved it, Day."

"Rosie, how'd you like to feel it?"

My eyes shoot open. The fae Prince of Summer is gazing down at me with a predatory grin. "Feel what?"

"The open air on your skin." Dayton drops one of his hands, but neither Farron nor I move. The top laces of my leather corset dangle between Dayton's fingers.

"Kel and Ez are going to come back any minute," I stutter. "They're going to—"

"Then stop me." He leans down to kiss me.

His lips are fire, the pressure pushing me against Farron. Dayton draws the string completely out of the front of the corset in a fluid movement. The front falls open, leaving me covered only by the loose cream blouse. A cold wind whips over the newly exposed skin, and my breasts feel heavy and loose without the support of the corset.

"Fucking perfect," Dayton gleams. "Touch her, Fare."

Farron lets out a pained sound, but then Dayton grips the Autumn Prince's hand, moving it over me. Lightly, Farron's fingers touch the soft skin of my breast.

He lets out a shuddering gasp, and even the briefest contact with him has me clenching my legs shut.

"I know that look," Dayton says. "Tell me, Blossom, is he hard?"

I gasp as he pushes me against Farron, and yes, his hard cock presses against my ass. Farron groans, his hand slowly moving down my breast.

Breaking branches sound, and we all scramble away from each other as Ezryn and Kel burst through the leaves.

"Anything to report?" Ezryn asks, looking at each of our guilty faces.

Kel's just staring at us. He doesn't look mad but ... pained. Then I remember he can feel what I do, or at least some version of it.

"Let's get moving," Ezryn says. "We have to report to the Princess."

Keldarion shakes his head, then turns. "And for stars' sake, lace your bodice, Rosalina."

I look down at the shirt Dayton unlaced. Yep, I'm indecent. Without the thick leather holding everything in, my breasts hang loose in the thin fabric.

But when Keldarion wants me to do something, it makes me want to do anything else. "If you want it laced so badly, do it yourself."

"It seems you are getting used to royal life, with servants dressing you," he growls. "Do you enjoy being treated like a princess?"

When you're the one treating me that way, I think. But I shake my head. "Whatever, I can do it—"

But he's in front of me now, swatting my hands down, and delicately picking up the laces. His fingers are rough and calloused, looping the thread through the eyelets of the corset, stitching it closed. Every brush of his hands against my sensitive skin sends skittering pulses of heat through me, and I clamp my legs shut.

Damn Dayton for starting this all. And damn Keldarion's hands for feeling so good against my skin.

The other princes move in a semicircle, watching as if in rapture. There's something predatory in their gazes. Chills run down my spine as if Kel and I are cornered by hungry animals.

Maybe we are.

I take a deep breath, causing my chest to rise. It presses Kel's hands against the delicate skin of my breasts.

His fingers tremble. "Rosalina," he says, a warning edge to his voice.

A warning I want nothing more than to ignore, so I tilt my head at him, hair falling over my shoulders. *So easy to tear, so easy to rip apart ...* Words I wish he'd say filter through my mind, and it's like I can hear his deep voice etching a place within me. *Lay you bare and have you here upon the forest floor.*

"Move your hair," he says. One of his fingers dip between the valley of my breasts. I press my thighs together, sensing I'm going to soak through my underclothes.

There's a heavy presence behind me. Ezryn. "Let me." A rough, gloved hand caresses my neck as he sweeps my hair away from my face.

Oh stars. *Ohh stars.* Kel's gaze shifts from me to Ezryn. It's like there's a silent conversation between the two of them. I can't handle this. I've already been pressed between two fae princes today.

I can't help but let out a soft groan as Kel's rough fingers delicately touch the last of my exposed skin, tying my corset together.

A small, matching growl escapes his lips, then he snatches my face. "Are you satisfied?"

My eyes flit over him, down the hard planes of his chest, until I see the obvious outline of his arousal. Hard and yearning. Yearning for me.

Ezryn gives a tight yank on my hair, and I fall against his hard metal frame. "Careful what you say next, Petal."

But I don't want to be careful. Not around them. "I could ask you the same question." My voice comes out husky, dripping with desire.

Kel's grip tightens on my jaw. Wild thoughts race through my mind as my body trembles. He just did up my laces, but I want to throw off my top, all my clothes, and toss myself naked onto the forest floor until one of these muscled idiots fills my aching—

Keldarion loosens his hold and turns. "You are going to be the death of me."

Dayton clears his throat. "You know what I'm feeling? Forest orgy. Hear me out, we all get naked and—"

Keldarion storms away, and Ezryn gives a dissatisfied sigh, letting go of my hair and following Keldarion.

I giggle. Did he read my mind or something? I walk over to Dayton. "Sorry, Day, no forest orgies today."

"It's alright." Dayton throws his arms around me and Farron. "There's always tomorrow."

40

ROSALINA

T hank goodness for the cold breeze because my skin is seriously heated from that last encounter. Being pressed between Day and Fare, then Kel's hands over me, Ezryn pulling my hair ... I need to get my head on straight. We have real actual problems here. I can't constantly be lusting after these princes like Marigold.

I step cautiously through the dense undergrowth, my feet sinking into the earth. The air is thick with the scent of decaying leaves and the distant sound of trickling water. Between twisted trees and tangled roots, a bog gleams in the dappled sunlight.

I stop in place. "There's something out there."

A light bounces at the edge of the water—not the shimmer of sunlight, but something floating. It oscillates back and forth, resembling a dancing flame on the wind.

Almost in a trance, I step closer to it, mud squelching beneath my boots as I approach. I peer into the blackness, trying to see through the thick mist.

"Careful." Kel grips my forearm.

"I've read about this," I say.

Farron nods as he creeps up beside me, then gestures for the others to be quiet.

"Is this a will-o'-wisp?" I whisper, turning to him.

His broad smile is the only answer I need. "It might be. This is only the second time I've come across one."

"A will-o'-what?" Dayton asks.

"A will-o'-wisp," Farron says. "They're said to be the wayward hearts of mated souls who never completed their bond."

"Stars," Dayton says. "Better break that celibate streak of yours, Kel, or you're soon going to look a little more ... flamey."

Kel growls, but I ignore them, nearly vibrating with excitement as the little blue flame dances.

"They're not dangerous," Farron continues. "Well, unless you're—"

"Professor Thaddeus Goldstorm," I finish. "Man, his book was dry. He spent half of it explaining his research credentials. Every single night, he camped out looking for the wisps. His book was pages upon pages of his injuries, from eating the wrong mushrooms, to animal attacks, to getting stuck in his own traps."

"After a thousand pages, he finally admits he never found one." Farron laughs, and his eyes sparkle as he looks over at me. "I think we were darn near ready to throw his book in the fire after that."

"As cute as you two are, being all smart," Dayton drawls, "are you sure these things aren't dangerous? Because this one's got some friends."

Two more blue flames flicker to life. Farron lets out a long sigh. "The Harvest Goddess must truly be blessing us to see so many."

"They're not dangerous," I reiterate. "Legends say they can be mischievous, leading bewildered travelers off the path. But others say they're leading you toward your destiny."

"And why do you both know so much about these ... things?" Ezryn asks, swatting one away that bounces too close to him. Farron utters a pained hiss at Ezryn's movement. The flame weaves back, skittering blue light over his armor.

"We looked them up while we were researching mates." An idea sparks in my mind. We've been so busy trying to figure out this frost, I haven't spent as much time on my original goal: finding a way to break the princes' curse. Finding their mates.

Warmth blooms on my skin. Maybe there's another reason I've been avoiding that mission.

But I have to stop being selfish. This is for the entire Enchanted Vale.

"Farron," I say, "do you remember that legend about catching a will-o'-wisp?"

"The lighting of the mate bond." He nods. "One myth says that if you catch a will-o'-wisp, it will temporarily alight your mate bond, and you can see a path to the other half of your soul."

Keldarion grumbles as if the whole thing is ridiculous. He already knows his destiny and hates it.

"Come on," I urge the others. "It can't hurt."

Slowly, they follow my instructions and creep toward the will-o'-wisps.

"Any legends about catching one and being consumed in its creepy fire?" Dayton asks as he perches beneath one.

"Only one way to find out." Cautiously, Farron holds out his hand. He closes his eyes, steadying his breath. A little chime sounds through the air, and the wisp floats onto his palm. "Hello." He smiles at it, eyes crinkling.

Following his lead, both Ezryn and Dayton catch their own. The three of them return, little flames dancing happily above their palms.

"That was surprisingly easy," Dayton says.

"They appeared," I say, remembering the lore. "They wanted us to see them."

"I think that one's waiting for you." Farron nods to my left, where a blue flame floats beside my head.

"Be careful, Rosalina," Keldarion says sternly. He, unsurprisingly, stands back.

"I'll go first," Farron says. "If I remember correctly, you place it on your chest, and its fire will merge with you for a short while."

My heart pounds nervously as Farron carefully holds the wisp to his body. Magic crackles, and his chest glows with unearthly light. It's as if we can peer inside him, not to his skin or bones, but to something else. Something soul deep.

And beside his heart is a cracked circle, tangled with dark lines, like black yarn woven around a miniature star. Every few seconds there's a burst of light, and then it dims, the darkness strangling it.

"That's kind of strange." Farron gulps.

"Here goes nothing." Dayton brings the wisp closer. Ezryn gives a frustrated sigh and mimics the movement.

I gasp as both their flames spread out over their chests and reveal the same strangled ball of light. Dissatisfaction lingers in my heart.

"Maybe this is what it looks like when the mate bond is dormant," I muse. "We need to wake up those balls of light. I'm pretty sure I didn't feel my connection with Kel until he was trapped beneath the ice."

Kel gives a displeased sigh as he does anytime our tie is brought up.

"Why don't you try, Rosie?" Farron says. "Then we can see what an awakened bond looks like."

I glance over at Kel, but he's avoiding my gaze, so I gently place the blue flame over my chest. A tickling warmth spreads from my heart as the wisp's fire expands. I tilt my chin down, and my heart sinks when I see the same strangled light as the others. Maybe the wisps don't show mate bonds at all.

Then a spark ignites, bursting forth like a shooting star and slamming straight into Keldarion. He looks down at the glowing yellow thread as if it's offended him. It glimmers between us, a living tether.

"Well, it does work," Farron says. "Seems there's something wrong with us."

I march over to Dayton, who is closest to me, and examine the strangled light inside his breast. It doesn't make sense. Mine looks the same as his, besides the tether connecting me to Kel. Does it appear that way regardless of whether the bond has awakened?

"Wake up, mate bond." I slam my hands onto his chest. A burst of his wisp's fire tingles through me. "I could … I could be your mate, too."

But as my hands settle on his chest and nothing happens, I flush and laugh, embarrassed. "Worth a try. But I guess fae don't have two mates, let alone a human."

Farron gives me a soft, sympathetic smile. "It's happened before. Remember the legend of Princess Eurydice Erato? She had two mates. At least she did if we untangled that poem correctly."

"Sorry, Sweetheart." Dayton takes my chin in his hand. "I don't think it works that way. But for the record, if I was your mate, I'd be honored. Even if it meant sharing you with that icy bastard." He winks at Kel, who rolls his eyes.

"Rosalina," Ezryn says. "Your light. It's splitting."

I stare down at the luminosity radiating from my chest. It diverges into two threads: one leading to Kel, and the other into the forest.

"Wait, *do* you actually have a second mate?" Dayton's eyes widen.

Something blooms in my chest, because yes … Yes, I do. I know it with my entire heart.

I take off in a run, following the shimmering thread.

"Rosalina, wait!" Keldarion yells.

I break through the foliage. Leaves crackle beneath my feet. The princes clamber behind me, but a part of me desperately wants to get away from them, away from their bonds that haven't awakened. Their mates are far, far away, waiting to be found. Maybe a little foolish part of me thought they'd awaken for me, that the belonging I felt for them meant something more.

"Wait, Rosie!" Farron calls. "Be careful! Even if you have another mate, it's highly—ouch, watch out for that log—it's highly unlikely he's in this forest. It could be leading you anywhere in the Enchanted Vale!"

I ignore him, feeling like it's close.

Because even though I know Kel is my mate, there's still an emptiness in my heart that needs to be filled. Is it because he refuses to accept our bond … or something else? Someone else waiting for me?

The light twines through the trees, and I break out into an open clearing. The end of the thread. Slowly, I step into the sunlight to see where it's leading me, but it's not to a person. It's just a patch of flowers. They're bright blue with luminescent petals, appearing like roses without thorns.

I fall to my knees in the mud, staring at the three flowers, the light thread in my chest pointing to each of them. I don't understand. Tears drip down my face.

Branches crack behind me as the others approach.

"Oh fiddlesticks," Farron says.

"No second mate, eh?" Dayton says gently. "Don't cry, Rosalina. If I had Kel as my only mate, I'd be sad, too."

Kel stays silent.

I wipe my eyes with the back of my hands. What do I say to them? How do I tell them I'm crying because I thought I'd belong to them?

"These flowers are called Friar's Lanterns," Farron says, leaning down beside me. "Do you remember reading about them?"

I shake my head.

"They're also known as the Deceiver's Bloom or the Lonely Lover's Flower," he continues. "There's something in the nectar that attracts the will-o'-wisps. Many wayward souls have had their search for their mate end with these blossoms."

"I guess I was wrong about what I felt," I whisper, an embarrassed sob breaking out of my chest. I had been so certain...

"Come on," Keldarion says, and there's a soft expression on his face as he holds a hand out for Farron and I, helping us to our feet.

"You cannot escape the magic either, Kel," Ezryn says, gesturing at one last will-o'-wisp floating by Keldarion's head.

He gives an annoyed sigh, but I whisper, "I want to see if it points to me."

"You know it will," he says gruffly, but slowly moves the flickering flame to his chest.

I blink against the brightness as his mate bond sparkles to life. There are no shadows at all, no woven threads of darkness strangling his light. Something sparkles forth within him, and strikes me in the heart, and a tingling happy sensation courses through my body.

"Hey, why does he get to be all sparkly?" Dayton chides.

I can't answer, lost in the warm light of our tether, the strength of the starlight beaming in Kel's chest.

"Rosalina, I'm not the mate you deserve," he says slowly. Then he bends down and picks up three of the Friar's Lanterns flowers. "But tonight, you can pretend to have a bond with those much more worthy of your affection than me."

My mate proceeds to tuck a flower behind Farron's ear, one between the slats of Ezryn's armor, then one into the messy knot of Dayton's bun.

The light in my chest splits more, a golden line pointing to each of the flowers, to each of my princes. Tears brim in my eyes, and Keldarion reaches out to squeeze my hand.

"You bastards better give her a good dance tonight," he says, then his voice grows more serious. "And protect her with your lives if I cannot."

"Of course," Farron says.

"On my sword." Dayton smirks.

Ezryn bows his head slightly as he mutters words in another language.

I grip Dayton's hand, who grabs Ezryn's, who takes Farron's, who connects the circle by holding Keldarion's hand.

The will-o'-wisp burns brightly in my chest, bursting forth a light to my mate beside me, but also to the flowers on each of my princes. It lights their faces in gold, as if there truly was a bond there. There must be more fallen flowers on the ground, because a fifth light darts down through the brush below.

I give a secret silly wish to the fire blooming in my heart that I can keep us woven together like this for always.

41

ROSALINA

Arm in arm with Marigold and Astrid, I stroll through the grandest pumpkin patch I've ever seen in my entire life. There's to be a festival tonight, celebrating the Harvest Moon.

I'm so grateful for a full moon tonight. It will give Farron a much needed semblance of normalcy.

We've been given the very important task of picking the perfect pumpkin for the centerpiece at tonight's festival.

Truthfully, I think the Autumn staff just wanted to get Marigold out of their hair for a while.

"No sense of order in that Keep," she continues to complain as we walk. "Not like when I ran Keep Hammergarden in Spring. There, we had everything in shipshape."

Astrid and I both laugh, and I can't help but be grateful to be out here with my friends. They've helped lighten my mood since the encounter with the will-o'-wisps in the forest, and all of us are looking forward to the festival tonight. Excitement is palpable in the air, and we're greeted with smiles and waves from other fae gathering crops.

This patch lies outside of the gates of Coppershire. The pumpkins, in all shapes and sizes, are scattered like jewels waiting to be discovered. Some are small and round, while others stretch into peculiar shapes. They're strange colors, as well. Most are orange, but others are white, red, and even blue.

"We'll show them we can find the best pumpkin," I say, kneeling and running my fingers over the hard ridges of one.

"Oh no!" Astrid peeps and clutches the back of my cloak.

"What is it?"

"Over there. It's the twins! I just know Dom is going to ask me to the festival tonight!"

"What's wrong with that?" Marigold cocks a brow. "He *is* a prince."

Astrid wrinkles her nose. "An annoying little prince who tried to assassinate the ruler of Winter."

I straighten and can't keep the smile from my face. "You two go get a cider from the wagon at the edge of the patch. I'll distract them."

"Are you sure?" Astrid asks, tugging on my sleeve.

"Of course. I'll meet you there."

"You're the best, Rosalina!" Astrid gives me a quick hug before she grabs Marigold, and they scamper across the grounds.

I'm still chuckling when Billy and Dom emerge from behind a particularly hefty gourd.

"Fair Astrid!" Dom stretches out his hand. "Where did she go?"

I cross my arms and stare them down. "You weren't going to ask her to the harvest festival, were you?"

Dom gives me a determined smile. "What if I was?"

I can tell from the devious look in his eye, he's not going to be easily deterred. I'll have to go about this a different way. "Astrid is from Winter, and you know they have special customs for extending a formal invitation."

Dom stares me down. "What do you mean?"

I pause, allowing myself one breath to make something up. A custom of the Winter Realm ... My eyes flicker closed, and for a moment, it's almost like I can feel snowflakes on my cheeks.

In the moonlit holly grove, where starlight softly weaves,
Two hearts entwine, beneath frosty leaves.

A whispered exchange during night's hush,
Scarlet promises, a binding touch.

"You have to present her with a bushel of holly berries, each one a promise of how you will treat her." I open my eyes. "Scarlet promises, a binding touch."

Billy smacks his brother on the head. "Yeah, you doofus. It's like the lullaby Mom used to sing." His eyes light up and he starts to murmur a tune:

"Through frost-kissed dawns and dusk's veiled embrace,
Holly berries hold our secrets in a sacred space.
For far off days, in Summer's radiant gleam,
When Autumn gold falls, echoes of forgotten dreams."

Dom nods enthusiastically at his brother's words. "Yes, that's it."

"The only problem is," Billy says, "how am I to get holly in Autumn?"

"We'll crush up some raspberries and dye some acorns red," Dom says eagerly. "That'll do that the trick."

They thank me and wander off, contriving their plan. I stay rooted to the spot. Billy had sung the song in the same melody I'd heard in my head. But I'd made it all up ... Hadn't I? How could I have known a fae song from the Enchanted Vale?

The Autumn breeze suddenly carries a coldness, and I wrap my arms tight around myself. Songs, thorns ... What other secrets are inside me?

A PUMPKIN VINE twining around my ankle breaks me from my haze, and I tear my boot free. But when I look down, I don't see the twisting green, but rather purple thorns.

My breath catches in my throat as I watch the briar retreat through a tangle of green and orange. I look around. Astrid and Marigold are still sipping cider in wooden chairs on the outskirts of the patch. The rest of the fae don't seem to noticed the oddity.

I follow the thorn as it twines through the pumpkins, leading me to the edge of the field. And there stands a cloaked figure, the thorny vine circling his feet.

Storming over, I grab his arm. "What are you doing here?"

The Prince of Thorns whirls, his hood falling off, dark hair catching in the breeze. "Finding a pumpkin, of course."

"You're not—" I begin but pause when I notice the basket slung over the crook of his elbow, a little blue pumpkin poking out.

"See for yourself."

He holds out the basket. I look around to see if anyone's watching us, but we're on the outskirts of the field. I snatch the basket and peer inside. There's an odd assortment of trinkets—an empty cup they served cider in, leaves, acorns, and roots. There are also two jars, one emitting a strange blue glow.

"What is all this for?"

"Presents for my little bird," he says.

Pushing aside the brittle leaves, I notice one of the jars is filled with luminescent blue flowers, while the other contains three fluttering will-o'-wisps. Their glow sets the whole basket ablaze with light.

"What could you possibly need with the wisps?" I ask, pulling out the jar.

Caspian tilts his head. "You'd be surprised how valuable things from the world above are to those in the Below. Just like how you surface folk are so fascinated with us."

"I'm not fascinated with anything from the Below."

He closes the distance between us, hovering over me. "Then tell me, Princess, why are you looking at *me* like that?"

I should tell him he's being ridiculous, that of course I'm not looking at him like *that*. But when I meet his gaze and see those midnight eyes, it's like I've stepped off the edge of the world, fallen in an endless void, and thrown away my map.

"Caspian." His name on my lips sounds like a beginning, but I've forgotten the ending, because all I see are briars rising around us, as if they want to push us even closer. "What are you doing?"

"I'm not doing anything."

Me. It's me. I somehow took control of his thorns, like I was able to do at Castletree. They encircle us like an extension of my consciousness.

Though, it is certainly troubling that my subconsciousness thinks pushing me and the Prince of Thorns this close is a good idea. Letting the thorns fall among the green vines, I steady myself with a deep breath.

Trying to look anywhere but him, I study the jar in my hands. The little will-o'-wisps flutter. In the basket, their flight had been lazy, but now they're desperate to get out. I don't know much about them, but I'm sure Autumn wouldn't be happy with their wisps being taken to the Below.

"Well, you can't have these," I say and unscrew the top of the jar.

Caspian pushes away from me with such urgency, I can't help but let out a small giggle. "They're not dangerous."

He runs a casual hand through his hair, watching with a calculating gaze as the three blue lights flutter into a nearby cluster of trees. "Do you know how hard those were to catch?"

Throwing the empty jar back into the basket, I hand it back to him. "Find something else for your bird."

He watches the wisps until they're out of sight before reaching into his basket. "There's a gift in here for you, too." He pulls out a cluster of holly berries framed by an emerald green leaf.

"How did you ..." I ask breathlessly.

"What's the distance between realms when you have thorns?"

"You were listening to me."

"Thought it only polite. You are attending my party."

The berries gleam red as blood in his palm. "More like you're forcing me there through your bargain with Farron."

"Fine," he says, annoyance flashing on his features, and he withdraws his hand.

"Wait," I gasp, reaching out to clutch his wrist. "What do the berries mean?"

"Different songs, different meanings. Vows, promises, secrets."

Cautiously, I press my finger down on one of the berries. "What does this one mean?"

He tugs me closer, so we're chest to chest. "That one is a secret."

"What secret?"

A dazzling smile spreads over his plush lips. "Take it and find out."

Scarlet promises, a binding touch. "Is this some sort of trick?" He doesn't answer and when I look up at him, it's like he hasn't even heard me, his eyes so intent. Intent on me. "Tell me this isn't a trick, Caspian."

He tilts his head, gaze shaded shrouded by his hair, and he says so lowly I'm not sure he even knows he's speaking out loud, "You believe I can think straight enough for tricks when I'm around you?"

Carefully, I take the bushels of berries from his palm. "This secret better be worth it."

"It is," Caspian says. "A secret Kel doesn't even know."

"Can't be that good then," I say, tucking the holly behind my ear. "I doubt Kel knows many of your secrets."

Caspian quirks his head as if implying I have no idea what I'm talking about. He and Keldarion do seem to have a rapport, a history that I don't quite understand. Just how close were Kel and Caspian? As close as Kel and Ezryn? Closer?

"Tell me your secret."

Caspian's gaze flicks from his basket up to me. "I have a younger sister."

"Really?" I ask. "If she's anything like you, I can't wait to meet her."

"She's not like me," he says, staring at me for several beats of my heart before continuing. "She's worse."

"I always wished I had a sibling," I say, not certain how else to respond. "But it was just me and Papa."

"I never wanted one," Caspian says. "Maybe she changed my mind. I haven't decided yet."

Then he's just staring at me, and I'm not sure why I'm not leaving. A late afternoon fog has crept through the field, curling around our feet. This is the first thing close to a normal conversation I've ever had with the Prince of Thorns.

He saved me from Lucas. His bargain is helping Farron …

"Keep that on for the festival." He gestures to the holly leaves behind my ear.

"Hardly fits the harvest aesthetic."

His dark eyes narrow. "Humor me."

"Why?"

"Maybe I don't like the idea of everyone else getting to touch you tonight with no piece of me there."

"Not going to crash this party?"

"I've already been above too long." He steps closer, and almost tentatively reaches out to caress my ear. "Tell me, Rosalina, do you remember the rest of the song?"

Caspian's lips dip to my ear as he begins to softly murmur in a tune I've only just remembered:

"So sleep, Princess, in the holly's keep,

Where oaths linger, in shadows deep,

Through Winter's shroud and Spring's gentle glow,

In the tapestry of time, where thorns may grow."

"As the moon weaves tales, and the sun takes its cue," I whisper, breath catching the

melody. *"Our bond, like the holly, forever true."*

Briars rise around us, entangling his arms and legs. As he pulls away, he says, *"In this eternal dance, a melody divine, So dream, my love, as the seasons entwine."*

42

ROSALINA

Despite all the tragedy they've been through, the Autumn fae sure know how to celebrate. I sit on a log off to the side, a cup of spiced cider in my hands. The clay mug warms my cold fingers as I observe the festival.

The smell of cinnamon, roasted pumpkins, and wood smoke fills the air. The party is outside the city walls in a grove of twisting trees. Golden ribbon wraps the trunks, and lanterns dangle from the branches. A crackling bonfire lights the center. Tables of food, wine, and ale dot the clearing, while logs and squishy mushrooms have been positioned around the perimeter to rest upon. The music is a merry jig played on flutes and pipes. Fae dance in the flickering light of the fire.

After my encounter with Caspian, I'd had just enough time to get ready with Astrid and Marigold. I chose a beautiful gown, the bodice adorned with intricate beadwork that shimmers and sparkles in the firelight. The skirt is full and flowing, with layers of tulle and chiffon that resemble the changing of leaves with hues of red, orange, and gold. Even the fabric rustles like crispy leaves in a breeze. My hair falls over my shoulders in cascading waves.

I'm not sure why, but I've kept the holly berries tucked behind my ear.

This time, Marigold and Astrid also got ready with me. In fact, I spy Marigold dancing with a burly fae man with bright red hair. *Trust me, girlie,* she'd told me as we headed to the party, *you've never truly been fucked until you've had one of these wild Autumn fae.*

I'd laughed and reminded her she'd said the same thing about the Summer fae. Now, another giggle bubbles up from my chest as I watch her. I hope she has a fantastic time tonight.

"Enjoying the party?" a voice asks, the command in it drawing me from my thoughts.

I look up at Farron's mother, the former High Princess of Autumn. She's wearing an elegant green dress, her silver and brown hair woven in a crown atop her head.

"Oh! Yes, very much so," I tell her. "It's magical."

She takes a seat beside me, and I flush, cupping tight to my drink. I've only seen her a handful of times since we've been here. She might be content to let us roam free now, but I'm under no illusion that at the first hint of trouble she won't hesitate to slap Keldarion—and the rest of us—back in chains.

"I've been watching you," she says, her golden eyes so similar to Farron's.

"Watching me?"

"Yes. Tonight, you've made everyone you've talked to happier than they were before."

"I've just been having fun." I shake my head. "It's the atmosphere."

It truly has felt magical. Like Kel made them promise, I danced with all three princes. Farron was so sweet, teaching me the steps in time to the music. I had to remind Dayton to grab my waist and not my ass, though I didn't really mind. Ezryn and I finally got to have the dance Caspian interrupted at the Winter Solstice Ball. Though, I can't help but wonder if he's going to show up, even though he said he wouldn't.

Most of the fae opted for no shoes, so I did the same, feeling the leaves crack beneath my feet. I felt the energy of the Enchanted Vale as we moved to the beat of the music, and for a moment, I was a part of this world.

After the dancing, Papa and I ravaged the buffet table, stuffing ourselves with candied apples and rhubarb pie. We feasted on roasted nuts, soft bread, and strangely shaped mushrooms. Papa particularly liked the sweet and spicy pumpkin beer, and I was inclined to agree.

I even caught up with Farron's little brothers. Acorns painted as holly berries were a failure at wooing Astrid, but they seemed to have recovered. I found them rehearsing a jig and they pulled me in to dance with them. We performed twice for a gaggle of small fae children before we all agreed our masterpiece deserved to be shared with everyone. They pulled me up on a table in the middle of the party, and we sang and danced our hearts out. I can definitely thank the pumpkin beer for that one.

It must have been decent—or perhaps people are inclined to clap for princes—because we got a round of applause. I was a bit unsteady after that. Ez helped me off the table with praise that it was the best song he'd ever heard in his life. Maybe he'd had some pumpkin beer, too. The thought makes me nearly burst out laughing as I imagine Ez tucking a huge curly straw under his helmet.

Of course, Kel hasn't danced with me. He's been standing in the shadows, calmly sipping his ale. Though, I suspect he's having fun. Every now and again I catch his stare, watching me and the princes through the firelight.

"It's a magical celebration," I breathe again.

"Mother." Farron breaks through the crowd, his cheeks rosy and flushed. "Are you interrogating Rosalina?"

"Absolutely not," she says, moving aside for him to sit.

Farron's dressed as befits a prince. A crown of gilded leaves rests across his soft brown hair. A regal deep green tunic fits across his lean, muscled chest. A golden cuff that twists like a blazing flame adorns one of his pointed ears.

"She was telling me all sorts of embarrassing stories about you," I say, poking his cheek.

His eyes widen. "Wait, what? Really?"

"I'm teasing you." I laugh.

But Princess Niamh's eyes sparkle with a mischievous glint. "I would never tell anyone about the time you got stuck in the alder tree until your father had to carry you down."

There's a lightness in her tone revealing a strange side of the Princess I've never seen before. More of the mother, less of the leader holding her realm together.

Farron lifts his chin. "I was attempting to see if the leaves exposed to the most light were more potent."

"Of course." She nods seriously, but there's the tremble of a smile on her lips. "And what about that 'love' potion you mixed trying to gain the affections of one of your schoolmates, and instead that unicorn followed you all the way home?"

I can't help but giggle and Farron crosses his arms, trying to hide his smile. "You know, that unicorn could have been a beautiful girl; we never saw her in the light of a crescent moon."

"These memories lighten my heart," Niamh says, smoothing down his hair. "But there is also the time you cared for the baby bird that plummeted from its nest. You stayed up all night watching over it. Even fashioned a splint for its wing."

"What else was I to do?" He shakes his head.

"Or when Nori was sick with fever, you built a puppet theater for her and spent the whole day performing plays." Niamh smiles fondly.

"I even made Dom and Billy laugh like an audience." He turns to me. "Though I'm sure my jokes were hilarious, anyway."

Princess Niamh clasps Farron's hand in her own. "I would not trade a single memory of you for all the gold in the Enchanted Vale. I treasure each deeply."

Farron lets out a long sigh. "I love you, Mother, even if you know every embarrassing thing about me."

"I love you too, my clove." She kisses the top of his head as he rests on her shoulder.

I stare at the two of them, marveling in the complexity of it all. She had her son in chains only a month ago and had threatened to take back the Blessing. And yet, I can tell her love runs deep and vast for him. If only he trusted her enduring love.

Another emotion flickers within me. What would it be like to have experienced a mother's love?

My gaze drifts across the party to find my father. He's been recruited by the musicians and bangs on some acorn drums, while Farron's father and Dayton sing a sea shanty that must be from the Summer Realm. My heart warms that Papa's finding himself here. But I know he'll never truly be happy unless we find my mother.

If she even wants to be found.

Dayton taps out of the musical festivities and wanders over to us. "How are the three most beautiful people in the Enchanted Vale?"

"Can you not flirt with my mother?" Farron glares up at him. But Niamh pushes Farron to the side and gestures for Dayton to sit beside her, kissing his cheek with motherly affection.

"Are you enjoying the party, my dear?"

"Of course." He grins. "Taught Paddy some new songs."

"Oh yes, I heard. He'll be singing them all night." Niamh smiles. "I received a letter from Eleanor the other day,"

I've heard that Farron's youngest sibling, Eleanor—Nori—is currently a ward in the Summer Realm. Something shifts in Dayton's expression. "Did she mention Delphia?"

Delphia, Dayton's little sister, and current steward of the Summer Realm.

"By mention, you mean complain about every single aspect of her," Niamh says. "You know them, getting on like oil and water."

Dayton gives a charming laugh. "Sounds about right."

"Delphia's well. The very spirit of the sun inside that one. Though," Princess Niamh's voice drops to a low tone, "the Summer Realm is a great expanse. There will be a time soon when she'll need you, Daytonales. She will need the Blessing of Summer and her older brother."

Dayton heaves in a breath. "Yes, alright." He stands, pulling Farron with him. "But tonight, we dance."

Farron shrugs before he's towed away into the throng with Dayton.

I can't resist grinning as I watch them, the way Farron's whole body melts into Day's chest as they hold each other.

I chance a glance over at Niamh, who watches them with a matching expression of fondness.

"Your family," I say softly, more to myself, "is so close. I can tell how much you love each other."

"Of course," she says. "Love stokes a mighty fire within us, one able to summon armies, create magic, and break spells. It is the greatest strength we possess."

"And you're wise as well," I say, "with words like that."

"Well, I can't take all the credit for it." She taps the side of her nose. "Long ago, when I was only a small child, I met Queen Aurelia herself. I asked her how to help my people and that is what she replied."

"Wow, like *the* Queen? The one who built Castletree? What was she like?"

"Mighty," Niamh says, then her eyes narrow as she looks at me. "And beautiful. And ... kind."

"Well, for the record, I think you're an amazing ruler. I'm sure the Queen would be proud."

Niamh smiles, gaze returning to Farron. He and Dayton have been pulled into a jig with Dom and Billy now.

"Can I ask you something?" I whisper.

"Of course."

I inhale deeply, hoping she doesn't get offended. "You're such an amazing ruler and the people love you. How come you passed the Blessing to Farron instead of continuing to reign?"

Niamh doesn't hesitate as she says, "Because when I looked at him, I knew he could be a better ruler than I. Though, there are times I wonder if the burden of Autumn's Blessing is too great for his gentle heart."

Our eyes meet. "No, you weren't wrong. I know he'll make the Autumn Realm proud. I know he'll make you proud." Emotion wells within me at the trueness of my words. "Farron's gentle heart makes him mighty."

43

KELDARION

Even though it's past midnight, the band still plays a light, lazy tune. Many of the Autumn folk are retiring back to the keep. Ezryn left a while ago, and I see Rosalina, Dayton, and Farron on the edge of the festival. Dayton has his arm around Farron and whispers something in Rosalina's ear that causes a pink flush across her cheeks. Is she going to go to them tonight while the full moon reigns and our beasts do not take hold?

My grip tightens on my cup. It shouldn't matter to me. I can never have her in that way. Shouldn't think of her in such a manner. It will only drive me further into torment. But she surely does make it hard when she twirls around in such a manner, casting her smile like rays of sun.

She belongs here.

Curiously, she hugs Dayton and Farron goodnight. She wanders off to the edge of the party, running a hand along some of the tall mushroom seats. Her gaze is far away as she tilts her head to the sky. Something's bothering her.

"Something is bothering her," a voice says.

I startle, turning to see George O'Connell standing beside me, a foaming pumpkin beer in his hands. He's a tall man, almost my height. Like Rosalina, he's had no trouble fitting into the world of the fae.

"Yes," I finally agree when the silence stretches out too long.

"Well, let's see to it then." George grabs my arm and starts dragging me toward her.

"Really, I doubt there's anything I can—"

"Nonsense," George says, unruffled. "You're her mate, aren't you?"

"Yes, but I'm hardly—" *I'm hardly capable of taking care of her.*

"Rosalina, dear, you've got that look," George says when we arrive in front of her. "What's on your mind?"

"Oh, Papa, it's just—" Rosalina whirls to us, but she pauses as she sees George's hand on my arm. "Keldarion."

"Rose."

She swallows and sits down. I almost want to leave—she'd never confide in me. I'm not sure why her father even brought me over. He doesn't understand I can never have a true bond with Rosalina.

But I can't help but take in the worry etched across her features.

Gingerly, I sit down on a bright purple mushroom seat opposite of her. "What's wrong?"

She tucks her knees up into her skirt. "Earlier, I thought I made up a song. Turns out, it's some fae lullaby. The words all came to me like a memory. Where did it come from?"

George raises a brow, leaning back in his own mushroom chair. "Hmm, what was the song?"

Rosalina looks between us, before she begins to hum a few notes. I know the song instantly, a common children's bedtime song, *Holly's Keep*.

George blinks his blue eyes several times, before a smile breaks across his face. "Your mother used to sing that song to you." he says. "My dear An—Au—"

"Anya," Rosalina says.

"Right." George gives an awkward laugh. "I didn't forget my own wife's name. Just stumbled over it for a moment. Now, that song … I can't believe I'd ever forget it. Anya would sing it to you before bed, rock you on the porch to the chorus of crickets."

Rosalina gives a smile, and a silent tear runs down her cheek. For a moment, I consider reaching out to wipe it away, but quickly dash the notion.

"I used to ask her what *Autumn's gold* meant." George leans down to pick up a bright yellow leaf. "She'd say, 'George, you've never experienced a true autumn until you've seen gold fall from the sky, leaves so gold they'd be fit to wear around your neck." George's gaze is far off as he twirls the leaf in his hand.

Rosalina quirks her head. "Like Farron's necklace. He wears a golden leaf around his neck."

"I suppose he does." George sighs and lets the leaf drift to the ground.

"How did Mom know the song?" Rosalina asks.

"Sometimes fae from the Vale wander into the human world," I say. "Perhaps someone passed on the lullaby."

Rosalina looks up at me. "What if it's more than that? Could she have been to the Vale before? That's how she knew the way."

"I knew your mother's heart inside and out," George insists. "She would have told me if she had come to this place."

But there's something sparking in Rosalina's gaze. "Papa, what if you didn't know everything? Could she ... could she have been fae?"

I cast a glance at George before weighing in. It's an interesting concept. Our Rose certainly has her fair share of mysteries.

"Darling," George says quietly, "I met her as a young woman. I watched her age. We struggled with bills and car problems and all the mundanity of life. I'm afraid her magic only extended to how much joy she brought me. And how she gave me you."

Rosalina gives a sad smile. "It was a wild idea, anyway."

I lean forward, tucking her hair behind her ear. There's a holly leaf tucked in her braid. "It's not an impossible theory. There have been half-fae in the Vale. It's rare. Though, they don't normally look—"

"Don't look quite so human. I get it." She pulls away from me.

I grip her chin to keep her close. "Fae or human, I have never seen anyone quite as beautiful as you, Rosalina. You are perfect."

She sucks in a tight breath, cheeks turning pink.

George clears his throat. "Well, I'll leave you two kids to your deliberations. I should head to bed." He rubs his temple.

"Are you alright, Papa?"

"Oh yes, perfectly fine. I thought I remembered something, but it's gone ..." He gives a half-hearted wave as he wanders off.

Rosalina watches him until he disappears, then blows out a breath. "Sorry about all this rambling. I just wish I knew what happened to her."

"That's understandable," I say. "If anyone can find her, it'll be your father."

"I know, but even if he does, what then?" she asks. "What if she left on purpose?"

Who could ever leave you? I almost say but stop myself. Because I did. I left her. Instead, I reach out and clasp her hand. Her fingers are soft, and she rubs a circle on my palm. "In your heart, do you believe that's true?"

"No, I don't." She shakes her and the piece of holly falls free, landing next to our hands.

"Holly, like from the lullaby. How did you find that here?"

She doesn't reply, her face turning bright red.

"Rosalina," I growl, tugging her closer to me.

She bites her lip. "I ran into Caspian before the festival. He gave it to me as a formal invite to his birthday party."

It takes everything in me not to spirit her back into the keep. I inhale a deep breath. She must sense my discontent because she squeezes my hand.

"He didn't hurt me. I don't think he even meant to run into me. I caught him gathering strange items for some bird. He even had some will-o'-wisps, but I released them."

I shake my head. At first, I believed his obsession with her was simply because she was *my* mate. But it's growing more dangerous. I'll have to be extra watchful of my Rose when we visit the Below next moon.

"You have to be careful around him, Rosalina," we both say the same time, though she's dropped her voice considerably to mimic mine.

It's so adorable that I can't help but laugh and throw my arm over her. "I'm serious."

"I know," she says, leaning against me. "And I will be careful. I promise."

We're silent for a moment, and I can't make myself let her go yet. Her gaze drifts back to the celebration grounds where only a few fae still linger. Even the musicians and entertainers have left. The lights are dimmed, and the bright full moon casts its silvery glow.

"What about it, Kel?" she says. "How about one dance?"

"There's no more music."

She hops up and holds out her hand. I take it. "Are you sure? I can still hear it."

I let her drag me past the near empty tables to the edge of the forest, to the dark line of trees. There, I move our hands into proper position.

"Can you hear it now?" she asks.

"No."

She quirks her head, brown waves falling over her shoulder. "Maybe you're not listening hard enough."

I move her through the steps of a waltz. Dew drops sparkle up from the grass.

"I can hear it in the crickets chirping," Rosalina says softly. "In the crackle of the leaves beneath our feet, the distance melody of the river. If I listen hard enough, I can even hear the twinkling of stars."

"The hoot of the owl," I say. "The breaking of boughs. Sometimes, I can hear melody of the moon, whisper that tonight I am free."

Her skirt billows as I twirl her, and she crashes back into me, grinning. She rests her head on my chest. "This is my favorite tune of the night."

"What is?"

"The beat of your heart."

I wrap my arms around her, letting myself have this one moment to simply hold her.

"I feel like there's two versions of you," she whispers. "For the record, I like this side the best."

She's not wrong. And the problem is, I like this side of me, too. A man who could dance with his mate beneath the stars. A man who could love her.

But he cannot keep her safe. Loving her will only bring her more danger.

I only wish it didn't feel so right.

Blue light flickers in my vision, and for a moment, I think that maybe the stars have descended to dance around us. But then I see ...

"Rosalina," I whisper. "Open your eyes."

She does, and her lips part in a soft gasp. A sapphire glow plays across her features and sparkles in her eyes. "The will-o'-wisps."

Fluttering from the forest, a cluster of small flames have come to bob around us, almost as if they're swaying in time with our dance.

"Maybe they're coming to thank me," she whispers, a beautiful smile on her face, "for rescuing their friends earlier."

"Perhaps," I agree. But as I watch Rosalina, the magic of the Autumn Realm quivering around her, I know it's something deeper. Wherever she goes in the Enchanted Vale, it comes alive.

44

ROSALINA

I should be exhausted after the party tonight, yet sleep eludes me.
I've been tossing and turning for an hour at least.

Maybe it's because this is the first night in the last month
I've actually spent alone. Every other night, I've been curled up in a
nest of pillows and blankets outside of Farron's door surrounded by
my wolves. It's lonely without their comforting scent, the warm fur, or
in Keldarion's case, skin...

I'd been startled the first time I'd woken up embraced by a man
rather than a wolf. But fast asleep is the only time Keldarion gives in
to our mate bond, holding me with utmost ferocity.

And some nights, when I'm sure he's deeply in his dreams, I roll
over and study the lines of his face, or touch the hard panes of his
chest, and nuzzle into his embrace.

But since there are no wolves tonight, we're in our own rooms, and
it's not just loneliness that's keeping me from sleep.

A pressing ache throbs within my lower body. Heat radiates from
my core, and I rub my legs together in an effort to relieve the tension.

The thing about being surrounded by four incredibly sexy men but
also dealing with ice zombies and a beastly curse is that there's not a
ton of time to enjoy them.

I take in a slow breath and trace my hands up my body. I'm wearing a cream nightdress that hugs tight to my soft curves, falling just above my knees. It's got a cute little bow right at the bust, and lacey cap sleeves that show off the arms I've kept hidden away for years.

It's a shame there's no one to appreciate how pretty it is.

My palms clasp the soft fabric. My heart picks up pace, and a throbbing urgency circles deeper inside of me. This is strange. There's something pressing about this lust, like it's growing hotter and hotter without me even doing anything.

I close my eyes, turning my sight inward at this building desire. I can feel it ... Rough hands, uneven breath. Not mine.

His.

Keldarion.

This lust is his.

Whatever he's doing is affecting me. Traveling through that invisible mate bond that tethers us together.

I should try to ignore it. Instead, my bare feet pad across the floor, and I slowly creep out into our joint living space. Keldarion's bedroom is on the farthest side. I peer through the dark. Everyone's doors are closed, but there's a thin line of light from underneath his.

Lust shoots up my body, and I stifle a moan by biting into my hand. I ache for something I'm not sure of yet. But as soon as I see him, I'll figure it out.

I walk over and quietly turn the knob. "Kel—"

All the air leaves me. Keldarion's lying on his massive bed on top of the blankets, his shape illuminated by the dim candle on the bedside table.

His huge body is laid bare, every inch of him covered in corded muscle. He looks like a work of art, reclining there with eyes closed, long white hair like a halo around his face.

One hand is under the back of his head, revealing every bulging muscle in his bicep. And the other ... It's wrapped tight around the enormous expanse of his cock. It curves upward, impossibly thick and achingly hard. A rush of pleasure flits through me. *His pleasure.*

The bed creaks with the movement of his hand rhythmically pumping up and down, a satisfied *slap* each time he reaches the base. I stumble forward as if drawn to him by an invisible string.

His eyes spring open, and his hand stills. He stares at me, a silent moment passing between us.

"You knew I'd feel you," I whisper.

He draws his hand up his cock, so slowly. "I wondered."

Breath comes ragged out of my throat as I quickly click the door shut and stumble to the edge of the bed. He does nothing to welcome me closer, nor does he chase me away. He just stares, face stern, and continues to coax his cock in a gentle rhythm.

"I can help you," I whisper. I can't decide where to look; at those beautiful eyes that seem to see through to my very bones, to his chest rising and falling with each precious breath, or to the monstrous girth in his hand.

The expression on Kel's face … It's not anger. It's predatory. Like the rabbit has just wandered into the wolf's den.

"Listen very carefully, Rosalina," he growls. I notice his eyes have left my face and dip down to my low-cut bodice, to the thin fabric that shows the points of my breasts, the curves of my hips. "Do you remember when you first came to Castletree?"

"Of course." I crawl closer, my hands on the edge of the bed now, right between his feet. His toes curl and stretch. He makes a feral sound, warning me not to get closer.

"You agreed to obey me, the master of Castletree. We no longer have a bargain. And we're not in Castletree." His voice is rich with dark promise. "But am I still your master?"

"Yes," I answer without even needing to think. "Always."

He pumps his cock quickly, satisfied. "Then you must do exactly as I tell you, and you must not act without my explicit instruction. Do you understand me?"

The ache inside of me has only grown as I jealously watch his hand touch what I so desperately want to be mine. "Yes, Keldarion," I say. "But please don't ask me to leave."

He closes his eyes and sinks his head deeper into the pillow. "I'm only fae, not a god."

My legs tremble so badly, I fear they will fall straight out from under me as I crawl up on the bed.

"Stop," he says.

I obey.

"Kneel before me."

I do, sitting on my heels on the soft bed, caged in by his huge legs. My heart races as I stare at his throbbing form. Though I've seen Keldarion naked—and felt his hardness against me—this is the first time I've truly been able to take in the High Prince of Winter. Thick veins curve up its length, and I imagine running my tongue along each one, tasting the sweetness. My breath quickens as I fight the urge to pounce on it.

"Stars be damned," he rasps, his eyes running up my body. "You are gorgeous."

I sweep my tongue over my lips. "Careful, Keldarion," I say huskily. "If you compliment me like that, I might get confused and assume you like me."

His lip curls, and he brings his other hand down to cup his balls. "You do enjoy torturing me, don't you?"

I lean down, eyes half-closed and mouth open. "I could find other ways to torture you that are more to your liking—"

"Sit up," he says.

I do, heat flushing to my cheeks.

He never stops stroking himself as he says, "You may not touch me. And I will not touch you. Do you understand?"

I glare at him through my lashes, but his face is all business. He grits his teeth and squeezes the base of his cock. It's so thick, I can only imagine what it would be like to sit on top of him, to try to push all of that inside of me...

His voice is low, husky. "Do you understand?"

I shake my head, refocusing. "Yes. But if I can't touch you and you won't touch—"

"Raise your skirt."

With featherlight touches, I push the edge of my nightdress further up, slowly revealing the soft flesh of my thighs.

"Are you wet?" he asks gruffly.

"Yes."

"Show me."

I gather the nightdress around my waist, and he sucks in a tight breath. Then I slide a finger through my center, shivering at the contact. When I pull my hand away, the candlelight dances off my arousal.

"Does this please you?" I ask.

He runs a tongue over his teeth, and I'm half expecting to see sharp canines by the predatory look in his gaze. "Very much."

I shift my weight forward, bringing my shimmering hand close to his straining cock. "Would you like to feel for yourself?"

He closes his eyes and grunts, his hand pumping hard. "Don't … tempt me."

"Why not—"

"Suck it off," he orders.

I do, placing my fingers deep in my throat, holding his gaze the entire time. My heart skips in my chest as he holds me in that piercing blue stare. His face is a work of art, a perfect blend of rugged masculinity and refined elegance.

There's an intensity in his gaze that draws me in. His eyes seem to hold secrets, and I want to unravel them all. The way his brow furrows as he watches me sucking my own fingers deep makes my core burn. Is he picturing my mouth wrapped around him like I am?

Kel's jaw tightens. "Put that hand back where it belongs."

I drift it to my aching cunt, running my fingers up and down. "It belongs to you, Kel."

His nostrils flare and he pushes himself up on his forearms, hand slowly working on his swollen member. "Tell me what you're thinking."

I laugh, flinging my head back, brown waves tumbling over my shoulders. "What aren't I thinking? I'm wondering what it would feel like to have you inside me."

There's that flash of fire in his icy gaze. "And?"

"How the rough stubble on your jaw would feel between my legs."

"And?"

My breathing becomes labored as I rub my clit faster, more desperately. "And I'm wondering how you would react if I licked the tip of your cock."

He shudders, and I'm washed with the scent of him: pine, cedar, and the musk of arousal. There's something primal about his smell, something that speaks to a deep, instinctual part of me. "I would be very angry."

"I'm used to you being angry with me." I lean forward.

"You said you would obey me," he growls, and I flop on my heels. "Touch your breasts."

My pussy is nearly aching with the need for release, but I pull my hand away and cup myself. Kel's eyelids flutter as I knead the soft flesh. My dress is so thin, I know he can see the points of my nipples. I pinch and pull, wanting to show this stubborn High Prince exactly what he's missing.

He shakes his head, and his face is twisted in anger. *But it's not anger.* I feel it through the bond: desperate, hungry need.

"Show me," he says.

I take my time inching the pretty lacey sleeves off before revealing the mounds of my breasts.

Kel sits forward, eyes wide and unblinking, devouring me in a gaze. For a second, I think he's about to leap on top of me. I close my eyes and enjoy my own hands, my soft fingers tracing over my nipples. I take a deep breath, his scent enveloping me in a shroud of desire. It's as if every inhalation I take is infused with his essence.

"I need to see your body. I need all of you," he says. "To see all of you," he amends quickly.

I allow myself a smirk as I pull the shift over my head, stretching my whole body out for him to see. He was the one who called himself master when I came in the room, and yet, I feel like I'm holding so much power. And as I sit at his feet, completely bare before him, it's the strangest feeling. Normally, I would be so self-conscious, my soft belly swelling over my thick thighs, but I don't feel insecure at all.

Because I can feel it. His lust through the bond. He thinks I'm beautiful ... and I believe him.

"Fuck, Rosalina." He throws himself flat on the bed. "Why did you come in here?"

I test him again, crawling further between his legs. "You called me."

"I did not."

"Your bond." I trail a hand up to the thick hair covering his chest. He snatches my wrist. "It was begging for me."

He holds my wrist tight, but his gaze holds me tighter. I push myself up over him, legs on either side of his hips, chest hovering above his. "Inconvenient little thing, isn't it?" he says.

"I couldn't agree more," I whisper.

But it's a lie. Because this thing between us isn't little at all. It's a living tether, a throbbing swell that threatens to consume me anytime I allow it the smallest bit of purchase in my heart. It's bigger than I can comprehend, a connection beyond any physical desire. I saw it today, like a star blooming between us. I am terrified and desperate to follow where it leads.

"Rose," he says.

"What are you thinking?"

His head dips to the side, soft strands of white hair cresting his brow. "That I am bespelled by you."

"Keldarion," I whisper, staring into his eyes.

"I'm thinking," his thumb lightly grazes my wrist, his eyes fixed on mine with an intensity that sends shivers down my spine, "it would be no great wonder if you bore a loathing for this world. But you, my dear, find enchantment in the smallest things, and you shower kindness as though it's an endless supply, plentiful as the spring rain that melts the snow."

His words stir something within me, a warmth that spreads from my core to my fingertips. Our bond shines brightly between us. I'm bare before him, but it's like he sees deeper than my body, into my soul. His words give me something I've craved for so long. He's seen my scars but does not pity me for it. He thinks I'm stronger for bearing them, and with his words, I believe it, too.

I am undone by my love for you. The words filter through my mind. Our souls are so close together, even my thoughts are plagued by his voice.

Our bodies are so close, touching and not touching, together and not. A burst of rageful lust sweeps through me as I stare at what should be mine. He grips his cock harder and pumps. "I am at my edge."

I stay overtop of him, my fingers returning to my pulsing slit. "Come with me, Keldarion."

His breathing becomes ragged. "Where?"

"Cover me," I say lowly. "Paint me with your desire. Mark me and let me be yours, just for this one night."

My words seem to alight him. His chest heaves, and our skin nearly touches. "Rose," he rasps. A primal heat shudders through me as my hand feverishly rubs my clit. And I feel it, not just my own orgasm rising inside but his.

He roars, body arcing with the power of his release as spurts of cum cover my body. I cry out, my orgasm wracking me like a star shower. A delicious satisfaction shivers up my spine as I revel in the heat of his load dripping off my skin. I bat my eyes, trying to come back to reality.

Kel lies beneath me, blinking and panting. My heart rises. *I did that. I did that for my mate.* Our bond pulses between us with its own heartbeat.

I need more of him, all of him.

I lower onto my forearms, still not touching but a breath away.

"I can't do this halfway devotion," I whisper across his lips. "Kiss me, Kel. Kiss me and claim me and—"

He pushes against my chest. "Get out."

I fall onto the mattress. "W-what?"

He gets up and strides to the attached privy. I hear water running and then a wet towel is chucked at my head. Angrily, I wipe his arousal from my skin.

"Return to your room." He comes out in loose trousers, his hair tied back into a knot at the base of his neck. He looks so fucking delicious, I want to scream.

"You can't be serious." I cross my arms and glower at him. "You can't pretend you didn't like that." I gesture to my boobs, splattered with his desire only seconds ago. "I fucking felt it."

He intakes a breath. He knows what I mean. Not just our mutual pleasure, but the desire that sparked through our bond. *Not only desire. Love. There was love there.*

He grabs my nightdress and throws it at me. It hits me like a slap in the face. A knot forms in my stomach as I pull it on. "You are serious."

The mattress dips as he sits. The usual fury in his face when talking about this is gone. Instead, he just looks exhausted. "You know where I stand, Rose," he says, voice a gruff rasp. "I wouldn't bed you if my last breath depended on it."

That's the thing. I don't know where he stands. Earlier this evening, we danced to the beat of our hearts. Now, he's kicking me out of his bedroom. I storm to the doorway. "I'm sorry I'm such an inconvenience to you, High Prince. I didn't choose this bond. If I could, I'd rip it out."

He buries his head in his hands. "I only wish that you could."

A lump settles in my throat, and my eyes water. "Fine. See what I care, Keldarion. If you hate me so much, I'll go be with someone who actually wants me."

I slam his door and march out to the middle of the living area. I know I should go to bed. I know that nothing good happens after two a.m. But I want to keep my promise: someone else *does* want me.

I head to the Summer Prince's bedroom.

45

ROSALINA

I throw open the door to Dayton's room without knocking. Slits of moonlight dance over the bed, illuminating the sleeping fae. A muscular arm drapes over his face, and the blankets fall low on his hips, revealing his toned chest. Breath surges in my lungs. I shut the door behind me and cross to his bed.

"Dayton," I whisper.

He groans, eyes slowly blinking open. "Blossom? What are you doing here?"

"I want you, Day." Biting my lip, I reach down and bring the dress over my head, baring myself completely for him.

He rises to his forearms, mouth agape. "Is this some sort of fucking dream?"

A shiver of sinful pleasure races through me as his eyes devour my figure. I slink onto the mattress. "Touch me and find out."

In a second, I'm flung on my back, the air knocked out of me. Delicately, he cups my cheek. His other hand grazes over my breasts and down the soft curves of my stomach. "Your body feels like a dream."

My eyes flutter closed as he kisses me. Yes, yes, *yes*, this is what I need. Someone not afraid to touch me. My hips rise, and I gasp, realizing he's not wearing anything.

"So, you sleep naked?" I giggle.

"Why not? You never know when a beautiful girl is going to crawl into your bed."

I kiss a trail along his neck, tasting sweet nutmeg and clove. "Farron was here earlier."

"Of course." His large hand squeezes my leg, inching closer to my core. "I'm not going to waste the one night he's not surrounded by that bastard's thorns. You should have left early with us instead of dancing."

"Then where is he?"

"In his room. We don't do the whole sleepover thing."

"So, I shouldn't expect cuddles after we fuck?"

His fingers dance across my upper thigh, sending skittering shots of desire through me. "Well, Rosalina—"

"It's okay," I say quickly before he thinks I'm a clingy weirdo. "I came here for your cock, after all."

His laugh radiates through the room. "I knew you had a dirty mouth behind that sweet façade. Tell me what you want with my cock."

I press my palms on his hard chest, pushing him down to the bed, then straddle his hips. "I want you to fill me like you promised when we went to the Summer Realm. The night you cut off another man's hands for touching me."

"That was me in control. I hadn't even kissed you yet—you won't find me so merciful again." He grabs my hips. "But this cock is for good girls. Can you be a good girl, Rosie?"

Something flutters in my breast, and I nod.

"Suck my cock," he says, voice all dominance.

Happiness churns through me. I had ached to please Kel, but Dayton wants me. I can make him happy. I grip his thighs and lower my head; a spill of hair falls over my shoulder. Dayton reaches forward, twining it into a rope. My lips part and I take his cock in my mouth. He tastes of salt and sweat. I lick and swirl my tongue around the head before drawing down his length. His hands tighten in my hair. He groans deeply, and I take him deeper into my throat.

269

"Does this feel good?" I moan, mouth dripping with saliva.

"Oh fuck." His hips rock upward. "Baby, you have no idea."

His words travel into my core, and wetness pools between my legs. His cock pushes so deep into my throat, tears spring from my eyes. But I can take it. I can take him.

With my free hand, I grip the base and stroke. Dayton's hold tightens in my hair, and he tugs my head up. I gasp, heaving in air, probably looking completely undone with my tongue hanging out, pre-cum dripping down my lips.

"Come here." He pulls me on top of him. I weave my fingers through his golden hair as we kiss. My legs spread out on either side of him, and I press my aching core against his stomach, desperate for any friction.

"Yes." He grips my hips, pulling me down so my wet pussy slides against the length of his cock.

I cry out, squeezing my eyes shut. Every nerve in my body is alight with the sensation.

"You're such a good fucking girl, Rosie. You almost made me cum. But you came looking for something, didn't you? You tell me, where do you want it?"

"Want it?" I blink.

"Your delectable lips?" He brushes a rough thumb over my mouth. "Your soft breasts?" He squeezes one. "Your perfect stomach? Or..." He drags a hand down my belly to slip between my legs.

"Yes," I moan, the word long and loud.

A devious smirk crawls up his face, and he pops a finger inside me. My hips instinctively rock against him.

"I want you to fill me. I want you to come inside me." The idea consumes me. I pitch harder against his hand. "Day, I need you."

He doesn't say anything, but he doesn't stop pleasuring me. I flutter my eyes open, and my body tingles. There's an oddly serious look on his face. "Wait, is that not what you meant? Do you not finish in your lovers?"

"No," he says, and he pulls his fingers out of me. "Not usually."

"I'm sorry, I—"

"Lie back," he demands.

I do, sinking into the soft sheets.

He kneels at my feet. I can't help but admire his physique, painted silver in the moonlight, the incredible definition of his muscles, the strong curve of his jaw. He runs a hand along my leg, then raises one up, placing a kiss to my calf before releasing it.

"I don't usually come in my lovers," he says. "Only Farron. But if you want me, all of me, then I'll fill you."

"I do," I gasp. "I want you."

He presses a large hand over my stomach. "And what about protection?"

I flush. "It's been a long time since I've actually had sex."

Dayton smiles, his golden waves catching in the light. "That's what I like to hear. I don't want to think about any human men touching you."

"Marigold mentioned some tea I can drink afterward," I whisper.

"That's right," he says. "Then you're going to take all of me, and I'll fill your fertile little pussy tonight."

He kisses my legs then drags his lips up to my pulsing core. When he licks me there, it's as glorious as I remember. He sucks, then his tongue darts over my sensitive clit. I grip the sheets, throwing my head back. He takes me to the edge, then stops.

"You're not coming," he commands, "until I feel you clench around my cock."

Desire courses through me. I wonder if Kel can feel this the way I felt his pleasure. A cruel part of me wants him too, but a bigger part wants to hold this special moment between myself and Day.

Dayton continues his worship of my body, kissing my stomach with a featherlight touch before he gets to my breasts. His wet tongue circles my nipple before he draws back, nipping in a way that sends fireworks through me. The way he's pleasuring me ... It's like he's touching something so much deeper than my skin. The reverent kisses fill a part of my heart I didn't know was empty. His fingers thread through my hair, and his lips brush against mine, tasting of salt and sunshine. He deepens the kiss until I'm lost in his embrace, until I've forgotten everything except him.

"Are you sure about this, Rosalina?"

I blink my eyes open to see his turquoise gaze sparkling, his full lips parted in that strange smile of his, the one just for me.

"I know you have a mate. I'd understand if you only want him." He looks almost embarrassed. My heart bleeds from the vulnerability he's showing me.

I take his face between my palms, knowing I've never been so sure of anything in my life.

"You make me smile even when the whole world seems dark," I tell him. "You protect those you care about with a fierceness I admire. You're brave and clever, and every time you laugh I do too, and I want —I want you, Day."

"Careful, Blossom," he whispers, and there's a warmth on his face that could light up an entire room. "If you keep talking like that, I might just fall in love with you."

That would be convenient because I'm pretty sure I've already leapt off the edge for him.

Slowly, he lifts my hips as I spread my legs, and he positions himself. Then I feel it—the rounded tip of his cock, lightly pressing against my aching center. I throw my head back, my whole self erupting with the sensation of being so close.

But he doesn't move. "Is everything okay?"

"Yeah, huh? Maybe I'm nervous." He shakes his head, then brings a hand to clutch at his chest. "It's, uh, a feeling—"

Something wild flits through me bursting to life beside my heart, a deep uncoiling. Euphoria leaks from my fingertips as I stroke his face. Because I know this feeling, this innate want. It's the same as it is with Kel—

It's the same. I *knew* Dayton belonged to me. I need to complete it and tell him I'm a part of him.

I grip Dayton's face and bring my lips to his ears. "Kel, it's the same."

He stiffens, then pushes away from me. "What did you call me?"

A giant pit opens in my stomach, and I feel like I've been shoved into a dark room with the loss of his touch. I blink stupidly, my mind, which had just felt light and sparkly, suddenly murky. "I—"

"I should have known this was all about him." Anger laces through Dayton's voice, and he stands, throwing on a pair of pants.

He's getting dressed? No. I need to bring us together. "Wait—"

"You even smell like him." He gestures to me. "But I ignored it because, fuck, *look* at you."

I sit up. Can't he see I belong to him too? "Dayton, I didn't mean—"

"You didn't mean to call me by your mate's name?" He grips the bedpost. "Then what did you mean, Rosalina?"

"I meant..." My mind clears more. How can I tell him, I felt—no, I *feel*—the same for him as I do my mate? How will Dayton react to that? Dayton, who won't even spend the night with Farron, who he's been with for years? Dayton, who implied there would be no cuddling after sex?

There's no way I can admit to him the intensity of my feelings.

"What do you even care anyway?" I grab my nightdress off the floor. "Isn't this just about sex for you?"

His face blanches, and he storms over to the wall, resting his hands upon it, muscles tense. "Yeah, that's what I'm good for, isn't it? A fun time? Excuse me for at least wanting my partner to know my name."

"Look, I'm sorry, okay?" I cross my arms over my chest. "I know your name. Can we—"

"I'm not going to have you while you're pretending I'm someone else."

I take a step toward him, wishing I could explain.

He turns away. "Leave, Rosie."

Angry tears fill my eyes, and I stalk out of the room, slamming the door hard behind me. A frustrated growl bubbles from my chest. I prowl over to Kel's door, pound my fist against it and snarl, "You can go to sleep now, you stupid smug bastard. Hope you're fucking happy."

I make it to my room, alone. Rejected by two fae princes in the same night. Throwing myself down on the bed, I clutch my chest, feeling that tight coil beside my heart.

How could my feelings for both of them be so similar? It's as magical as it is terrifying.

One tear slips down my cheek, followed by a stream until I can't help but curl into myself and sob. Finally, exhaustion takes over and I drift off to sleep.

46

ROSALINA

"I 've read the same paragraph three times." I rub my eyes. "You'd think the ancient Autumn scholars could have livened their literature up somewhat."

Farron exhales sharply out his nose and smiles but doesn't look up from his own text. "Rosalina calling a book boring? You've been spending too much time with Kel."

I bury my face in the book to hide my blush. I haven't been spending *any* time with Kel lately, or at least as little as I can manage. We've all gone back to sleeping in our own rooms. It's easier this way. Besides, the last few days Farron and I have been totally engrossed in our research.

The library in Keep Oakheart is beautiful, the shelves made of twisted bark that stretch up toward the ceiling dotted with glowing orbs that cast warm, amber light throughout the room. The air is heavy with the scent of old parchment and the musky aroma of aged leather. As I look at the man sitting beside me at the table, a sense of contentment washes through me. Everything outside of this room is confusing and dangerous and messy. But this feels like home.

"It's not boring, just dense," I say.

"Autumn scholars are not known for their brevity." Farron adjusts the gold-rimmed reading glasses that have fallen down his long nose.

When we first arrived in the Autumn Realm last month, he was still wearing the usual vests and suspenders he wore at Castletree. But a few days ago, I heard Marigold scolding him: "You're the High Prince, Farron. You ought to dress like it!" Now, he's donned a shirt of spider silk in an iridescent burnt orange, draped by a long coat of fiery red. Tight-fitting trousers hug his lean legs, leading to boots of polished chestnut leather.

Though Marigold hadn't been able to convince him to cut his hair. For that, I'm grateful. I'd miss the way his fluffy auburn locks fall over his eyes, or how they curl at the base of his neck.

I shut the tome with a thud. "This book doesn't have what I'm looking for. I'll try another." I walk to the far end of the library and scan the titles. Bless the ancient Queen who created the Enchanted Vale; Farron told me long ago that one of the many charms she laid on the land was of universal language. Without it, the words in these books would be like gibberish to me.

"Rumor has it the Queen had a real soft spot for humans," Farron had informed me when I questioned him about it. "She wanted to make sure they could flourish in the Enchanted Vale."

"So, I can understand any fae language while I'm here?"

"Mostly," he replied. "There are some dialects that were created after she placed the enchantment. Spring has a particular tongue they speak in their monasteries. Sometimes, Ezryn swears in it when he's mad, and I have no idea what he's saying."

I had suppressed a laugh, remembering how I'd been on the other end of a deluge like that back in the human world. I wonder what he'd said.

Now, I skim each title, trying to find a book I haven't read yet. I come up empty.

"I don't get it," I say, collapsing back at the table beside Farron. "Everyone talks about Autumn's legendary researchers and the brilliant spells encased in parchment. But this library is small. It's not even half the size of Castletree's." I hold my arms out wide. "Where are all the books?"

Farron stills, eyes drifting off the page and looking inward to a faraway place I can't get to. He opens his mouth, but no words come out.

"Farron?" I touch his shoulder. "Is everything alright?"

"There ... was a fire," he whispers. "Much of Autumn's ancient knowledge was lost."

"Oh no. I'm sorry." A shameful blush heats my cheeks. "This library's plenty big. I'm sure we'll find answers here. We just have to keep looking."

Farron sighs. "I was hoping something would have been saved that could help one of us."

We've both been researching different things. As pressing as the frost is, I can't forget about my promise to help the princes. And after seeing their strange, tangled mate bonds, I thought I could find more meaning if there was a text on the legendary will-o'-wisps. But I've had no such luck.

Farron, on the other hand, has been searching the spell books for an incantation that can help against the wraiths. Princess Niamh has sent successful parties out with torches and magic to eliminate some of the ice creatures invading the lands, but without finding the source, more keep coming.

When the frost reaches the capital, Autumn will go to war with Winter.

And though Farron may be High Prince, he does not have control or sway over his people the way Princess Niamh does.

"Here's a passage on the Emberwood," I say, running my hand over the finely lined page. "But it doesn't say anything about the will-o'-wisps."

"Maybe they showed us everything we need to know," Farron says. "Dayton, Ez, and I are just broken on the inside."

"Don't say that." I grab his hand. "Never say that."

He gives his head a shake and smiles. "Truly, if anyone's broken, it's Keldarion. I can't imagine seeing my mate bond in front of me and not..."

My eyes meet his, a strike of lightning between us. "Wanting to consummate it right there," I finish quietly.

Farron sucks in a tight breath through his nose. "He would be free. All he has to do is accept the mate bond."

The way Farron is looking at me ... It's a look of pure anguish. I don't know why, but I can't bear it. I turn away from him, pretending to bury myself in my reading. "Kel took me to his bed the other night and then sent me away before anything really happened. He would rather watch all his magic drain away and be stuck as a beast forever than mate with me."

"Well, Keldarion is a fool," Farron mutters. Without me realizing it, he's scooted closer, and we're arm to arm, both staring down at our books, but not reading.

I know I should keep my mouth shut, but I feel raw with rejection. I can't help but lament. "I don't know. He's not the only one who doesn't want to be with me."

Farron looks at me through long waves of auburn.

I can't stop it: the word vomit. It rushes out in a pathetic and ridiculous deluge. "Dayton rejected me the other night. Do you understand how that feels? He'll be with any random person he finds, but he says no to me. And yes, it happened because I accidentally said Kel's name, but not like *that*. I was just thinking about Kel, but not because I was pretending Dayton was him—"

Farron's staring at me wide-eyed, brows raised.

I can't help it. The word vomit's still coming. "I thought I knew where I stood with Dayton, but now I'm not sure. And talking about where I stand with people, a month ago, Ezryn and I ... Well, I don't really know what we did. But it was a thing. A *thing-thing*, you know? But he's back to acting like I'm some pariah he can barely look at! Honestly, I should be grateful for Keldarion's actions because at least I know he hates me. The wondering ... That's the hardest part."

Farron blinks once, twice, then shakes his head. He laughs joylessly to himself. "Yeah, tell me about it," he grumbles. "The wondering is the hardest part."

He shuts the book and stands up.

"Farron?" I reach after him. "Did I say something that hurt you?"

He turns away from me, shoulders slumped. "No, Rosie. It's me. I'm thinking of all the things I should have done differently." He looks over his shoulder. "I really should have decided sooner in the hot springs, huh?"

"What are you talking about?" I drift over to him and grab his hand.

"Dayton, Ezryn, Kel ... At least they had enough courage to act on their feelings once, so they won't ever live with that regret." He stares up at the ceiling, a gold-crested mural of dusk-drenched clouds. "The Enchantress's curse is right again."

I shake my head, totally lost. "Farron?"

He closes his eyes and takes a shuddering breath. "Come on." He pulls me toward the door. "I'm going to show you why I was cursed."

47

FARRON

"We're almost there," I say.

We walked just outside of the keep to a grove of trees. Rosalina is quiet, and I'm grateful for her patience with me.

She's too patient. You took too long, Farron. I close my eyes at the thought. It wasn't jealousy that spurred me earlier in the library, at least not in the traditional sense. Rosalina's affections for the other princes are both understandable and comforting—though she laments their rejections. Instead, I'm filled with anger at myself.

How often have I been in her presence, aching to hold her, to press my lips against hers and whisper my longing? Every moment we've spent together burns in my mind, all the different times I could have let her know she is not just a companion to me, but the absolute focus of my affections.

But instead, I've hesitated. Restrained myself.

"Are you going to tell me where we're going yet?" she asks.

I take a deep breath. "To Coppershire's first library."

"Oh!" Rosalina flutters with excitement. "Where is it?"

"It was treated as a sacred space built right outside Keep Oakheart.

You might have seen it from your room, though after the fire, a grove of trees was planted around it to hide the remains from view."

We slip between the tightly knit trees into an opening drenched in cool sunlight.

"Welcome to the Great Scriptorium of Alder," I say. "Or what's left of it."

The remnants of a once grand structure lies in the clearing before us. Fire has reduced the building's outer walls to charred rubble, leaving only a few pillars and arches standing. The roof has collapsed entirely, now a warped mass of wooden beams and ash. Through the twisted trees, I can just see the towers of the keep, including the balcony connected to our chamber.

Despite the destruction, I can still make out the remains of intricate carvings on the surviving pillars. Fragments of once-beautiful stained-glass windows litter the ground. The treasures held here—the books and pages—have long turned to ash.

Carefully, Rosalina steps toward the wreckage. She looks out of place, too much beauty for such devastation.

I don't know why my mother never ordered the removal of these ruins. Maybe she wants it to remain as a reminder to me.

A massive alder tree stands in the middle of the rubble, its trunk a stout pillar that stretches up to the blue sky. The tree's canopy is ablaze with fiery hues, the leaves transformed into a tapestry of golds, oranges, and reds that shimmer in the sunlight.

I hold Rosalina's hand and walk into the burned remains. I can practically see it take shape around me: the old entranceway so familiar, the smell of books and ink, a sanctuary in itself.

My boots crack over the burnt rubble. "I used to spend every moment here. If only you could have seen it, Rosie. The ceiling stretched so tall, it seemed to blend in with the sky. The bookstacks moved, and you only had to change your thoughts to find the proper shelves in front of you. This place was home to writers and visionaries, philosophers and strategists."

Rosalina touches what may once have been the leather cover of a tome. Her fingers come away black. "There was more knowledge here than at Castletree?"

"Yes." I spin, images coming to life: gold-plated shelves, political debates, the grinding gears of a printing press. "But it held more than history or spells. Much of our culture was recorded here, and of civilizations long past. Tales of the world Above, a place so old only the Queen knew of it."

Rosalina blinks up at the sky. Her hand stretches upward. "The world Above…"

My eyes rest on the huge alder tree. "And the Scriptorium was home to many rare grimoires."

"What's a grimoire?"

"A book of spells. But not the usual kind that we write on parchment and share with one another. The spells recorded in a grimoire are … more advanced."

She grabs my arm. "Could there be a spell in one of them that might dispel the frost?"

"Possibly," I say. "But if it was, it's more than likely nothing but ash now."

"Farron, how did the library burn down?"

My chest clenches, and I can't meet her gaze. Everyone in Autumn knows this story. The other princes know. But to tell Rosalina…

But she takes my chin in her hand and guides me to look back at her. The softest smile caresses her face.

"It's my fault," I say. "I let the library burn to the ground."

Rosalina opens her mouth to respond, but I cut her off before she can say anything. "I told you my mother was the High Princess before me. She'd grown tired of the role and decided to pass the title on. She asked if I was ready. I said yes, not because I wanted it or because I thought I would be a good leader, but because I didn't want to disappoint her."

I shake my head and move deeper into the rubble. "I hated the responsibility, the pressure. Everyone always needed me to fix something. How could I fix the realm when I couldn't even tell my mother the truth?" I throw my head back, staring into the sun until my eyes burn.

Rosalina stays silent but hovers close.

"Things only got worse during the War of Thorns. I was High Prince in a time of war." I grab Rosalina's hand and squeeze. "It is hard to describe the horrors that were unleashed by the Below. Of the choices that had to be made."

"I can't imagine," she whispers. "What did you do?"

I laugh joylessly. "What did I do? I hid. Every day, I held up in the scriptorium and let my mother make the hard decisions. The ones that cost some lives to save others. But she had passed her magic onto me, and without Autumn's Blessing, the realm became harder and harder to hold."

Rosalina's face scrunches up. "I understand what it's like to be afraid. To be unable to act even though your whole being is screaming at you to do something, *anything*. I'm ... still working on it."

"Rosalina," I say softly and stroke the smooth skin where her scar used to be, "you willingly became a prisoner to the fae to save your father. You are no coward."

Something twists in her expression, but she shakes her head and looks back at me. "The library..."

"There was an assault on Coppershire by an army of goblins and other creatures created in the Below. They weren't looking for terms of surrender; it was a pillage, plain and simple." I can see and hear it all in my mind's eye: the screams, the fire, the dark shapes scrambling through the night.

"My mother rallied the forces, but it wasn't enough. She needed the magic of Autumn's Blessing." The words tear up my throat. "She needed me."

"Where were you, Farron?" Rosalina whispers.

"I was here!" All energy drains from me, and I sink into the charcoal. "When I saw the assault, I ran. My mother needed me on the front lines to protect the people, but I fled to the one place I always thought was safe. But the thing about being High Prince is you've always got the magic with you. And those creatures can smell it like a stink. They knew I was hiding." Shards of ashen wood crush beneath my fingers. "So, they tried to smoke me out."

"Oh," Rosalina whispers. She drifts to her knees to sit beside me. "They set fire to the library."

"Every text with irreplaceable knowledge, every map of lands now lost, every piece of precious artwork … Gone."

"But you survived. And you are most important of all." She grabs my shoulders, then looks around. "How did you endure the fire?"

I stand on shaky legs and walk over to the huge alder tree. Leaves whisper in the wind, carrying a magic I know only I can feel. The tree is untouched by any damage, its roots anchoring deep in the ground, stretching out amongst the ruins.

There is an image carved into the trunk, the outline of the ram's head: a symbol of the royal family. I place my palm over it, and golden light floods through the etching.

The trunk shimmers, fading away to reveal a luminescent doorway.

Rosalina gasps and I grab her hand, pulling her with me inside the tree. We step into a dimly lit room, cramped with old shelves and even older books.

"A secret library?" Rosalina asks.

"The Queen planted the alder tree when she first created Autumn. It's enchanted so that only the royal family can enter. It's protected by a very ancient warding spell, so the fire didn't affect it. I stayed in here for hours, but I could hear the fire blazing, the walls collapsing around me. The goblins, laughing."

Rosalina stares at a space between the stacks. Could she know that's where I'd curled into a ball, hands pressed to my ears, listening to my realm's destruction but doing nothing to stop it? The memories keep flooding back, unwanted and unbidden. I try to push them away, but they propel at me, one after the other. Each feeling like a weight pressing down on my chest, suffocating me. *Coward, coward, coward.*

My heart races faster, and I want nothing more than to get out of this cramped space, but my legs have forgotten how to work. I shuffle backward, smacking into a bookshelf. My eyes are wide but unseeing, and I think my lungs may burst from my chest—

"Farron, it's okay. I'm here. We're safe right now. Nothing like that's going to happen again, alright?" Rosalina's hands are on the side of my face, and she guides me down to a sitting position. "Let's breathe together. Deep breath in, hold at the top, and out."

I close my eyes and concentrate on her voice, letting her guide me. Finally, my heart feels like it's not going to rip free from my chest, and I bat my eyes open.

She's right in front of me, smiling softly.

"You're still here. Even though you know the truth about me."

"Oh, Farron," she whispers. "You came for me when I was at my lowest. That's what we do. We stay together."

I lean against her chest. "Do you understand now why my mother doesn't trust me? Why the people have no faith in me?" My voice wavers. "Why I won't be able to stop this winter?"

She pulls me to my feet and puts her hands on her hips. "You're not alone, Farron. You've got three other High Princes and one human to help you. Besides," she spins around and stares up into the towering trunk, "think of this tree. It's thriving in adversity, still growing amidst the destruction. You have the same resilience." Her eyes sparkle with determination. "Bloom among the ashes."

"I wish I had your optimism."

She turns to the stacks. "What are all these books? They must have been important if they were kept within the tree."

"After the fire, the most precious books kept at Keep Oakheart were moved in here for safekeeping. Family histories, diaries of ancient rulers, that sort of thing. But most of these books were kept hidden for good reason. Some knowledge should not be pursued, for the rewards are too uncertain."

"You mean these are evil books?"

"Grimoires," I correct, "filled with twisted and dark spells. Unfortunately, we will find no aid here."

"But maybe there's something—"

My heart pounds in my chest, and I tug at the collar of my shirt. "Rosalina, I've already tampered with enough dark magic. If you do something wrong with one of these spells, it could make everything worse."

Rosalina runs a finger down the spine of one of the books. "The goblins that attacked the library ... Did Caspian send them?"

"Maybe. He'd betrayed Kel at that point and had fully joined the Below's forces. But I think more likely it was Sira."

"Sira?"

My throat tenses to even speak her name. "Yes. Someone even Caspian is afraid of."

Before I can tell her more of the Queen of the Below, Rosalina leans against a shelf, her shoulders shaking. "Rosie? What's wrong?"

"I've been keeping a secret from everyone. I think I'm afraid of the answer."

"What?"

Her brown eyes sparkle as she turns to me. "I can hear him in my head. Caspian. He talks *inside* of me."

At first, I'm about to laugh. It's an impossible notion. But the fear in her gaze stops me. She's serious. "When did this begin?"

"At the Solstice Ball."

Cold slithers through my body. I've read about telepathic conversations before. Read about them when we were researching ... No. I shake my head, refusing to dwell on the thought. It must be another one of his tricks, another seed of his foul magic.

I knead the bridge of my nose, careful to keep my expression neutral. I don't want to worry Rosalina until I've researched this myself. "There's so much we don't know, especially about the Below. I'm sure there's some sort of reason for it. But ... I wouldn't tell Kel."

"Caspian did something really terrible to him, didn't he?"

I sigh. "You have no idea."

A brightness returns to her voice, and she smiles, though I know it pains her. "Maybe one day he'll trust me enough to tell me why."

I take her hand and lead her out of the tree and into the bright sunlight. The trees rustle with ancient songs the fae no longer have the words for. "I hope so."

"Maybe I'm wrong, but at the dinner last month, it seemed like there was a history between the five of you. Almost like you were all once … friends."

I touch the thorn choker around my neck. Though I hate the hideous thing, Caspian has been true to his word. It has controlled my beast each night and kept my loved ones safe. "We all learned the hard way that there can be no true friendship with someone from the Below. They're not like us, Rose. They see the world as something to be conquered."

Her gaze is faraway, staring down into the ash-covered dirt. "I don't know. Sometimes, I get the feeling he's really lonely."

"Trust me. Even if Caspian wanted to abandon the Below, he couldn't." She opens her mouth to press me further, but I can't stand to think of Caspian anymore, of his goblins raiding our villages, of his thorns draining Castletree. Draining me. Quickly, I say, "Hey, I almost forgot. I have something for you."

I fish in my pocket and pull out the moonstone rose locket.

"Oh my gosh." She snatches it from me, holding it up to the sun until it glitters like a prism. "You did it! You really fixed it."

"I'm pretty good with my hands," I mumble, face suddenly hot.

She passes it back and turns around, moving her braid aside. I trail it over her chest and take my time doing the clasp, savoring the beauty of her long neck, of the smell of roses each time she swishes her hair. "You know, this is the sigil of the Queen."

"What?"

"This rose." I dust my fingers over it. "How did your father come by it, anyway?"

"It belonged to my mother. She was an anthropologist, and he was an archeologist. They worked together on a bunch of different sites. I bet she found it on one of her expeditions."

"It's a strange miracle you can use it," I say.

"Well, maybe there's more to both of us than we give ourselves credit for."

"I hope you're right."

We head away from the wreckage. I thought I'd feel lighter after telling her, but I've only reminded myself what a coward the Autumn Realm has for a ruler.

Rosalina looks over her shoulder. "You know, my father did several excavations recovering artifacts from burned sites. He might find something salvageable."

"He's more than welcome to look, but I'm afraid it's a futile cause." I close my eyes. "The spells that could have stopped this frost are lost."

I blink open when I feel her soft touch against my cheek. "Fire may have destroyed the past, but it's what will save our future. We only have to be brave enough to discover it."

Light filters through the trees, creating pockets of brightness and shadow across her skin. She's so beautiful. The way the sunlight flickers off her hair, her long dark lashes as she lowers her gaze. I've laid before her my most seared edges, and she hasn't run. She only draws closer …

I wish I could tell her she's right, that I'm not afraid anymore. I wish I could sweep her into my arms and kiss her. I want to know her in the way I know my favorite books, read her front to back and savor every sentence, learn every secret between the lines of her life. I wish I could discover all the ways to love someone with her.

But she is Kel's mate, and my own bond is a tangled mess inside of me. We don't have a future together.

And if we do, it's only one that will end in heartbreak for the both of us.

48

KELDARION

"On your left," I growl and swing my sword in an arc just as Ez slides along the frost-covered ground. My blade embeds in the shoulder of a winter wraith, its face a terrifying mask of frozen bone and frostbitten skin. I grab its skull in my hand and blue flame lights across my palm. The creature screeches as its flesh melts beneath my touch.

Rain *tings* off Ezryn's armor as his boots squelch in the mud. "Behind you!" he roars, and I turn, scarcely managing to raise my sword up to stop the slashing claws of another frozen corpse.

The hideous wraith gasps, then drops, the fiery burn of an oil-soaked throwing ax sticking out of its back. I nod at Ez, and he turns back to the other four aberrations.

The two of us have ridden out to the Ambardon Moors, a section of sprawling purple hills, in search of more winter wraiths. Following a trail of frost, we'd found more than we bargained for. A whole herd of winter wraiths ambling across the grasslands, their blighted frost trailing them with each step.

We'd lost our steeds between the twelfth and twentieth wraith we killed. I feel my power weakening. And Ezryn's panting with each strike of his flaming blade, imbued with oil, not magic. The pounding rain isn't helping.

More amble toward us, their dead eyes so intent for creatures of ice and rot.

"Where are you bastards coming from?" I charge them. I'd gone to patrol the border between Autumn and Winter only a few days ago, but Perth's report was true. None of Winter's border villages have been attacked by the frost.

Ezryn runs beside me, but he slips on the frosted grass.

"Ez!" I call as he falls, tumbling over himself down the icy hill. He lands in a metal heap, adjusting his helmet as he sits up. But his sword's flame went out in the fall. With a growl, I turn away from the wraiths in front of me and sprint toward him.

But there are blights at the bottom of the knoll, shuffling on their stiff legs. His hands move frantically, pulling out the vial of oil and pouring it over his blade, then trying to light a match. Water sloshes down his helm. The flame flicks, then dies, flicks, then dies.

Why didn't you learn the magic? I think. *Stubborn bastard.*

He can't get the match to ignite, and one wraith moves with astonishing speed, rushing on top of him. Fractals of frost glitter from its fingertips as it reaches for his helm. Ez holds up his hands to stop the creature—

But I launch a blue flaming orb at its head. The projectile connects, and the abomination shrieks, clutching its blazing face.

I skid on the ice next to Ez and yank him to his feet. We stand back-to-back, trapped in the valley between two frosted hills as more wraiths pour down on either side.

"Thanks for the save," Ez says.

"I just bought you a little more time."

We raise our swords defensively, moving with the synchronization that only two people who have fought together in hundreds of battles could achieve. "I'll take the east hill, you take the west?" he asks.

"And we'll hope Farron can find our frozen corpses," I grunt.

A strange melancholy floods through me. Ezryn and I have been in countless impossible situations before. We've been outnumbered by fae, by goblins, by monstrosities so vile I dare not think of them any longer.

But facing these wraiths swarming down the hills … For the first time, fear flickers in my chest.

Fear strong enough that I wonder if Rosalina can feel it.

There's no way I'll allow myself to fall here. Not when I still have a duty to protect her. Even those nights surrounded by my brothers and wrapped in her warm arms, I never allowed myself to fall asleep before she did.

I know I make her feel alone. But that's the only way I can truly shield her.

But even I have my limits. I look to Ezryn. There are so many things I should have said. We've been in the Autumn Realm for two months now; I've had more than enough time.

But I still have a chance to make at least one thing right.

Ezryn's body tenses against mine, and I know he's readying to charge into the fray.

"Ez," I say. "I'm so—"

A screech fills the air, not of a wraith but of an animal. A high-pitched cry. Then arrows cascade around us, tipped with flames.

One wraith goes down, then another. I look up to the sky. The giant white wings of an owl crest through the clouds. Atop the beast, a fae ranger clad in blue fur peers over the feathers, bow drawn. She unleashes another fiery arrow.

A rumble sounds and the ground shakes.

A shadowy silhouette of cavalry thunders over the hill and into the valley toward us. They ride a variety of creatures, and my heart pounds with anticipation. Reindeers storm at the forefront with antlers raised high, while the rear guard is comprised of lumbering polar bears. Giant white foxes dart in and out of the formation with ease. And leading the troop is a massive moose, its mighty legs propelling down the hill with grace and power.

Atop each of these beasts is a fae soldier, dressed in the sapphire blue regalia of Winter.

The soldiers rip through the wraiths, distracting them with blade and spear and rounding them into a tight circle. From above, the ranger atop the snowy owl shoots flaming arrows into the mix. A rider on a polar bear throws a flask into the ring of wraiths, and blue fire explodes around them. Whatever they've done to their weapons has made their fire impervious to the relentless downfall.

Ezryn and I back up against each other. "It's the Kryodian Riders," I breathe.

49

FARRON

I haven't seen a storm like this in years. The clouds, heavy with rain, loom low over the realmlands, sparking with lightning. Rosalina sits in front of me atop my great elk, Thrand. Amalthea, Rosalina's white mare was spooked by the thunder and now trots behind us on a lead.

"This certainly came on quickly," Rosalina calls above the wind.

When we embarked this morning, the sky had been clear, that gray-blue color I've only seen in this realm. Rosalina and I had set forth to a village frozen by wraiths.

Kel had barely batted an eye at Rosalina and I traveling alone. *He trusts me,* I realize. *He trusts that my magic is enough to protect his mate.* A warmth blooms in my chest.

With Autumn's Blessing, I'm the only one strong enough to unfreeze an entire village on my own. With the rest of our forces spread thin, I'm happy to take these missions. Traveling to the village today took the better part of the morning, but the relieved faces of the citizens had been worth it.

As grateful as the villagers were for my magic and presence, it was Rosalina who had truly comforted them. There was a feeling of harmony in the way she handed out the supplies, a trust and comfort in her words that didn't sound forced but brimmed with genuine optimism. I might have used my flames to clear the frost, but Rosalina left something else gleaming in their eyes.

The spark of hope.

It's her faith in all of us to make this right, I think. *Her faith in me.*

Faith that I've had a hard time finding lately.

"The weather can be temperamental here. The storm probably won't last long." I urge my steed forward. His giant hooves splatter in the mud. The wind pelts my face, and my clothes are completely drenched.

And not just mine. Rosalina's beige tunic is soaked, and through the light material, I see the dark shape of her pointed nipples. My thoughts run wild with need. I want to spin her around, take her breast in my mouth, wet fabric and all, and suck her until she's aching.

My elk starts up a rocky incline, and the shift in gravity presses Rosie flush against me. My riding pants do little to hide my engorged cock as it rubs against her ass.

"Oh." Rosalina lets out a breathy sound, and it's as if she's deciding on whether to move away. Her hand drifts up into the rain. "There's beauty to the storm, isn't there? Something wild and uninhibited."

"You mean dangerous," I say.

"Or is it only perceived that way? Storms renew ecosystems, enrich the soil, and help prevent fires. The calamity of a storm heals." She leans against me, pushing herself into my bulge. "Imagine being that way: wild and unafraid, if only while the rain falls."

"A stroke of lightning," I murmur, my hands moving around her body. "A flash, and then it's gone."

"But what a flash it could be." Her voice is low, hungry.

I know what she's doing. These moments alone together have only made me doubt when I failed to touch her in the hot springs or when I couldn't kiss her at the burned library.

My logical brain knows I made the right choices then.

But while the rain falls...

"Hold these for a moment." I hand her the reins and lead. Thrand is so well-trained he doesn't require much guidance, and Amalthea trots dutifully behind. "I should stretch."

I splay my fingers on Rosie's soft stomach. She leans her head back against my chest, admiring the scenery. The red and gold trees bend and creak, their branches lashing out in the gale. Bursts of lightning illuminate the dark noon sky.

"Are you cold?"

"Not too bad," Rosalina says, but her shiver tells me otherwise.

I run my hands up and down her arms. *Just keeping her warm,* I tell myself. But when my fingers graze the side of her breast, we both make an anguished sound. We're playing a game, but we both know the truth. I want her. She wants me.

"Please touch me," she says, lightly, tentatively. Rosie's been trying to show me how she feels for months. Her heart is right there for me to take.

The problem is: I know I won't want to give it back.

I dip my head to the crook of her neck, my wet hair falling in a tangle as I let go of control. I brush my hands over the mounds of her chest. Slippery fabric slides beneath my fingers, and Rosie lets out a soft moan as I caress her pointed nipples, no doubt sensitive from the cold.

"I wish I could peel this off," I whisper, "and lick every drop of rain from your body."

"Farron." Rosalina drops the reins and lead to her lap, grasping each of my thighs.

Her caress has me wanting to strip her bare and take her on this elk. I move my lips to her neck.

"Are you sure you're okay with this?" she murmurs. She knows my hesitations.

But I can't find it in myself to care. "I'm just helping you get warm," I say.

Slowly, I let my hands slip beneath the cloth. Her skin is so silky.

She squirms as I knead the soft flesh. She arches her hips, and between the wet constraints of my pants, my cock is painfully hard.

I can't help but imagine it, how heated and glorious it would be to sheathe myself inside her. Ezryn hasn't touched her that way. I'm surprised even Dayton hasn't. Her own fucking mate won't claim her.

Her pussy is begging to be fucked, and the scent of her arousal near consumes me.

"Fare." The word is a plea. "More, please. If you can."

I would give her the whole world if I could. My hand drifts over her stomach to her equally wet leggings. Softly, I rub the slick fabric. A raw whimper escapes her lips, and I answer it with a growl as I squeeze her breast. *She needs to be fucked.*

"Yes," she says. But she's shaking against me, and not from pleasure.

"Rosie, you're freezing."

"No, I-I'm f-fine." But she can't keep the chatter out of her voice now. Sometimes I forget she's human, that her needs differ from us fae.

I blink and try to find a landmark through the sheet of rain. I take Thrand's reins and Amalthea's lead and slightly alter our course to descend into a small valley.

"There's a tavern," I tell her. "We can wait out the worst of the storm before returning to Coppershire."

Rosie nods. Thrand makes his way carefully down the hill, and I adjust Rosie's shirt to properly cover her. The buttery orange glow of the tavern cuts through the mist, the light reminding me of the will-o'-wisps we once saw.

The wisps that showed me my mate bond is nothing but a tangled mess. Not surprising, really. I always knew there was something broken inside of me. Our research hasn't turned up any answers for it yet, but I know Rosie won't stop looking.

Wood smoke billowing from a chimney mixes with the smell of damp earth. At the side of the building, we board Rosalina's horse in the stable, while Thrand trots off to the cover of the woods, preferring the freedom. He'll return at a simple whistle when it's time to depart.

The tavern is for travelers, situated between towns off the main road to Coppershire. It's a sturdy wooden structure with a thatched roof and a large, welcoming door painted bright yellow. The windows glow with the light of candles, and I can hear raucous laughter and clinking tankards from within. A sign that reads "The Wandering Bard" above the entrance swings back and forth in the wind, creaking loudly.

A rush of warm air swirls around us as we enter. It's busy and dimly lit, with rough wooden tables and benches strewn chaotically throughout the space. A fire crackles in the hearth, casting flickering shadows on the walls.

The tavern owner, a stout and stern woman, greets us. "Don't have much space left. We're crowded with so many people escaping the frost." Her eyes narrow. "Prince Farron?"

I flush and feel the sudden direct attention of the tavern. I instinctively pull Rosie closer, though their gazes are more curious, not hostile. "We don't need a room, just a place to dry off and wait out the storm."

The owner scowls, determination crossing her features. Within a moment, she ushers us up the stairs with arms full of dry clothes we tried to insist we didn't need. But she wouldn't take no for an answer.

"Got some hot water ready," she says, stopping in front of a simple brown door. "Stay as long as you need."

"We only intend to wait out the storm," Rosalina says. "We have to return to Coppershire before nightfall."

My heart sinks. Of course we do. And it's not to hide my beast. It's a full moon tonight, the one night a month the wolf doesn't have dominion over me. But someone else does. I unconsciously tug the chain of thorns around my neck. Tonight, we all fulfill my bargain with Caspian.

"Thank you again," Rosalina says, taking the clothes from her.

"No, thank you, Lady Rosalina and Prince Farron." She smiles. "Word's spread about what you're doing across the realmlands. We won't let that frost win."

I give a weak smile and thank the owner myself before following

Rosalina inside the room. Outside, the shutters rattle with wind, and rain patters against the panes of glass.

The warmth of the blazing hearth washes over me as I take in the small room. There's one bed, laid with plush pillows. But it's the object in the middle of the space that draws my attention.

A wooden tub, wisps of steam rising in the air.

50

ROSALINA

This room has one bed and one bath. I'd be lying if they both weren't appealing to me right now.

Slowly, I place the dry clothes we've been given on the bed. There are clean towels on the comforter. A bright pink blush stains Farron's cheeks as he softly closes the door behind him. "I'll go downstairs while you bathe," he says. "You're shivering."

"Don't be ridiculous. I mean, it's not like you haven't seen…"

And there it is spread out before us: the time in the hot springs when Dayton pleasured me while Farron watched … and refused to join.

"Just turn around," I say. He nods, and I slowly peel off my soaking clothes, my breasts feeling extra tender from where he touched me. I live for those moments when he breaks free and *acts*. But I know it's not fair of me to think like that, not when he has to find his mate.

A small gasp escapes me as I dip my toes into the clear water. Pin pricks alight over my cold skin as I slide in.

"How's the temperature?" Farron asks.

"It's perfect," I sigh. "The sound of the rain, a warm bath … Give me a good book and some chocolate and it'd be a dream."

He chuckles. "I think we left our books in Thea's saddle. But chocolate I'll remember for next time."

I glide a hand through the steam. Farron shivers, dripping by the door.

Slowly, I rise out of the tub. "That felt amazing. Your turn—I don't want the water to get cold before you have a chance."

"Get back in, Rosie," Farron says. "I'm fine."

I lower myself into the water. "What if I face one way and you face the other? We won't even touch."

He lets out a sound part way between a growl and a moan. "That's probably a bad idea."

"Well, either that or I'll get out so you can get in. I can't just sit here, watching you shiver."

He tilts his head, auburn hair dripping down his back. "Fine. Face the bed."

There's the wet slap of clothing on the ground, and I scoot myself to the edge of the tub, knees drawn to my chest.

The water rises close to the top as Farron steps in. This wooden tub is deep, but definitely not long enough for a nearly six-foot human and a six-foot-something fae prince. He slides in and his back brushes against mine, skin freezing.

I hiss in a breath, resisting the urge to lean against him.

"The water is warm," Farron says.

"It is."

Rain pitters against the window and in the distance, thunder rumbles. But inside, the hearth crackles comfortably.

"If it were any other night, this wouldn't be such a bad place to stay," Farron says.

My eyes drift to the corner. "There's only one bed."

"I know, Rosalina."

I sink deeper into the water. The movement slides my spine against his. The thought of him so close, his lean body bare ... Is his cock hard? *Do you want me as much as I want you?*

My hand dips between my legs. I brush the sensitive bundle of nerves, and a sharp gasp escapes me.

Farron stiffens, and I immediately remove my hands from the water. "I wasn't doing anything."

He laughs lightly. "Would you like me to get the knots out of your hair?"

Gingerly, I touch the rat's nest on my head. "Okay."

"I'm going to turn around. Stay where you are."

The water splashes over the edge, and then his hands are on my shoulders. He tips my head into the water. I clasp my arms over my stomach as Farron delicately untangles my hair.

I squint up at him, his face soft, cheeks red from the warm water, the brown freckles like constellations across his nose. Even the thin collar of thorns around his neck looks enchanting.

"You're really beautiful, Fare," I whisper.

His fingers still, but there's the quirk of a smile at the edge of his lips. "Sit up." His elegant hands stroke through my hair and he begins to weave it into a braid.

"Wow, you're really good at this," I say.

"In Autumn, the idea of weaving or binding things together is very important," he says, hands dancing through my hair.

"This idea is celebrated in many places in the human world, too," I say. "Where I'm from in the Pacific Northwest, the Coast Salish Peoples create beautiful textiles by weaving wool. And my father once told me of an ancient Celtic ritual called handfasting. Two people have their hands tied together to symbolize the binding of their lives."

"Your world is beautiful," Farron says. He lowers his head and whispers something too low for me to hear.

"Hmm?" I ask.

"Here, it's customary when you braid someone's hair or offer a bracelet or other woven item to imbue the braid with well wishes and good thoughts for the person."

"What were you saying about me?" I whisper.

He places the braid over my shoulder. "That's a secret."

I turn in the tub, water sloshing over the side, until we're looking at each other. "You braid Dayton's hair all the time. What do you imbue then?"

He smirks. "Lots of things. Sometimes I wish for him to stop being such a dumbass. But most of the time, I speak of the love I feel for him, and a wish that he could feel the same."

The breath catches in my throat. The way Farron's looking at me, it's as if he's telling me the same. "Farron…"

"Why are you holding your arms that way?"

"Oh," I say. "Not exactly the most attractive position. My stomach's all scrunched up."

Anger flashes across Farron's face, and he reaches under the water to pull my hands away. "Stand up."

"I—"

"Do it, Rosalina," he says, command rippling in his words. I bite my lip and slowly stand up before him in the bath, the warm water sliding down the curves of my body.

"You are absolutely perfect," he says.

There's not only lust, but something reverent in his gaze. Like he wants to devour me down to my very essence—body, mind, and soul.

Every part of me aches to give him that. To merge ourselves so completely, I don't know where he ends and I begin.

"Can I sit down now?"

"No. I'm admiring the view." Farron smirks and leans back, arms spread on either side of the tub. The move and air of confidence seems like something he must have learned from our dear Summer Prince.

At the thought of Dayton, my heart pangs for him in a sudden desperate beat, and I wish he were here. *Not that he wants anything to do with me.*

"I know the others find me attractive," I say, shifting from foot to foot. "Kel probably can't help it because of the mate bond, but when he saw me this way, his desire was intense."

Farron licks his lips, and his hand dips beneath the water as he adjusts. Does the idea of my mate seeing me like this turn him on? "Ezryn is the only one who hasn't seen me naked."

"Witnessing you unclothed would send Ezryn into the panic of a century. Honestly, I would love to see it."

So Farron doesn't just like the idea of seeing me with Kel, but with

Ezryn, too. And he might not have joined in, but I think he enjoyed watching Dayton and me in the hot springs. "Ezryn has seen naked women before."

"They aren't you." His eyes darken. "Are you really so unaware of the effect you have on them? The effect you have on me? Sit."

I do, closer now, between his bent knees.

"Who made you think such a way about yourself?" His voice drops from flirty to serious, and then his gaze shifts to my wrist.

"I didn't want to admit what Lucas truly was. Couldn't let myself see the monster behind his smile." At the mention of Lucas, the water seems to drop in temperature.

Farron brings my wrist to his lips. "Ezryn may have healed the wound, but only you can heal the scar. And some scars go deeper than your skin."

"I should have let him die. The things he said when I tried to help him ... How he attempted to hurt me again..."

Farron shakes his head. "Kindness and empathy aren't weakness, Rosalina. Those things will always prevail."

"I kept making the same mistakes with him, over and over. I thought I'd changed in the Enchanted Vale, that I'd learned everything I needed to know about myself. But when I got back to Orca Cove, I couldn't even say no outright to the engagement." Thoughts I've locked away in the deepest part of my mind spill out. But sharing them with Farron isn't scary. I know he won't judge me, no matter how much I regret my past choices. "Sometimes, I hate her. The girl I was. Sometimes, I'm worried she's all I'll ever be."

"There's no timeline for healing, Rosalina. You can be courageous one day and fearful the next." He lets my hand fall and cups my cheek, leaning closer across the steaming water. "You're on your journey, and that's all that matters."

"Same for you, Farron. Forgive the boy who was scared."

His lips tremble. "But what if I'm still that scared boy?"

I place my hand over his. "What if I'll always hate who I was before?"

We stay there for a heartbeat that feels like a thousand years, and I see myself reflected in his amber eyes. Bare and raw before each other. "I could be brave for you, Farron."

He leans closer, his forehead resting against mine. "And what if I could love you? Past, present, and future? Every part of you, Rosalina."

A gasp sounds in my chest, and I blink up at him. But before I can speak, he grabs my face and pulls me into a kiss.

51

KELDARION

"What are the Kryodian Riders doing outside Winter?" I ask.

Ez gives a shuddering laugh. "I don't care. I'm just fucking glad to see them." Then his match strikes true, and his oiled blade ignites with fire, blazing against the rain. He charges into battle with the riders, immediately slicing through the head of a wraith.

A smile finds me, and I roar, rushing after him.

Within minutes, the knoll has been cleared of the herd, their frozen corpses littering the ground. Fire licks at the grasslands, burning away much of the blighted frost. I pull my flaming hand back from the monster and straighten, assessing our surroundings to ensure there are no stragglers.

Ezryn walks up to me, blade extinguished. "I think we got them—"

Thundering hooves sound, and the snowy owl above screeches again. The entire cavalry moves into formation, encircling Ezryn and me. The rangers hold out pikes and spears, caging us between them.

A growl rises in my throat, but I find the eyes of their leader atop the towering moose. He leaps down and removes his silver helmet, revealing a tangle of wet long, blond hair and a thick beard.

"Eirik Vargsaxa," I say. "Do you not recall the High Prince who named you captain of this cavalry?"

Eirik's blue eyes flash. "Your Majesty." He waves his hand, and his soldiers lower their weapons. Then he drops to one knee. "I was not certain it was you. It has been so long since I have beheld the High Prince of Winter."

I hold out a hand to help him stand. "I see the Kryodian Riders have lost none of their abilities."

Eirik sighs deeply. "We have become quite skilled at killing the corpses. Unfortunately, it has turned into a necessity."

"Explain yourself, soldier. Why are you on Autumn's land?"

Eirik looks around at his soldiers, and a pained expression crosses his features. "You ... do not know, Your Highness?"

Cold apprehension laces through me. "Know what?"

"We are banished, High Prince," Eirik breathes, "by Vizier Quellos himself."

There has to be some sort of confusion. Quellos wouldn't betray me. He served my grandfather and my father with such loyalty.

Ezryn stirs beside me, body tensing. He's always hated my vizier, and the stars know Dayton and Farron carry no love for him. I could even feel my mate's apprehension through the bond when she was close to him.

Have I once again failed in my beliefs, misplaced my trust? *Father, I wanted to do right by you. Wanted to finally make a decision you would agree with. Please, say that my loyalty is not once again betrayed.*

"Why would Quellos banish you?" I ask. "The Kryodian has always loyally served the throne."

"It happened only a fortnight ago. Several of us heard word from friends and family in Autumn of this deadly frost. I wanted to take the Riders to investigate, but Quellos said he'd sent his own soldiers out. But every time they returned, they said there was no danger." Fury etches across Eirik's features. "We went over the border without permission and found dozens of these monsters. When I returned to the capital to confront the vizier, he banished our entire unit for warmongering."

A polar bear stomps its huge paws and huffs. I take in a shaky breath, my mind roaring with anger and confusion. "Quellos cannot make such decisions. Please, I urge you to come back to Coppershire. I have aligned with the High Prince of Autumn to find an end to this devastation."

"With all due respect, Your Highness," Eirik says as he leaps back upon the moose, "we have been banished from Winter. Now, we no longer serve a High Prince. We are on our own quest to purge the lands of these monstrosities." He puts on his helmet and shakes his head solemnly. "Quellos betrayed our loyalty. And the Protector of the Realms has not shown himself to be faithful to the people of Winter. So, we will remain on our own." He turns his steed and gives me one final look. "I wish you well, Keldarion." Then he raises his hand in the air. "Riders, with me!"

In a roaring crescendo, the cavalry thunders away, disappearing over the hill.

I stand still, unable to move. Thoughts hover at the back of my mind, but it's like a frosted glaze separates them from my awareness. "My own people would rather be renegades than serve me."

Ezryn grabs my shoulders. "Kel, listen to me. Quellos is keeping something from you. His stewardship of Winter must be called into question."

"You're right." Long have I held onto the Winter my father left me. What right did I have to assign a new steward, considering all the poor decisions I'd made? Though now, I don't feel quite so alone as when I first came into my Blessing. The princes stood by Farron, and they will stand by me. And even if I can never truly be the mate she deserves, Rosalina is there for me. I will do right by her. "Quellos has been allowed too much power. I will go to him at once and see this made right."

"Tomorrow," Ezryn says and looks to the sky. The sun is hidden by the dark clouds, casting shadows over the rolling hills. "Tonight, we have a bargain to uphold."

The full moon. Caspian's Revelry Day party. As much as this business with Quellos troubles me, I will take no chances with Farron's bargain. I will not give the Prince of Thorns a reason to break his deal with the Autumn Prince.

Ezryn sheathes his sword and starts walking south in the direction of Coppershire. I trail him in silence, when suddenly he tilts his helm toward me. "Kel?"

"Hmm?"

"For what it's worth," he mumbles, "I may not be your people. But I will follow you."

"Even to the Below?"

"Even to the Below."

52

ROSALINA

Farron's kiss crests over me like an inferno. I sigh into him, wrapping my arms around his shoulders, feeling the hard press of his chest. I don't want to break away, afraid he'll change his mind.

When we finally separate, there is an almost delirious smile on his face.

"You kissed me," I giggle.

He blinks, water dripping from his wet lashes. "I kissed you."

"Well, are you going to again?"

"What?"

"Kiss me?"

He lets out a breathy laugh. My hands find their way to his face, tracing his sharp jawline, savoring the feel of his stubble against my fingertips. His lips are warm and soft, moving in sync with mine as if we've been doing this for years.

"What changed?" I murmur.

"I'm tired of being afraid," he says. "I want that bravery you offered. I want you."

"I want you too."

He pulls me against him, and his hard cock presses against my stomach. I can't help but reach down and touch it, feeling the silken steel beneath my palm as I slide up, up, up. "Oh, Baby," I say, noticing my own bit of Dayton confidence. "You feel so good."

He doesn't reply in anything more than gasps and moans. His head tilts back, his eyes close, and he offers a contented smile as I stroke him.

Then he surges toward me, capturing me in a hard kiss. Every inch of my body is on fire, the water almost scalding. Our kiss grows more intense, more passionate, as if we're trying to convey all the emotions we've kept hidden for so long.

When we finally break apart, gasping for breath, our foreheads still pressed together, I feel tears streaming down my face. This is what I've wanted, what I've dreamed about, but now that it's happening, I'm afraid it'll disappear like a mirage.

Farron brushes the tears away with his thumb, his eyes searching mine for any sign of doubt. Without saying a word, he picks me up in his arms and carries me out of the bath. My legs wrap around his waist. Sometimes I forget how strong the Autumn Prince is because he's always so gentle, always so ready to follow the other princes' lead.

But it's just him and I. And Farron's in complete control.

He lifts me with ease, as if I were no heavier than a ragdoll. Then he tosses me on the bed. My breath surges with the movement and the power of his stance. He stands before me, naked and glistening with water.

Well, naked except for the thorn choker around his neck. There are some things you can't strip away completely.

"Listen, Rosalina." His voice carries an air of dominance. "In this room, there is just you and me. There's no one else. So right now, you are mine."

"I'm yours," I echo, feeling the sensation light through me.

"Remember what I said about the rain?" A smile curves up his face. "I think licking bathwater off your skin will be just as pleasant."

I run my hands over my curves, empowered by the confidence he's given me. He lowers himself, and our tongues dance together in a wild, passionate rhythm as we explore each other's mouths.

"Now, there's something I've wanted to do for a very long time," he says as he takes one of my nipples into his mouth.

The sensation is electric, and I moan in pleasure as he sucks and nibbles on my breasts. His arousal grows against my palm as I stroke his long length again.

Farron pulls back slightly, eyes flashing with wildness. "I need all of you, Rosalina. Is that something you desire?"

The answer is so clear. "Yes, I do."

His eyes darken. "Show me."

I spread my knees, revealing my slick entrance.

A growl sounds in his throat, and I feel a shift in his demeanor. *It's his. I'm his.*

He drags his hand down my breast and over my stomach to grip my thigh. "Do you know what I think when I see that pussy?"

"What?"

"That you need to be fucked, made love to, worshipped. Call it what you want—I am going to have you in every way."

He takes his cock and slaps it against my entrance, sending a kaleidoscope of stars into my vision before he gathers me in his arms. Our kisses grow frantic, almost animalistic. I need every inch of his skin.

This is a different side to Farron, one I've only glimpsed. His movements are sure, positioning me where he wants me, ready to claim what's his. And I am more than happy to be at his mercy.

"Farron," I moan.

He pushes me back down to the bed and rubs his palm between my legs. "They haven't fucked you. How long has your pussy been aching for a cock, Sweetheart?"

I whimper beneath him, writhing in pain with the longing for it, for his cock deep inside me. "I need it."

He licks his lips, a positively devious smile on his sweet face. "And you'll have it. I'm going to fuck you and fill you. You'll be dripping with my cum, and when we go to the Below tonight, Caspian won't be able to tell where I end and you begin. My scent will consume you, and everyone will know it."

I squirm beneath the dominance in his gaze. "Take me, Farron."

"Now," he growls, voice deeper than I've ever heard it. "Mine."

He positions his cock at my entrance, hands shaking, a feral jerk to his movements. But I'm not scared—I'm desperately craving more of him. My body is so warm, something blooming like a wildfire beside my heart. I want every untamed piece of this. There's a glint in his eyes, something not entirely human, an expression I've seen before.

Wait. His emotions are too strong. The thing between us is too strong.

I realize with sickening fear, it's not only fear or anger that can change him.

The beast is here.

And I'm naked and bare before him.

Farron stutters, eyes shining with the bright yellow of the monster. His body ripples, and his face contorts in wild panic.

Then in a truly horrific sight, I watch as the thorn collar writhes, then shoots out, spearing into his neck. Two more wrap around his wrists. Farron screams, blood streaking across his skin as he falls to the ground.

I wait a breath, and then slowly creep to the edge of the bed, afraid of what I will see there. Will it be the beast covered in briars or...

My heart weeps. Farron is curled up. The thorns have recoiled, but small cuts line his arms and waist, and blood drips from his neck.

Caspian's thorns stopped his shift. And they saved my life.

SUN SPARKLES in through the window, and I clasp my cloak over my new clothes. Farron gazes out, a somber expression clouding his features.

The storm has passed, and it's time to return to Coppershire. I find myself drawn to the now cold bath and tousled bed, lingering like an unkept promise.

I pad across the room to him. "Ready to go?"

"Yes."

"Farron..." I reach for his arm, and he dances out of my grasp.

"Rosie, don't."

"I wasn't—"

"Forget it, okay?" He shakes his head, mussed hair falling over his brow. "I thought I could be brave, but I forgot my greatest fear of all is of myself. Take away the fact I must find my mate, that *you* already have a mate, us being together could kill you."

I swallow in a dry throat. "You don't know that—"

"I do. And *he* does, too." Farron's expression darkens, and he pushes past me toward the door. "It's time to submit and go Below, to show the Prince of Thorns just another way he owns me."

53

ROSALINA

"How long is this going to take? I'm freezing." I cross my arms over my bare chest.

"Almost mixed," Astrid assures, flicking her red eyes up from whatever strange potion she's got brewing on the side table.

I shift from foot to foot, completely naked except for my underpants. Strewn fabric, pots of makeup, and glitter cover my room in Keep Oakheart. Tonight's the big event. The five of us are going to fulfill Farron's end of the bargain.

Tonight, we're attending Caspian's birthday party in the Below.

Marigold and Astrid are determined to make me fit in. Marigold has been taking some shears to a skirt for a precariously long time. Astrid's working on some weird potion she picked up from Flavia, Castletree's seamstress, when she tagged along on one of Kel's visits back to the castle. It looks like a big pot of ink, so I'm not sure what it has to do with my outfit.

They've already completed my makeup and hair, painting my eyes in dark shadows and my lips crimson. My hair is pinned into a loose bun, tied with silvery thread, a few curled pieces left out to frame my face.

Maybe I'd be nervous about tonight if my mind was less occupied with thoughts of Farron from earlier. Guilt wracks my thoughts; I should be making things easier for him, not harder. But a stronger emotion has taken hold.

Anger.

I want more than anything for Farron to break his curse and be free, but I can't stand the idea of him finding his mate. The thought of him with some stranger makes me want to scream. It's just not *right*. There's something thrashing inside of me, desperate to grab him and tell him he's mine and mine alone.

But that's selfish.

I have to push these thoughts away and focus. We'll need to be on guard tonight.

"How are you two spending your full moon?" I ask, trying to distract myself.

"Avoiding Farron's little brothers," Astrid groans, black paint splashed over her hands and hair. "Dom left a heart-shaped leaf outside my door the other day with a piece of parchment that said: *I'm falling for you.*"

A giggle escapes my lips. "That's kind of cute."

"They're way too young for me. Besides, I heard them muttering the other day how much they love rabbit stew." She grimaces.

"I, for one, will be partaking in all the delights of Autumn," Marigold says in a sing-song voice. "Remember that farmer I danced with at the festival last moon? Turns out he knows how to plow more than a field."

"Marigold!" Astrid chides.

"The poor lad has been after me all month," Marigold continues. "He thinks I'm playing hard to get. Maybe I should thank my raccoon. She's been making him all hot and bothered with this waiting business."

Astrid leaps up. "It's done! Flavia said this is the latest fashion in the Summer Realm when someone wants to look fancy without getting too warm. Apparently, the fae of Summer mix in gold and pastels, but I think black will be perfect for tonight."

"What exactly is this?" I raise a skeptical brow.

"It'll be easier to show you." Astrid sits on a stool before me and puts her little pot on the side table. "Drop your hands."

I do with a sigh, pretty used to being undressed around these two at this point. Astrid dips a paint brush into the inky goo, then slides it along my stomach in a twirling arc.

"Body paint?" I gasp. "I think I need more than that."

"Just wait," she says.

In the strangest sensation, the paint dries, then turns into a taut, almost silk-like material.

"I'm going to paint the bodice." Astrid gleams. "I have the perfect design in mind."

"Okay," I tell her, more confident now that it feels like actual fabric. Astrid works quickly, swirling lines up and down my torso. The substance tightens to my body, giving support as she delicately covers all the important areas.

"Is it going to be strange?" I ask. "The four princes attending a celebration in the Below?"

"Well, the realms aren't technically at war," Marigold says.

"But what about all the goblin raids? Caspian's thorns siphoning Castletree?"

"The Below claims to have no control over the goblins," Astrid sneers. "They insist they're wild animals. Everyone knows that's a lie, though. As for Caspian's thorns, the princes don't want to declare war again while their magic is depleted by the curse."

"Maybe this can be a diplomatic mission," I say hopefully. Or maybe if Caspian's guard is lowered, I can figure out what he wants with Castletree's magic. What's his purpose for smothering the tree?

"There's not going to be much diplomacy transpiring in a Below party." Marigold breezes over with gauzy fabric.

"Have you been to one before?"

"A few in my younger years." She gives a breathy sigh. "I was part of the staff accompanying Prince Ezryn when he descended to the Below."

"What? Why would Ez go?"

"To see Keldarion, of course." Marigold gestures for me to step as she slides a skirt up my legs. "He was always worried about the master spending so much time there."

My heart quickens. They've never given me this much information, and I'm eager to learn anything I can about Keldarion's past. "I didn't know Kel spent a lot of time there."

"His father was still High Prince," Astrid says, face pinched in concentration as she works the paint brush across my chest. "Keldarion and the Prince of Thorns were searching for a great weapon said to be lost there."

"Oh dear." Marigold looks at me with a displeased expression. "Now this won't do at all."

I look down at the beautiful skirt. Marigold cut the chiffon in thin ribbons that flow down my legs. The material is dark black near my hips, fading to a transparent gray by my ankles.

"This is lovely," I tell her, "but a little revealing."

She tsks and pushes the material aside to uncover my bright pink polka dot panties.

I flush. "I guess they don't exactly match."

"Take those off." Marigold winks. "I have just the thing."

I shimmy out of my underpants, and Astrid gives an annoyed grimace at the interruption of her work.

Marigold waltzes over with the daintiest little black lace undies in her hand. "I have a feeling my girl is going to get lucky tonight."

"I don't know about that." A month ago, I was kicked out of both Kel and Dayton's rooms. Ez continues his routine of ignoring me as much as he can. And Farron...

My heart stutters. If his beast hadn't emerged, something magical could have happened between us. But now, he'll never trust himself around me.

"You might be too oblivious, but those men look at you like a flute of faerie wine in a sea of swill." Marigold pats my cheek then sets the black panties on the bed.

"Done!" Astrid says.

I turn to the full-length mirror. Astrid has painted the most amazing designs using swirling lines. No, not lines. Thorns crawl up my torso, giving the illusion that my chest is covered in briars. The paint has stitched into tight black fabric, holding me in. But between the lines, my skin is bare.

It pairs perfectly with the gauzy skirt, which cinches high on my waist. When I move, it exposes my legs all the way to the top of my thighs. I always thought they were too big, but damn, I look sexy.

"This is..." I shake my head, telling myself I won't cry. "This is amazing."

"How do you want the sleeves?" Astrid asks.

I study the design in the mirror. Right now, the bodice curves up along the top of my chest, my shoulders and arms bare. My moonstone rose necklace, fixed by Farron, hangs between my cleavage.

Gently, I touch my exposed left wrist. *A fresh start.* I'm not sure I'll ever be able to express to Ezryn the gift he gave me. "This is perfect."

They both smile, and Marigold places shoes at my feet, deep purple heels. I've been practicing in them the last few days, so I won't embarrass myself down there.

"Wait, how do I take this off?" I gesture to the top.

"I like your thinking, girlie." Marigold's chest heaves with her laughter.

"It's actually very malleable," Astrid says. "Try it."

I gently caress the soft fabric across my chest. It sways, brushing aside to reveal my breast. I release my hand and it snaps back.

"If you want it off for good, gather it and pull."

"Alright." I turn one last time to look in the mirror. I barely recognize myself.

"You could be mistaken for the Princess of Thorns," Marigold coos.

"Don't say things like that," Astrid hisses. "And don't let the master hear you."

But it gives me an idea. I rush over to my bag with all my most precious treasures and carefully pull out the thorn crown Caspian gifted me at the Winter Solstice Ball. I place it on my head. "Did someone say Princess of Thorns?"

A knock sounds on my door, and we all jolt.

"Rosalina?" It's Ezryn. "Are you almost ready? We're set to depart."

"One moment," I call.

"Here, wear this." Marigold fastens a heavy cloak around my shoulders, pulling the hood over my hair.

"Thanks." I quickly grab my bag. "It's probably cold out there."

"That," Marigold says, "and if the princes see you dressed in such a fashion, they're not going to let you out of this keep."

WE MAKE our way to the ruined library. Caspian had suggested a place where no one would see our thorn-ridden passage, and Farron agreed this would be the best spot. The rest of the Autumn royals think we're returning to Castletree for the full moon, so nobody will be looking for us.

Moonlight illuminates the broken pillars, and ash wafts in the breeze. Tension shivers through the group as Farron pulls the thorn seed from his pocket, then kneels, digging a hole in the ash.

Keldarion fixes me with a stern glare. "You do not leave our side. One of us must always be with you. Do you understand, Rosalina?"

I nod, wringing my hands together. Nerves flutter in my stomach. I have no idea what to expect from this party.

The Winter Prince then settles his gaze on the others. "She is not to be alone."

Ezryn and Dayton both nod.

Farron stands, stepping back from the seed he'd buried. "Here goes nothing."

A sharp crackle of magic shudders through me. Giant thorn vines burst forth from the earth, looking so much like the ones that ensnare Castletree, a painful longing for home pangs in my chest.

The thorns twine around each other to form an arch. As soon as they connect, a ripple of enchantment flows down to the ground, resembling a wavering mirror.

"The way to the Below is open." Ezryn says.

ELIZABETH HELEN

I step forward, placing a palm on the thorns. "This passage goes both ways."

"Thank fuck for that," Dayton says. "I don't want to spend a moment longer in that place than we have to."

My fingers dig into the plant. I know it must open on both sides so we can return home, but something doesn't sit right with me.

"Thank you," Farron says softly. "Thank you all for doing this with me."

Dayton places a hand on his shoulder, and Ez follows his lead. Kel steps forward next and says, "We will bear this burden with you."

"We stand with you, Farron," I say.

He gives a rueful smirk. "Then let's go wish that bastard a happy birthday."

With that, he steps through the portal, followed by Dayton and Ez, until it's just Keldarion and me standing beneath the moonlight.

His face is a firm line, but I see the pain flashing in his eyes. What must it be like for him to attend a celebration for someone who betrayed him?

"And I'm with you," I say, offering my hand. Even if I'm still mad at him, I know he needs my support tonight.

"Thank you, Rose," he says, taking my hand. Together, we step through the portal.

A cold breeze whips through me, and a chill flickers through my legs.

Then I realize something.

I totally forgot to put on my panties.

PART FOUR
THE DESCENT

54

ROSALINA

Light shimmers in my vision, and the cold breeze flutters to a stop as I walk through the portal and into the Below. Kel's hand is tight in mine.

I inhale the thick air, rich with a sweet and almost floral scent. We're in a cavern. Crystals line the walls, emitting a gentle glow of pink, blue, and purple. A small pool of water lies to our left, iridescent plant life gleaming at the bottom.

"This is beautiful," I say, turning as I try to take it all in.

"Not nearly so beautiful as you," a smooth voice says, "Princess."

Kel's grip tightens on my hand, tugging me back. Because standing at the opposite side of the cavern is the Prince of Thorns himself.

How long has he been waiting there?

Farron shoots a wary glance at all of us, then advances. "Caspian, I'm here to uphold my end of the bargain."

A dark chuckle reverberates through the cavern, and Caspian steps into the light. My breath catches. The gems' glow casts off a beautiful silver circlet, adorned with a sapphire stone. He wears a black jacket cinched at his slim waist, with swirls of purple thread embroidered at the cuffs. A brilliant silver cravat billows at his neck. His pants are tight, tucked into shining knee-high boots. He stops before us, sliding his hands into his pockets, long dark hair falling across his eyes. "Welcome, residents of Castletree, to the Below."

No one says anything. Not a single thing.

"Happy birthday," I blurt.

His eyes widen, and he smiles. He should not be allowed to have a smile that beautiful. "Let's be sure to celebrate it." He winks at Farron. "Nice pants. Taking inspiration from Kel now, little pup?"

Farron flushes. "What? No!" He's wearing a long-sleeved white shirt, laces undone, tucked into high-waisted leather pants. My gaze drifts from him to Kel, who's wearing his similar tight navy shirt and leather pants.

"They're dressed quite similarly." Dayton gives Farron a little pat on his ass. "Cute."

"Shut up," Farron growls.

"Let's get this over with," Ezryn says, black armor shining, his movements stiff and precise.

Keldarion doesn't let go of my hand as we follow behind the Prince of Thorns to the other end of the cave. It's completely enclosed. Where is he taking us? I cast a quick glance at our thorn portal, still shining. Twelve hours, that's how long Caspian said it would stay open.

He stops in front of a shimmering cave wall. "I thought I'd plant the matching seed somewhere out of the way. Didn't want your arrival to cause a scene."

He taps a crystal three times and the wall groans then shifts open into a small passage. Kel gives me a slight nod and we follow him through. It leads to a hallway. The walls are the same stone as the cave, but they've been smoothed flat, the ceiling low above us. The ground, too, is polished and covered in a plush blue rug. Crystals light the way, set into elegant mounts on the wall.

Behind us, the stone door slams to a close. Our exit, gone.

"This way," Caspian drawls.

"Wait." I stop. "How do we get back in there?"

Caspian glances over his shoulder. "I'll open it for you when you're ready to leave."

If the mirror in Castletree can't bring us here, then what if the princes' necklaces can't bring us back? Like hell I'm letting us get trapped.

"Show me how to open it," I say.

Caspian sighs, then storms past the princes. He grabs my arm, tugging me away from Kel. "See those stones in the wall? Tap the green one twice, then the pink once, and then the blue three times."

His hand over mine, we go through the movements until the door creaks open. "Green twice, pink once, blue thrice," I whisper.

"Aren't you clever?" He drops my hand, then continues to lead us down the hall.

Kel prowls up to him and snatches his arm. "If you touch her again so callously, I will—"

"Chop my arms off? Behead me? Give me a talking to?" Caspian rolls his eyes.

I slow my pace, falling in step beside Dayton.

He doesn't acknowledge me, just trails a hand along the smooth wall. Every so often, the wall dips into the shape of stone doors. Sometimes an odd clang comes from behind one of them, and I swear I hear the chitter of goblins.

I turn my attention back to Dayton. Only a few weeks ago it had felt like my soul was brushing against his. Now he feels a million miles away even as we walk side-by-side.

I know he's been busy. Everyone's been busy. But he's barely spoken to me since that night.

Tugging my cloak tighter, I blink and ask, "Have you ever been to the Below before?"

"Hmm?" He raises a dark brow as if he didn't realize I was there. "Oh, not like this."

"Are you ... Are we okay?"

"Why wouldn't we be?"

I glance ahead, but Caspian and Kel are still arguing, and Farron and Ezryn are hopelessly trying to mediate.

"I didn't mean to hurt you," I say, knowing I have to explain. "The reason I said Kel's name—"

"Rosie." Dayton draws my name out like a sigh. "Is that what's got your pretty little face all scrunched up? Did you bruise my ego a little? Sure, I'm a man after all."

"But all these weeks…" *You've barely even looked at me.*

"Have been a bore." He tilts his head, golden hair cascading over his shoulders. "Work, killing frozen things, traversing across the hills, training. Boring. As much as I *loathe* Cas, his parties are revered around the realms. I am ready to wet my throat and other things." He winks.

I flush. "Oh."

He walks backward, throwing out his hands. "And didn't you say we need to surround ourselves with people? Who knows, maybe my mate is in the Below, and they'll fall on my dick tonight."

I struggle to swallow, let alone form words. This isn't the reaction I thought he'd have. But maybe it's the one I should have expected. All I can do is nod.

"Rosalina." Kel stops and turns, and I wonder if he can feel the pang of heartbreak through our bond. I scurry up past Dayton and join the rest of the group.

"We're almost there," Caspian says.

Ahead, the hall ends in two silver doors. Caspian pushes them open, and a blast of cold air hits me. It's like we're going outside, but we're still beneath the surface.

We step into a massive cavern. The ceiling disappears into a murky gray mist.

A bridge of white stone weaves gracefully across the grand expanse. Glowing jewels light the railing, giving off a warm pink hue that lights the path to the other side of the massive chasm. I tread onto the bridge and peek over the edge. There's a whole city down there, a labyrinth of serpentine paths and soaring buildings that spreads as far as I can see.

I finally shift my gaze to the far side of the bridge. There sits a marble castle. The entire structure is adorned with intricate carvings, arched windows glowing with opalescent light, and high silver towers reaching for the mist. It's reminiscent of a fairy tale, not a nightmare.

"Welcome to Cryptgarden," Caspian says. His dark eyes sparkle as he whispers in my mind, *Make yourself at home, Princess.*

55

ROSALINA

udity. Nudity everywhere. And sex. My breath convulses, and I can barely concentrate on anything else as Caspian leads us into Cryptgarden, his home.

We traverse the great bridge and venture into the castle grounds, avoiding the long line coiling around attempting to be allowed in.

He takes us to a grand courtyard, open air, with towers and balconies encircling the area. The courtyard is just as beautiful as any I've seen in the fae realms, everything cast in blue and purple tones. Crystallized trees are draped with gauzy fabric, and glowing enclosures feature plush seating and beds. Elegant silver tables line the edges, filled with all manner of bubbling concoctions, sweets, and fruit. Several fountains spurt brightly colored liquid, and people fill their cups with it. There's so much going on, I can hardly comprehend. Every available inch is crowded with fae.

And they're all fucking.

Okay, that's not true. But my cheeks burn at the sheer amount of debauchery around us. Fae move and flow together in the enclosed space. They dance half-naked along a marble stage in the middle of the courtyard. A chorus of pleasure rises to match the haunting music that drifts down from a gathering of fae on one of the upper balconies, the musicians all masked in skulls.

"Come along," Caspian says, leading us through the throng.

It's like electricity sparks through everyone as the Prince of Thorns enters his own party. Fae start to surround him, but he waves them away. As we trail behind, I hear the names of my princes whispered among the fae.

Keldarion throws a protective arm around me, drawing me against his massive body. These fae are dressed in everything from fine gowns, to crowns of thorns, to leather beaked masks. Others wear only paint or binding jewelry. Some wear nothing at all.

Nope, I don't think my outfit will stand out at all. In fact, maybe I'm a little overdressed, even with forgetting my panties.

Keldarion spins me around, eyes narrowed.

"You forgot what?" he whispers.

My whole body goes red. "Uh, nothing. What are you talking about?" How could he possibly know that? His large hands reach for the folds of my cloak, and I smack him away with a scowl. "You'll never find out."

I rush to catch up with the others.

Caspian stands almost shyly beside a willow tree carved of jewels, with strings of glowing gems for the branches. Fondness pangs in my chest; it reminds me so much of the tree I love back in Orca Cove. "This is a private area if you need a reprieve from the party," he says. "No one will bother you here."

The willow's jeweled vines enclose an area of plush pillows and a low table. Fabric drapes add to the privacy. It's a strangely thoughtful gesture, to reserve such a beautiful spot for us. Keldarion ducks inside, a pained expression on his face. Ezryn quickly follows, and I drift in after them.

"I know being back here is hard for you, brother," Ezryn says, low enough to be out of earshot of the others outside.

"I'm fine, Ez," Kel says gruffly.

Ezryn places a metallic hand on Keldarion's shoulder. "Tonight, I shall abstain from any spirits or elixirs. I swear on my life, I will not let her out of my sight for a single moment—"

"Hey, I'm not a baby," I say indignantly. But I don't press. Keldarion may want nothing to do with our mate bond, but I've done enough research to know he probably feels a need to keep me safe at the very least.

Ezryn leans closer to Keldarion. "Partake in food and drink and trust me to keep what is dearest to you safe."

Dearest to him? Yeah, right. Before I can roll my eyes, Dayton barges into our willow enclosure. "Did someone mention drinks?" A tray of bubbling blue glasses balances in his hands. "Found these on my way here."

Dayton places them down on the low table. Keldarion snags one and quickly shoots it back. Even Caspian raises a brow as he slinks his way into the nook with us. "Trust the Summer Prince to begin the celebration."

"The party seems well and truly underway." Dayton takes his own shot. "We're catching up. Oh, that's not very strong. You serving weak drinks here, Princey-Poo?"

"Please." Caspian levels Dayton with a glare, and the two start arguing.

"Can I take your cloak, Rosie?" Farron comes up alongside me, and my heart nearly beats out of my chest. The feel of his naked body against mine is too fresh.

But he's trying to be normal so I will, too. "Thanks." I take off my bag slung around my chest.

Farron grabs it and smiles. "This is heavy. What have you got in here?"

"My emotional support book. I mean, I know I probably won't have time to read, but I like to have it with me just in case." My throat tightens thinking of the second book in my bag.

"I get it." Farron gives me a soft smile. He's likely the only one who would understand. He moves to remove my cloak.

I guess I can't hide behind it all night. I'll have to hope Marigold's skirt is solid enough to hide my forgetful mistake...

The moment Farron slips my cloak off, all the voices silence. I look down at my dress, the thin briars elegantly covering my breasts, the delicate swirling skirt. I squeeze my thighs together. But when I think of the crown of thorns on my head, I make myself straighten.

I'm met with five pairs of eyes on me.

"I'm going to murder that raccoon," Ezryn says.

"Really?" Dayton says, almost dreamily. "Maybe I'll actually give her that kiss she's always demanding."

Farron shakes his head, gazing down. "Rosie, you look…"

But it's Caspian's gaze I meet next. He's … furious. Did he not think I'd keep his crown? Mustering all the stupid confidence I can, I hold his stare and delicately touch the thorns atop my head. "What? Didn't you say it looked better on me?"

Thorns and shadows erupt from the ground, but they don't dive toward me. They wrap around Kel's legs, pinning his arms to his side.

All the princes tense, waiting. But they're going to let Kel make the first move.

"I always knew you were a mindless brute, but to bring her here dressed like *that*." A dark chuckle rises from Caspian's chest. "She's going to get eaten alive."

I cross my arms self-consciously over my chest. I thought I looked nice.

Kel's gaze is fire as he studies me, then he rips free of the briars. Ice crackles over the thorns, snapping them immediately. Kel grabs the collar of Caspian's shirt, lifting the Prince of Thorns off the ground. "My *mate* may dress however she sees fit. So, if you value any of your minions' lives, you will tell them not to touch her. Anyone who does will answer to me."

Caspian sucks in a hard breath before pushing Kel away and dropping to the floor. He smooths his suit, composure instantly regained. "Very well. Enjoy the festivities. There are many delights in Cryptgarden. Do take care to sample them all."

With that, the Prince of Thorns turns and leaves.

The breath is heavy in my throat as Keldarion slides up beside me, and I feel the light touch of his hand on my spine. "The Lady of

Castletree is truly embodying her namesake tonight. You look as deadly as you are beautiful."

But I didn't need to hear your thoughts to know you forgot your panties, Rose, Kel's voice sounds in my mind. *I would have smelled you the moment you removed your cloak.*

Ice floods my body. "How are you doing that?" I whisper. "You can hear me?"

"Only bits and pieces," he says gruffly. "I wasn't sure it would take effect. But the bond is growing the more time we spend together. I remember my grandparents having whole conversations without our family at the dining table."

"Wait, what?"

"Mates can speak within each other's minds."

The words rattle in my mind as the fact comes back to me. I read about this. My gaze shifts beyond the willow tree and locks on the dark figure walking away.

Because Keldarion is not the only one I can hear in my mind.

56

ROSALINA

Peering through the sheer curtains around the willow tree, I can't stop watching the fae—they're captivating and beautiful in a horrific way. Some dresses seem crafted from cobwebs, while others look dipped in liquid gold.

Even the air feels different in the Below, soupy and heavy with desire. Farron hypothesized that there's an aphrodisiac added to the atmosphere, the wine, or perhaps the delectable food. Whatever it is, Cryptgarden is engulfed by an unrelenting wave of lust. The sensation is intoxicating as everyone's inhibitions are swept away.

Well, almost everyone.

Everyone except for the two fae men sitting with me in this enclosure. Positioned by the entrance, Ezryn sits on a large bench made of false bark. His metal leg taps up and down as he observes the party, a sentinel on duty. And Keldarion's only interested in the drinks.

At first, Dayton thought it was great as the pair of them tilted back shot after shot. But once Dayton realized all the alcohol in the world can't change Keldarion into a fun time, he dragged Farron out onto the dance floor.

I watch them now. It seems Day's lost his shirt, and they're doing a lot more kissing than dancing. Happiness swirls in my stomach. I'd been worried Dayton would fuck the next fae who blinked at him.

I take a sip of my own drink. This one is a deep red, strawberry sweet with a sourness that tingles the back of my throat.

Why don't I care when Dayton's with Farron, but the thought of him with some random fae makes me angry beyond comprehension? Maybe it's the same reason why they don't get jealous about me being with the other princes. I thought about going to dance with them, but every instinct in me screamed to stay here with Kel. Not because I want to indulge his weird desire to keep an eye on me, but because I feel like *he* needs *me*.

He's not acting drunk, but he hasn't uttered a single word except for a couple grunts. Something is clearly wrong.

I crawl across our alcove to where Keldarion is slumped over the table, a small crystal glass in his large hands. Gently, I touch his arm. "How are you doing?"

"Fine." He finishes his drink and slams the cup down on the table. "A little longer and we can leave."

I nod and follow his gaze out to the party. Caspian has emerged from the dance floor, where he'd moved as fluid as a living shadow. His hair is mussed now, a tangle in front of his face. He's being led by the collar of his shirt by a fae woman. She's stunning. Her dark hair is long and curled, matching the spiral patterns adorning her red dress that hug her generous hips. There's a man too, drunkenly hanging off Caspian's jacket tail. He's beautiful as well, with light blond hair and full lips. Not to mention it looks like he lost half his clothes.

They head past our willow tree toward a towering structure near the far edge of the courtyard. There's a staircase made of twisted thorns, resembling the briars in Castletree. As I look around, I realize these are the only thorns in all Cryptgarden. The briars lead up to a plateau where a beautiful throne stands crafted by more briars. He falls onto the crafted seat and pulls the fae woman onto his lap.

I finish my drink and quickly swig back another one that's on the table. I've avoided looking at the Prince of Thorns all night. Yes, after Keldarion mentioned mates speaking in one another's heads, I recalled reading something similar during my research. But that's not what's going on between me and Caspian.

For many, many, many, reasons.

One, I already have a mate. A growly, angry, frosty mate who refuses to touch me. But he's my mate all the same.

Two, so what if Farron said sometimes people have more than one mate? That's not me. Because then I would have had another line of light when we used the will-o'-wisps, wouldn't I?

And three, it's *Caspian*. The Prince of Thorns. The fae that betrayed Kel, that is hurting Castletree. There's no way I could be bonded to someone as cruel as that.

I need to shift my train of thought. I look at Ezryn. "Are you enjoying the party, Ez?"

"No." His voice is flat and final.

Alrighty then. Caspian is lounging on the throne, wearing only a thin white shirt, with the top laces of his pants undone. The fae woman writhes on his lap.

"He wouldn't," I mutter. Sure, there are people having sex all around us, but he's the prince of these lands. It would be so inappropriate—

A sharp gasp escapes my lips, and my hands curl into fists.

Caspian starts fucking her on his throne in front of everyone. It's hard to see through the layers of her red dress, but her thighs are spread wide, and he's got his hands on her hips as she bounces up and down on his lap. I feel it—or rather, imagine how it would feel—as his cock slips into her. A delighted, almost joyful emotion, like when you tell a joke and everyone laughs.

Kel's staring them down so hard, I'm surprised the entire throne doesn't turn into a giant ice sculpture. In fact, the drink in his hand is entirely frozen, and ice creeps out beneath his fingers.

"Hey." I grip Kel's arm. "Stop staring; you're acting like a perv. Just chill … Or actually, chill *less*, okay?"

A shiver runs through my body. Simultaneously, the fae woman on Caspian's lap cries out. Keldarion and I both look to the throne. Guess we're both pervs. But it's the stupid prince who's putting it on full display.

She's bouncing quicker now, facing away from Caspian. He reaches around and undoes the laces of her dress, breasts falling free. The blond man beside them leans over and kisses her, groping at her tits. Caspian unlaces the fae man's pants, and they drop around his ankles. He strokes the fae's cock twice before guiding it to the woman's mouth, who takes him greedily.

A shocked sound escapes me, and a powerful wave of lust coils in my core. But another emotion ripples, more powerful than the other. Anger, deep and fiery. This isn't just the thick air, it's something else.

It's like there's music and a TV playing at the same time, two different sounds, two different emotions cluttering my mind, and neither of them feel like my own.

Kel grips my thigh, fingers trembling. I grasp the sleeve of his shirt to steady myself. Cum spills into the woman's mouth as the blond man whips back his head. She smiles, and he backs away, almost tentatively presenting his limp cock to the Prince of Thorns. But Caspian waves him away dismissively, instead tightening his hold on the woman's hips, moving her faster and faster upon his lap.

I swallow, feeling dizzy, hate and lust and something deeper swirling through me, something that cuts at my heart. Sadness. I don't understand this. I just know I want him to stop. *Stop fucking her or I'll die.*

A voice caresses the inside of my mind: *As you wish.*

Caspian moves the woman off his lap, then tilts his head, the smuggest expression on his face. And even though his body is hidden by the fae, who's looking slightly confused, I know he's releasing his pleasure. *But he didn't finish in her.*

Kel's fingertips grip my thigh hard enough to bruise. The idea sends a tingle of desire through me, one I know has no influence from the Below. I lay my hand over his. "Okay, I agree. This place sucks."

Ezryn shows the most emotion I've heard all night as he chuckles, "Heh, he didn't last long."

I whirl to Caspian, conversing with the fae woman. He looks past her, down to us, and winks.

Thorns crawl around the woman. Then they fall away, dipping into the ground in a wave of shadows, leaving only Caspian, lacing his pants.

"Where did she go—" I start before a swirl of shadow and thorns weave before us.

Ezryn stands, drawing his sword. I let out a startled gasp, and Kel reaches across the table for another drink. The shadows fall away to reveal her, Caspian's latest conquest.

57

ROSALINA

Why would Caspian send the woman he fucked to our alcove?

I stand, ready to tell her to get out. But she pushes into our willow grove, completely ignoring me and oblivious of the giant man with a sword. She throws herself on top of Kel, grabbing his shirt, and blinking up at him with big doe eyes.

"Keldarion?" Her voice is a low rasp. "I'm here for you."

I take a single breath, watching in horror as her bare breasts push against Kel's chest, hands stroking his face.

A fiery beast bursts forth from inside my chest, and I snarl, "Get off of him."

Thorns break through the ground and wrap around her arms, tugging her back. She clatters over the table, glasses falling to the side, shattering and spilling.

What … What did I just do? The thorns release. Thankfully, it doesn't appear like any pierced her skin.

The fae woman sits up, unbothered, and doesn't even glance at me as she searches the room, finally landing on Kel again. "Keldarion, I belong to you."

Kel's face remains impassive, but my anger flares.

"He doesn't belong to *you*," I snarl. Spending so much time with these fae princes has rubbed off on me. "Take your eyes off him or I'll claw them out."

She behaves as if she doesn't hear me and clambers toward him.

"You are not wanted here," Keldarion growls.

The woman pauses, then sits up, blinking. A confused expression crosses her face as she looks around. "So, are you guys round two?" She tilts her head, pouting. "I thought he'd at least let me finish."

"Get out of here." My vines sprout from the ground, their razor-sharp tips glinting in the gray light. "Touch *my* mate again, and I'll use these thorns to shred you to ribbons." The briars coil around my arms, awaiting my command.

"Who the fuck are you?" the fae woman stammers, scrambling up.

"Someone you don't want to anger." Ezryn gives the woman a gentle nudge out of our alcove.

I drop my hold on the thorns as soon as she leaves, feeling something relax in my chest. I'm swept up in strong arms, the scent of pine and winter. Keldarion pushes me against the willow tree's jeweled trunk, and my legs instinctively wrap around his waist.

He grips my chin. A strange satisfaction simmers in my heart at chasing that woman away from my mate.

"Did you want her?" I ask, knowing the answer.

Kel's gaze drifts up and down my body. "Never."

"Did I frighten you?" I'm less sure of this answer. Briars now lace around our willow. It reminds me of Castletree.

Kel's pupils are dilated, breath sweet from the drinks. "You are ferocious and beautiful, my Rose. You deserve to claim what is yours after that display."

"Claim what is mine," I echo. *You're mine, Kel. I'm yours.*

His hands roam over my body as I melt in his arms, letting go of all the worries and pent-up energy. "I have never wanted anyone the way I want you right now." His mouth dips to my neck, teeth skittering along the sensitive skin. "I have never longed so desperately to show you."

"Show me what?"

His lips are a hair away from mine. "My devotion to you."

I sigh, becoming limp in his arms. My hips rock, feeling his steel length through the thin ribbons of my skirt. His hand snakes around to grip my waist, pulling me against him.

Spitefully, I think, *Feel this, asshole. This is what it's supposed to be like.*

A beat passes, and Caspian's familiar purr caresses my mind. *And isn't it delicious?*

I press my lips to the exposed skin along Kel's collarbone. A purely male rumble emits from his chest. I twist my head to give him better access to my neck and see Ezryn near the entrance of our enclosure.

He's watching us.

A strange smile skitters across my lips as I continue to taste Kel's skin while looking at Ezryn. It doesn't feel strange that he's here during this intimate moment. In fact, I can't help but remember the time in the forest when he wound my hair around his hand as Kel laced up my bodice.

A deep moan escapes my lips, and I lick my way up Kel's throat. A thrum of satisfaction crawls through my body at the sounds he makes with each press of my mouth. I look up at him through my lashes. How many times can I ask him to kiss me? So, I don't ask. I rise up, lips parting, eyes closing.

He slaps a hand over my mouth as he growls, "I need to leave, or I am going to take you against this tree."

He drops me, then stumbles, reaching out to a branch to steady himself. Ezryn darts forward, holding him up. "Don't go out there right now, Kel."

Kel grips Ezryn's shoulders, his face a pained grimace. "I can't be in here with her like this. Just look at her."

Ezryn tilts his metal helm and regards me. "I'll take her for a walk."

"She—"

"I will not let harm come to her," Ezryn says. "Trust me."

Kel grits his teeth before he nods.

I tap Ezryn hard on his gauntleted arm. "Hey, do I not get a say in this?"

"No."

"Did I mention how annoying it is when you two gang up on me?"

Ezryn leads me into the fray of the party, and I don't look back. Stupid icy prick. Kel gets to storm around when he's angry, but the moment my mating bond takes over a little bit, I get banished like a child?

"I'll find us a quiet place away from the crowd—"

I break out of Ezryn's grip. Rage bubbles in each of my steps. I know exactly where I'm going.

I march toward the thorn staircase.

Ezryn leaps in step with me "What are you doing?"

"I'm going to talk to the Prince of Thorns."

"I can't let you go up there."

I spin and fix Ezryn with a glare. "I won't let Caspian keep tormenting my mate. Trust me, Ezryn. Let me do this."

"I do trust you. It's Caspian I don't trust." A deep, reluctant sigh comes from beneath his helm. "I'll be right here watching."

"Good." It's time to face the Prince of Thorns.

58

ROSALINA

I make my way up the staircase of briars.

Caspian's still lounging on his throne and raises a dark brow at my approach. The fae man from the dance floor stands beside him. Thank god he's tucked his limp dick away.

From this high, I have a view of the whole party, including our willow tree where Kel watches me with an intense gaze. I'm sure he's not happy about this.

"Princess, how wonderful of you to pay your respects to the guest of honor. *Me.*"

I don't let a hint of emotion pass over my face as I stand before him. "Enough with the games. Stop sending Keldarion your rejects—"

"You can't talk to His Majesty that way, *human.*" The man beside Caspian glowers.

Caspian releases a long sigh. "Get out of my sight."

The man with the long ice blond hair flashes a satisfied smirk. But within a heartbeat, Caspian pierces him with a glare. "You. Now."

The fae man's mouth opens and closes. Then he tilts his pointy chin in the air. "I see how it is. I suppose the human does look fuck-able." As he walks past me, he slaps me hard on the ass. I whirl, ready to rip his head off.

But I don't get the chance.

Caspian stands and shoves the man off the raised platform. His face twists in horror, and he doesn't have time to scream before a sharp thorn rises from the ground and impales him.

Blood and guts splatter as his ruined body slides down the thorn.

The music stops. Kel's rushing out of the alcove. Ezryn's halfway up the stairs. Even Dayton and Farron sprint off the dance floor.

But Caspian gently steps in front of me and eyes the crowd. "This is Rosalina O'Connell," he says, not needing to shout to capture the attention of everyone in the courtyard.

I wave down my princes, not wanting them to get caught up in this. They slow their movements, watching me intently.

"She is a very special guest. If any of you touch her, you'll join," Caspian furrows his brow down at the bloody thorn, "whoever that was, as a party decoration. And since you have a warning, I won't let you die quickly. I'll enjoy your screams alongside the music as you're slowly ripped apart by my thorns."

The crowd is still and silent, looking from the Prince of Thorns to the dead man hanging off the briars.

Caspian falls back in his throne as if exasperated, then waves an idle hand. "Carry on." The music picks up its haunting elegance again, and the guests return to their activities.

I make eye contact with the princes, letting them know I'm okay. Caspian waves a hand and the throne he sits on twists, becoming larger. Large enough for me to sit beside him.

"Take a seat, Princess." A crafted smile spreads across his lips, "I've been waiting for you."

Gulping, I take a seat.

This is ... weird. I'm sitting on a throne of thorns with Caspian at his birthday party. And I'm not afraid. Which doesn't really make sense considering I just watched him toss a man off his pedestal.

Though, I am nervous. Invisible wrinkles flee beneath my fingers as I smooth down my skirt for the hundredth time.

"It's prettier here than I thought it would be," I say.

"And how exactly did you picture the underworld?"

"I don't know." I shrug. "Blood dripping from the ceiling. Skeletons leaning against the walls. The sound of your victims screaming."

"Sorry to disappoint." He gives a wry smile. "What can I say? This is where I reside, and I've always been a fan of beauty. As for those other things you mentioned, you'll have to go deeper."

"I came to you for a reason. It's about Keldarion," I tell him. "We need to talk."

"On my birthday, truly? Princess, you're a constant thorn in my side, but for some reason," he leans closer, "I can't bring myself to pluck you out."

"You have to stop sending those fae to us after you, uh, sleep with them. It's cruel to them, and it upsets Keldarion. And me. It upsets me, as well. Why do you bother telling them to throw themselves at Kel? He's not going to be mated with them. He's already found me."

Caspian rolls his eyes. "You're yelling at me like I have a choice."

"You do have a choice," I say. "A choice not to be evil and twisted."

"Twisted?" He slides closer.

I hold up a hand to halt his advance. "And it makes you smell terrible."

He tucks his chin, looking down at his chest. As always in the world of the fae, my senses are on high alert. I can smell him, his own scent mixed with that fae female.

Caspian narrows his dark eyes. "Don't go anywhere."

Briars twist up around him. In a mixture of shadows and thorns, he disappears, and I'm alone on the throne.

Ezryn looks up at me, not having moved from his post on the staircase. I shrug at him. Where did Caspian go? I adjust the thorn crown on my brow and survey the party. For a single heartbeat, I pretend I'm an evil queen looking for my minions. All I need is a raven and a cool staff.

After a few minutes, thorns rise before the throne and Caspian steps out. His hair is wet, the silver circlet with the blue gem tilted. He's changed, now wearing a dark tunic and tight breeches.

"You..." My words fall away as he braces his hands on either side of the throne, leaning over me, wet hair dripping.

"Is this more to your satisfaction?"

I can't help but inhale deeply. He smells like flowers, earth, and something else: sea and sunshine. "You were in Dayton's hot springs. How?"

He smiles and falls back to the throne. "Your princes have their little mirrors to take them to Castletree. I, however, can travel anywhere my thorns are. There are quite a lot of them in Castletree, as you know."

I shouldn't have said anything. He smells nice now ... Too nice. The way his damp hair curves along his sculpted jaw sends a shiver through me. "So, do you agree to stop? Because I brought you a birthday present, but I don't think I'm going to give it to you after what you did."

A muscle in his cheek tremors, confusion on his face.

"Do you not exchange presents in the fae realms?"

"The fae realms have a tradition like that," Caspian says, his fingers sliding over his hair, stopping on the silver circlet. "Not ... in the Below."

"Well," I say, raising my chin, "perhaps you should have been kinder. Though I appreciate you sticking up for me with that creep. But you didn't need to kill him."

"Oh, I didn't do that for you," Caspian drawls. "I did that for me. Self-preservation. Last thing I need is a frosty ass coming up here to kill me for allowing someone to touch you."

My gaze shifts to check on my princes. Farron and Dayton are eating at the table, but they keep glancing up. Ezryn is back at the bottom of the stair, an unmoving guardian, and Kel's got that piercing stare fixed on us from the willow tree.

There are so many things I need to ask Caspian, like how he speaks in my mind. But I can't make myself voice the question.

"Why aren't you afraid of me?" I turn to him, the words surprising myself.

"Who says I'm not?" Caspian replies. "I saw what you did to my little present."

"No, I mean, you saved my life. I know you did, the first day I arrived in the Briar." My voice trembles, but not with fear. "You killed your own goblins, then brought me to Castletree. Did you know I was Keldarion's mate?"

He blinks, clearly surprised.

"Don't lie to me, Caspian."

"I knew," he answers slowly.

My breath stutters in my chest. "How?" How could he have known before I did? I don't think it's possible to feel someone else's bond.

"Well, you can't expect me to give up all my secrets now, can you?"

"We can break this curse anytime. Kel could get his magic back. I don't understand why you aren't trying to stop me."

"Hmm." Caspian's gaze looks far away, on the horizon of the courtyard or lost in a memory. "He doesn't seem to be in a great hurry, does he? I wonder why that is."

My fingers tighten in my skirt, and my shoulders shake as I try to hold back tears. Shit, I do not want to cry in front of the Prince of Thorns. Why did we have to start talking about this?

"What?" Caspian raises a surprised brow. "Why in the stars are you crying?"

I quickly wipe my eyes with my palm. "Because I know why."

"You realize why he won't break the curse? Do tell."

I sniff, regaining composure. "Kel's heart is too broken from when he was in love before."

Caspian is silent for a beat, then he breaks into a laugh. It's deep and long, and above all else, cruel.

"Why are you—"

Caspian puts a hand on each of my shoulders, the first time he's touched me all night. But there's nothing sensual about this. "Now, who told you that?"

"Dayton said—"

"That mutt is even dumber than I realized." Caspian's laugh continues. "Listen carefully when I tell you, Princess, Keldarion has never been in love before."

"But—"

"And if he ever tricks you into believing you're the shore his star washed upon, remember he's nothing but a selfish liar."

Slowly, I push Caspian's hands off my shoulders, and they drop like lead to the side. "You really hate him, don't you?"

"I hate him more than a rain that falls on Midsummer's Eve, more than an early frost that kills the harvest, more than a plague that tears across the realmlands, more than the fires that ravage the forest." He pauses, and for a moment, there is a look of unhinged darkness in his features. "There is no end to how much I hate Keldarion."

I stand quickly looking down at him, breath heavy, and that fiery anger rising. "Then why bring him here? Why come to Castletree? What is this all about?"

"Because," he snarls, "I will not stop until he has suffered as he made me suffer."

I grab his arm, shoving up his sleeve to reveal his bargain bracelet with Keldarion, the chain of frosted thorns. But there's something else there on his wrist, higher, a golden linked bracelet, a dangling gem in the familiar shape of a rose.

I pause for a heartbeat. Farron had told me bargains could be any circular object. *Who else have you made a bargain with, Caspian?*

His eyes flick up. He heard me. *A gift, not a bargain. But the consequences certainly do resemble that of a curse.*

"Why can I hear you in my mind?" I ask.

"Asking questions only the stars know the answers to, Rosalina." He doesn't flinch, just leans forward so we're nose to nose.

"Why can I control the briars like you?"

His smile deepens. "Gift or legacy, the magic is the same, wouldn't you agree?"

"That doesn't make any sense." I take a deep breath in through my nose. He'll lead me around in circles if I let him. I need to focus on my most important question. "Tell me what your bargain with my mate is. Tell me about your bargain with Keldarion."

He rips his arm away. "Oh, it won't be that easy." He spreads his legs wide. "Come, sit on my lap. It'll help you figure it out."

"You're disgusting," I spit. "Why would I want to do that? You can't even make your lovers finish."

He rolls up his sleeves, the frosted thorn bracelet on full display. "Just because I don't, doesn't mean I can't. Unlace my pants for me. Stars know you don't have any barriers beneath that skirt."

I press my legs tight together, hating the burning heat in my body as his gaze rakes over me. He tugs the band of my skirt, so I shuffle between his legs.

"Sit, Princess. Let me sheathe myself in you. I promise you'll see stars you've only glimpsed in your dreams." One hand lazily swishes the black ribbons. "And don't worry about your precious mate. Even while you're still trembling from my touch, you'll find yourself back in his cold arms."

I move away. "You're ridiculous. I'm not going to sleep with you to learn the bargain. You probably wouldn't even tell me, anyway."

"On the contrary," Caspian stands, so much taller than me, "I just answered three of your questions."

"What—"

Caspian steps around me to address the crowd. They gaze up at him reverently. "I think the music has gotten a little dull. How about a taste of the deep? I've got a grand show planned. You don't want to miss this." He inclines his head to the empty seat next to him as he sits.

But I cannot stand another second in his conniving presence. I scramble down the thorn staircase, fleeing the Prince of Thorns and his riddles in the dark.

59

ROSALINA

My heart thunders as I make my way down the thorn staircase. I thought Ezryn had been at the bottom of the stairs. Where is he? At Caspian's words, the dance floor has become even more crowded.

Revelers push forward. Skin slicks against mine as I get pulled into the shuffle. Everyone must be attempting to get a good view of this show. I turn around and stand on my tiptoes, trying to find our willow tree. A sea of crazy-eyed partygoers stands between me and it. *Shit*.

As the music swells, a deep mechanical rumble echoes through the courtyard. I spin to look. The dance floor splits apart, revealing a gaping rift. Out from the darkness arises a large aquarium.

Its sleek, glassy surface gleams in the flickering jewel-light. Clear water splashes against the edge. Pipes and valves snake across the bottom like veins, pulsing with energy. In the middle of the tank is a creature of stunning beauty: a siren.

I gasp, not even caring as drunk and half-dressed fae shove me to get closer. She's so mesmerizing, with a shimmering tail of powder blue and a mane of pink hair. I step forward, entranced by the gleam of her scales.

But more fae crowd around me until I'm pinned on all sides by bodies. I try to catch a glimpse of the princes, suddenly feeling vulnerable without them nearby. *I need to get back to our tree.*

A commotion sounds from behind me, and fae offer curses and exclamations. Ezryn shoves through the crowd with the subtlety of a bull in a porcelain shop. His dark armor shimmers with the fuchsia, emerald, and sapphire of the glowing jewels from the tank.

"Get out of my way," he growls at the fae standing at my back. Then he grabs the fae man by the shoulder and shoves him to the side.

As soon as his cool armor presses against me, I feel relief. His large arms wrap around my body, and I melt into him. "It's too crowded," I say.

"I know. I got caught up in the crowd when Caspian announced his show. The shadowfolk obsess over creatures from the realms above. Hold tight to me." Ezryn takes my hand in his huge, leather one, and shoves through the masses. My hand looks so tiny in his, and I press myself tight to the rough fabric of his cape, so we don't get separated.

For a small moment, I catch Keldarion's eyes through a gap in the crowd. His features soften when he realizes the Spring Prince is beside me.

Ezryn swears under his breath. "There's too many of them. We'll make it back to our tree after the show."

The siren's tail flicks in a captivating rhythm. "I kind of want to watch."

Ezryn surveys the courtyard. There are obsidian benches along the edge of the tank, but they're filled with people lucky enough to get a seat. But that doesn't deter Ez. He goes up to a skinny fae with dark circles under his eyes sitting on the end of the bench. "Move."

The fae looks up at him. "Fuck off—"

Ezryn grabs his shirt and drags him off the bench before shoving him into the crowd. No one seems to notice or care. The fae man shoots us a dirty look then fades away into the sea of people.

Ezryn takes a seat on the bench, then places his hands on my hips. I can feel his smooth leather gloves through the ribbons of my skirt, and my breath hitches. "Sit here," he says huskily. "You'll have a better view."

Then he pulls me down onto his lap. I gasp as the shock of his cold armor hits my bare thighs. Damn Marigold and her overzealousness with those scissors; the fabric is so thin and the hardness of his metal cuisse shoots right through me.

"Are you comfortable?" he asks.

You wouldn't think sitting on steel would be, but he's holding me with one hand tight around my hips, the other resting on my knee. I feel so safe amid the chaos around us. "Yes. Am I squishing you?"

"Not at all."

I lean back against him, my head in the crook of his neck, right below his helmet. He smells so freaking good, like walking in the woods right after rain.

The music halts, and a hush falls over the crowd. The tank rises higher upon a pedestal, so I'm able to see the mermaid clearly.

Her skin is pale, pearlescent white, as if she's been carved from the purest ivory. There are jewels stuck to her torso and chest, but her breasts are bare.

Her hair is long and flowing, with shades of pale pink and light lavender blending together in a soft pastel hue. And her ears … I'm used to the pointed tips of the fae, but hers have delicate ridges and curves that mimic the shape and movement of a fin. They seem to move independently, twitching as she watches the crowd.

I lean my head against Ez's helm. "Why is she here? Do you think she's trapped?"

"Look at her arm."

She moves her body in a graceful rhythm, but I catch sight of a steel band emblazoned with stars around her forearm. *A bargain circle.*

"She's probably upholding her end of a contract with someone from down here," Ez says. "Whatever she bargained for must have been important."

For some reason, it makes me sad.

The siren flicks her large tail and ascends to the top of the tank. She grabs onto the side and hoists her torso above the water. The crowd gasps in awe at her every movement. Then she opens her mouth and sings.

The sound is ethereal, mesmerizing. My heart seems to rise and fall with each note. I don't understand the language, yet the haunting beauty of her words sink into me like an anchor.

"Do you understand her?" I whisper.

Ezryn leans forward, helm resting on my shoulder. "It's a seafaring language from the Summer Realm. She sings of a lost lover." His voice takes on a deep rumbling melody in tune with the mermaid, *"I met you on the ocean's edge, beneath the moonlit sky. We danced among the waves that night, our love a lullaby. But then the storm clouds rolled on in and tore us apart. And now I sing this mournful song, with my broken seabound heart."*

"You can speak a language unique to Summer?"

"I speak over ten languages."

"Oh..." My skin shivers, yet heat flips in my belly. I wonder what it would be like to listen to him in one of these beautiful tongues.

The siren's voice carries throughout the entire ballroom, rendering the crowd speechless.

"Oh, my love, my sweetest love," Ezryn murmurs, *"lost to the deep blue sea. I'll sing this song of longing until you return to me."*

I intake a breath, and my gaze drifts from the beautiful creature in the water to Ezryn. The dark makes his visor even more impenetrably black than usual, but I can sense his gaze on me.

He pulls off his leather gloves and stuffs them into his belt. "It's hot down here," he mutters, but then his bare hand returns to its spot on my hip.

"What else is she saying?" I whisper.

His finger traces a circle, slipping between the slits of fabric until they touch my bare skin. *"For though the tides may ebb and flow, and the winds may ever blow, my love for you will never fade, like the starlight's gentle glow."*

I close my eyes and lean my head back, reveling in the warm caress of his voice and the touch of his hand on my skin. It's too gentle, too teasing, only small circles.

His breath reverberates within his helm, and he shifts, leg pressing harder against me. My hips quiver and I writhe, suddenly desperate for more friction. The crevice between my legs pulses, and the crowd disappears. There's only the bewitching siren song and Ezryn's broad thigh beneath me.

His left hand trails up my knee, and his right hand pushes aside the strips of fabric to grip the soft flesh of my thigh. He presses so powerfully, indentations form. My breast shudders with my rapid breath. He's pretending to watch the show, but those deft fingers skirt higher and higher.

My hand drifts up to caress the side of his helmet. "Say something to me in the language of Spring."

He tilts his head, and I can almost picture him—that strange, face-less yet familiar image I have—lowering his brows and staring at me with a seductive gaze.

"Please." The word comes out more plea than pleasantry.

"Anon caria mirel baelorin," he whispers. "Yavanthy caeotin. Daris-feli em onore, *Rosalina*."

Each syllable drips with a musical lilt, and there's a hint of mischief that has me screaming to know what he said. I grind against him with more conviction, and he continues to speak to me, each word seeming to dance upon the air.

The siren's still singing, and the guests are lost in her pull, but I can barely hear her. Ezryn drives his leg up, and I bounce on his lap until I'm sitting with my back pressed to his chest, my thighs on either side of one of his. This angle makes the pressure of the steel plate over his leg even more punishing on my throbbing center.

I should adjust, but the thought of losing this delicious friction makes me only want to rub harder against him.

The cold metal of his helmet leans into the crook between my neck and my bare shoulder. I so badly wish I could feel his breath upon my skin, know the sound of his voice without the reverberation of the helm. But these thoughts take a back seat as he drapes an arm over my waist and pulls me tighter to him.

My slit heats as he drags me over his thigh, and I bite my bottom lip hard to avoid a moan. Does he know exactly what he's doing? He's pretending to watch the songstress, but his hands keep finding their way to my skin—

"I've searched the reefs and caverns deep, calling out your name," Ezryn hums, *"I've swum across the four realms' seas, but nothing's ever been the same. For every night I dream of you,"* his voice becomes a breathy rasp, *"and our love so true."*

"Oh, Ezryn," I breathe. His hands feel too light on me; I want them hard and disciplining, the way I know he can touch me. The way he grabbed me the very first time we met.

I arch my ass back against him, wishing he wasn't wearing this damned armor. Is he hard? Or is he wondering why I can't just sit still and watch the siren?

Every nerve in my body feels on fire. Sparks of pleasure surge through me each time I rock my hips over him. The slits of my skirt have fanned out all around his leg until there's only my soaked panties pressing against his metal thigh.

Then a realization hits me.

I've forgotten to wear panties. I've been grinding my bare wetness against him, drenching his thigh in my arousal.

Oh god. A wave of shame rushes to my cheeks as I imagine Ezryn's repulsion when he realizes there's been nothing between me and his armor. I whip my head around until I catch sight of the alleyway leading out of the courtyard. There's an opening in the crowd.

The siren stops singing and everyone erupts into thunderous applause. I take the opportunity to leap from Ezryn's lap and run away.

60

EZRYN

I inhale a deep, rattling breath. Every nerve of my body stands on edge, but I hold myself perfectly still. Rosalina darts through the crowd, but I don't move to follow her. Not yet. I allow a single moment to bring myself under control.

Because if I don't, I'm likely to devour her in the middle of the party.

My cock throbs against my steel armor. Her skin, soft as a petal, feels imprinted upon my fingertips. I barely grazed her and yet that touch was enough to make an untamed craving flare within me, something both thrilling and terrifying. The gleam of her arousal on my armor only fuels my need.

I stand and move through the crowd with slow but deliberate purpose. I lost her in the throng, but I'll find her quickly enough. Her scent drives me forward. My senses zero in on that delicious smell, letting the din of the party die away. She's here…

Brown hair flashes before me, and I spot the familiar profile of her nose. *Mine.* I reach out and snag her arm.

"Don't touch me," the woman snarls, and I release her. This is a fae, not Rosalina. I notice now her hair is much shorter, and her eyes flash with a feral glint that would never match Rose's sweet demeanor.

"Apologies, I thought you were someone else."

The fae woman looks me up and down, and a smirk darts up her wild face. "Interesting."

"Excuse me." I push past her and give my head a shake. My senses must have been confused among all these people. But it doesn't take long for me to pick up her trail. She ducks into a passage that connects the courtyard to the rest of the castle.

I slip into the shadows behind her, taking a moment to watch as she catches her breath in the quiet. *Beautiful.* I'd said I was going to murder Marigold for dressing her in such an outfit, but only because no one's eyes are deserving to stare upon the majesty of her radiance. Not that I am more worthy … But she is the mate of my brother-in-arms.

That does not make her yours, I tell myself. *So why are you torturing yourself like this?*

The answer comes with a flick of her dark hair over her shoulder, the sway of her thick hips.

Because the pleasure is worth the pain.

In a single swift movement, I'm pushing her back against the stone wall. My hand wraps around her small wrists and pull her arms over her head. The act causes her chest to shudder in and out, beautiful breasts barely hidden by the inky black designs dripping down her bodice. "Rosalina, what did we say about going off by yourself?"

Her eyes are wide and unblinking. She licks her lips and flicks her gaze down to my leg. "Ez—"

"Eyes on me when I'm talking to you," I growl.

A flash of mischief crosses her face. "What if I don't obey? Are you going to choke me, tin can?"

I can't help my smile. "Only if you ask nicely."

Her perfect mouth drops into a delicious O. I tighten my grip on her wrists. "Where did you think you were going?"

"Away," she whispers. "I was … embarrassed."

I trace the hand that isn't holding her wrists up along her jaw. "Now, why would you feel something so ridiculous as that?"

Her breasts heave close enough to touch my chest plate. Suddenly, I understand Dayton and his preference for going without a shirt. "Because I couldn't help myself—"

"And you should never have to." I inhale deeply, tilting my helmet to curve into the dip between her neck and shoulder. "It is a privilege and pleasure to be at the beck and call of your arousal."

She squirms beneath me. I tighten my hold on her in response and push in closer, trapping her between my body and the wall. "Ezryn..."

I drop my hand from her jaw down the line of her neck. "You deserve to be satisfied, Petal."

She barks a laugh, which is quickly cut off by the light press of my hand on her neck. "Did I say something humorous?"

She gasps, and I feel the delicious bob of her throat against my hand. Her heart beats in a nervous cadence, but she swivels her hips to brush against mine. "Well, not everyone thinks that way."

A growl rumbles through my chest. "Who dared not satisfy our lady?"

She looks sheepishly to the side. "Dayton—"

I swirl her in my arms, reveling in the press of her body against mine. She looks up at me with wide eyes and a genuine smile, and for a moment I'm mesmerized that I'm finding joy in such an evil place.

I dip her, and she throws her head back, long hair dusting the ground. "Dayton is a fool," I say. "His mistake should be rectified immediately."

I stand her straight and lace my fingers through hers. And then I pull her down the hall.

It's been decades since I've been to Cryptgarden. My last memory of my time here—Kel's rage, the hurt in his eyes when he saw me and his army—threatens to overtake my mind, but I shove it away. Right now, I will stay present in this moment. For her. For me.

Though it's been forever, I know my way through these halls. And things don't change much down in the bowels of the Vale. *It's probably still here.*

I lead us up a staircase that winds round and round one of the towers.

She says nothing, but excitement lights up her face. My heart thunders.

The stairs land us on the ramparts of the castle, the walls lined by a series of violet doors. "The residents of Cryptgarden Castle have a bit of an obsession with the world above. Many consider themselves collectors. They keep treasures from the surface within this section of the castle."

"Wouldn't the residents prefer to move to one of the realms?" Rosalina asks.

I bite the inside of my cheek, trying to remember the right door. "It's not so simple. Many are considered traitors from conflicts predating the War of Thorns. Others seek refuge; it's a place where smugglers, illegal merchants, or shunned nobility can disappear."

Rosalina looks over the edge of the railing, staring out beyond the castle to the vast city below. An image flashes unbidden into my mind: Kel standing on the top of this very tower. *"Admit it, Ez. There's a certain beauty here."*

I never saw it. The jewels shine with magic sapped from the earth, the purple and sapphire light has no natural source, no sky, only hazy fog above.

I breathe in, trying to detect the scent of wood and dirt. "Through this door."

Rosalina squeezes my hand tight and follows me. I try the door handle. Locked.

"Let me." Rosalina pulls a thorn from her crown and leans down to the lock.

I place my hand on her hips, my groin pressed against her ass.

"You're distracting me," she says, though her voice is low and husky. The lock clicks open, and she looks up at me, giddy pride on her face.

I run a hand along her cheek. "So that's how you escaped from your room all those months ago. You got me in a lot of trouble."

She examines me with a half-veiled gaze. "I could make it up to you."

My hand grips her jaw, and I push her against the doorframe. "Not *could*. You *will*, Petal."

Her only response is her rapid breath and a delicious red flush over her cheeks and across her nose. I can't wait another second. I need her alone *now*.

Opening the door, I grip Rosalina by the hair and gently push her inside.

"Oh my god," she gasps. "What is this?"

Thank the stars Caspian truly hasn't changed. I knew he'd still have this place. We walk into a small indoor arboretum. The room is dim but lit by huge crystals growing out of the ground like trees, gleaming with an ethereal blue and purple light. The air is thick with the heady scent of flowers from each of the four realms: only the rarest and most beautiful. Some shimmer like precious gems, their petals infused with an inner light.

Iridescent ferns glow like fireflies and leaves the size of dinner plates appear like emeralds ready to be plucked from the earth. A mossy bed lies in the middle, wavering with prismatic light.

"It's a secret garden," Rosalina whispers, turning in a circle.

"No one can deny Caspian loves beautiful things." I lock the door, then feel for my magic. It's so weak down here, far from Castletree, but I'm still able to grow a thick spiderweb of vines across the door frame. I can't risk anyone finding us.

Not with what I plan to do.

"Some of the plants look a little withered," she notes.

A little withered is kind. Many of the plants look sickly, near death. "Things aren't meant to grow down here. It's a miracle this garden exists at all."

I can only imagine what magic Caspian has sapped to keep these alive. But I don't want to think any more about the Below. I only want to think about her.

Now that we're alone and the clamor of the party is far away, an odd, antsy sensation stirs in my chest. *Am I … nervous?*

Rosalina raises a brow. "So, Prince Ezryn, may I ask why you've just locked me in a room alone with you?" Her hips sway side to side as she approaches me. She walks her fingers up my chest plate. "You should know, I'm a very dangerous human."

Her playfulness washes over me, and my nervousness quells. I weave my fingers through her hair. "Trust me. I'm terrified."

"Don't worry. I'll go easy on you." Her fingers dance to the bare skin between my armor and my helm. "Unless you beg for it otherwise."

A primal need surges through my body, and I twirl her against the planter of a large fern. "Now, don't get ahead of yourself, little human. My honor is the most important thing to me." I lower beside her ear, voice low and smoky. "And I made you a promise."

She folds against me, and I heave her legs around my hips. At the contact between my cold armor and her bare sex, she cries out, and I nearly moan from the sweetness of the sound. I grip her thighs, and she wraps her arms around the back of my neck.

I've kissed her before, but this is what it's like to truly have her in my arms, to hold her as tightly as I've always dreamed. All those months at the castle when we sat across from each other at Keldarion's forced dinners, I could barely muster up a word to her. And all the months she'd been away from us, I hated myself for my coldness. This is what I'd been missing.

I lower us down to the mossy bed. The shimmering light from the crystals paint her skin like a canvas of stardust. "You are a work of art. I'll try not to tarnish you."

She whimpers and laces her hands into the moss. Her body arches, head back, revealing her gorgeous long neck.

She sits up, eyes wide and frantic, and grips the side of my helmet. "Ruin me. I am yours to do with as you like. Take me and discard me, as long as I can be yours for a moment."

The idea fills me with delirious heat: the idea of my sweet woman, in all her softness and humor, willing to be debased by me. The beast inside me thrashes against my chest. *Take her. Take her.*

"Ezryn—" she whines, but I silence her with a finger to her lips.

Her expression flashes with annoyance and she wraps her mouth around my finger. I close my eyes and groan as her tongue swirls up and down, her eyes never leaving mine.

"Here I was, going to be so nice to you," I say. "And you're being very bad."

She frees my finger with a *pop*. "What are you going to do about it, Tin Man?"

I prowl my full body over hers and place a hand softly on her throat. "Call me that one more time."

A teasing smirk tugs at the corners of her lips. "Or what ... Tin Man?"

Fire ignites throughout my body, and I mount her, pinning her to the ground with my legs. One of my hands grips the base of her hair *hard*. The other one wraps tighter around her throat. "Is this what you wanted, naughty girl?"

Her mouth opens in a soft gasp, and her eyes nearly roll to the back of her head. "Oh, yes," she whimpers.

"You can still talk. I must not be squeezing tight enough." I press more of my weight down upon her. "Blink twice if it's too much, alright, Baby Girl?"

She bucks her hips up against me in response. I growl, my cock raging against the restraints of my armor. Fuck, she looks exquisite with my hand necklaced around her throat. I pull her hair harder, and see the movement mimicked by her own hands in the moss. *Sorry, Caspian.*

I release my hold on her and sit back. She gasps for breath, and her eyes are wet and shiny. "Ezryn..."

I run a hand across her cheek. "What a good girl."

She lets out a frustrated mewl and starts clawing at my armor. "How do I take this off?"

I laugh and ease her arms back down to her side. "Close your eyes."

She raises that brow again, her mouth soft and questioning. But then she does.

I take in a shaky breath. I've ... I've never done this before. Never with any other lover. But I've also never been with someone who sees the world with such joy and positivity; never known anyone who cares for everyone, even those they barely know. I've never known someone willing to face the world with the innocent bravery in which she does. Never had anyone seen *me* that way. *I want to be in your world.*

Carefully, I grip the edges of my helmet and pull up. The cool air in the arboretum catches my hair. For the first time, I look at her not through the tinted lenses of my visor, but with my own eyes. Stars, she is beautiful.

I am stupid. If she disobeys me and opens her eyes, I will dishonor my house. I will be banished from the Spring Realm, and worst of all, I will betray every commitment I have made to our creed and way of life.

But one moment to look at her like this is worth the risk. I set my helmet down and place my hand over her eyes. She exhales quickly, and I bend to capture her sweet breath. Then I lay the softest kiss upon her mouth.

"Ezryn," she whispers against my mouth.

The kiss is slow, intimate, tender. A kiss as vulnerable as I am. Aching, I pull away. "Keep your eyes closed."

I pick up my helmet and ease it over her head. My hands are tender as I lift her by the base of her neck, twisting the helmet so the visor is at the back.

Within the depths of my sacred steel, she is blind.

Her hands tentatively come up to feel the helmet. Yearning tremors through my body; her gorgeous soft skin draped in the inky black fabric, crowned by a helm of the Spring Realm ... I can only imagine her drifting through the cherry blossoms outside of Meadowmere dressed in only her own helm and nothing else.

"Wait." Realization trembles through her voice. She sits up, movements frantic, and reaches for me. Her fingertips dust over my face, across my eyebrows, along the curve of my nose. I sigh against her touch, softly kissing her hands anytime they drift by my lips.

"It's like I can see you," she whispers. "I mean, I can't actually see you. But when I touch your face, I can see you in here." Her hand hovers over her heart.

A knot forms in the back of my throat, and I need to do something before I'm eaten alive by my thoughts. Her hands tangle in my hair. I push her back to the mossy bed and run my lips all over her throat.

"Now, Petal, I am starving for you."

Slowly, I work my way down her body, raining kisses and nips on each piece of bare flesh. It's as if she can't bear to take her hands from my hair. I have to pull my head free as I lower to the mound between her thighs.

I push aside the ribbons of her skirt, revealing her dripping heat. Stars, she smells good. I nuzzle my face against her, inhaling deeply.

She moans as the cold air hits her skin, and her hips undulate toward me. My mouth waters with need. *I am going to devour you.*

"Ezryn," she whimpers. "Please. I need—"

She doesn't have to finish the sentence; I know what she needs.

I cover her heat with my mouth. Her hands find my hair again, and she pulls hard. I grin against her wetness and tease her with the tip of my tongue, swirling and dipping, before plunging it deep into her warmth.

She bucks against me. The slick heat sends my head spinning, and I savor every moan and cry as I feast upon her. She tastes delightful, salty and sweet all at once. With each lick and suck, she gets wetter and hotter. It's so delicious, I'm afraid I've bespelled myself with an addiction.

I lap at her clit, her thighs squeezing around my head. My cock is stiff against my armor, and I imagine tearing free of it all and taking her now.

Thankfully, I retain some sense within this ecstasy.

But she hasn't. "Take this off, Ez," she begs, pounding at my shoulder plates. The backwards helmet muffles her voice. "I want you inside me. Please."

I tear myself away from her pussy and drift my hands over her breasts. As much as I want to rip off this beautiful dress and suck her beautiful breasts into my mouth, I can't destroy her fragile outfit.

There's no way I'm walking her out of here naked. "When I take you, it will be among the cherry blossoms and the wildflowers. It will be under the cloud-dusted sky, with only the birds to hear your screams." I sink my teeth into her collar bone. "Not buried under the dirt like two corpses."

She lets out a frustrated growl and pulls at the back of my hair. "But—"

"No buts." I descend back down between her thighs. "You'll have to be satisfied with this for now, Baby Girl."

I plunge two fingers deep within her warmth and curl. She releases a desperate, nearly feral cry and arches her back. I bury my face in her again, sucking deeply on her clit. My fingers and mouth work in rhythmic tandem, making her legs tense and untense around me.

"Ez … Ez, oh my god."

I can't stop the smile forming as I press harder and she unravels, her sweet nectar dripping over my tongue.

And it's like her climax sends a rush through me, a tumbling of joy and wonder that blooms from my heart and extends out my fingers.

Her release sends her body quivering, but I don't stop, eagerly lapping up every drop I can until she's rigid and panting beneath me.

"Oh, Ez," she whispers. "This is a heck of a party."

I laugh and shuffle up beside her. I pull her body against mine, the steel helm resting on my chest. Her hand drifts down between my thighs. "I want to please you."

I grab her wrist. Though my cock aches, I know we've been gone too long. "The others are going to send out a search party if we don't get back soon. Besides, tonight is for you. Think of it as retribution for Dayton's foolishness."

"Okay," she whispers, but curls tighter against me.

"I should probably take this back." I knock on the helmet.

"My eyes are closed."

I pop the helmet off her face, savoring the delicious flush of her cheeks, the mess of her hair. The face of a lady well satisfied. With a new heaviness, I place the helm back over my head. "You can open your eyes now."

She blinks and looks around. "Ezryn…"

"Hmm?"

"The flowers," she whispers. "They look healthier."

I turn and stare around the arboretum. She's right. The plants, once wilted and dying, now bloom in a way that would rival any meadow of Spring.

I look down at my hands and notice a fading green shimmer. "I … I did something."

But as I meet Rosalina's gaze, the thought corrects in my head. *We did something.*

61

KELDARION

The music envelops me like a lover's embrace, awakening my senses as I wander through Cryptgarden. My eyes drift to the drink table, every corner filled with brightly colored concoctions promising freedom. I take three bubbly shots before grabbing two more drinks in my hands to take back to the willow tree.

Now, where is that tree? My vision fades in and out. The only thing I can focus on is the twisted thorns and the throne above it where *he* sits.

"What are you doing out here?" a stern, metallic voice cuts through the din.

I spin. Wavering before me are Rosalina and Ezryn. They've got their arms around each other.

The strangest joy blooms in my body at seeing my best friend holding my mate so protectively. I realize I haven't even been worried about her; I knew she was with him; knew he would protect her as fiercely as I ever could.

A deep desire to get closer to them cuts through everything else. I drop my drinks and stagger toward Ez, clasping his hard shoulders, feeling his solid weight support me.

I'm so happy he's here. He's never here. He loves to leave. Because he hates Castletree. Hates me. But he always comes back.

"Ez, I missed you." I think I might be speaking loudly, but it doesn't matter. I place a kiss on the front of his metal helm. Still using him as support, I lean down to the woman wrapped around his waist.

She blinks up at me, the most adorable expression on her face. I'll kiss her, too. I snatch her jaw, and she sighs, the sound igniting my body.

No. I pull away from her, my eyes cutting across the courtyard to the staircase of thorns. *I'll never let him have her.*

"I think he had more drinks while we were gone," Rosalina says.

Ezryn gives a deep sigh. "I've never seen him this drunk."

"I'm perfectly fine," I tell them. But my words don't have the desired effect because Rosalina giggles.

"We've stayed long enough." Ez tightens his grip on me and the three of us are moving. It must look odd to an outsider that Ezryn is dragging two stumbling people through the party. I'm sure I could walk if I wanted to, but I happen to like leaning on him.

The familiar glowing branches of the willow tree rustle, and Ezryn deposits us on the soft cushions. I topple down, somehow finding myself on my back and Rosalina lands beside me, her hair falling in dark waves. She has one leg up, and the skirt melts away, revealing her beautiful thigh, the smooth curve of her calf.

I want to taste every inch of her body.

"Keldarion." Ezryn's harsh voice cuts through my hazy mind, and I blink up to see him standing above us. "Where are Dayton and Farron?"

I search through the clouds of my mind. "I think they went to find somewhere to fuck."

"Of course they did." Ezryn sighs. "Where?"

I shrug.

"I'll find them, and then it's time to go. We've more than fulfilled Farron's bargain," Ezryn says. "Rosalina, you're in charge."

She sits up, nodding obediently. "So, I can boss Kel around?"

"Do whatever you wish. Just do not leave here. Understand?"

She smiles and nods, and he gently bends to caress her cheek, then turns to me. "Don't do anything stupid."

"When have I ever done that?"

After another long sigh, Ezryn leaves Rosalina and me alone.

And I'm certain it was him who did something stupid.

"Ez left me in charge," Rosalina purrs, and she draws nearer to where I'm still sprawled on the pile of cushions.

Her beautiful breasts are covered only in inky thorns. Her knees push through the panels of her skirt with each movement. And I know there's nothing between that bit of fabric and her pussy.

A deep groan rumbles through me at the thought. She is perfect. The night she came into my room, sensing my pleasure, was the first time I ever glimpsed her truly bare. Every part of me ached to touch her, to bury myself inside her and never leave.

I know the mating bond makes her crave me too. Makes her crave a monster. And each day it's getting harder not to give in to this need.

She rests her head on my shoulder, pressing the softness of her breasts against my side. One leg drapes over mine.

"Ez said I could do anything I wanted to you," she whispers.

"Hmm." I drift a finger down her spine until I cup her ass. "I'm sure you're planning something devious."

She pushes her bottom into my touch. My hand slips through the panels of fabric and caresses her bare skin.

"Fuck," I groan, and then I can't stop myself. I pull her on top of me, her thighs spread on either side of my hips, her bare heat pressing against me. "Do you feel that, Rose? Do you feel how weak I am for you?"

A sound of deep desire ripples through her, and she rocks along my cock. "You know what I want, Kel." She presses her lips to my jaw. "But I'll start with a kiss."

I angle my face toward hers, lips a hair from mine. "Tell me what you were doing with Ez. His scent is all over you."

Her eyes widen, and she flushes. "We were—"

"I hope he was good to you, Rose." The thought of my best friend satisfying her in a way I'll never be able to fills an ache in my burning chest.

"He kissed me *there*." Her eyes flick down.

Slowly, I slide my hand between the folds of her skirt. My fingertips graze her hot core. So soft and wet. I need to be inside her. "Rose—"

"Well, isn't this the most delicious sight in all the Below," a smooth voice says.

I sit up, cradling Rosalina in my arms as I take in Caspian leaning by the entrance of the alcove. "Careful, Kel, or you might just break your twenty-five year streak."

He's all mocking smile and sharp angles. Twenty-five years. Has it really been that long? But it hadn't been hard, not at all. Not with knowing the harm it would cause.

That is until Rosalina entered Castletree. The answer to my curse. And the doom of my realm.

"Room for one more?" Caspian sits down beside us.

Rosalina fixes him with a glare. "What are you doing here?"

"Why, I do believe you mentioned you had a present for me."

"You don't deserve it for being a pig."

He pouts his full lips. "But it's my birthday."

She wavers, whether it's from her unyielding kindness or she's just as weak to his charm as everyone else. "You can have it if you promise to stop sending fae you fucked to Castletree."

"How can I promise that? I may be a prince, but I'm also a man with certain needs."

"Find a new kink other than offering up naked people." Rosalina slides off my lap, and I instantly miss her touch.

"Something new," he muses. "Want to help me discover it?"

Thorns wriggle out from the ground. Almost affectionately, they encircle her wrists, connecting them together, and lifting them above her head. Two more vines snake out and bind each ankle.

Caspian gives her the slightest poke in the sternum, and she falls among the cushions with a peep.

"Let her go," I warn.

"That's the thing, my dear Kel," Caspian purrs. "She is able to tame these briars, the same as I. You can break free, can't you?"

Rosalina seems to test them, chest heaving. The only emotion pulsing through the bond between us I s... lust. *Damn him.*

"Sometimes it feels good to surrender, doesn't it, little princess?" Caspian licks his lips. "Because deep down you know I'm not going to hurt you. That I'll only bring you pleasure. Thought about my proposal? I can offer you the answer you so desperately seek."

"You think this is how you'll get your present?" she bites out, but her voice is raspy, low.

"I be nice to you. You be nice to me." The briars holding her ankles move, opening her legs slightly. Her skirt shifts to the side, and through the panels, I glimpse her bare pussy, the light line of hair before her dripping center. The smell of her arousal is intoxicating.

I fly closer to them in a fury, grabbing his shirt. "She'll never be yours, Cas."

"You're adorable, Kel." A sly smile crawls up his face, and instead of fighting my hold, he melts into me. His legs drop to either side of my knees and his hand glides down my chest, my stomach, then a featherlight touch over my cock. "You're aching for her."

He speaks like he knows my very soul. Maybe he does.

"You shouldn't be touching me," I growl. "The last person who did that got thrown across the room."

"She doesn't seem to mind." Caspian flits his gaze toward Rosalina. She's shimmied out of the vines and now digs in her bag.

Rosalina rolls her eyes. "You know, the only reason *he* hasn't thrown you across the room is because he's hopelessly drunk."

"And what will you do?" Caspian takes his hands off me and hangs them limp in front of himself. "Go on, tie me up with your thorns."

"Here." Rosalina holds out a wrapped package.

Caspian slinks onto the cushioned ground with the fluidity of a black cat.

"I told her not to bring you anything," I say, searching the table for another drink.

"Of course you did," Caspian says, inspecting the simple brown package.

Rosalina sits down on his other side, also reaching for a drink. "It's not right to go to a party without a gift," she says. "Besides, it's nothing much."

Caspian's long fingers tear at the paper to reveal a small leather-bound book.

Rosalina's flush deepens. "You see, Farron and I crafted these notebooks to help organize our research. But I made an extra one."

The front has an inked drawing of a holly and his name written in handwriting.

"Back home, whenever I got sad, I would write in my journal." I note her nervous rambling. "Not that I think you're sad. Well, that's a lie. I do think you're sad."

Only the flicker of amusement crosses his features. He carefully opens the book. On the top of the page are the words: *Things that make me smile.*

He raises a brow at her, and I lean closer to see what else she's already written:

1. *Dancing to beautiful music*
2. *Fine clothing*
3. *Competitive board games*
4. *Annoying Keldarion*

Caspian flicks his dark gaze to me. "I suppose I do enjoy the last one."

"It's good to remind yourself of what makes you happy," Rosalina says. "You can fill out the rest yourself."

I take a moment to admire her, the ability to show such kindness to someone so undeserving of it. He's holding her home hostage, and yet she's filled with empathy for him.

Caspian thumbs through the blank pages of the rest of the book, then carefully places it on the table. "How quaint."

Rosalina's features dim as he coldly disregards her gift. But she doesn't see his veiled vulnerability: the slight quiver of his lip, the glimmer of tenderness in his gaze. She has reached a place within him I didn't think existed anymore. My heart rages as I stare into his eyes.

Believing that, seeing those traits in him, is what got me into this mess to begin with.

My eyes meet his, and a flash of fear shatters his face. Like I have caught him wide open.

"Oh, what happened?" Rosalina touches the crown of thorns on her head. Except it's not just a crown of thorns anymore. Brilliant black roses bloom around it. She gently lifts it off, smiling at the flowers. "Pretty. Thanks, Caspian."

Caspian looks down at his hands. "No ... I didn't do that. My thorns may be the briars of a rosebush, but they don't bloom with flowers."

Delicately, Rosalina touches the silken petals. "But it wasn't me. It *feels* like you."

Before I can ask how she knows what Cas *feels* like, she places the crown atop his head then grabs his hand. He stiffens beneath her touch, but she guides their fingers down to the thorns that still lace along the floor.

"Relax. You're trembling," she whispers, then looks up at him with a smirk. "I'm not going to hurt you."

"Oh—" He swallows. I've only seen Cas nervous a handful of times, and every time it was adora—

I grab another drink and down it in a single gulp.

Rosalina holds their hands above the thorn. She gasps as light flickers beneath their palms. "Can you feel that?" she breathes. "It knows we're talking to it."

Caspian looks over at her, brows lowered. "We're ... talking to it?"

Then slowly something sprouts from the light. A tiny bud.

"Caspian," a stern female voice says. Looking in from the entrance to our alcove is a fae woman. A dark hood and a mask shield most of her face, and a cloak covers her body.

Caspian rips his hand away from Rosalina and stands, prowling over to her. "What are you doing here?"

"I could ask you the same thing."

Caspian doesn't look back as he grabs her arm and drags her from the enclosure.

"Who was that?" Rosalina asks.

"I'm not sure," I admit. "I've never seen her before."

Rosalina creeps to the edge of the willow tree. I follow, leaning my body protectively over hers. "I wonder what he did to upset her," she says.

Caspian and the woman stand in the shadow of the thorn staircase. She has her arms crossed and glares up at him. They seem to be in a heated argument.

Finally, the woman throws her hands up and storms away through the crowd. Caspian stands still for a moment, running a hand through his hair. Then he turns toward us.

Rosalina tugs me inside, and we fall back to the cushions right as Caspian steps through the sheer curtains.

"What was that about?" Rosalina asks.

He's silent for a heartbeat, something softening in his expression as he gazes down at her. "A minor disagreement on tonight's entertainment schedule. Nothing to be—"

A clamor sounds at the entrance, and Ezryn and Dayton walk in.

"Why are you here?" Dayton growls at Caspian.

Caspian bends to swipe the book Rosalina made off the table. "Collecting my present."

Ezryn crosses his arms. "We'll be departing shortly. Have we satisfied our end of Farron's bargain?"

"Oh, yes. Where is he, anyway?" Caspian asks.

"Getting one last drink," Dayton says.

"You finally left the little pup alone. You two were hardly separated all night," Caspian says slowly, then something dark flickers in his gaze. "Well, enjoy the rest of the party."

Rosalina crawls to me, grabbing my hand. "We did it," she says. "See? Not so bad."

Ezryn looks out at the revelry. "We're not home yet."

62

FARRON

Purple liquid spouts from the fountain like an amethyst waterfall. My head is fuzzy, and staring into the shimmering cascade is easier than trying to take in the party. I have partaken in little drink, but the din of music and chatter, the bright lights shining in the darkness, and the ever-present press of the crowd makes my mind feel muddled.

One more drink and we can leave. I fill the obsidian goblet from the fountain. Even though I haven't talked to anyone outside of my group, this has been enough socializing for a long time. I yearn for my bed, a quiet room, and stillness.

I turn away when someone slams a hand down on the stone counter, stopping my departure.

Caspian.

He stares at me with an enigmatic smirk, dark eyes twinkling mischievously, dark hair garlanded by a crown of black roses. "Well, well, we finally have an opportunity to talk. I haven't been able to get a moment alone with you all night."

"What do you want, Caspian?" I try to push past him, but he stands in my way. He's right—I haven't left Dayton's side since we've arrived.

Usually, a revel with this much debauchery would have him with a different fae on his lap all night. But he was in a terrible mood. Nothing cheered him up. Not dancing, not kissing. We didn't even fuck. Day barely drank at all; his emotions ranged from anxious to sour.

It's my fault. We're here because of me. Because of this bargain. He hasn't said it, but I wonder if he thinks I'm a coward for this, for not being brave enough to find another way.

"What do I want?" Caspian puts a mock offended hand on his heart. "Farron, you wound me. You and I share a bond."

"One I will be glad to rid myself of," I grumble and make to pass him.

Again, he moves in front of me, blocking my path. "I only wanted to thank you for attending my party. I wasn't sure you would all show up."

"We had to show up. It's part of the bargain." The thorn collar around my neck seems to tighten at the thought. I resist the urge to scratch it.

Caspian looks down at a small notebook he's carrying. "Come now, Farron. It wasn't only about the bargain, was it?"

"Trust me. It was." I peer through the crowd to the willow tree in the courtyard's corner. Rosalina sits surrounded by the other princes, and an intense longing to be near her throbs in my heart.

Caspian follows my gaze. "This is how it is for men like us. The watchers and the waiters. The poets and the philosophers. Always on the outside looking in."

They're laughing, all four of them. I'm not an outsider; I belong there with them.

"They are men who take what they want," Caspian says. "But you and I hide in the shadows. Never truly part of the living. So often betrayed by our very bodies."

"I'm nothing like you," I say. Slamming the goblet on the counter, I reach up and pry my fingers under the thorn collar. Barbs dig into my hands, and a warm trickle of blood drips down my neck.

Caspian runs a finger through the blood. "I've protected you each night, Farron. Do you feel me when my thorns cradle you in the dark?"

"No..."

"How about when your control slips?"

My breath hitches. He couldn't know about earlier today and yet ... I'm there again, in the best moment of my life. Until I felt my beast clawing at me from the inside out, and all I could think was *I'm going to kill her.* And it was him who stopped it all.

"What would have happened if it wasn't for our little bargain?" He pops his finger into his mouth, sucking deeply. Then he opens to a wicked smile, teeth painted red. "Would you have devoured her or ... devoured her?"

"Shut up." My voice is raspy and raw. How could he know about Rosalina and I in the tavern? There was only the two of us.

And the beast and briars.

"But I know your secret," Caspian continues. "There's a part of you that craves to let the beast win. You know it, don't you, Farron? You'll never be truly free until you do."

My eyes widen, and panic laces through me. "That's not—"

"In many ways, we are one and the same. Monsters within our family."

My heart hammers in my chest, and I rip my hands away from the collar. "You're nothing like me, Caspian. Even back before the War of Thorns, you were never truly one of us. We all sensed it, all except Kel. It's like there's a doom on you, something vile and condemned. I don't know what game you're playing with us now, showing up at our home, making us come to your stupid party." My voice is ragged, breath too fast. "You're not part of our family, Caspian. You never were. And you never will be."

Caspian steps back, eyes wide and shimmering.

Sometimes when I look at him, I forget just how wicked he is. But he nearly destroyed Kel. He's bringing ruin to Castletree. Plus, he's tormenting Rosalina.

I am the High Prince of Autumn, and the Below is an enemy to the realm. Caspian is an enemy. If I can't stand up for those I love, I'll never be able to defend all of Autumn.

I snatch Caspian by the lapel and shove him against the stone counter. "And stop speaking in Rosalina's mind. Whatever dark sorcery you've conjured, leave her out of it."

His eyes flick down to the notebook he's holding. I recognize it now, one of the blank pads we use during our research. Rosalina's handwriting is scrawled over the front—

I snatch the book from him, and he cries out, reaching for it. And with all the anger built in me, I rip the pad in two and throw it to the ground.

Caspian lets out a strangled sound and falls to his knees, gathering the shredded pieces. Then he glowers up at me. "You were all so quick to bestow me with the role of villain. Well then, Farron dear, if it is between that and outcast, I accept. I'll play the part to perfection, and you'll rue the day you ever cast me in it."

The thorns around my neck shiver and all goes black.

63

ROSALINA

"Blossom," Dayton raises a dark brow from where he's lounging on the cushions, "are you going to tell me why you smell like the meadows of Spring or am I going to have to guess?"

My entire body heats, and Ezryn stiffens.

"Oh, come on," Dayton drawls. "Now you have to tell me."

I open my mouth, knowing something awkward is going to sputter out. But Ezryn steps forward. "I was correcting an error most grievous, Summer Prince. How dare you not satisfy the Lady of Castletree?"

The Summer Prince doesn't look intimidated in the slightest. His grin only widens. "So that's what it's all about. Our noble knight committed to justice, both in and out of the bedroom." He places a hand on his chest. "But did the fair maiden proclaim how she wounded me so?"

I bury my face in my hands.

"I only hope, brother, she remembered your name in the throes of passion. Or did the name of our Sworn Protector grace your ears as well?"

I peek out between my fingers. Kel watches them both with a hint of amusement while sipping the water I gave him. There's not a flicker of jealousy on his features.

Ezryn grabs Dayton by his shirt, lifting him up so they're nose to helm. "I don't care if she calls you Goblin," Ezryn says. "If our woman requests pleasure, you give it to her."

Dayton clasps his hands tight over Ezryn's bracers. He smirks, wavy strands of blond hair falling across his brow. "If you say so, Daddy."

Ezryn drops him with a long sigh, and Dayton springs lightly to his feet, laughing. We've been at a party for hours and he's not drunk. Strange.

Dayton saunters over to me and throws his arm around my shoulders. I've missed the warm touch of his skin. "What do you say? Can you forgive me?" he breathes in my ear. "Jane?"

"You're ridiculous." I laugh. "Where is Farron to calm you down?"

A hushed silence settles over our alcove, and Kel says, "Where is Farron?"

He's been gone too long. Apprehension tickles in my stomach. Outside, the party is winding down. The music has slowed to a haunting melody, and low moans of sex have replaced the earlier loud cries.

Ez shakes his head. "I'll go look for him."

"No." I grasp Ezryn's arm. "I don't think we should split up."

Ezryn nods. "He probably got turned around. Farron's never been much good at directions." His voice has lost its usual confidence.

I glance up at the throne, but the Prince of Thorns isn't there. The rocks settling in my gut sink deeper. "I want to go home," I whisper.

"He might have gotten frustrated with me," Dayton says, remorse audible in his words. "He kind of wandered off, saying he needed a drink. I thought he wanted some space."

You've barely left him alone all night. Caspian's words to Dayton ring sharply in my ear.

"Dayton, is it true you and Farron were together all night?"

"Yes."

It's like we both feel it at the same time. Something is wrong.

Farron is in trouble.

"We need to find him," Dayton says, voice low and commanding, all hints of merriment gone.

"Ez, can you help Kel?" I ask.

Ezryn gives a nod, not questioning our sudden seriousness. He hoists Kel's arm over his shoulder as we make our way through the party.

Dayton grabs my hand, clutching it tight. *It'll be fine,* I tell myself. *We'll find Farron and get home. It's okay, we'll find him.*

We don't. Not after three laps of the courtyard or searching the surrounding passages. There are halls within halls in this castle, but why would Farron wander down any of them?

"He wouldn't leave without us," Dayton says, panic lacing his words.

"We can find him," Ezryn says. "We'll grid Cryptgarden, every hall, every room—"

"He's not here," I say.

They all stare at me. I'm not sure how to explain it. But I knew after we lapped the courtyard once. Farron isn't in Cryptgarden. He isn't even in the Below. I *know* it.

"What are you thinking, Rosie?" Dayton asks. I know he's trying to remain strong, but I can see it in his eyes. He's terrified.

"We need to get to our portal."

"The portal remains open for twelve hours," Ez says. "If he's not in Autumn, we can return here to search."

Keldarion vomits behind a bench.

We sprint out of Cryptgarden Castle and across the expansive bridge over the city, passing drunken partygoers and unconscious bodies. Back into the main hall, my heart lurches in my chest.

The carpeted corridor is unnervingly quiet. No soldiers, no revelers. We stop in front of the rock wall where Caspian revealed the hidden door. Quickly, I tap the crystals in the order Caspian showed me.

It doesn't open.

"No..." I breathe. "I know that was correct. It should work."

Dayton steps up, tapping the same ones. Nothing happens. "That was the sequence."

"The bastard did something to it," Ezryn growls. Kel's still slumped over his shoulder, slowly coming back to himself.

"I hear something." Dayton presses his ear against the rock. "Goblins."

I follow his lead. Faintly, there's the clash of steel and a hungry chitter.

"What are goblins doing by our portal?" Dayton asks.

"Maybe this is the wrong place." Frantically, I look up and down the narrow corridor. No, it was here.

Footsteps sound from around the bend. "Who goes there?"

My heart stutters at the sight of guards rounding the corner. Their armor is a cacophony of jewel-tones, helms wrought with sharp spikes. The opaque visors hide any glimpse of their true intentions.

"Who are they?" I whisper.

"The Dreadknights. Soldiers of the Below." Ezryn leans Kel against the wall, then steps in front of us, hand casually resting on the hilt of his sword.

Behind us, Dayton has taken off his necklace, desperately trying to get the mirror to catch the light. "These never work down here," he hisses.

I inhale a shaky breath. "We're guests of the Prince of Thorns."

"Oh, really?" a husky feminine voice purrs. "I don't see him. Do you?"

The female glides forth from the cluster of soldiers like an encroaching shadow. For a moment, I am spellbound by her presence. Her black cape flicks behind her, resembling a tail of raven feathers. A large hood shrouds her features, and a mask conceals the bottom half of her face, leaving only her blue eyes visible.

She was the one arguing with Caspian below the staircase of thorns.

"Do I know you?" Ezryn asks, venom lacing his words.

She moves closer with a haunting grace, each step fluid and silent. Her armor is adorned with intricate plates of jewel-toned metal, each one a glittering gemstone of a different hue. Blades are strapped to her waist and around her legs.

"They call me the Nightingale," she says. "Commander of the Dreadknights, and the one who will finally deliver the useless fae princes and their human pet to the Queen of the Below."

"We are guests. Detaining us will have dire consequences," Ezryn says, though I think it's more a stalling tactic at this point. His helm moves ever so slightly. He's taking count of the soldiers.

Dayton abandons working on his necklace and rushes forward. "What the fuck have you done with Farron?"

Where's Caspian? I grip the wall, and something pulses beneath my hand—

The heartbeat of the Below.

I kneel on the ground, pretending to check on Keldarion. The Nightingale and her soldiers move closer to my princes.

I press my palm to the hard earth. *Your princes have their little mirrors to take them to Castletree. I, however, can travel anywhere my thorns are.*

Caspian can leave the Below as he wishes. He doesn't need mirrors or portals. He has everything at his fingertips.

And so do I.

Beneath my hands sprouts a vine of thorns.

PART FIVE
DEATH OF LIFE

64

ROSALINA

ou are mine. A possessive fierceness radiates through me as I bury my hands in the earth. Thorns rise around me. I've controlled these briars before. Even Caspian admitted I could do it.

But I've never summoned them like this.

A well of magic courses deep within me, my connection to the thorns stronger than I've ever felt it before. There must be some tie to the Below, some vicinity to this underworld that fuels this link between me and the magic. Whatever the case, I need it now more than ever.

Caspian uses the thorns as transport, appearing and disappearing wherever his thorns have grown. And there are thorns in the Autumn Realm: the ones we planted.

Take me to the surface, I roar inside my mind. *Take me to Caspian.*

The thorns trickle over to us. Kel immediately kicks out, breaking one apart as it nears him. Pain flicks through me as if they are an extension of my nervous system. They wrap up my legs and around my waist, and I will them to do the same to the princes.

Kel rips them off as soon as they touch his skin, and even Ezryn backs away defensively.

"Are you idiots?" Dayton snaps. His arms are outstretched, head up toward the surface. "There's no time for your fear. Farron needs us. Rosalina's going to get us to him."

I offer an appreciative smile while Ez and Kel exchange looks. Mercifully, they stay still, and the thorns wind tight around each of us.

I catch one final glance of the Nightingale, her blue eyes wide with surprise.

Let's give this a go.

Picturing the thorns that grew from the seed we planted in the burned library, I allow my energy to pulse out of me, lacing through the vines. I am both here and everywhere, my consciousness spreading like light scattered through a prism. *Up, up, up.*

We rocket through the earth.

A network of briars rushes past, and we're like fish caught in the net. The underground thicket opens into a tunnel, and we whip through, thorns snagging at my skin and hair. My stomach loops at our speed, only briars dashing by in my peripheral. Up, then left, then right, then down, and up again, the briars shoot us through tunnels I never knew existed.

The thorns twist away from us, responding with a violent surge of energy. But silvery moonlight gleams in a pinprick on the horizon. *The surface.*

My head spins as we're shot out of the thicket, landing in a heap upon hard, charcoal-drenched ground.

"Is everyone alright?" Ezryn asks, voice slightly queasy.

I lift my hands up. Black. Ash everywhere. We're at the burned library, where we planted the seed to allow us to travel to the Below.

"Farron?" Dayton cries, staggering to his feet.

We all clamber up. My knees shake, my body completely spent from the rush of magic. A bone-deep weariness fills me, and even standing is an effort.

Dayton's voice cracks. "Fare..."

A massive brown wolf lopes out of the hidden door in the sacred alder tree. And in his mouth, he carries a grimoire, one of the books containing dark magic.

"This shouldn't be happening. It's the full moon—" I begin before a gasp takes over, and my hands cover my mouth. Through the open entrance into the hidden library, I see ... destruction. All the precious books that had been saved from the first disaster—the family histories, the diaries, the grimoires—are ripped apart, destroyed by fang and claw. Papers fly in the breeze, and tears spring to my eyes.

"Prince of Thorns!" Dayton roars. "What did you do to him?"

Then I see him, sitting in a branch of the alder tree, swinging one leg down, looking perfectly nonchalant. He picks at a nail. "It was such a lovely birthday party. Farron thought he'd give me one last present."

Farron sits at the base of the tree, eyes glazed. The thorn collar weaves tightly through his fur. A vine erupts from the ground and wraps around the book in his mouth before rising to Caspian.

A sharp metallic ring sounds through the night as Ezryn unsheathes his sword. "Another betrayal, Caspian? You're getting predictable."

The Prince of Thorns smiles. "I wouldn't count on it."

Keldarion falls to his knees, ash billowing up around him.

"You've got your stupid book," Dayton says. "Let him go."

"Oh, you really wouldn't want me to do that."

The princes banter back and forth, and I creep toward the tree, willing my heart to slow. Farron's wolf seems like a statue, sitting so still. "Farron, are you in there? It's me. Rosalina. Can you hear me?"

But the wolf doesn't even blink.

"Release him or I'll tear your fucking face off!" Dayton yells.

Caspian clicks his tongue. "Perhaps you're upset because you didn't receive a party favor. Don't worry, I have a present for all of you as well."

The portal to the Below flickers with purple light, and then a pungent, acrid smell wafts from its bellows.

"No," I whisper. "No, no, no—"

Goblins pour out. Emerging in a chaotic, writhing mass, they run toward us, their movements frenzied and wild. Ten, twenty, more and more keep coming, their skin in sickly shades of green or white, their hair tangled messes of oily strands that point out in each direction. Moonlight gleams off their crude weapons.

"Rosalina!" My name is shouted over and over again, but I can barely comprehend. I must help Farron. If he's trapped by the Prince of Thorns—

Dayton shoots a blast of wind at the monsters. They stampede toward us with a primal rage, snarling and snapping at each other as they jostle for position.

"You're dead." Ezryn leaps into the branches.

He lands beside Caspian, but the Prince of Thorns doesn't look afraid. "I know you've wanted to kill me for a long time, metal man, but you'll have to be patient."

With the grace of a cat, Caspian springs from the tree and lands before Farron. The mischief disappears from his face. "You ruined my book. I ruined all of yours. Fair is fair, friend."

Ezryn hurdles down, sword drawn, but a thorny vine whips up, knocking him to the side. Dayton gives a booming cry and runs forward, but thorns wrap around his ankles, yanking him to the ground.

Caspian never takes his eyes off Farron. "You came to my birthday party. I've controlled your beast. Let us consider the bargain complete." Magic sparks in the air, so electric I can taste it on my tongue. Light shimmers around them. The thorn collar snaps and falls from Farron's neck.

Caspian looks to me and Kel, then winks. "Until next time, lovers." The briars wrap around his body, and he sinks deep into the earth.

"What's the plan?" Dayton cries, breaking free of the vines and pulling me against him.

Kel's still on his knees, motionless.

The goblins are almost upon us. They move with an uncanny grace, darting and weaving around the remains of the library. Some leap onto the ruined shelves, their claws digging into the charred wood. Others skitter across the ground like insects.

But my mind races. What had Caspian said when they'd made the bargain? *This spell will ensure you remain under control.* Yeah. Under *Caspian's* control.

And we'd never clarified that Caspian had to continue helping Farron even after the birthday party. If the bargain is complete, Farron's no longer enthralled by Caspian's magic. That means...

"Watch out!" I scream.

But it's too late.

Farron's eyes glow with feral rage as he shakes his head, then charges.

65

DAYTON

I'll be the first to admit I've been in some bad fucking situations before. Alone in the middle of the ocean with only a little dingy and an ancient kraken circling the boat? Check. Waking up butt-ass naked in a barn and having to sneak into the castle unseen on a festival day? Check. Facing down eight soldiers and a couple mino-taurs in the Sun Colosseum while blindfolded? Check, check, and check.

But now I realize none of those moments had been bad at all.

Flames ignite from Farron's paws. The beast is summoning fire magic. If we don't do something, he'll set this whole place ablaze.

I'm terrified. All those other times, I was only trying to save my own dumb ass. But it's not just about me anymore. Rosalina's nearly collapsed on the ground; her body drained from wielding magic a human has no business being able to use. Keldarion's gaze is faraway, mind completely muddled with drink. Ezryn charges toward the space where Caspian disappeared, despite the fact there's no way to get to him.

And I have no idea what to do.

The world is a blur, movement I can't stop. Goblins charge toward us from out of the thorn portal. Through the grove of trees encircling the ruins, I catch glimpses of torches and golden armor. The Autumn Guard approaches. The wolf swipes its massive burning paws at the ruined library and any goblin that dares to get within its reach.

"We have to help him!" Rosalina yells. Something about her voice snaps me awake.

She moves to dart toward Farron, but I grab her arm. "Rosie, no. He'll never forgive himself if he hurts you."

We're dressed for sex, not a battle. Fuck, Kel is barely conscious. Funny to be on the other side of it for once. And a bit pitiful, realizing that's how I've appeared the majority of the time. The High Prince of Winter will be no help to us.

Ezryn marches back to our group, pure rage radiating off him like waves of heat.

"Get them out of here, Ez," I say. "I'll handle this."

"I'm not leaving Farron." Rosalina glares up at me. "I'm not leaving you."

It's a stupid thing to do, knowing she doesn't feel the same way. But fuck, this might be the last stupid thing I do. I grip her face and kiss her. She tastes like starlight and sun, and I know exactly what I need to do. "I'm going to keep him safe," I murmur against her lips. "But I can't do that with you here, alright?"

"Day..."

"Trust me, Rosalina. I won't let him get hurt."

Finally, she nods, and I push her into Ezryn's arms.

Ezryn looks desperately between Farron, the approaching soldiers, and the goblins. Then he heaves Kel over his shoulder with one hand and grabs Rosalina around the waist with the other. His helm tilts upward to the keep visible over the treeline. To Rosie's balcony.

A vine sprouts from beneath the palm of his gauntlet. It hurtles over the trees before twining around the balcony railing. With a quick tug, Ezryn tests the vine's strength, then tightens his grip on Rosalina and Kel as he uses the vine as a makeshift grappling hook, swinging them up toward the balcony with all the strength and finesse he can muster.

Something in my chest relaxes as they all safely clamber onto the balcony.

Now time to assess my own fucked-up situation. Goblins still pile out of the portal, currently occupied by the raging beast. There's no sign of that bastard Prince of Thorns.

We should have never trusted him. Attend his birthday party? Bull-shit. It was all a distraction so the Below could attack the Autumn Realm. We planted a fucking gateway right into the heart of the city.

I am a fighter. I am a gladiator of the Sun Colosseum. I am the High Prince of the Summer Realm. And I need a fucking weapon.

I sprint toward the goblins. A few of them stumble, startled at my approach. I draw my fist back and punch one straight in the jaw.

It lets out a chittering moan before collapsing. Quickly, I grab its long sword made of thorns and a small wooden shield.

Better than nothing.

It couldn't have come at a better time. Two goblins swing at me, but I easily deflect their blades. These creatures aren't as wild as those who dwell in the Briar; they must be one of the Below's special forces. Pieces of metal glint on their ashen bodies, and some clutch jagged steel weapons.

The goblins surround me. But this isn't the first time I've been outnumbered in a fight. It just takes another tactic. Deep within me, I feel for the Blessing of Summer. It barely stirs, buried within my chest. *The magic of Castletree is weak, barely able to reach me in Autumn.*

Then it catches, sparks to life. A barrier of wind erupts around me, keeping the monsters at bay.

Still within the fray of the burnt library, the wolf rages, tearing at the goblins. He needs to transform back, but even the light of the full moon will not calm his raging, especially with a host of goblins surrounding him.

I need to get him out of here. Leading him away from the library will only take him deeper into the city. I pierce my sword through two unsuspecting goblins, then retreat behind a rotting piece of wood.

Opening the seashell at my neck to reveal the mirror, I angle it to create a portal back to Castletree. I'll open a way home and force him through. Sure, a couple of wayward goblins might follow us, but I can easily dispose of them there.

Except nothing forms. No pool of light. I can't sense the magic of Castletree. I can't find the path home. Have our roses wilted?

Panic stutters in my chest, threatening to consume me. No, I remain a fae man. I can still feel the Blessing of Summer.

But I've been away from Castletree for too long; the magic is too weak to create the path between me and my home. I'll have to figure something else out.

I close my eyes, allowing myself one more breath before I jump back into the battle.

Shredded goblins lie at the wolf's burning feet, but even the giant beast is losing blood. There's too many of them. They swarm Farron, poking and prodding at him with thorn-tipped spears.

Gold glitters at the edges of the library, and the goblins cry in terror. Soldiers' shouts ring in the air. The Autumn Guard has arrived.

Many are on horseback, while others charge in on foot. Gleaming suits of armor, fashioned from interlocked golden leaves, adorn the valiant warriors. In their hands, they wield spears that cleave through the goblin horde with effortless precision, hardly halting their swift, synchronized maneuvers.

"Prince Dayton!" a guard calls to me. "What in the seven realms is happening?"

I can't very well tell him we opened a door for Caspian to bring his army into Coppershire. So, I lie my ass off. "I don't know. I heard goblins and I think I saw the Prince of Thorns."

The Autumn soldier nods, then flanks me as we take on another onslaught. These warriors are powerful, but will it be enough to stop the might of the Below?

Spears dart like lightning into goblin bodies. Swords slice through rotting flesh, and arrows whistle past my ears as they strike. An Autumn mage raises her arms. Enchanted by her magic, the trees enclosing the library spread their branches, making way for more rein-forcements. Archers flood the ramparts and roof of the keep.

Black blood sprays like rain, screams filling the air as goblins fall under Autumn's fury. We might win this. I glance over my shoulder; Farron tears a goblin's head from its body. At least he's currently helping with the problem.

"The big one!" one of the Autumn Guard calls, gesturing to the archers on the rafters. "Take it down."

The archers dip their arrows, then raise them, now writhed in flame. They pull back, aiming straight at—

Farron.

Abandoning my position, I sprint toward the brown wolf, shouting at the top of my lungs. "Stop! Don't shoot!"

They don't hear me. Swift arrows of fire fly down, embedding in the wolf's body. He snarls, and his eyes flash with pain. His focus shifts from the goblins to the golden soldiers.

"This creature isn't a danger to you!" I yell as a soldier prods the beast with his spear. Farron swipes out a paw, sending the soldier flying.

"He's not a danger as long as you don't get too close!" I amend quickly, though I'm not too sure about that. The flames around him expand. What's going to happen when he reaches the city?

"Oh fuck," I groan. *Where are you, Ez?*

Soldiers surround the Autumn Prince. One aims a javelin.

"No!" Water explodes from my palm, flinging the soldier back.

Her javelin clatters to the ground, and she fixes her gaze on me, wide-eyed. "What are you doing, Prince?"

"Don't hurt him! He's—" Proclaiming that this monster is their bloody High Prince will not help Farron's situation. Another member of the Autumn Guard shifts toward Farron, spear raised.

I move without thinking, blocking the soldier's advance. I kick him away from Farron.

And unfortunately, right into the path of a goblin. The creature chitters delightedly, then drag a jagged knife across the fae man's throat.

Shit.

Not exactly what I had in mind.

"You ... You really are all in league with the Below," the soldier on the ground gasps. Her words are loud enough, others look our way.

"No, that's not true," I say, backing up.

"You bear their weapons!" Another soldier points a condemning finger at me and my thorn sword. "Keldarion let the Prince of Thorns into the Winter Realm, and now you bring his monsters here!"

"No," I shout desperately. "Just don't hurt the wolf!"

The wolf, which is right behind me, not an ounce of recognition in its blazing eyes. It swipes a massive paw and strikes me across the chest.

Pain explodes through me as I sail through the air, toppling over myself before I land in a bloody heap on the ground.

Blinking through blurry eyes, five goblins waver above me. "Quick timeout?" I croak.

One goblin arcs its toothed dagger—then pauses, mouth sputtering with black blood, as a long silver sword protrudes from its belly.

The sword retracts, there's a swift whirl, and then all five of the goblins' heads fall cleanly to the ground.

A gloved hand reaches down to pull me to my feet, and damn if I've never been happier to see the Prince of Spring in my whole life.

"Had to get your swords," Ezryn says.

"Tardiness accepted," I say. "Are Rosie and Kel okay?"

"Safe in her room." Ezryn sheathes his own blade and grabs two short swords from his holster.

"My babies." I reach for them. "I could kiss you, Ez. In a mostly platonic way. The metal throws me off a wee bit."

But Ezryn is too still, and my attempt to escape the situation is short-lived, because I know what I'm going to see when I turn around.

Flames dance in the reflection of Ezryn's armor. Farron is coming for us.

"We have to protect him, Ez," I say finally.

"Farron made me promise that if he was ever out of control ... I would stop him."

Now it's my turn to still. I look up at the Prince of Spring. "Yeah, because he's an idiot." I tighten the grip on my swords, and my voice drops to a low growl. "If you want to get to him, you'll have to kill me first."

For a moment, I wonder if he's going to go through with it. Then he turns. "I'll destroy the portal and stop the goblins from coming through."

I nod at my brother. An understanding forms between us—we'll fight to the death to protect each other, even if one of us is fighting for the death of us.

I rush into the fray, moving with more agility and precision with my familiar blades. A sudden, piercing howl rips through the air. Farron writhes in pain, body thrashing amid the goblin swarm and encroaching soldiers. I promised Rosalina, I wouldn't let him get hurt.

The horde of goblins descends upon me from all angles, but I meet them head-on, cleaving and hacking through their ranks with deadly precision, leaving a trail of mangled bodies in my wake. I push to Farron's side, and my heart breaks at the sight of him.

The wolf is covered in goblin bites and scratches, his fur matted with blood. He looks up at me with pained, pleading eyes. *Do you know I'm here?*

Chaos surrounds us, but I crouch down and place a hand on his smoldering paws, even as the fire sears my skin.

"Fare, listen to me," I say, voice shaking. "You need to remember who you are."

Farron howls in agony as another volley of arrows pierces his skin. He thrashes, and I roll away, barely escaping a swipe of his paw. I've never been able to get through to him when he's like this. What kind of idiot am I to think I could do it now?

But I can do what I'm best at, and that's fight.

My world becomes a rush of blades. Soldiers, goblins, Farron. Fighting three enemies that all want to see your guts laid out and not hurting two of them shouldn't be that hard, right?

I try not to harm the Autumn Guard anymore than I must. I focus on knocking them out—which is unfortunate because I could really use their help against all these bloody goblins.

Through the swarm, Ezryn hacks at the portal of thorns, chipping away at it, piece by piece. Beyond him, smoke rises into the air.

The goblins are burning Coppershire.

"High Prince of Summer!" A commanding voice rises over the cacophony, and I whirl to see Princess Niamh in full battle regalia, surrounded by armored knights. "Where is my son? Why do I hear reports you are in league with fiends of the Below?"

"You don't understand, Princess. You can't hurt the wolf."

"Tell me where my son is and lay down your sword, Daytonales." Fury emboldens Niamh's voice. "Or I will show no hesitation with mine."

"I'm protecting him!" I shout. "We were cursed! This *is* your son!"

There's no flicker of recognition in her dark gaze. *She doesn't believe me.*

I drop my swords and close my eyes. I delve deep within myself, feeling for my wolf.

Farron may not know I'm here, but I'll use every ounce of power to protect him. Even if it means revealing our greatest secret.

My body shifts, the golden wolf breaking free of my fae skin. The goblins scatter as I let out a ferocious howl.

Unfortunately, the massive brown wolf and Autumn Guard seem equally unimpressed. Princess Niamh and her knights stare at me in shock.

"I will not allow you to harm him," I growl.

"You are a monster," she hisses, drawing her sword. "What have you done with my son?"

A sickle-shaped claw slices into my side. The brown wolf opens its jaws, teeth gnashing at my soft underbelly.

"Trickery of the Below!" Niamh's voice careens through the air. "Take it down! Fire!"

Arrows pierce my flesh. It's too late. She already thought Keldarion was a traitor, now she believes we all are.

Distantly, I see Ezryn abandon the portal, but there's a huge cluster of goblins between us. And the bastards, seeing I'm mortal, push aside their fear and attack.

Soldiers, goblins, and a beast—their collective force is too overwhelming for me to face. But I have no choice but to try. Farron's safety is vital, and I'll do whatever it takes to keep him from harm. With a deep breath, I steel my resolve and charge the goblins, teeth and claws bared. A rusty sword whistles toward me, but I deftly dodge and sink my fangs into the goblin's neck. The taste of its foul blood fills my mouth, fueling my determination. Yet, more goblins swarm around me, and every time I fend them off, the brown wolf lunges at my legs or the archers rain down another barrage of arrows.

The full moon loosens my hold on the beast. I'm so hurt, my body ripples, shifting back into a fae.

Naked and bloody, I land on my knees. The beast seizes the opportunity and claws my back.

It's so deep, I can feel my blood seeping out of the wound like a waterfall.

"He's defenseless," the archers cry. "Fire!"

The pain of the first arrow in my chest is the worst, piercing deep, hard enough my head flings back. But my body must go numb because I barely feel the next two arrows that hit me, one in my gut, one in the opposite shoulder.

"You have chosen this fate, High Prince of Summer." Niamh's voice is cold as stone. "Whatever bargain you've made with the Below to gain such awful power shall rot away with you in death. I only hope your sister will be more responsible with the Blessing."

I can't stay up anymore, so I fall to the hard earth, landing in something moist. There's enough vision left for me to realize what it is. A shaky laugh escapes my throat. I've always known I'd die in my own blood, but I thought it'd be on the sands of the arena. Never thought it'd be here in the Autumn Realm beside the man I love.

Now that's a funny thought.

The wolf—Farron—stalks closer to me, and even if he's the one who's going to kill me, I'm glad he's here. At the end of it all.

66

ROSALINA

A terrible cry escapes my throat as I watch Dayton fall. I collapse on the balcony, clutching the railing. My body trembles, like the arrows pierce my own chest. "Dayton!"

"Lady Rosalina!" Astrid runs up to my side. "You shouldn't be out here."

Thankfully, she and Marigold are safe, and Papa is secure in the keep.

"I can't just watch this," I say, tears streaming down my face. Below, Coppershire is burning, Farron is trapped inside his beast, Ezryn's surrounded by a sea of goblins, and Dayton's fallen. I don't know if he'll ever get up...

And inside, safe after throwing up in a bucket, is the High Prince of Winter.

Something seethes within me, and I crawl toward him on shaking arms. Traveling through the briars has left my body so weak.

"Oh, dearie," Marigold says, and she and Astrid hoist me up under my arms.

"Take me to my mate," I snarl.

They exchange a worried glance and carry me into the room.

Kel's on the floor, knees to his chest, a glass of water and an empty bucket beside him. At least the vomiting has stopped.

Carefully, Marigold and Astrid lower me to the ground, then back away.

Keldarion turns to me, eyes glassy and rimmed with red, his expression one of twisted torment.

"I shouldn't have let him make that bargain," he says. "I knew better. I *know* better."

His large hands are wrapped over his forearms. Red scratch lines score beneath the bargain bracelet on his wrist, as if he tried to peel off his very skin.

The utter agony erupting from his soul ebbs into mine. I can hardly bear it. "This is my fault, too." I shake my head. "I thought I could get through to him. That maybe somewhere deep down, there was goodness in Caspian."

But I was wrong about him. I should have listened to Kel. There is no sympathy left in me for the Prince of Thorns.

"Do not degrade yourself because he took advantage of your kind heart," Keldarion mumbles. "I should have shielded you from his darkness."

I glance at the window. "They're out there, Kel. Farron, Dayton, and Ez." Tears pool down my cheeks. "We need to help them."

"You drained yourself freeing us from the Below." Keldarion sighs. "The revelry poisoned me. There is nothing I am capable of. I corrupt whatever I touch."

"Start by standing." I grip his shirt, trying to heave him up, but my arms are so weak and he's so heavy.

"After what I've done? I've failed my realm, failed Farron. I've failed you. How can you bear to look at me?"

"I'm not looking at you." I clutch his face. "I *see* you."

He tries to pull away, but I hold him firm. "No, listen. You pretend to hide in Castletree because you don't care. But that's not true. All you do is care. For the realm, for the princes, for me."

"Do not paint me as a hero."

"It is the truth of who you are. You came for me on the ice, then sent me away, even resisting our bond, to keep me safe. You've distanced yourself from your realm since you were cursed. Was it shame? Or were you afraid Caspian would turn his thorns upon Winter if you spent too much time there? You came to defend Autumn against a frost despite the accusations. And you let Farron make his own decisions, setting aside your own desires."

"All that has only led us here," he says.

"Where we can still make this right. They're hurt and lost and frightened. Can't you feel them? They need us."

"My Rose," he rasps, "if you only knew how selfish my wretched heart truly is."

"Wretched or not, I know what your heart does best." I drop my forehead to his in surrender. "Shelter those you care about."

I kiss him gently, feeling my shattered heart blazing to life against his touch. His mouth opens to mine in a longing sigh. The fire grows. The bond between us stirs in pleasure and might. "Kel, my mate, you are the Protector of the Realms," I say. "So, protect them."

67

EZRYN

Splintering pain radiates through my shoulder as I collide with the massive brown wolf. Farron's thrown off balance, and he sails through the air, landing in a cadre of assailing goblins. *That'll keep you busy.*

My heart thuds in my throat as I scamper around, looking for Dayton's body amongst the chaos. I find him bloody and gasping for breath. If I had gotten here a second later...

Farron would have ripped him apart.

Goblins ascend upon him and with a growl, I grab one and twist its neck until it snaps. *Snap. Snap. Snap.* Then I sink to my knees, blood and mud coating my armor. "I'm here, Day."

His eyes look unseeing into the dark sky. Rattling breaths wheeze out of his throat, becoming shallower and faster, like the fluttering of a dying bird's wings fighting to stay adrift. Distantly, I hear the clash of swords and screams of the wounded—goblin and fae alike. An arrow rings off my armor, but I ignore it, not even bothering to check if it is the crooked shaft and crude fletching of the goblins or the fine craftsmanship of the fae.

"I'm here," I say again. Stars Above, the blood. It sputters out of his mouth with each breath. I need to work fast, but there's so much going on. I barely have time to bring my hands to his chest before having to block a goblin's sword with my gauntlet.

"Hold on, Day," I growl as I crush my thumbs into the goblin's eye sockets and drop its dead body. "I'm going to fix you."

I need to stop his bleeding, but my magic feels so far away, trapped within the sick bark of Castletree. Even the most elaborate healing I've done before seems nothing compared to the chest of my brother, struck with arrows. I sit on my heels, blood flinging from my leather gloves as my hands shake.

All around is death, death, and more death. Fire rages, and the sickly smell of burning goblin flesh stings the air. Farron roars as an arrow sinks deep into his shoulder. From across the burned library, Princess Niamh lowers her bow and stares at him with hatred.

My vision tunnels to blackness. Everything feels muted and distant as Dayton's gaze flicks to me. "Ez," he gasps, voice barely intelligible, "I-I'm afraid."

"Day." I wrap my arms around my brother and heave him to my chest. Dayton is dying. Farron will be shot. And I will roast within my armor until I am nothing more than a charred skeleton upon this field.

Dayton's blood splatters over me and I can't help it: an inhuman scream tears out of my throat. I never wanted to hold the dying body of anyone I loved ever again. My gaze shifts up to Farron. *Not Farron. The beast.*

He asked me to kill him if he lost control. I failed my promise. Now, when the sun cuts over the horizon and the wolf retreats, Farron will have to live with knowing he caused the death of his beloved. He will have to stare into Dayton's lifeless eyes and know the truth of his destruction.

It is a sorrow I would not wish upon my most hated enemy.

A sorrow I cannot let Farron carry for the rest of his life.

I drop Dayton in the mud. With a deep breath, I reach for the first arrow, my fingers finding purchase on the slick shaft. The sound of the battle fades into nothingness as I pull the arrow out with a sharp, sudden yank. Dayton's blood spurts out in a thick stream, soaking my hands and armor. He arches off the ground, his back bowing as he screams in agony. My hands shake as I toss the arrow aside and grab the second one, tearing it out with another violent pull. Dayton's body writhes beneath me, and his screams echo in my ears. I reach for the third arrow, hesitating for a moment before gritting my teeth and ripping it out in one swift motion. Dayton's body goes limp. Blood oozes from the gaping wounds in his chest.

I need to stop the bleeding. I tear off my gloves and place my hand over the first wound. My magic is far away. But Autumn's magic is close; Farron is close.

"Let me do this," I whisper to the Above, to myself. "Let me save him."

You'll only kill him too, a voice whispers inside me. But this time, I don't listen.

Heat bursts within my heart, a burning reserve that fills my veins. I know this power is devastating, but I grit my teeth, temper it.

Fire bursts forth from my fingertips, blazing and bright. A comforting warmth blankets my skin. I focus my energy on the first wound, and the flames respond, licking the jagged edges of flesh. Dayton lurches, crying out, but I don't stop. The heat cauterizes, sealing the gash and renewing it, like a forest regrowing after a terrible wildfire.

Red, raw skin emerges from beneath the flames, and Dayton collapses to the mud. I do the second wound. Then the third. My vision swims as the fire fades, but somehow, I'm able to wedge my fingers into the crook of his neck to find his heartbeat. *Steady.*

Vertigo hits me from the exertion, and I collapse over Dayton's body.

Beyond the darkening edges of my vision, goblins grimace down at me. There are so many... *At least Farron won't die thinking it was he who killed Dayton.*

I can barely stay conscious, but I know we're at the end of all things now. A terrible howl fills the night as mounted fae surround Farron, including his mother. She raises a golden sword above her head.

I need to get to him, but I can scarcely move. The magic needed to heal my brother has dried all the wells of power within me. A goblin's thorny hammer smacks against my chest plate, and I cry out from the impact. I need to ... I need to ... I need—

A burst of white shines across my vision, and a man leaps down into the chaos, magic radiating around him like flashes of lightning.

Keldarion, High Prince of Winter and Protector of the Realms, has come for us.

He moves like a hunting cat, streaming through the hordes of goblins with long knives crafted of ice. Beneath each step, fractals spread over the ground, extinguishing the flames with a hiss. A feral rage claims his features.

My bones ache as I try to sit up. With a wave of Kel's hand, the surrounding air crystallizes. Cold energy ripples outward, and a swell of frozen spikes erupt from the earth. The goblins shriek, fleeing before him, some pierced upon the spikes, others caught in the spreading frost. I watch with horror as their bodies stiffen and gleam with ice. The same as if they were attacked by a winter wraith.

"Kel," I try to call, but my voice is weak, raspy. "Enough."

Ice shoots from his every step, claiming whatever is in its path. The charred remains of the library, the fleeing goblins ... the Autumn Guard. A horse whinnies and rears, nearly throwing its rider off, but Keldarion's terror takes them first, freezing its hooves to the ground.

With growing horror, I regard the frost crawling toward us. "Dayton, we have to go." I force myself to my hands and knees, ignoring the nausea swimming through me from using so much power. But Dayton's unconscious head lolls to the side. I grip him under the arms and pull. Stars, he's so damned heavy. Frost licks at his boots.

"Kel!" I rasp, but he can't hear me. He is a winter storm, tearing through the battlefield as an icy tempest spirals around his hands. Huge, jagged shards of ice spring from the ground, and goblins and fae alike flee from his power. This is his magic at its weakest...

"Fuck," I swear and drop Dayton. Using the very last dregs of my energy, I raise my hands through the air, causing root and vine to propel up in a thick barrier between us and the frost.

I collapse to the ground, begging the Above that it will hold. Huge pillars of ice burst through the thorn-crusted portal which we created hours ago. Kel stands, shoulders heaving.

"Kel," I say, and it's like my voice carries on the icy breeze. "It's enough." He turns to me, and something flashes in his gaze.

The frost stops crawling forward, and Kel looks down at his hands, a horrified expression on his face. My root barrier cracks and falls to the earth. I wish I could sit up, but even that is beyond me. All I can do is stare at the frozen wasteland: horrific ice statues of screaming goblins, fae, and steeds litter the area.

A blood-curdling scream pierces the air. Princess Niamh. She emerges from behind her guards, frozen sentinels with their shields out. But she's not looking at them. She gapes up at the alder tree.

It is completely frozen, a skeletal ice structure. And sitting at its base is Farron's wolf. He stares up at it, many arrows piercing his fur. His head tips back, and he howls, a forlorn and lonesome sound. Deep within my chest, I feel my own wolf desperate to join the call.

Princess Niamh's eyes hold a fevered look as she turns to Keldarion. "The truth reveals itself. I opened my doors to you. I offered you mercy. And behold what you've done!"

Kel steps back. "I am not the frost tearing across the Autumn Realm. I will not apologize for protecting the High Princes of Castletree."

Darkness covers Niamh's gaze. She looks behind her at the remaining soldiers who narrowly avoided Kel's frost. "Arrest the traitorous High Prince of Winter." Then she turns to me and Dayton. "And the High Princes of Spring and Summer for conspiring with him."

Guards surround Kel, swords raised. He lets himself be pushed to his knees. His hair sticks to his sweat-strewn face, and he grits his teeth. "I surrender because I am not your enemy. We are not aligned with the Below."

I'm pulled up by my arms. Ropes are roughly bound around my wrists. Two guards heave Dayton up. "Careful with him. He's injured." The soldiers ignore me.

"Take them to the dungeon," Princess Niamh orders. She turns, her dark red cape snapping in the moonlight. "And kill the beast."

"That is your son!" Kel cries. "That beast is Farron. You cannot kill him—"

Niamh's face flashes with heartbreak and horror. "If this is true," Niamh says quietly, "then he has fallen to darkness. He is a shame to his people. To his home. To me." Her eyes shine and her lip quivers. "I wish I had never passed on Autumn's Blessing, for then such evil would never have come to Autumn. With his death, I could take back the Blessing to protect our realm."

The wolf trembles, its own eyes blazing. Then it sprints away from the burnt library.

One of the soldiers raises a bow, arrow notched, but Niamh waves him down. "Let the beast go. We will hunt it in due time." She turns and stares at us. "We have enough executions to worry about."

68

ROSALINA

"Oh! I can't watch!" Astrid throws her hands over her face. "Describe what's happening."

"Well," Marigold leans her busty body over the balcony, "everything is particularly icy. And, oh dear…" Her voice drops sensually. "Oh my my my."

"What could possibly make you say that?" I run up beside them.

"The master and the other princes… They're being handcuffed."

"Marigold!" Astrid scolds.

"What? I can't help it. Danger really gets the juices flowing, if you know what I mean."

"Marigold," I sigh, "we *always* know what you mean."

But hey, we all deal with terrible situations in our own way, and I'm not one to judge. Because this is the most terrible of all terrible situations. Farron has fled, and the princes are in chains.

A clattering sounds from outside my room. After Kel literally jumped off our balcony, I felt my energy return slightly. I'm not sure if it was because of whatever fire passed between our mate bond or if my body kicked me with a shot of adrenaline, but I'm grateful for the boost.

Cracking the door, I peer out into the living chambers. A host of guards searches the area. They bust into Ezryn's room. I quickly close the door and lock it, though I doubt that'll do any good.

"I think you're about to change your opinion on handcuffs, Marigold," I hiss, "because we're about to be in some."

"Oh goodie." She winks, then frowns. "Though it's not as fun if I'm clothed."

"We need to think. We won't be able to help anyone if we're caught."

"Marigold and I can turn into our animals to hide," Astrid suggests.

"That might work for a bit." I kneel and place a palm on the floor, trying to feel for the thorns. If only I hadn't forgotten my crown on Caspian's betraying head. They felt so easy to connect to in the Below and at Castletree. But Castletree was already rife with briars, and there had to be some reserve of power in the Below I was pulling on, a supply I can't reach here.

My hands drift over the rose necklace at my breast. Maybe...

A commotion sounds outside the door: the clash of metal, a guard crying out, the clunk of armor hitting the ground. Astrid and Marigold both gasp. My heart pounds, but I steel myself. "We have to see what's going on—"

The door caves in. Astrid gives a loud peep and transforms into a white hare. I catch her in my arms.

But standing there isn't the host of Autumn soldiers.

"Billy and Dom?" I gasp. "Papa?"

"Looked like you were in need of rescue." Billy grins.

"Oh well, well, well." Marigold bats her eyelashes. "I've always wanted to be saved by a strong hero."

My father gives an awkward huff and places a firm hand on my shoulder. "How are you doing, my girl?"

"Better now that you're here," I tell him. "Hey, is that a frying pan?"

"Oh yes." Papa holds up the cast iron proudly. "I was having a wee midnight snack with the lads when some foul creature came charging in and bit the hand off the chef. This thing gave it a mighty good smart."

I hurry back to the door, still clutching Astrid to my chest. Outside, I see the guards tied up with rope, gags in their mouths. "These are your men."

Darkness clouds Billy's face. "After goblins attacked the kitchen, we crept to the hubbub in the ruins of the old library. We saw Dayton fighting like a warrior trying to protect that big wolf. He kept yelling it was Farron."

"At first, we thought he was crazy. Corrupted by the Below like our mother said." Dom's voice wavers. "But then I saw the beast's eyes."

"Day wouldn't leave him," Billy says. "It's Farron, isn't it? That wolf is our brother?"

I nod solemnly. "It is. He's under a curse. He can't control himself when he's like that. Caspian tricked us into letting the goblins into Coppershire. It was our fault, but we're trying to do what's best for the city, for Farron."

"That's what we thought," Dom says. "But Mother won't listen to any of it. She thinks it's connected to the Below. All the princes and you."

"Kel only froze the keep to protect Farron and stop the goblins," I urge. "Believe me."

They both nod. "That's why we're getting you out of here. But we don't know where to go. Outside the city, that frost has gotten close."

Absently, I pat Astrid's soft white fur. "This is such a mess. The High Princes are prisoners, the frost is nearly upon the city, and Farron … He's so lost."

"That wolf was powerful," Billy says. "All that fire. Why can't Farron use that when he's not foaming at the mouth?"

"Fire…" Images flash before me: flickering pages in the wind, the grimoires of the alder tree. "Farron mentioned powerful but dark spells in the alder tree. I think he was frightened of them, but we've got nothing to lose now. Do you think there could be something useful?" I give a deep sigh. "Never mind. Even if there was, the wolf tore the place to shreds. It's all in ruins."

"Hey." Papa holds both my shoulders. "I've been piecing together ruins my whole life. Take me there, and I'll find what you need."

"As royal blood, we can get you in," Dom says.

"Problem is," Billy adds, "only a High Prince would be powerful enough to use any of the spells in there."

I look out the window. "I'll find him."

"Rose," Papa says, "I saw that beast. It's too dangerous."

"Farron always turns back into a man at dawn. The sun will soon crest over the horizon, and he'll wake up scared and alone. I have to be there for him."

Papa considers me. "My brave girl. You remind me of your mother with that look. Such fierce determination."

I turn to Marigold. "You and Astrid are going to use all your wiles to get down to the dungeon. Tell the princes I'm safe. I don't want them to do anything rash on my behalf. Right now, they have to show Princess Niamh they're not the enemy."

Fear still courses through me, but having a plan kindles my hope. Its spark catches in the others' gazes as well.

"I'm always good at doing what I'm told, darling." Marigold winks.

"We'll do right by you, Rose," Papa says. "I'll be here for you now. Whatever you need."

I squeeze his hand. "Have courage, and don't give up hope."

"Ah, but sweet Astrid," Dom mumbles. "Where is she?"

There's an explosion of fur in my arms, and then Astrid's thin naked frame stands in front of me. She pumps a fist in the air. "I'm here and ready to save the princes!"

Dom and Billy go completely red.

Despite it all, a smile creeps up my face. Marigold gently places a blanket over Astrid, and I survey our team. The High Princes, the most powerful men in the Enchanted Vale are in trouble, and it might just take a human archeologist, two young pranksters, a timid hare, a lusty raccoon, and me—the Lady of Castletree—to save them.

69

ROSALINA

Wind tears at the strands of my hair as Amalthea streaks across the fields outside of Coppershire. Hands shaking on the reins, I gulp down a breath, feeling the power of my mount beneath me. I've never taken a horse beyond a canter before, but now I urge my steed forward, barely holding on.

I need to find him.

Normally, mornings in the Autumn Realm are filled with cool sunshine, painting the hills in orange and red. But dark clouds cover the sky, and a crack sounds in the distance.

After I changed into proper travel gear and quickly packed a bag of clothes for Farron, Dominic and Billagin snuck me and my horse out of Coppershire. They've returned to join my father in the remains of the burned library. Maybe, just maybe, they can find something amidst the wreckage.

Where is he? Farron's wolf had torn off through the city and up the hills, but dawn has long spread over the Autumn Realm. I can only imagine him, naked and afraid, huddled into himself.

It's like I can feel it in my chest: the grief, the terror, the sadness. He's alone out there, and I won't stop until he's in my arms.

A trail of burned grass leading up a hill alerts me that I'm on the right track, but it's deeper than that. An invisible tether pulls me forward. *This way, this way, this way,* the wind seems to whisper, tugging at my braid. *This way, this way, this way,* the rhythm of my horse's hooves says. *This way, this way, this way,* rings in every beat of my heart.

We crest the top of a hill when I see the ruined Shrine of Nymphia, the forest, and the graves of the fallen soldiers among the chrysanthemums. I pull to a stop. We were here two months ago when we first learned of the winter wraiths. My horse paces anxiously. A dark shadow creeps over my heart, weaving around that unseen string. Now, I can't hear the heartsong guiding me forward. Now, the world seems to scream at me to stay away.

The clouds crack open, and rain trembles to the earth.

I blink the water out of my eyes, staring deep into the ruins. "Come on," I urge Amalthea. "This way."

But my mount will have none of it. She whinnies frantically and shuffles on the spot.

"Come on. To the ruins," I say with more command this time, giving the reins a snap for good measure. My horse responds with a desperate bray.

"Fine then." I slip off, pulling my pack with me. Somehow, I know I've found what I'm looking for.

As soon as I'm on the ground, Amalthea turns and sprints away from the ruins.

I shiver in the growing downpour. With only the wild realmlands surrounding me, I am truly alone.

Taking careful steps, I make my way over to Nymphia's ancient shrine. A putrid smell wafts through the air, the stench of decay and molding earth. I gag and cover my mouth. It's like I can *taste* it, an acrid metallic tang of blood and rot that clings to my tongue. *What is that?*

I step into the ruins, my travel boots sinking into the layer of water pooling on the stony ground. "Farron?" I whisper, but my voice has no power.

Then I hear it: deep, guttural breathing like the bellows of a roaring fire. My heart hammers against my ribs, and my mouth has gone dry. I tuck my body tight to a pillar and peek around.

And there he is. The beast of Autumn.

Farron.

My hands lurch to my lips to cover my scream. Because despite it being day, the fae man is nowhere in sight. There's not even the usual brown wolf I've become accustomed to.

There is only a monster.

This wolf is a repulsive behemoth of death and decay. Matted fur the color of rusted iron bristles with each ragged breath. Rotten chunks of apple and pear tangle in its coat, their sickly scent mixing with the other stenches. Cobwebs stretch across the mass of his body, and I swear I see the skitter of bugs around its ears. Patches of molding leaves create a hideous tapestry over its face.

I swallow down vomit, my fingers gripping tightly into the stone, so I don't fall apart. Where is he? Where is Farron?

Maybe the grief was too much. Maybe it was his own self-loathing. Or maybe his rose has finally given up. But this monster is not my Farron.

I need to get out of here before it sees me. My calf throbs from a long-healed wound. I saw what it did to Dayton, and there is no one here to save me if the beast sets its sights on me. Slowly, I creep away from the pillar.

I'm nearly out of the ruins when something blue flashes in my peripheral. That invisible tether snaps taut in my chest, and I turn one last time to stare at the beast.

It's staring back at me.

I stumble away. The eyes are deep amber, like smoldering embers in a fire, and they flicker with fierce intelligence.

The wolf prowls to its feet, revealing its true size. Farron's form before had been but a dog compared to this creature; in fact, now it would overshadow even Kel's giant wolf.

It lowers its head and bares its sharp fangs, the face of pure preda-tory evil. Its body shakes with a deep and primal hunger. I am paralyzed in its wake, unable to stop as it measures me against some wild and unknowable standard.

Maybe … Maybe he's still in there.

"Farron," I whisper. "It's me." My voice is barely audible over the pounding rain. Huge, hot clouds of breath shudder out of its maw.

It was a mistake to come here. I thought I could be brave. I thought I could save him.

But there's nothing left to be saved.

I turn on my heel, water splashing up, and sprint from the ruins.

A howl sounds behind me, loud enough to send pebbles skittering over the stony ground. If I can get to the Emberwood, maybe I can hide among the trees.

The wolf's thundering gait pounds in my ears, but I can't turn around. I run across the grasslands, ribs aching with the force of my heart. My fear threatens to paralyze me, but I can't let it. I have to keep running, keep moving, or I'll die.

My legs burn, and I swear my lungs may burst before I reach the treeline. I dare a look back to see the great beast snarling down the hill, teeth shimmering with saliva.

Its fetid scent drags closer, and I throw myself into the forest, pushing bracken and bushes out of my way. With the storm clouds and the towering trees, the forest is dark, and branches pull at my braid and clothes.

The wolf charges behind me, eyes wild with hunger. Brush flattens beneath its great weight, and it has no care for the bushes that snag its fur. It is made entirely of coiled muscle and sinew, and if I don't think of something quick, I'll be dead.

I dodge between trees, jumping over fallen logs and dipping under low-hanging branches. A scream pulls at the edges of my throat, but there's no one to hear me. I need every precious breath. The wolf is close, too close, its rancid breath heating the back of my neck.

Never in my life have I ever run so fast: the forest is a kaleidoscope, trees whipping past, their leaves rustling in a chorus of warning.

My legs will tire. My lungs will give out.

He will keep hunting me until I am claimed.

The trees condense to a thicket ahead. Briars have sheltered me before; perhaps I can lose the beast in the dense underbrush. With a desperate cry, I fling myself into a small gap in the brambles. I belly crawl deep into the tangle of thorns, ignoring the pain as they scrape along my cheeks and hands.

A frustrated growl sounds as the wolf snaps at the entrance, its colossal shape hindered by the briars. It pulls out and stares at me with an intensity beyond any animal, as if to say, *I will have you.*

My whole body thuds with my rapid heartbeat. To my left, the brambles shake with thundering steps, and a powerful sniff, sounds. It's searching the thicket for a way in.

Tears and blood stream down my face. No, no. It wasn't supposed to be like this. It wasn't supposed to *end* like this. I was meant to find Farron. *My* Farron. Not this beast that has stolen his body and soul.

I clasp my knees and curl up. What else is left? The beast has taken Farron, and it will take me too. I'll never find him, never see that sweet smile again or hear his laugh or spend another moment in his quiet company.

He'll be lost forever in the dark, trapped inside the rage and desolation of the beast. He'll never realize what he's capable of. How there is strength in stillness. How peace is his power.

My body shakes, but it's not from fear. It's from anger. My hands grip the wet ground, and I stare up into the brambles, letting the rain that filters through splatter my face.

"Who are you to judge him?" I whisper into the void, speaking to the Enchantress wherever she may be. "How can you say his heart deserves this curse when you have not seen how he struggles each day to be worthy of his realm? When you have not heard the kindness in his voice when he speaks to his family, both his blood and his chosen? When you have not felt what it is to be *loved by him?*"

Now, my voice is not a whisper. I don't care if the wolf hears. Let him. Let the whole damn realm hear me. I push to my hands and knees, eyes wide and focused.

That aching *thing* inside my chest reverberates like sparks cracking from a hearth. Farron. He's here somewhere, and he's alone and lost and scared.

I will show him that the fire burns within us. I will show myself.

I creep out from the brambles and stand up among the rain-drenched woods. The wolf digs at the end of the thicket but straightens as it sees me. It bares its maw in a vicious snarl.

That blue light from earlier flashes in my vision again. Moving with graceful fluidity, a shimmering will-o'-wisp dances through the air between us.

I realize why it's here.

"I know you're there, Farron," I say. "I've come to find you. I will *always* find you. And I'm not frightened. You don't have to be either."

The wolf growls and snaps at the will-o'-wisp that flutters around its snout.

"You and I are alike, Fare. The world has always been too big for us, hasn't it? Too loud. Too bright. But when we're together, I can face the whole damned realm and everyone in it. Because you are my strength. You are my courage. I feel it here, within my chest." I clutch at my heart, reveling in its steady beat. "My fire is within. I've always been afraid to see what happens when it burns. But I will light the whole world up for you." I take a step toward him, chin held high. "I will light up for you."

The beast lowers its head to the ground, stalking forward. Something flashes in its golden eyes. Eyes I know so well. Eyes that I love.

Blue light surrounds me. More will-o'-wisps. They paint my body with shimmering light. A single teardrop whispers down my face, but I've never felt stronger. "The fires of your heart cannot burn me, Farron. I have felt their warmth, and I would have them engulf me."

The wolf lunges, and so do I. I wrap my arms around its massive neck, letting it tackle me to the ground. My face burrows into its fur. I barely notice the putrid scent, or the sticky feel of rotten leaves on my fingertips. All I care about is that he's in my arms.

"I love you, Farron," I whisper. "I love you."

At first, there is only the wolf's guttural snarl, its hot breath on my skin, the pounding rain.

And then there is a spark.

It shudders through me, shifting and twisting, that invisible tether that's been guiding me all morning. The wolf pulls back to stare at me, gaze wild but in a different way than before. More will-o'-wisps descend, now covering the wolf, too. A glow burns within my skin, calling to a kindred flame.

To the wolf's flame.

Farron's flame.

His body shimmers and shivers, the fur becoming flesh, claws to tender hands. All the while, the eyes remain the same. Magic ignites around us, and I can hear our hearts like a chorus: not separate, but a single entity, beating stronger than I've ever heard.

Farron's fae body collapses against mine, still covered by the will-o'-wisps. Through their wavering blue flames, I see something that makes my heart take flight.

His body is healed, the wounds of the wolf faded away. And his mate bond … It's not tangled anymore. It's bright and beaming and beautiful. A glowing star.

I reach for him, and the will-o'-wisps disperse, their movements playful as they dance away into the forest. I clutch Farron's face in my hands, staring at him with eyes that seem to see for the very first time.

Rain slicks his hair to his forehead, runs over his lips.

"You found me," he finally says.

"No, Farron," I say, "you found me."

Farron, High Prince of Autumn and my mate, kisses me. A kiss born from the ashes.

70

FARRON

There is nothing but the taste of her lips, her sweet breath whispering over my face, the tangle of her wet hair in my hands. Everything that I once was, has floated away like cinders in the wind, and now there are only the parts of me held together by her.

She and I.

Woven together for eternity.

We kneel in front of each other, mindless of the mud and rain. I brush the damp strands of hair off her forehead. I have gazed upon the most precious art in the history of the Enchanted Vale, read poetry that would make the ancient gods weep, and studied maps of every wonder in the fae and human worlds.

But nothing compares to Rosalina's beauty. It's as if I can see her heart—her kindness, her joy, her humor, her generosity—wavering around like spirals of color. She's glowing.

Mate.

My mate.

Born from the same star.

I know it, deep within every piece of me, that she is why I'm still here. Why the Enchantress did not allow me to cower away forever.

The Enchantress gave me a second chance. So, I could love Rosalina.

So, I could be loved by her.

Tears mix with rain, and I blink rapidly so I don't lose one second of staring at her. A million thoughts compete in my mind: How did I get so lucky to find my fated mate, and that it is Rosalina? My best friend? And how had we found each other when I was caged within the darkness of the beast? I'd heard her calling for me, and for the first time, there was something beyond the shadows.

Something worth fighting for.

Other thoughts threaten to crowd my consciousness: flashes of tooth and blood and ice.

But Rosalina cups my face and smiles, and it's as if daybreak spreads over my mind.

Only one thought is left.

Mate.

My mate.

I must claim her.

There is too much space between us; my lip curls back in an act too familiar to the wolf inside me. A visceral need that goes far beyond hunger or thirst. Rosalina undoubtedly senses the change in me as her pupils dilate, and her chest heaves with breath. As the rich scent of her arousal floods my senses, my control slips away.

Not in the usual way where I lose to the wolf.

This time, I'm losing to her. And she can have me.

My hands rake down her neck, her arms. She hurries to unbutton her blouse, and I pull it off and toss it to the side. Frantically, she reaches behind her back and unhooks her brassière.

My breath catches in my throat. Rain drips down the tip of her nose, over her collarbone, over the peaks of her breasts. Joy radiates from her beaming face.

I rise up on my knees and stare down at her. I wind her braid round and round my hand, then pull it gently so she's looking up at me.

"You are my mate," I say. "Submit to me. Let me claim you as mine. And in return, I will show you our love has always been inevitable."

Her lip tremors, eyelashes kissed with rain, but her gaze is fully on me. "Farron, darling," she whispers, "I will always be yours. Take me now. Take me forever."

With her permission, I give myself to the bond. I push her to the ground and pull off her skirt and undergarments in one swift motion. Stars, she looks gorgeous, her pale, soft body squirming in the mud. Rain pounds my back as I crawl over her, but I don't care. There's a wildness in us; the press of the earth, crisp scent of the trees, and the rain only heightens this feeling of *aliveness*. Alive in a way I've never been before.

Our bodies tangle together. Closer, closer, I crave her skin on mine, my mouth aching for her lips, her throat, her collarbone, her breasts. Everything all at once. She giggles as I move her so she's on top of me, then laughs harder, noticing she's painted in muddy handprints. Gods, I love her laugh, but I need her mouth, and I take it.

"Farron," she murmurs against my lips. "Mine. *Mine.*"

We roll again, and I pin her beneath me, an unconscious growl erupting as my length presses against her. Deep within my heart, I know I will spend every moment of her life discovering her body, finding new ways to worship her.

But I've waited too long already. I *must* claim her.

She peers up at me through her lashes, a look both sensual and intimate. A dare and a need all at once. I position myself at her entrance and inhale.

There is a deep and ancient knowing in my chest. When we do this, nothing will ever be the same. All the walls I've built to shelter myself will tear down. I will never just be Farron anymore.

I will be hers. Forever.

I will be yours. Forever. Her soft voice drifts into my mind. In her eyes, I see the weavings of the cosmos, the flickered breaking of a star that knew we would one day be reunited.

I sheathe myself within her.

7I

ROSALINA

A cry escapes my lips as my mate fills me: a sound of pleasure, of completion, of letting in his divine love.

Farron cradles my head, and I loop my arms around his neck to tether myself to the earth.

The space between us feels alight, our breath and gazes weaving together.

He thrusts.

Tears stream down my face as he moves inside me. There's a strange sense of beginning. It's the first time I've ever been with Farron like this, but also the first time I've ever *made love*. Nothing in my past could compare.

His pace increases, and I lose myself to the wildness. He's loving me and fucking me all at once. We're both two feral creatures in the mud, and one intertwined being that *is* the mud, and the rain, and the canopy of maple leaves. I see his realm as he sees it: images of golden hills and bursting fields painting the edges of my vision which is filled with him. His beautiful face, gasping in bliss.

My mate.

I arch my back, his body fitting so perfectly with mine, pain and pleasure entwining from the mass of his manhood. My legs wrap around his hips, and I pull him harder into me, wishing I could dissolve within his skin.

With each thrust, a ferocity steals his gaze, his pupils blown. His pace increases; my fingernails scrape down his spine as growing heat spreads over my body. "Fare—"

He slams to the hilt, his voice now a throaty roar. Farron may be a prince, but he fucks me like a beast.

The invisible tie between us sings, and I claw at his neck to bring him down to my lips. "Kiss me," I beg.

I know by the flash of surrender in his eyes, this is our moment. This is where we descend into the divine.

My body erupts with release as he explodes within me. A pure, unbridled ecstasy floods my heart. Words spark in my mind amidst the bursting color and beauty of his face: *Starlight igniting your body, having the empty part of your heart filled.*

That's what's happening and more, so much more, as if the sparkling energy of the cosmos flows through my veins. My soul has been reaching out to Farron, from the moment I first found him in the dungeon. How my body knew how to find him when I didn't have the words to understand. And he's always been reaching back.

Now, the rest of the world melts away in a distant, insignificant blur, leaving only the pulsing intensity of our bond. A love that ignited the darkest corners of ourselves.

Farron collapses on top of me. I revel in the steady beat of his heart against mine.

"The rain has stopped," I murmur as I slowly drift my hands through his hair, over the sharp point of his ear.

He rolls to the side, staring up at the tree canopy. I mimic him, marveling that the dark clouds have passed so quickly. Golden light shivers through the trees, making their wet leaves glimmer.

"Rosalina," he murmurs and rubs his chest.

"Farron," I reply and lie on my side so I can hold his hand. "I love you."

He blinks at me.

The words come out of me in an unhurried breath. "I love you in the starlight way."

The softest smile pulls at the corners of his lips. "I love you in the starlight way."

"And I'm honored to be your mate."

Something shifts on his face, and he sits up. "Rosie..." He staggers to his feet, steps unbalanced.

"Are you okay?"

A beam of orange-gold bursts through the trees, painting his skin in brilliant light. He turns to look at me before his body shines with thousands of iridescent sparkles.

"Farron!"

His back arches and celestial light streams from all around him. Then with a great howl, the silhouette of a wolf shines behind him before dissipating like motes of dust in a sunbeam.

Farron falls to the ground, and I scramble over. "Farron?"

He lifts his head, and his auburn hair falls away from his face. I gasp.

His eyes sparkle with newfound joy, and his skin seems to gleam as if lit from within.

"Rosalina," he says and cups my face.

Through the bond, I feel our shared realization.

Farron's curse has been broken.

72

ROSALINA

Farron and I walk through the forest hand in hand. I can't help sneaking glances up at him; he's always been handsome, but there's a luminance to him that wasn't there before. A tinge of nervousness flickers in my belly, and Farron chuckles to himself.

Thankfully, I brought two extra sets of clothes in my pack, so I didn't have to put on my soaked outfit. We're both dressed in simple traveler's attire—trousers, long tunics, and Autumn cloaks—but he's never looked more princely.

My body hums as we walk, a satisfied ache pulsing between my legs. *So that's what sex is supposed to be like.* I'll have to drink that tea Marigold told me about.

Other issues press on my mind. I have to ask Farron if he will return to Coppershire to confront his mother, his people. I informed him of what happened while he was lost in his beast, and that Dayton is safe, but we need to free the other princes.

"Watch out." Farron pushes me back as we step out of the treeline. The edge of the forest shines with ice, and the hills are covered in blue frost. Tendrils leach down, weaving their way out of the woods like sickly veins.

"It's all such a mess," Farron whispers. "The frost is so close to

Coppershire now. Kel, Dayton, and Ez are imprisoned by my own realm. My people are on the brink of war. And my mother believes me to be nothing more than a monster." He shakes his head. "What can we do against such obstacles?"

I squeeze his hand three times. "Unite. Coppershire needs their High Prince."

Farron opens his mouth to respond when a rumble shakes the ground. The sound of muffled shouts and commands carry over the wind, and a flock of birds screech up into the sky.

We exchange a look and run up the crest of the hill. Farron lies flat and pulls me down beside him. I gasp, fear thundering through me.

A war camp spreads out on the chrysanthemum field beside the old ruins, a teeming mass of tents and soldiers. My heart sinks at the sight of the telltale blue fabric of their shelters and armor. "These are Winter troops," I say.

"Dissenters, by the looks of it," Farron whispers. "They bear no sigil nor flag."

My gaze is drawn to an icy dais in the center of the camp. Standing atop it is none other than the vizier himself, Perth Quellos.

Even from so far above, I can see the conniving glint in his eye as he observes the gathering. On his head sits a metal crown encircling a bright green gem; I remember seeing him wear it back at Castletree. Emerald mist writhes and shifts around it like a living thing.

A cloaked figure stands beside him. Though their face is hidden by the hood, the same green glow emanates from the shadows. Do they wear a crown of the same?

"What's going on?" I whisper to Farron.

"I don't know." Anger flashes in his gaze. "They're camped upon the burial grounds from the War of Thorns. Such utter disrespect to our history, to our dead."

The crowd hushes as the vizier raises his hands. Dark charisma oozes out of him, a very different presence than I've ever seen him possess.

"Beloved denizens of Winter," Perth begins, his voice carrying across the wind with a magically amplified force, "long have you

430

waited for our prodigal prince to return and lead our realm to right-eous deliverance. Standing before me are those of you who were brave enough to cast off your shackles of loyalty and instead stand for what is right."

A booming applause rages up from the soldiers. Some clatter swords to shields.

"Long have the realms been at the whims of the High Rulers. Long have we pretended they are the tenets of Queen Aurelia herself! But the Queen abandoned us, and Keldarion has followed suit. It is time for us to stop believing the lie that the High Princes want what is best for us. Instead, we must carve our own fate into history!"

I can barely hear the roar of applause over my pounding heart. If this is a Winter rebellion, why are they in Autumn?

The vizier spreads his fingers wide, voice hoarse and raspy. "I have seen with my own eyes what evil has befallen the Winter Prince! In my quest to free the Vale of its attachments to these futile leaders, my designs accidentally crossed into Autumn territory. But now, word comes that Coppershire shelters the High Princes, and they intend to make war on Winter. So, we shall strike first!"

Farron grabs my shaking hands in his. A fervor takes the crowd, and Perth's crown blinks with that poisonous inward light.

"Coppershire will be the first to fall, but the rest of Autumn will soon follow. Then we shall take Spring and Summer. All the realms will know of the mercy of living under a free Winter. A Winter not led by a useless boy, but by the people!"

The crowd begins another uproarious cheer, but Perth holds up a single finger. "It is you who must do this thing. You who must sacri-fice your mortal body to become something greater. Something worthy of the great destiny that awaits Winter. Who shall be the first?" He surveys the crowd. "Who stands brave enough to deliver Winter's grace?"

"I do." A young soldier steps out of the crowd and onto the dais.

A sliver of a smile crawls up Perth's face. From out of the wide sleeves of his robe, he pulls a dagger. "Then you know what must be done."

The man takes the dagger with shaking fingers and holds it to his breast.

"What's happening?" I whisper to Farron.

"I don't—"

A horrible squelch sounds in the valley. The man's hands fall from the dagger that he plunged into his own heart, and he hits the icy dais with a thud.

"Do not mourn him," Perth calls to the crowd, "for he is to be reborn as something greater."

His crown pulses with green energy, and his cold eyes gleam with anticipation. He mutters an incantation and raises his arms out to the sides. A frigid wind swirls around him, carrying the unmistakable stench of death.

The fallen body twitches and convulses. Frost forms on the skin, and the limbs jerk, then stiffen. The dead man's eyes shoot open, but they are no longer filled with the warmth of life. Instead, they are glazed over with cold, soulless emptiness.

A winter wraith. This is how they're created. It's been Perth Quellos's doing all along.

"Kel trusted him," I manage.

Farron's face scrunches with anger. "Quellos framed him. He allowed these creatures to ravage Autumn."

The wraith rises, its movements jerky and uncoordinated, the skin a sickly shade of blue.

It stands obediently beside the hooded figure on the dais.

"Now," Perth says, "who is next?"

Farron and I watch in horror as soldier after soldier volunteers. Each one drives a dagger through their own heart, only to be resurrected into something unnatural and obedient.

"We have to warn the city," I urge and Farron nods.

The terrified voice of a soldier halts our escape. "Your Eminence, with all due respect, there are not enough of us here to take the capital! Should we not gather more troops?"

Perth gives a sinister grin. "Why, my good man, you are surrounded by the rest of your comrades."

Frosty light pulses from Perth's crown, and green mist seems to stream from his eyes, his nostrils, his mouth, as he raises his arms. A rotten stench of death and decay fills the air as the ground around the camp rumbles. The earth stirs, turning over and over itself until...

Hands. Bony hands shoot up from the ground. Skeletons claw their way to the surface, their limbs creaking and cracking as they pry themselves loose from dirt. Not just fae, but the skeletons of goblins, too. All the fighters who were taken during the mudslide during the War of Thorns.

Icicles protrude from the bones as they shamble toward the base of camp, hollow eye sockets fixed on their master. Hundreds and hundreds shuffle forward, falling into rank.

Farron's breathing quickens. "No ... It can't be."

Perth purposely camped upon the mass grave. He planned this.

His voice beams with reverent pride. "At dawn, we march on Coppershire!"

Anger and grief war in Farron's eyes, but I grab his arm and yank him away from the army. We take off at a run, finding shelter in the treeline once again.

"Those are our dead," Farron says. "Those are the bones of our fallen soldiers!"

"He's going to use them to take your living ones." I grab my mate's face between my hands. "We must warn Coppershire at once."

Farron closes his eyes and nods.

"My horse ran off. We'll have to find a way back to the city, and quickly," I say.

Something sparks in Farron's gaze. He looks up at the burning sun. "I know a way." He touches the space above his heart. "We broke the curse, but I think the Enchantress left something. A gift."

Slowly, he unclasps his cloak, letting it fall to the ground. Then he pulls off his shirt and pants. Standing in the bare golden light, my mate looks angelic.

His fae body melts away, revealing a majestic wolf with fur the color of fallen leaves and rippling flame. He shakes himself, and the air encircling him shimmers with energy.

Gone is the beast. Before me stands a guardian.

I glide over to the wolf and tentatively reach out to touch his snout. He nuzzles against me. Then he lowers his body and motions for me to get on. I mount the wolf, weaving my fingers through his rich fur. And as the great beast dashes across the Autumn realmlands, he lets loose such a howl that it shakes the very hills themselves.

73

FARRON

I am strong.

Not the wolf. Not the beast.

I, Farron, High Prince of Autumn, am strong.

For now, the wolf and I are one and the same.

My powerful legs bound through the streets of Coppershire and toward Keep Oakheart. My mate's thighs clutch tight around me, her hands woven into my fur.

Everything is heightened. I know where each guard is before I even see them: I smell their leather armor, hear the patter of their feet on the cobblestone. The beating of my great heart is both new and familiar all at once. *You were always inside me.*

The guards I can't avoid are too astonished to spot a beautiful woman atop a massive wolf to pose any threat.

With each step of my massive paws, heat radiates from me. I run to the ruins of the library. My warmth thaws Keldarion's frost. A crack sounds, and the soldiers and horses frozen by his attempt to save me shudder forth from their icy binds.

Flames flicker from my paws, and I direct my power up to the alder tree. Water drips down the trunk as the frost melts. The tree begins to breathe once more, leaves unfurling toward the sun.

One day, I will rebuild its sacred library. But I have to do something else first.

I run toward the keep. As we approach, a near-painful sensation tugs in my chest.

"Over there," Rosalina says, but I don't need her to tell me. I can feel him too—mate of my mate.

Keldarion.

He's not in the dungeon.

I change course.

A large chamber lies within the grounds of Keep Oakheart, a place I've long avoided, one of justice and decision. But now, I charge toward it, heart beating with purpose. Rosalina tenses atop me as if she too steels herself.

Great mahogany doors lead into the building, and I rise on my hind legs to push them open with my huge paws. Rosalina gives a yelp but hangs on.

The doors burst open, and I enter the Autumn Realm's throne room.

The large chamber bristles with nobles dressed in their finest attire. Smooth, dark wood makes up the walls, but the ground is a tapestry of foliage. At the far end, the throne looms atop a platform: a seat carved into a massive tree, its bark polished to a shine and engraved with runes. It rises up into a canopy of vibrant leaves, the branches covering the ceiling.

Upon the throne sits my mother, adorned by the golden ram's crown of the High Ruler. My father stands off to the side.

Familiar smells assault my nose: pine and steel and salt. The princes are on their knees before my mother, hands chained. A guard with a pointed sword stands behind each one. In the corner of the room is a small cage stuffed with a plump racoon and shivering white hare.

My feet land firm against the ground. I know I have but a single moment to decide before the guards are sent after Rosalina and me.

Do I attack to free my brothers like the beast would?

Do I run as Farron has before?

But I'm not the beast. And I'm no longer only Farron.

I am Rosalina's mate. A receiver of the Enchantress's gift. A scholar, a brother, a son.

I am High Prince of the Autumn Realm.

It's time for me to act like it.

With a powerful surge, I leap over the screaming nobles and land in the space between the princes and my mother. Fear and anger flash in her eyes, and she raises a hand to summon the guards.

But Rosalina's calm strength flows through me. She slides off my body, and I turn to stare at my mother. I want her to see me like this: not the rabid beast from before, but a guardian. Can she recognize her son's eyes within the wolf?

Then I look at the crowd, holding each gaze in turn. Fear makes way to curiosity, slowly growing to...

Awe.

I feel for the connection between my fae self and the wolf. It's so clear, I wonder how I never found it before. With a shiver, my body shifts back to my fae form. Instead of standing before them in nakedness, I reach into my magic reserves. A majestic robe of leaves rises from the ground and drapes over me.

The crowd gasps as their High Prince stands before them.

But none are so shocked as Keldarion, Ezryn, and Dayton.

Rosalina laces her fingers through mine as I meet their gazes. They sense it, our mate bond.

But more than that, they can feel that I'm free.

A single tear streaks down Dayton's face. He lets loose a smile as radiant as the very sun itself. *He's so happy for me.*

I'll have to explain all of this to them soon, but first I need to do something I should have done long ago.

Rosalina squeezes my hand three times and peers up at me through her dark lashes. "You can do this," she whispers.

I take a deep breath and step forward, the focus of the entire throne room on me. My mother regards me with a mix of curiosity and skepticism. My father beams and looks as if he's about to rush to me, but mother slaps a hand on his arm. I cannot let her break me with disdain. My words will be my armor.

"Princess Niamh, Prince Padraig, and nobles of the Autumn Realm," I begin, voice ringing across the chamber, "I stand before you today to ask for something I have been undeserving of in the past. I have failed you, and for that, I am deeply sorry. But the man who stands here now is different from the boy who first received the honor of being crowned your leader."

The room is silent, tension and doubt swirling in the air. But I press on, my voice growing stronger with each passing moment.

"The man before you now wields a heart filled with hope. Because I have seen what we can do when we stand together." I look to Rosalina. "When we are united."

She shines up at me, breathtaking in her beauty.

I stare at my brothers. My heart leaps as my gaze meets Kel's, mate of my mate. "The man before you today, has learned to stand for what he believes in, no matter the cost. To trust in his own resolve. To take action."

I drift my eyes over to the shining visor of Ez's helmet. "The man before you today embraces the fear. Honors it. Welcomes it. Lets it pass through. And rises from the dark trail it blazed."

I look to Dayton. A tremor shakes through my chest, and I try to keep it out of my voice. "The man before you today, stands here because he knows what it means to love. And I will fight for that. Today and every day. I will never let it go."

I turn to my mother. "So, I ask for something the boy was undeserving of. Trust. Trust the man. I will stand with you. Fight with you. Lead you with honor and valor. And I will not rest until our enemies are vanquished and our realm is safe once more."

A thundering silence fills the throne room, the only sound my pounding heart.

Then my mother walks toward me, her steps echoing. Her eyes shine as we stand nearly chest to chest. She's so much shorter than me, yet I feel like a child beneath her gaze. But I hold myself steady.

Princess Niamh takes the ram crown off her head and places it on mine. A great weight settles over my brow.

"I bestowed this crown to you many decades ago," she says. "I always knew you were deserving of it."

Then she falls to one knee in a deep bow.

One by one, the throne room joins her. My father, the guards, even the princes bow their heads. Rosalina flashes me a wink as she drifts to one knee.

Everyone here … They're offering me their trust.

I hope I am worthy of it.

74

ROSALINA

I take a few deep breaths outside of the throne room, staring up at the late afternoon sky. The princes are still inside, finishing up a discussion with Princess Niamh. After Farron's proclamation and his mother's endorsement, we freed the princes—and poor Astrid and Marigold, who'd been captured in a tiny cage before they could turn back into their fae forms. We warned the Princess of the army preparing to march at dawn.

I also connected with my father and Farron's brothers. They escaped capture by hiding in the alder tree and are still there now, trying to see if any spells survived that might help Farron against Perth's army. Papa was overjoyed when I told him about my mate bond with Farron. But there's no time to dwell on celebration while the city needs protecting.

Anxiety riots in my chest. Tomorrow, Coppershire will be under attack. Farron called for a war council meeting this afternoon to devise a strategy. I know there is great magic in the Autumn Realm, but Perth Quellos *raised the dead*. His minions can create a frost that can freeze any living thing. There's no time to ask for reinforcements from the other realms.

I squeeze my eyes shut. I have faith in Farron. In the strength of Autumn. I have to hold on to that.

The doors creak open, and the four princes file out, faces grim. But Farron softens as he sees me. "Rosalina."

A sense of peace floods my nervous body as soon as he wraps an arm around my waist. I lean against his chest.

But I feel their gazes like a spotlight.

"So, uh, I guess we should talk about this," I say, trying not to sound awkward. "Something happened with Farron and I..."

"Rosie." Farron weaves his fingers through mine. "I'm pretty sure they already know."

My gaze locks with Keldarion's. "You felt it, didn't you?"

To my surprise, only a rueful grin breaks across his face. There isn't a hint of jealousy or possessiveness in his features. "You are mates. Of course, I felt it."

"Your curse?" Dayton asks.

Farron looks at me with a look of genuine love, then turns to the princes. "My curse is broken."

Water brims in Dayton's eyes, and he pulls us both into a massive hug. "Fare, I'm happy for you." He presses his lips quickly to Farron's cheek, before turning to me and whispering in my ear, "Thank you, Rosie."

I clutch him tight, feeling his salty tears on my face. Relief floods through me. I was worried about how he would react to me and Farron being mated. But his joy is so pure, it's like I can feel it coursing through me. I'm so relieved to see that Dayton is okay ... I don't think my heart could take it if we lost him.

Ezryn clutches Farron's shoulder. My mate wraps an arm around his waist. "Ezryn," I say, "please tell me, is there a smile beneath your helm?"

"There is, Petal." I hear the truth of it in the light reverberation of his voice. "I'm overjoyed for you both."

Only Keldarion does not join the embrace. "We should make a quick return to Castletree before the war council and observe the state of High Tower. We can return through the door to Keep Oakheart."

"Wonderful." Farron pops his head out of the group hug. "I want to observe what's happening with our roses."

"My necklace was a no-go last night," Dayton says. "Been too long since I was at Castletree. Kel, you were there most recently, so try yours."

Keldarion reaches beneath his shirt to pull out his snowflake necklace. Like a weight, I feel the rose locket at my breast. "I want to try something."

"By all means," he says.

I slip the necklace over my head and open the locket, revealing the mirror. "My mother always wore this. But it's a part of Castletree, a part of all of you. I was able to use it to contact Ezryn even when it was broken. So maybe I can use it to get us home."

"As with all our experiments, Rosalina," Farron steps up beside me, "you can certainly try."

"Right." I angle the necklace and try to catch the light like I've seen the princes do before. I draw in a deep breath, centering my thoughts. I am a vessel, and pinpricks of magic shudder through my body, filling and emptying me all at once.

Castletree, I want to go home.

My bond with both Farron and Keldarion blooms bright within me, but there's other magic here, the magic of the High Princes of Spring and Summer.

Castletree, take me home.

The light catches and bounces, forming a shimmering oval. Energy builds within me, a fire growing hotter with each passing moment.

"I did it," I whisper.

The princes stare at me, faces cast in the bright glimmer of the portal.

"To Castletree," Farron says. He's the first one to step through, trusting me, trusting my strange magic.

The others quickly pass through the shimmering glow. A rush of exhilaration flows through me, as if I've tapped into a wellspring of power and knowledge. It's a feeling of connection to something greater than myself, a sense of belonging to the Enchanted Vale that is all my own.

The world shifts and blurs as I follow them. My stomach lurches with the sudden movement. And I'm home.

We emerge through the mirror into the grand entrance hall. There's still ice on the ground, though it's dissipated a bit with Kel spending so much time in the Autumn Realm. The thorns are as present as ever.

"Masters!" Rintoulo the butler rushes up, followed by several other staff members. "We're so glad to see you. Something's going on with us Autumn staff. We felt ... strange this morning. In a good way. There's a change stirring."

"It's my curse." Farron smiles. "It's broken. Lady Rosalina is my mate."

Rintoulo's eyes widen, and there is a collective gasp from the surrounding servants.

"I can yet sense the bear inside me," Rintoulo says, "but it's different."

"My wolf no longer has dominion over me, but the magic remains," Farron continues, voice full of confidence. "I believe the curse that forces you to turn into an animal has dissipated, leaving the gift of shifting at will."

Farron places his hand on Rintoulo's shoulder, and the butler pulls him into a hug.

More of the Autumn staff surround us and tug me into the embrace. "Thank yous" ring in the air, and my heart warms. This is about more than just freeing the princes; it's about freeing the people of Castletree, as well.

This curse can be broken for all of us.

THE STAIRCASE UP to High Tower is still tangled with interlocking thorns. A strange anticipation fills my chest. I know Farron's curse is broken with all my heart, but I wonder what remains in the

Enchantress' wake. What will we find where the seeds of torment were sown?

The High Tower is very much the same, thorns lining every wall except for the line of dirt where the four roses grow. But Farron's rose is tall, bright, and glowing, as though life radiates from it. The petals, which were once orange, are now gilded gold.

It is so beautiful, but that's not what has me clutching my chest. The thorns around his rose have changed too ... The purple briars have turned golden, blooming with yellow and red roses.

"It must be Rosalina's own magic," Ezryn says cautiously. "She has a strange connection to these thorns."

Farron casts a wary glance before kneeling beside one vine and tugging on it. It barely moves. "Very sturdy," he says.

"So, Rosalina's magic made Caspian's thorns stronger?" Dayton asks, raising a dark brow. "That doesn't make any sense."

Keldarion steps into the room, observing silently with a keen eye, his jaw locked and rigid.

Farron gently touches the new golden briars. His eyes flutter closed. "It feels like Rosie, but her magic is *good*. I know it."

Fearful uncertainty wavers inside me. Why do I have power over the briars? Why did some of them change color and strengthen around Farron's rose?

And there's the ever-plaguing doubt of why can I hear Caspian in my mind?

Asking questions only the stars know the answer to. That's what he told me. I clutch my chest. Caspian is a liar and a traitor. He betrayed us and nearly got Dayton killed. I'll never forgive him for that.

"The briars don't seem to harm your rose," Ezryn says. "Rejoice, for your curse has been broken for your people and yourself."

Farron walks over to the wall, the sturdy mix of stone and bark that runs with sickly black lines. "I knew it the moment we accepted the mating bond. The beast remains in me. My magic feels ... richer. The well deeper. Yet, something's still not right. Castletree is the source of our magic, and it's still sick. Until Caspian releases his hold on us, I don't think I will understand my true might."

Ezryn presses a firm hand on his shoulder. "Trust in what power you have earned. You'll need every bit of it for the battle to come."

"I can't do this without my brothers," Farron says. "Will you ride out and stand beside me to face our enemy?"

"I stand with you," Ezryn says, "High Prince of Autumn."

Dayton ruffles Farron's hair and gives him a rueful grin. "Like I'd let you go out there without me."

But Kel turns away, staring at the sun drifting through the window. "You know I would be by your side, Farron. But I cannot stand with you tomorrow. There is something else I must do."

"Kel—" Ezryn and Dayton both start.

But Farron holds up a hand. "You will not fight with Autumn tomorrow, Keldarion?"

Kel doesn't meet his gaze. "There are things I must set right."

Then he turns and storms out the door and down the stairs.

I exchange glances with the other princes.

"No," Dayton snarls. "He doesn't get to fucking do that. It's his damned vizier who's attacking Autumn! He can't abandon us. Not now."

Farron looks to the floor. "I thought Kel might have finally found something worth fighting for."

A joyless, muffled laugh escapes Ezryn. "Kel proves again he only fights for traitors and villains."

No ... No, they can't be right. Kel can't truly be leaving on the edge of battle. For all his faults, he *loves* us.

Or at least, he loves them.

"Stay here," I say and rush out of the tower. I finally catch him just as he exits the stairwell to the ramparts above the entrance hall.

"Kel," I snap, "where are you going?"

His shoulders stiffen. "I'm leaving."

"Why?"

He turns to face me, and for a moment, a strange softness settles over his gaze.

"Are you leaving because of me and Farron?" I ask, my voice breaking. "Because I have another mate?"

"Of course not." He drifts a hand to my chin, and his voice is low as he murmurs, "I am so grateful that you will know the love of a good man."

I place my hand over his, holding onto it as if I could keep him here with me. "*You* are a good man. Prove it, Kel. Stand with Autumn tomorrow. Fight for—"

"Rosalina," Kel says, his voice quiet but filled with purpose, "do you have faith I will come back?"

I stare into his eyes, losing myself in the delicate swirls of ice blue. The one part of him that seems fragile. "Yes," I whisper.

Kel pulls me into him and captures my mouth. All the anger and wanting and pain that our mate bond has brought us surges between our lips. My hands tangle in his hair, and his hands grip me roughly around my waist, pulling me tighter and tighter. I kiss him with everything I am, the act a plea not to go, and a surrender all at once.

Finally, he tears away. "My Rose," he says, and then nothing else. He strides to the mirror, and it ripples, revealing the Autumn realmlands. With a shiver, his body shifts into that of the cursed Winter wolf. The beast charges into the mirror.

"You'll come back," I whisper to the wind. "Because I did."

75

ROSALINA

I tumble into a soft cloud of pillows and sheets. After staying up all night, a nap is certainly in order.

The curtains are shuttered closed, but the golden sun seeps in through the cracks. Though my body is exhausted and sore, I don't know if I'll be able to sleep. Not with an impending army on our doorstep.

My door creeps open, and the familiar clank of metal sounds as Ezryn steps in. I start to rise, but he says softly, "Don't get up."

I settle back to the pillows. He sits beside me, running a gentle gloved hand over my cheek.

"I hope I didn't wake you," he says.

"Not at all."

His visor tilts down. "It's hard to rest on the edge of battle. No matter how many wars I've fought, it never gets any easier."

"Maybe we'll rest easier together." I tug on his arm. "Lay down with me."

A breathy sigh reverberates from his helm. "I wish I could, Petal. But I came to say goodbye."

"Goodbye?" I force my blurry eyes to focus. "You're not leaving too, are you?"

"No, I'll be back by sunset. There's a scouting party riding out to spy on Quellos's numbers and weapons. I'm going to accompany them."

The thought of Ezryn leaving so soon after Kel causes a hollow pit to form in my stomach. "I'm sure Autumn has capable scouts."

"I would prefer to see for myself."

I sigh. "You can just say you don't trust anyone else to do the job."

He gives a little snort of amusement. "When I return, I'll also assist in preparing the land around the wall for the attack."

"Is there anything I can do?"

"You've already rescued the High Prince of Autumn," Ezryn says. "You, Farron, and Dayton need to rest. No one fights in close combat like the Prince of Summer, and your mate will need all his strength to lead tomorrow. This is the best use of my power."

I'm silent for a moment, musing on his words, before I put my hand over his. "Will you stay with me for just a little while longer?"

He tilts his helm. I feel his hidden gaze on me like a caress. "Until you fall asleep."

The bed sinks as he lays beside me, his body stiff. I curl over him, nestling my head into the crook of his shoulder and laying my leg over his. My finger swirls lazy patterns over the intricate designs on his chest plate.

"This can't be comfier than the bed," he murmurs, but his arm has wrapped around my body.

"It is," I mumble. "I could stay here forever."

His fingers drift through my hair. "If only."

"If only," I echo, trying not to let my eyes droop. If this is my last quiet moment with Ezryn before the battle, I want to cherish it for as long as I can.

But sleep claims me anyway. As I'm fading away, I hear Ezryn whisper, "Trust in me, Rosalina. This is how I can show you, Farron, Dayton, and Kel that I ... I can protect you all."

THE SETTING SUN shines brightly on the horizon, casting Coppershire in golden light.

I cross my arms over my chest. "This is the worst part, the waiting."

Farron lets out a long sigh. "I know what you mean. I almost wish they would arrive now."

It's agony, knowing Perth Quellos's legion of monsters will be here by tomorrow. We've prepared the city. The soldiers are armed, defenses manned, and supplies stocked. I woke from my nap after a couple hours. Ezryn has left with the scouting team to gather intel on numbers and capabilities. Keldarion is gone without even a hint of where he went. Some whisper he won't return ... But in my heart, I know he'll come back.

"Even my books fail to keep my attention," I say finally. "I must really be nervous."

Farron pulls me against his chest, lips dipping to my neck. "Well, I could think of a few things to distract you."

I giggle, melting into his arms and savoring the taste of my mate's lips over my skin.

Farron, my mate. The thought still lights my whole self. I take his face in my hands and kiss him, knowing with every part of me that he's mine. It was meant to be. From the first moment I met him, slumped in that dungeon cell, I was called to him.

"Rosie, I can't just have you once. I need you again."

I let my arms loop around his shoulders. Though I've only napped for a few hours, I feel surprisingly awake. I wonder how long Ezryn stayed with me after I'd fallen asleep. "Wasn't the order to rest before tomorrow?"

"You, me, the bed? That's restful."

My core heats, aching for him.

"Farron, wait. There's something we should do."

His face furrows in a grimace, already knowing what I'm going to say.

"We need to talk to Dayton."

Farron shakes his head, and I feel the turmoil pass through him, though I'm not sure if it's from almost killing the Summer Prince in his wolf form or facing the man he loves after the awakening of his mate bond.

Placing a gentle hand on his arm, I try to ease some of his worries. "I hope you know I would never want you to give him up."

"I'm your mate. I belong to you."

"And because of that, I know your heart is big enough for both of us. Plus, I have another mate. Not that he wants anything to do with me."

"I know Kel. Before he left, there was a deep pain in parting from you."

"It's just the dumb bond."

"Hey, you don't get to call it a dumb bond now." He places a kiss on my ear.

"Remember what we spoke of in the hot springs ... Does this bond change any of it for you?"

Farron pulls back. "You mean when Day said that if you were with anyone else, he'd kill them and fuck you in their blood?"

Crimson stains my cheeks. "Yes. That!"

Farron tilts his head to the side, considering. "Kel is your mate. I know Dayton well enough to see how much he cares about you. And Ez is so important to me. The idea of you being there for him makes me happy. So no, it hasn't changed at all."

"Okay," I say.

"Unless you want me to growl and get all jealous. I could try that."

"Well, one of the guards does like staring at my chest—"

Farron grips my shoulders. "Nope, I don't like that at all."

"I'm only kidding."

"I know, but it still makes me want to tear his throat out."

I shake my head, but my smile turns serious. "It doesn't bother me if you're with Dayton, but the thought of you with anyone else—"

Farron places a firm kiss on my lips. "Sweetheart, there is no one in the world for me but you." He tilts his head back and groans. "And that stupid bag of muscle in the other room."

"Who we should go see."

Farron takes my hand, and together, we find the Prince of Summer.

HE'S LAYING out his armor on a large table: a beaten gold breast plate and a bronze helmet with the engraved motif of shells. The crest is shaped like waves silhouetted by a ray of sun. He's twirling two short swords.

Dayton turns to us, his golden hair loose and tumbling over his shoulders. I feel an overwhelming sense of love through the bond—Farron's feelings for Day. But it's not just his. My own burns bright beside it.

Dayton seemed so happy for Farron when he found out about the curse being broken. But does he secretly resent me for being Farron's mate?

Silence looms in the room, and I feel his heavy gaze. The short swords clatter over the armor as he drops then, then moves toward us.

Dayton cups a hand to my cheek, the other tight on Farron's shoulder. His turquoise eyes sparkle with an unsaid question.

Farron presses his lips to Dayton's. As soft as a first kiss, slow, tentative, exploring. Dayton grasps the back of Farron's neck.

Surprise flickers in his eyes. "This better not be a dream."

"It's not, Day," Farron says. "Nothing will ever part us."

Dayton swallows, then he turns to me, and a shadow falls over his expression. "And what about you, Blossom?"

Nerves bubble in my stomach. His gaze is so intense, but I force myself to meet it. "Dayton. Daytonales." I say his true name firmly, proudly. "You are brave and fierce and protective, and I cannot keep away from you any more than the tides can resist the pull of the moon."

The warmest wave of emotion travels through the bond. But Dayton doesn't reply.

Oh shit. I've gone too far. "Of course, if you want to continue with only Farron, that's okay, too." My cheeks burn, and I quickly move toward the exit, not looking at either of them. "And I totally won't creep in anymore doorways—"

Dayton crosses the room in a flash, and pulls the door shut. He cages me in with his arms.

"You think I'd let you leave?" The scent of sunshine and sea washes over me.

Dayton towers above me, and behind him, Farron has a knowing smirk.

"Rosalina." Dayton grips my chin. "Look at me."

I drift my eyes from his chest to meet his striking gaze.

His voice is a rough rasp. "If you're the tide and I'm the moon, pull me deep into your waves. I want to drown in you."

Then he kisses me.

76

DAYTON

The room disappears, and all I feel is her. I claim her lips with an unyielding hunger, pulling her into my embrace. Her taste and touch overpower my thoughts. Her tongue moves with an insatiable desire, while her hands roam over my body. I lift her up and press her against the door, yearning for more, needing her like air.

How is this possible? How can there be this much fire between us? How can she still want me when her mate is here? I pull back slightly and glance over my shoulder at Farron. He's staring at me with an equally hungry expression.

"Come here, pup," I say.

He crosses in two steps, kissing my back and gliding his lips to my neck. Rosie is pinned against the wall. She's wearing a light tunic and dark leggings. But as my hand drifts between her legs, I realize she's wet already. "You're soaking, Baby. Tell me how badly you want this."

"I need this." It's almost like I can sense her desire, and it's not just for Farron. *She wants me, too. They both do.*

Farron snakes his hand between us, touching both my aching cock and her wetness. "Can we get to the bed, please?"

We make our way across the room, clothes flying off. Lips caress my body and hands slide over my skin until we land in a tangle of limbs. Rosie kisses me and laughs, the sweetest fucking smile on her face.

I'd kill for that smile.

Stars, I'd burn worlds for it.

"Fare." I grab him and notice he's trembling.

Slowly, I sit up on my forearms. His eyes are wide, shining, staring at my chest.

But when you fight a cursed wolf and get shot with arrows tipped with steel from the Spring Realm, well, it leaves a mark.

Or in my case, several.

Gashes crisscross my torso and back, and puckered wounds dot my chest where the arrowheads went through. Rosalina tentatively traces a hand across my flesh.

"These are not sad scars," she says. "These are marks of your devotion, of your bravery and unyielding courage."

"But Day—" Farron's voice cracks. "I hurt you. Hurt you again."

"Hey now." I pull him closer to Rosie and I. "Ez was there, it's all good."

Ez just about killed himself keeping me alive. Guess I'll have to lay off the metal jokes for a little while. Did he really think I was so worthy to live? Or was it all his righteous noble heart, the one I've made fun of for years? But even the High Prince of Spring's Blessing has its limits. The scars of a beast still stain my body.

Tears slip down Farron's cheeks.

"I need to know, are you crying because you hurt me? Or because you have marred the most gorgeous body in the world?"

"You're such an idiot." He shakes his head, messy locks of brown hair falling across his brow. "You'll always be perfect to me."

"Then stop these tears. If I died for you, it would be the greatest glory of my worthless life."

I grab his face, pulling him into a fierce kiss, salty with his tears, before he can think too much about my words. Farron murmurs my name, and I roll, pushing him deep into the mattress.

A light kiss over a particularly gruesome scar on my back has me groaning. Blossom. Her mouth grazes along my spine, and she whispers, "Such bravery should be rewarded. What do you think, Farron?"

He gives a roguish smile.

Rosalina taps me on the chest. "Lie down."

I fall onto the pillows, putting my hands behind my head.

"Take his pants off," Rosalina orders.

"Damn, I like it when you're bossy," I say.

Farron grabs the band of my pants and pulls, revealing my hard cock.

"You both are too clothed." I gesture to them. Rosalina's lost her tunic and tights, but she's still wearing her panties and a light cream chemise. Lucky for me, the fabric is thin enough I can see the pointed tips of her nipples. My breathing becomes ragged at the thought of her breasts in my mouth.

Fare lost his pants, and dons a long, loose white shirt. That also needs to go.

"A problem for later," Rosie smirks.

A deep groan escapes me as her lips slide over the tip of my cock. I haven't forgotten that time in the hot springs. The thought of it haunts me daily.

Farron's soft hair brushes my stomach as he moves beside her. His wet tongue glides over my balls, sending the most incredible vibration through my body.

"Fuck," I moan. "You two are cruel. This is going to end with your faces covered in cum."

"You want to come in my mouth, Day?" Rosie looks up at me through dark lashes. "Beg for it."

"Now, where did my sweet girl learn such dirty words?" I stroke her cheek.

"From you."

Farron laughs before popping one of my balls into his mouth. I grind my teeth, bucking my hips before Rosie pushes me down. The silky fabric of her chemise rubs against my thigh.

"Ready to beg?" She drags her tongue from the base of my cock to the tip.

Farron watches her with a heady expression before he joins in. Both of them lick either side of my cock like it's the most delicious treat they've ever tasted. Their wet mouths are agonizing, the soft slurping sounds nearly sending me over the edge. "Fuck," I groan. "Someone put me in your mouth."

Rosie pulls away with a wet smack. "Beg."

I try to resist her command, but Farron is still slowly licking the side of my shaft.

"Put my cock in your mouth, Blossom. Take me deep. I need you."

She smiles at that, satisfied, and gathers her hair in the cutest damn ponytail before descending to suction her lips around my length.

Farron reclines, content to watch her as she works. Her mouth is wet, slippery bliss, and my balls tighten with each stroke.

"You like watching her mouth on me, Fare?"

"Stars, yes," he says. "Such a good girl taking your big cock."

Rosie moans from the praise, her speed increasing.

"Get rid of this thing." Farron reaches forward, and with a quick rip, the chemise is gone. I guess he was as frustrated with it as I was. Her breasts fall free, brushing my thighs as she moves.

"Oh, Rosie." Farron cups her, massaging deeply into the soft flesh. He rubs a nipple between his forefinger and thumb. I can't help but arch my hips in pleasure as the muscles of her throat tighten around my cock. I slide deeper, deeper, deeper.

She gags, but doesn't slow, eyes watering.

"Take him, Sweetheart," Farron says, a delicious edge of command to his voice. "Take him deep until he comes."

Gasping, Rosalina sucks harder, her throat stretching wide as she takes me all the way in. The slick wet heat of her mouth is pure bliss.

"Oh, fuck," I grunt. "I'm going to come for you, Rosie."

She keeps sucking, and I spill myself into her throat.

"Swallow it," Farron orders.

Groaning, I bury my cock deep. She gags and her body shakes, but she doesn't stop.

"You're so good, Baby. So good," I praise.

She pulls back, gasping. Her hair has fallen loose, her lips glistening with my pleasure. She's so fucking beautiful. *Damn, this is bad.*

Farron crawls to her, reverently touching her cheek, before running a thumb over her slick lips. "I didn't taste him on you before. I wish I had."

Then he licks the pleasure that's dripped down her chin before kissing her.

I fall back to the bed, trembling. That the hottest thing I've ever seen. Then in a heap, the mattress moves as both of them topple around me. I'm unable to resist kissing them deeply. I might never experience what they have, but if my body can bring them pleasure, I'll give myself to them. Every damn time.

"That was amazing," I sigh.

Farron rests his head on my shoulder. "Don't say you're done?"

"Oh, Summer Prince," Rosie says, "you didn't think we'd let you come only once?"

"Fuck," I groan.

"Tell me what you want," Rosalina says.

The bed smells like sex and roses, and I feel so content with their skin on mine. But I know what to ask for. "I want to see you two together," I say. "I want to watch my boy fuck you exactly how I tell him to."

77

ROSALINA

My body is nothing but bliss and pleasure. Dayton pushes me back on the bed. I lick my lips, still savoring the salty taste of him on my tongue.

Why does this feel so right? The three of us together...

"Before you take Farron's cock," Dayton says, "we need to make sure your sweet pussy is ready."

Farron lifts my hips as Dayton pulls my panties down.

"Hey." I grin at him. "I thought you were just going to dictate."

"After." He pushes my knees apart. "I'm not missing out on tasting you."

Farron leans on his forearms and places a gentle kiss on my inner thigh. "How fast do you think we can make her come, Day?"

"Oh love, the question isn't how fast," Dayton gently bites the sharp point of Farron's ear, "but how slow."

Farron smiles, and their expressions turn hungry as they gaze between my legs.

"You two look devious," I say, squirming in anticipation.

"Fair is fair," Dayton says.

"Relax," Farron says. "Let us worship you." Farron runs his warm tongue down my center.

"Oh god. Yes, yes," I moan, gripping tight to the sheets.

Farron pulls back and licks his slick lips, eyes shining with lust. Dayton watches us with a predatory grin before he deeply kisses Farron. "Delicious."

Farron returns to devouring me, and this time, Dayton joins him. They lick me greedily, only pausing when they get caught up in each other, with deep languishing kisses.

"I'm—I'm..." I whimper. Pleasure builds inside of me like a storm.

"Just wait, Rosie," Farron growls. "Feel this." They pull away, and I make a sound of protest, but Farron hooks his fingers into my pussy. He pumps rapidly before curling toward my G-spot. At the same time, Dayton's mouth sucks furiously on my clit.

Waves of pleasure wash over me as I orgasm, whispering their names like a prayer. Both the princes gently massage my legs as I come down from the high.

Dayton gives me a soft kiss before standing at the end of the bed. "Now, I think my favorite cock has been sorely ignored."

Farron flushes and sits up.

"Rosalina, take off his shirt and suck his cock three times."

Eagerly, I tug the tunic over Farron's head, displaying his lean body. His long length stands at full attention. I bow down to accept his cock, obeying Dayton's command.

Farron whines in protest as I pull away, but there's something in me eager to play this little game. I look to the Summer Prince for my next command.

"That's a good girl." He smirks. "Don't be grumpy. Lie down, Baby."

Farron does, his cock tall and glistening.

"Sit on it."

I crawl over to my mate and straddle him before easing him inside. Farron stares up at me with such love and devotion, my heart melts. His hair falls in messy waves, lips swollen from all the kissing.

"I love you," I mouth.

He reaches up and taps my heart three times.

Then I slowly lower myself, feeling my muscles stretch around his cock. I brace my hands on his chest, careful not to go too fast.

"Good," Dayton breathes, then, "Fuck."

The prince leans against the bedpost, eyes fluttered closed.

"What is it?" I ask.

He grips the bedpost, voice straining. "You're both so fucking beautiful. I don't think my heart can take it."

I giggle, pushing myself harder onto Farron's cock.

Farron shivers, obviously eager to go deeper, but letting me take charge. It's so long, it feels like if I push any further, it'll end up in my stomach. I bite my lip and whimper, "Day, I can't."

Dayton tsks and stands before me, his own massive cock hard again. "Yes, you can. His cock was made for you, and your body was made for him." Then Dayton yanks my chin up and kisses me roughly.

I moan deeply and push down. Something shifts within me, and I slide down fast on Farron's cock. I shout from the sensation of being filled so completely by my mate. My inner muscles clench and hold tight to his cock.

Farron lets out an animalistic growl. His fingers dig deep into my hips.

"Good," Dayton praises, lightly running his hands through Farron's hair. "It's going to be hard, pup, but don't move. Let her adjust to you."

My eyes close. Yes, I love this. How does Dayton know exactly what I need? The first time with Farron had been a rush of whirling emotions and near primal desire. But now I can savor every moment, every feeling, as I get to explore his body with mine.

"How do you feel, Farron?" I breathe.

"I would live inside you if I could."

Heat builds in my core, and I rock my hips, slowly beginning to sway up and down.

"Faster," Dayton says, voice low and throaty.

"Yes," Farron growls. "More, Rosie, more."

I move, each thrust harder, faster. My fingernails rake down Farron's chest, and I'm sure he's leaving bruises on my thighs.

My back arches as I lower closer to Farron, the angle hitting deep within.

"Suck her breasts," Dayton says, a desperate urgency to his voice.

My breasts now dangle before Farron's face, and he eagerly grabs one in his mouth. His wet tongue circles my nipple, then he bites gently and tugs.

My gaze shifts to stare at Dayton. He's watching me, eyes dark. My heart pounds in my chest, body on fire. I feel so alive.

Farron's cock rubs against my G-spot and I cry out, the pleasure overwhelming. I can't think—all I can do is keep moving.

Dayton cups my other breast, rubbing a calloused thumb around my hard nipple. "What are your thoughts on surrendering control to the High Prince of Autumn?"

"Yes."

"Tell him how you want him."

"Wildly," I gasp, feeling his cock throb inside me. "I'm yours to take, unbound. I want you to fill me."

Farron groans, and Dayton playfully slaps his cheek. "You heard our girl. Obey, pup."

Farron flips me on my back, and I let out a moan as he sinks deeper.

"You're so wet," he pants. "You feel so good, Rosie."

He thrusts slowly at first, then faster, pushing deeper and deeper until he's sheathed all the way. I wrap my legs around his hips, my ankles locking him in place.

"You like that?" Dayton asks. "You enjoy Farron's cock filling you?"

"Yes, yes." I nod, biting my lip. "More. Harder."

Dayton's hand tangles in my hair, and I lift my head to see him above me, red light shining in from the window, making him reminiscent of an ethereal god.

"I could watch you two forever." He kisses Farron before pushing my sweaty hair away from my brow and grazing my lips with his. "You both are going to be the end of me."

"Day," Farron gasps, pumping hard and fast, "you know this isn't ending without you. I'm aching for your cock."

Day straightens, an almost tentative expression crossing his features.

"Day, please," I whine, needing him with us.

"Fuck it." He runs a hand through his thick golden hair. Then he crosses to the bedside table and grabs a vial of oil.

Farron bends down to me, lips by my ear. "I'm not leaving you, Rosie. How do you feel about him fucking me while I'm inside you?"

My muscles squeeze tightly around him at the thought. "Yes," I whimper. "Yes."

Then Dayton is behind Farron, kneeling on the bed. He kisses his neck before whispering, "Ready, Fare?"

Farron stills his movement as Dayton enters him. I watch his face fracture in pleasure as he takes Dayton's massive cock. The pressure of it pushes Farron deeper inside me, and I release a cry of my own, clawing at his spine.

"Gods, you feel wonderful," Dayton breathes. We lie there, breathing together, intertwined. The beauty of it has tears pricking my eyes. My mate bond with Farron is glowing with so much pleasure, I think it could burn me completely. This is so *right*.

"Well, are we fucking or not?" Farron grins before thrusting into me then bucking his hips back into Dayton.

We both let out a cry and then we're moving together. Dayton pounds into Farron, his hand slapping Farron's ass. Farron's cock pumps in and out of me, slick and wet. It's like I can feel Dayton's movements in me through Farron. I watch Dayton work; he meets my gaze.

He leans around Farron, pushing deep into the Autumn Prince, and grabs my neck to pull me into a devastating kiss. I sigh into it. The movement forces all three of us closer than we've ever been.

It's beautiful.

We break the kiss, gasping in unison, our movements growing wilder and more frantic. Farron screams in pleasure, and dips his head to my neck, biting and kissing the sensitive skin. I tangle my hands in his soft hair. This is beyond anything I have ever felt before, and with the mate bond, my body feels overwhelmed with sensation in the best way.

"Yes," I cry out, arching my back. "Farron. Day!"

"You're so good, Rosie," Dayton rumbles. "So fucking good at taking that cock. You look like a goddess."

"And me?" Farron angles his head up, as hungry for the Summer Prince's approval as I am.

"Oh, Baby," Dayton groans. "I love being inside you. I love this. I love..."

My muscles tighten around Farron's cock.

"Ready, Sweetheart?" Farron says shakily. "I'm going to fill you."

My whole being quivers at his words, but I'm not alone. Dayton shouts to the heavens, his neck snapping back, golden hair flying, as he empties himself into Farron.

Farron gives a low moan, falling over the edge. His warm seed explodes within me. The sensation of their pleasure sends bursts of euphoria through me, and my body quakes with the most powerful orgasm I've ever had. I'm lost in it, completely and utterly consumed.

We collapse in a heap of tangled limbs, panting and sticky. Farron's still inside me, his cock softening, and Dayton lies on the other side, eyes closed.

"That was amazing," I whisper, lifting a hand to run it over his sweaty chest.

"I love... I love it," Dayton says. "You two are a vision."

I grin, my heart light.

"You were okay, I guess," Farron says sleepily, waving a hand.

We all laugh. I lie content with them. The fire in my soul still smolders. As I drift off to sweet oblivion, I wonder if it's my mating bond with Farron, or something else, something so bright it might consume me entirely in flames.

78

ROSALINA

I'm carried in someone's arms, maybe Farron's, to the attached privy where I'm washed. He throws a nightdress over me.

We've left the bed a *tad* messy, the scent of sex still in the air. The three of us shuffle over to Farron's room and slip beneath the crisp sheets. I wrap an arm around Farron's waist, his back to my chest. Dayton crawls in behind me and drapes an arm over both of us.

Feeling safe, sheltered, and utterly protected, I drift to my dreams.

Something wakes me up, and my eyes shoot open. I don't think I've been asleep long. Farron is still in front of me, breath steady and deep. Good, he'll need his rest for tomorrow.

There's a chill on my other side. I sit up and catch Dayton leaving the room.

I should let him go, but I softly pad out of bed and follow him into the main sitting area. Red sunbeams spill over the seats from the large windows.

"Dayton," I ask, "where are you going?"

He turns, flashing me a charming grin. "Light sleeper, eh, Blossom? You know Fare and I don't do the whole sleepover thing."

I level him with a measuring gaze.

"And," Dayton continues when I don't reply. "It's almost sunset."

"So? The bed's plenty big enough for you, even as a wolf. Or we could move all the pillows to the ground—"

"It's alright. Go and cuddle with Farron. Have a good sleep. We'll need to rest before tomorrow."

"But..." I say, my voice quavering. "I want you to stay. In whatever way you are. There's no form of you I don't—"

He quickly clutches my hands, cutting off my words. "Listen. What we did? Fucking fun. It was amazing, but it's just fun. You and Farron, do your whole mate thing. I'll happily join in on the other stuff."

I yank my hands away from him. "I don't buy it. You can't kiss us like that, make love to us like that, and say it's just fun."

He angles his head, still smiling, like my words are meaningless to him. "But we didn't fuck. Not technically, Rosie."

"I noticed that."

"Were you craving my cock?"

"I've been aching for you since the moment we met," I gasp out. "Dayton, can't you see that?"

He doesn't reply for a minute, then laughs. "You got my name right this time—"

"You said you were over that." I pace in front of him. "Do you want to know why I called you Kel? It wasn't because I wished you were him. It was because I was feeling the same thing for you that I had just felt with him. This burning spark in my chest and—"

"Stop it, Rosalina," Dayton says, and his words are suddenly so sharp, so commanding, my voice cuts off.

"Why?"

He's the one pacing now. "Because it's not fucking fair. You can't say stuff like that. Don't you think I wish a light could burst forth from my chest and bind me to you and Farron forever? But you're not my mate. The world doesn't work that way." He pinches the bridge of his nose. "Maybe Fare was right..."

His words tear something deep inside me. "Right about what?"

"Maybe it's better not to give in at all. I *can't* give in to you. I see that now. For the Summer Realm. For my people. I have to set them free, the way Fare did with you. Regain my full magic and help my sister."

Tears prick my eyes. "I'm sorry. I know you have to find your mate. It's just—"

Tenderly, he wipes away my tears with a calloused hand. "Here's the thing, Blossom. If I give in to you, I won't be able to stop. I'll stay by your side, by Fare, and I'll never want to find my mate."

"But—"

"Fuck, Rosie. I'm this close to falling in love with you. I'm teetering on the edge of the cliff, and one wrong step, and I'm going to drop and impale myself on your heart. There will be nothing for anyone else. So, it's got to be this way. But hey, it's still fun."

Logically, it makes sense. But everything in me fights to tell him he's an idiot. Because he belongs with Farron and me. I want to press my lips to his and drag him back into the room with us and prove it to him.

But before I can do anything, the setting sun dips below the horizon, and Dayton shimmers, becoming the sea-drowned golden wolf.

"Get some rest," he says, bowing his head. "Tomorrow, we fight for Autumn."

"You too, Day." Slowly, I return to the room, crawling in beside my mate.

Dayton's words still ring in my mind, and I know no matter what he says, it'll never be just fun between me and the Summer Prince.

Farron rolls toward me, pulling me into his embrace. I inhale his scent. Tomorrow, Coppershire fights for the realm. As I lie in Farron's arms, I know I'll be there, fighting for my princes however they need me.

79

ROSALINA

Golden sun gleams off the hills, and there's barely a cloud in the sky. Red, orange, and copper trees sway in the gentle breeze while dusty mist curls around their roots. *It feels wrong to have a battle on such a beautiful morning.*

It's silly to have such a thought. I have to be strong for my friends and family. I clasp my hands in front of me to keep them from shaking.

I've been given permission to watch from the gate's battlements, high above the fighting. I'm surrounded by soldiers. Farron's father is here, making use of the height to observe the entire battle and communicate orders as necessary. They only allowed me to get this close because Ezryn's scouting parties didn't report any signs of artillery or long-distance weapons.

Most of the citizens have moved to the inner city or the castle's barracks. Autumn soldiers line the outer walls with arrows, oil, and burning basins beside them. But it's the sight before the gates that is the most stunning.

Five hundred Autumn soldiers glisten in golden armor. Footmen with swords or long spears, cavalry, and magefighting units all stand at attention to the fae man atop a great elk at their head. Farron, the High Prince of Autumn.

My mate.

He's finally fighting for his realm. Farron has found his bravery. He looks so different from the person I first saw in the dungeon cell, the man who hid away in the library. *He's not hiding now.*

Beside him on her own great elk is Princess Niamh, fitted in gold armor, her helmet pointed with antlers. Dayton and Ez are on horses. Dayton's daggers shine as he twirls them, unable to keep still. Ezryn might as well be a statue on Dayton's opposite side.

My princes were loath to leave me, especially when I refused to stay in the castle barracks. But being close to Farron gives us both strength. I clutch the moonstone rose necklace; I promised them if things look bad, I'd use it to go back to Castletree. But how could I ever leave them?

And Keldarion ... He has still not returned.

Nervousness etches the troops' faces. Some fidget with their armor, adjusting straps and buckles, while others pace in place. Danger lies ahead for all of them. For all of us.

Despite their unease, the fae soldiers remain disciplined and focused, each one determined to defend their home and their people. I turn my attention toward the hill, steeling myself for the coming battle. All I can do now is watch and wait.

"Coppershire's not built for war," Padraig says, following my gaze. "Got stone walls, but they're not that tall and not that strong. Best to meet the enemy on the open field."

"Don't let them breach the city," I say, repeating what I've heard all morning.

The passing months have kindled within me a deep affection for Coppershire, Keep Oakheart, and the Autumn realmlands. I realize that like Castletree, the Autumn Realm is my home.

Despite the fact I'm only an observer for this battle, the High Prince has seen fit to dress me in armor—a combination of leather and metal that allows for ease of movement. The golden breastplate bears the ram horn emblem of Farron's house, while the bright copper bracers taper like the points of floating leaves. My leggings are tight, and my boots sturdy. It makes me feel like part of this story, a warrior defending her home.

Though a warrior probably wouldn't have packed an emotional support book in her battle satchel. I don't suspect I'll get much reading in, but I wanted to be prepared in case Perth decides not to show up.

"I wish there was more I could do to help," I say softly. "I'm not a fighter or a mage. I'm just a human."

Padraig's massive hand rests on my shoulder. "A human who is mated to the High Prince. You brought my boy back."

"Brought him back?" I say, surprised.

"Never thought I'd see Farron leading an army," Padraig says. "Not all battles are won with the strike of a sword. Sometimes all it takes is an inspiring word, a little spark. You, Rosalina, are that spark."

I flush, unsure of what to say. A battle horn bellows, and a deep chill passes over me. A warning.

The enemy has arrived.

Winter wraiths crest the golden hill, Perth Quellos at the helm. The eerie green light around his crown is visible even from here.

"Steady." Farron's voice rings out clear. "Hold!"

Perth points his hand. Thunder rumbles through the earth as his colossal force descends the rolling hill toward the city. Three thousand wraiths, that's what they estimated. Three thousand to Coppershire's five hundred.

But we have the High Princes.

The wraiths charge with an otherworldly grace, their movements almost liquid. Some still look like fae, with a sheen of frost over their armor. But the others—the long-dead fae and goblins who Perth rose from the grave—are nothing but skeletons strung together with ice.

Farron yells another command. The Autumn Guard stands steady.

I rush to the edge of the battlements, clutching the stone, as the wraiths draw close—

In a *whoosh*, the first line of wraiths fall, disappearing into a trench dug last night and hidden by leaves. Hundreds careen into the hole.

The wraiths behind them try to stop, but there's too many. They bump into each other, toppling down.

Farron spurs his elk forward, hooves thundering to the crevasse. With a sweep of his hand, fire bursts forth from the trench, igniting the tinder and oil placed at the bottom. Sizzling shrieks and pops reverberate in the air. A wall of fire now stands between Coppershire and the hill.

Magic burns tight in my chest as I feel Farron's power through the bond. He raises his chin, glare shooting out to Perth Quellos, who awaits at the top of the hill with the rest of his host.

"The Autumn Realm will not stand for your betrayal." Farron's voice is formidable, booming across the field. "Nor will we fall prey to your twisted magic. Surrender and I may consider mercy." He looks beautiful and deadly, his ram crown glittering like melting gold in the flaming light.

Silence. Silence except for the wraiths burning and sizzling.

Perth raises his hands high into the air, and his voice carries unnaturally, as if on the wind itself. "You have much to learn, young Prince, of magic beyond the Vale."

Terrible, keening death cries fill the air. Then a flaming skeletal hand claws from the trench. Farron's elk bucks, and he grips the reins. More hands, arms, and legs grasp the lip of the trench. Then full skeletons emerge, wreathed in fire, the twisted magic turning the flames an unnatural green.

"He's raising the dead again," I gasp.

"Now that's just unfair," Padraig grumbles, then rushes along the battlement. "Archers, ready!"

Farron kicks his elk and retreats to the line. "Brace yourselves!"

Dayton and Ezryn raise their swords. Princess Niamh thrusts her lance to the heavens, letting out a wild cry, echoed by the soldiers.

The burning skeletons charge, clashing with the Autumn soldiers. Screams mix with the ringing of metal on metal. Ice shards fly, and the smell of burning flesh fills the air. The wraiths' frosted swords slice clean through armor.

"FIRE!" Padraig calls.

A wave of flame-tipped arrows arc through the air like golden ribbons before colliding with a row of skeletons on the opposite side of the trench. Those struck in the head do not move again. So, they can be killed … until Perth raises them once more.

More and more of the fallen monsters crawl out of the trench, the dead unyielding. A hooded shadow emerges from a cluster of wraiths still trapped on the other side of the burning trench. A green glow lights the underside of his dark hood. Another one of those crowns … It's the same cloaked figure I saw before at Perth's camp.

The shadowed entity waves a hand, and that strange frost grows across the trench, cracking and smothering the flame. *He's creating a bridge.*

A horrible cheer rises from the dead, and they swarm over the trench, overtaking the Autumn soldiers like a wave.

Desperately, I search the battlefield for the princes. I catch sight of Ezryn. Still on horseback, he swings his great sword, covered in brilliant pink flames, and cleaves the heads from four wraiths at once in a wide arc.

Padraig has lost all humor, running up and down the rampart, commanding the archers, who unleash wave after wave of flaming arrows. He orders the use of ballistas, catapulting huge fireballs down into the wraiths.

The whole keep shudders as another line of winter wraiths marches down the hill.

My heart beats painfully. The Autumn soldiers are scattered dots amid a sea of frost. I lose sight of the princes amid the chaos. *Where are you?*

A familiar burn ignites in my chest, the faintest glimmer of a golden string. Then I see him, my mate. Farron's lost his mount and fights back-to-back with Dayton. The Autumn Prince casts out his hand, loosing a torrent of flames in the shape of leaves. Dayton pushes back a row of wraiths with a gust of wind before diving at them with flame-coated swords.

Keep fighting. I try to push my thoughts toward Farron, unsure if he'll be able to hear me. *I love you. Don't give up.*

Both look up at the same time. The flash of a quick smile from Farron and a wink from Dayton is all I get before they are swallowed from my sight in the chaos.

This enemy isn't like regular men. The arrows and ballistae have little effect on them. A fire arrow to the skull will take one down, and a fireball can flatten a whole section. But I would guess a real soldier would hesitate at least for a second after watching his allies fall.

These frost monsters have no such compunction. They press on as their comrades drop around them.

It's like they don't remember being alive.

Watching them, I notice patterns. The fae who sacrificed themselves for Perth appear as commanders. They seem to remember pieces of their old lives, shouting orders to the battalions. But most of them, the skeletons, are nothing more than raging monsters.

"Rosalina! Rosalina!" My father's voice.

I turn to see him, Billy, and Dom running up the ramparts.

"We found something," Dominic heaves, pulling a weathered scroll from his coat.

"In the alder tree?"

My father nods, breath heavy in his throat. "It was a bloody mess over there, but *this* is something."

Dominic places the scroll in my hands. It's been carefully glued back together, shredded pieces stitched. "What is it?"

"Well, we're not exactly sure," Billy says, his smile turning into a grimace.

"Weren't you supposed to find something useful?"

"This is useful," Papa says. "Trust me, when you've worked with as many artifacts as I have, you get a feeling for this sort of thing. This will turn the tide."

"Great deal about death and destruction in this little spell." Dominic nods. "No wonder it was banished to the alder tree. It's written in a way the ancient fae used to love, all cryptic and whatnot. But you know who loves to decipher texts like that."

"Our dear brother," Billy finishes.

"The lads will get this to your prince, Rosalina," my father says, "and he'll know what to do with it."

I look out at the raging battle. The last thing we need is more death ... but I trust Farron's brothers. I trust my father. "Okay."

"Only one wee problem." Billy leans over the battlement. "Where is he?"

My heart stutters rabbit-fast, but I can't hear it over the clangs and cries of the battle below. "I can find him; my mating bond will lead us."

"Rosalina," Papa says, "it's too dangerous. You could be hurt or worse."

I set my jaw, fighting back the fear. "Farron needs this, and I'm the only one who can locate him quickly."

"We'll protect you." Billy raises a short sword from his waist.

"We've been training for this our whole lives!" Dominic nods.

Steeling my gaze, I stare out over the battlefield and clutch the scroll. "All right then, let's go find the High Prince of Autumn."

80

FARRON

Heat bursts from my hands, sending a scorching wave over two wraiths. I spin, ducking under the sword of another and snatch its face with my fiery palm, melting its frost and bone beneath my grasp. Then I'm running again, lobbing a fireball through the air to scorch the back of the wraith attacking Dayton.

"I had that one!" Dayton calls as he slays another, his blades coated in turquoise flame.

"Trust me, there's more than enough for all of us," I say.

"Less chatting, more slaying." My mother's voice carries over the thundering hooves of her great elk. She's the only one of us to retain her steed. Thrand caught frost from a wraith I'd let too close, and I leapt off him before the frost overtook me too. Dayton's horse lays dead underneath a mound of massive icy bones.

Ezryn left to secure the western front in an attempt to spread our strength. I could hear the soldiers' cheers when he arrived, even across the battlefield. Ezryn's reputation as an elite general is known even in Autumn. My heart takes strength knowing his mere presence will raise the morale of my soldiers, and he will save as many lives as he can.

When I suggested Dayton take the eastern flank, he only rolled his eyes as if the idea of separating from me was preposterous.

I blink the sweat out of my eyes, trying to stare through the chaos of the battlefield to make sense of our numbers. *There's so many.* The ground is coated with bodies and bones, blood and frost. But unlike our soldiers who have laid their lives down, Quellos's army does not remain dead.

I stare up at him atop the hill before the field. His crown glows with a sickly green light. The bones of the wraiths we defeated jangle then rearrange, knitting themselves back together with hoarfrost. *The dead won't stay dead.*

"We're losing ground, Farron," my mother cries as she drives her lance into the rib cage of a spindly wraith. "If we don't do something soon, we'll have to retreat to the city."

As soon as we do that, they'll overtake our walls. All the citizens inside will be lost…

No. My people trusted me to lead them to safety. I won't let the dead take our home.

My eyes blaze as I stare up at Perth Quellos, the light of the green crown swimming in my vision. The crown…

"We have to take down their commander," I say. "Something about that crown is changing Quellos's magic. It's letting him bring the dead back to life."

"Cut off the head of the snake." Dayton crunches a skull beneath his boot. "We'll get you to him."

My mother nods. "And you, my son, will send him to the pyre."

Legions of dead stand between us and Quellos. *Why did Kel abandon us?* Casting spells from the side is a Farron job. Killing enemy commanders seems like a Kel job.

I force in a trembling breath. Quellos has spread frost over *my* lands. Entrapped *my* people in ice. Threatened *my* rule. It is me who must see this to its end.

I charge forward.

Whether by the strength of my family around me or the righteous purpose beckoning me forward, I fight with a fervor I've never known.

Autumn's Blessing courses through my skin, scorching ashen paths for us to follow. Dayton kills with a style that borders on elegant. And my mother's lance is more deadly than ten swords.

Bones crack beneath my boots as we approach the hill. I stare up at Perth, catching his serpentine gaze. Fire sparks in my own. *I'm coming for you.*

81

ROSALINA

I wonder what my old boss Richard would think of me now: Rosalina O'Connell, bookseller, dashing out into a battlefield of fae and monsters. I'm not sure why my mind drifts that way. Perhaps because I spent so many days hunched over a book, lost in an epic battle of good and evil, while rain pelted the streets of Orca Cove.

But my old life is far away, and now I must get to my mate. The scroll is tucked safely in my satchel, along with my water skin, snacks, and emotional support book.

The battle blazes around us. My heart pounds in my chest, and I follow the pull to Farron. I'm not a warrior, but I can't stand idly by while my friends fight for their lives. This spell *can* help. Billy and Dom are at my side, their flame-coated swords held high as they cut down the wraiths that cross our path.

The sound of steel ringing against steel resonates, and the acrid smell of smoke fills my nostrils. Billy and Dom battle with sharp ferocity. Gone are the young twins. Now, they move with the grace and speed of predators. I suppose that's how they were able to make it through the Briar all the way to Castletree.

Tension lines their faces as they fight, but they don't falter. They are determined to protect me, no matter what. The incessant tug pulls me onward.

"We're close!" I call out.

"Right then!" Billy grins, a burst of flame erupting from his palm as he hurls it at a nearby wraith.

"Let's not slow!" Dom dives, slicing the ankles of another creature so it topples in a clatter of bones.

A boom sounds, and the ground shakes beneath my feet as a gigantic winter wraith crosses our path. Not as fresh as the newly turned fae, nor as decayed as the skeletons, this monstrosity walks between. Its skin sags, nearly peeling off the bone, and it sways a massive, bloated stomach. Perhaps once it had been some form of gigantic goblin—or something worse. It carries a spiked club in one hand.

The stench of rot hits me. Dom and Billy give a determined nod to each other before engaging the monster. The monstrosity swings its arm, club scraping against the ground. The brothers dodge.

Despite their efforts, the massive wraith refuses to go down. Its rotting skin seems impervious to damage. Billy finally pierces its gut, tearing its thin flesh. A putrid ooze of black spills out. But it's not enough to deter the creature. It flails its club again, and Billy barely evades the hit.

"Keep going, Rosalina!" Dominic yells. "We're so close!"

"We'll hold it off! Don't stop running!"

Fear thumps wildly in my chest. They mean for me to go on alone? Suddenly, the sounds of the battlefield are so loud. But my mate bond sings within my chest; he's not far away.

Desperately, I survey my surroundings. Farron is northwest. I turn in that direction. There's an outcrop of rock near Coppershire's wall—I could sprint there and get my bearings before continuing.

I give a determined nod to Dom and Billy, then dart into the fray.

I run as fast as I can through the battlefield, my heart pounding in my chest. The fae soldiers fight with a fierce determination, their swords of fire clashing with the wraiths, but cries of the wounded and dying fill the space between.

A wraith falls in my path, an arrow to its head. I scream, stumbling back. A heartbeat later it's writhing in green flame then standing, body renewed by the foul magic of its master.

How can we fight an enemy that won't remain dead?

I scramble away; the rocks are close now. I can't see Farron, can barely feel him through my fear. I try to stay out of the way, dodging and weaving between the combatants.

A cloaked figure strides through the battle, seemingly unbothered by the destruction. He pulls down his hood.

My blood runs cold with a familiar fear.

A fear I've felt long before ever coming to the world of the fae.

The green glimmering crystal highlights the harsh jaw, that cruel smile. A smile I know all too well.

"It can't be," I whisper, rooted to the spot, unable to run. Unable to move. "He's dead. He's dead."

A sickening feeling courses through my blood. But this army we're fighting ... They're all dead, aren't they?

Lucas wears a similar crown to that of Perth Quellos. There's still a tinge of red in his hair, and the glowing crystal casts his frosted skin a sickly green. Vibrant blue lines etch up and down his neck like a haphazard stitch.

Keldarion tossed his dead body through Castletree's door to the Winter Realm. Perth must have seen the opportunity to create another one of his monsters.

I watch as an Autumn soldier rushes him, but Lucas raises his arm. When the sword touches his flesh, it freezes, the frost quickly crawling over the soldier. *That power...*

He's not like the other wraiths. That crown, and the waves of dreadful magic emanating from him, are proof of that.

What did Perth see in him to grant such horrid power? Did he want the thrill of turning a human? Or was there something inside of Lucas that made him the perfect vessel for such evil magic?

The battle rages around me. I know I need to run, but I'm frozen as Lucas turns to me. His once-familiar features are twisted, skin crusted with frost. "Rosalina."

Fear courses through me. I need to do something—

Get down!

A powerful command ripples through my mind, and I obey, throwing myself to the ground as the large ax of a winter wraith swings above my head. The skeletal monster surveys me, then arcs the ax down. I scream, throwing my hands over my face in a last-ditch effort to protect myself.

Steel clashes with steel. I open my eyes to see an Autumn soldier blocking the wraith's attack. Swiftly, he swings his sword, cleaving the wraith in two.

"Farron?" I gasp. A warmth bursts in my chest. *I found him.*

The soldier turns, and from beneath the helm, long dark hair blows in the wind. His eyes sparkle. "Would it really be a battle without a little princess to rescue?"

And who else smirks and holds out his hand to me but Caspian, the bloody Prince of Thorns.

82

ROSALINA

That warmth in my chest turns into a raging inferno at the sight of him. I smack Caspian's hand away. "I don't want anything from you."

Caspian looks both ways, then picks me up. I'm too startled to protest. By the time I manage to give him a swift kick—which does absolutely nothing—he drops me behind the outcrop of rock I'd been heading for.

I land in a heap. But there's something even more pressing than the Prince of Thorns. I peer out from behind the rock. No sign of Lucas. Was that even him? Or was my fear playing tricks on me? A sliver of relief washes through my body. Beyond this shelter, the fight rages on, but here is a tiny reprieve.

"And what's the little princess doing running into battle without even a sword to defend herself?"

I move back behind the cover of rock. "I have no clue how to use a sword."

"Those princes are ever foolish; they should have taught you to defend yourself."

"They defend me fine."

"Then where are they?"

"Fighting for freedom. For what's right," I snarl. "Something you know little of."

"Trust me. I had nothing to do with this." He gestures vaguely at the battle.

"No, you led a different attack on Coppershire with your goblins." The memory of that night is still vivid in my mind. He'd manipulated Farron, nearly killed Dayton...

Caspian gives a long sigh. "What does a guy have to do to get a little thank you?"

"Not be a betraying dick?" I smack him on the chest plate. "What are you wearing, anyway? You look ridiculous."

"Had to blend in." He taps the side of the Autumn helm. "Didn't think I'd be welcome."

"Well, that sort of happens when you attack a city with a goblin horde." My eyes catch on something between the plates of armor. It's the grimoire, the one Farron stole for him from the alder tree. He brought it here, even to the dangers of battle. "It was never about us attending the party, was it? Or helping Farron? It was always about stealing that book."

A sly smile crawls up Caspian's full lips. "I suppose the stupidity of the princes hasn't fully consumed you."

Slowly, I reach into my bag and flash my own book, a fae fairy tale I borrowed from the Autumn library. "I also brought a book into battle. But what's so important about that one? Why go to such lengths to trick Farron?"

Caspian checks that we're still concealed, then leans down. "I didn't trick him. I offered him a bargain. Control over his wolf were my terms. It pays to be specific in bargains, Flower, something our dear Autumn Prince learned the hard way."

"Don't speak about my mate that way," I spit, jabbing a finger against his chest.

"Right, your *mate*." Caspian flicks my hand away. "At the very least, you should be thanking me for helping you unlock that bond."

"Shut up." The breath is heavy in my throat. "Why are you here?"

"To offer you a bargain of your very own."

"Like I'd ever trust you."

"You don't have to." Caspian raises his hands. Two small thorns coil around his wrists as if they were wriggling snakes. "Remember how powerful you were when you helped that great oaf out of the ice? I've brought the briars to you. With these bracelets, you can keep the magic of the thorns with you always."

My heart pounds in my chest as a terrible but beautiful image passes through my mind. If I had thorns on this battlefield, I wouldn't be at the whims of the wraiths or need anyone's protection.

"I can summon the briars myself," I say, raising my chin. "I've done it before."

"Try."

I place my palm on the earth, trying to sense the sorcery of the briars like I did in the Below. I grit my teeth, willing to feel anything, but all I sense are the two thorns around Caspian's wrists.

He kneels and lightly raises my chin. "You've been able to use my briars. Perhaps some day, you'll be able to call them all the way from the depths of the Enchanted Vale. But while you're trapped in that human skin, the source of your magic is too far away. I'm the only one who can help you."

I look from the thorn bracelets to the battlefield. Distantly, I feel a tug in my heart pulling me to Farron, but he's so far away. Why had I felt like he was close? I need to get this scroll to him.

Gritting my teeth, I snarl at Caspian like a wild cat, "What do you want for them?"

"A kiss," he says, dark eyes sparkling. "From you. Lip to lip. It pays to be specific, you know."

My heart rages in my chest. Keldarion will hate me for this. The others will, too.

I know better than to make a deal with the Prince of Thorns. I sense there's a trick here. Maybe one neither of us sees.

But I will do everything in my power to save my mate, to save the Autumn Realm. So, I grasp Caspian's palm. "Deal."

His eyes widen in surprise, then he softens, letting out a long sigh.

The bracelets encircling his wrists uncoil, slithering forward. Only one vine remains on his wrist while the others wrap around each of mine, forming tight circles. A bargain.

I let out a small gasp as I sense the magic coursing through me. The thorns feel like an extension of myself, tapping into a deep well of power within. Testing their strength, I use the thorns at my wrist to cause vines to burst forth and slither over the ground.

"It works."

"Of course it does." Caspian hasn't blinked. He's just staring at me.

As I continue to test the power, the new vines detach from my wrist and weave through the earth. I feel a deep connection with each thorn. Bursting forth with even more energy, I create small vines that wrap the book I'm holding in my hand, hovering it above the ground.

"It's your turn to fulfill the deal," Caspian says, and there's a peculiar rasp in his voice.

My heart beats at an odd cadence. I send forth more briars, continuing to explore this magic, letting the vines playfully wind up his thighs.

"Now, that tickles." His smile shouldn't be that beautiful.

"I would know," I say, leaning forward. "You did that to me. Remember? The first day we met?"

He chuckles darkly. "I could never forget. But that wasn't the first day we met."

No, it was when I first passed into the Enchanted Vale ... He was the shadowy figure who had saved me from the goblins and delivered me to Castletree. "Why do you insist on rescuing me?"

"That was one time."

"But you spoke in my head the day I ran away from Castletree. You told me to run, that you couldn't get to me. I think ... I think you wanted to help me."

Caspian examines his clean, well-trimmed nails. "Yes, well, your mate had created quite a predicament for me at Castletree. I couldn't exactly step away."

"Ugh!" I drive my fingers into my hair. "You're so frustrating! Do you betray friend and foe alike? Is there anyone you're loyal to?"

"Like any good citizen of the Enchanted Vale, I am loyal to the Queen."

"Yeah, the Queen of the Below," I snap.

His eyes flash darkly, and he grasps the back of my neck, fingers running through my hair. "Are we going to continue to chat in the middle of a battlefield, or are you going to fulfill our bargain?"

But the battle feels far away, the shouts and cries distant, and I force myself to focus. Caspian looks so curious, dressed in the golden armor of Autumn. It makes him look younger, softer. I let him pull me close, so I'm in his lap. I take off his helm, and a tumble of dark hair frames his elegant face.

"A little kiss for such power?" I say softly, letting my thorns continue to weave up his body and through the plates of his armor. "You must have been thinking of this for some time."

His eyes close, long lashes sparkling in the golden light. "You have no idea, Princess."

Warmth blooms inside me, and I try to ignore the rush of feeling through my body. I lower my lips, a breath away from his. "I made a bargain to kiss you, Caspian."

Lightly, his fingers graze my spine. "Yes."

I pull back, taking my briars with me and stand, quickly shoving the book into my satchel.

Caspian opens his eyes, blinking, confused.

"I made a bargain to kiss you, but I didn't promise it would be now. It was you who failed to say where or when. It pays to be specific with bargains, you know."

For a moment I think he's going to be angry, but he only laughs, a dark rasp. "Ahh, Princess, you really were made for this world, weren't you?" His laugh turns into a cough, and black stains his lips.

"What—"

He wipes a finger through the dark ooze coating his mouth. "Use the power well, Rosalina," he says, then falls to the ground, as one might fall into ocean waves. Briars encircle him, and he vanishes into thorns and shadows.

But the vines encircling my wrists remain. It might be the magic of the Prince of Thorns, but it's mine now.

Mine to do with as I wish.

83

FARRON

Dayton, Mother, and I crash upon the top of the hill, a charging entity of gold and flame.

Perth snaps a hand, and three hideous creatures sally forth on either side of him. The decaying horses, their bodies blue and frostbitten, have manes crusted with jagged frost and empty eye sockets. Two are ridden by wraiths. Unlike the bare-boned skeleton soldiers, these riders are freshly made.

Perth hauls himself up on the third dead horse and holds out a hand, creating a glittering ice spear, the fractals shining with that otherworldly green glow.

"Looks like we got his attention," Dayton says.

I survey the battlefield, finding Ezryn in the fray. He's surrounded on all sides, his sword flashing against the enemy. His ranks have already shrunk. Soon, he'll be holding the western front by himself. I need to act now.

Thankfully, I don't have to wait. With a cry, Quellos and his riders charge.

"Take out the wraiths," I say, voice low. "Quellos belongs to Autumn."

My mother stops her steed beside me and lowers her lance. We steel ourselves. Quellos and his riders crash upon us like a blizzard: a flurry of cold and snapping wind and violence.

Terrible noises of equine pain shoot into the air; though I can't take my eyes off Quellos to check, I know Dayton has engaged the riders. My mother drives her lance into the visible ribs of Quellos's steed, and it bucks. I lunge forward, blazing fire from my hands.

Quellos cackles—half-laugh, half-cry—and stabs his spear toward me. I leap backward, feeling the hiss of wind as it barely misses.

He struggles to gain control over his steed as flames catch between its bones and it stumbles. "Well, isn't this touching?" Quellos winds his hands around the reins. "A High Prince finally finds something worthy of his presence."

"You don't have to do this, Quellos." I step back and lower my hands. "Call off your army. Autumn has no quarrel with the Winter Realm."

"Of course you don't," the traitor vizier snarls. "I'm sure Autumn loved watching Winter devour itself, being run by the pathetic excuse for a leader, Keldarion. Long did I serve him, thinking the fool would finally realize what was best for his realm and pass on Winter's Blessing to me, a deserving ruler!"

Flames lick my fingers. "So that's why you served Keldarion all those years. Not out of loyalty or a desire to help him succeed. Because you wanted him to grant you his power!"

My mother gives a cruel laugh. "You are an even bigger fool than I thought, Quellos. For all High Rulers know who is worthy of the realm and who is not." She swirls her lance in her hands. "You will never bring peace to Winter."

Quellos's steed gives a strangled cry and collapses to its front legs. The vizier shoots forward but hangs on. "That's where you're wrong, Niamh. I don't intend to bring peace to only Winter, but to all the realms. The peace of an endless frost." He gives a revenant look across the battlefield. "The calamity of growth in Spring shall freeze. Bitter winds will ease the scorching heat of Summer. And greatest of all, I shall remove the torment of Autumn: the constant death. Instead, all shall be at stasis. All shall be at peace."

I throw Quellos off his dying steed. His glittering spear falls to the ground. Body atop him, I lace my hands around his throat. "Autumn is death, is it?" Flames erupt from my hands, red light casting over his wizened face. "Then I will show you death."

But Quellos's eyes only shine with mirth, and an unsettling smile crosses his face.

More fire. I need more fire to burn this monster from Autumn's memory. To melt him into the ground and take all his walking bones with him. But the more fire I erupt from my hands, the larger he smiles. The red light of my flames is overtaken by the growing green from his crown.

"Your fire cannot hurt me, Prince," he hisses. "I am no frost. I am the creator, the harbinger of a new season. The season of the Green Flame!"

He's right. With growing horror, I realize my flames do nothing: he's not burning, or even hurting. I fall backward, staring at my useless hands. My one weapon against him...

Quellos leaps up, eyes glinting with wild joy.

"Then I shall strike you down with steel." My mother's voice. She charges on her elk, lance drawn, and drives it straight through Quellos's chest.

Blood spurts from his mouth, but his smile never fades. Instead, he throws his head back and howls with laughter as red flows from his blue-tinged lips. His crown glows again, and he snaps his head forward, eyes trained on my mother.

Without blinking, he wraps his hands around the lance and yanks it out of his body with a sickening squelch. The gaping wound in his chest festers with green light, then frosts over, ice cracking away to reveal new skin.

Absently, I notice Dayton smiting the wraith rider in flame, the other fallen at his feet. But I'm wholly focused on Quellos. A moment that seems to linger too long and not long enough—

"If you are so intent on death, Farron, son of Autumn, then I shall give it to you." Frost explodes from Quellos's hands, overtaking the lance, then elongating it, a hideous spire of jagged ice. And before the cry leaves my lips, Quellos hurls the lance through the air.

There's a dull thump as the ice lance crests through my mother's chest plate, then a soft, gurgling sound. My mother looks down, her own lance plunged through her heart. Tentatively, she feels the wound, eyes wide and unseeing. Then she slides off her steed and falls to the ground in a clang of metal.

Screaming. The swish of a sword. Dayton's voice, his blades locked in battle with Quellos. But I think the vizier has done something to me, too. I'm numb, as if the frost has taken me from the inside.

I fall to the charred earth and crawl. My mother's body convulses around the lance, and I flip her over, holding her hand in mine. Red stains her lips. I don't understand. She looks so small with this huge thing lodged in her chest. Not like my mother, but a scared girl.

"Mother." My words are a breathless cry. "It's going to be okay."

I grip the lance with the intention to pull it out, but her unseeing eyes find me, and she snatches my hand. "N-no—"

"Ez'll fix you. We'll get him and … He can heal—"

"It's in my heart, clove," Mother gasps. "No magic can save me now."

"No," I cry, desperately blinking away tears. This can't be happening. My mother, *my mother*. Her hands are so shaky against mine, her face too pale. I clutch her, as if I could weave her life thread back together. "Don't leave me. Please."

Warm blood gushes across my hands, and I curl over her chest, crying out, a sound more animal than man.

"Farron," she says, voice hitched with shaky breaths. "Let me see your face as I pass into the wind."

I take her hands in mine. She smiles softly, a smile I have not seen since my youth. So young, she looks so young. I gently lift her onto my lap, cradling my mother as she once cradled me.

Tears fall from my face and transfer onto hers. I can barely speak the words as she fades away. "What will the realm do without you?"

She reaches a shaky hand up to stroke my cheek. "Oh, Farron. The realm has you."

Her eyes drift skyward. Then she smiles, a look both joyful and content.

She slips from this realm to the next.

And I am left alone.

84

ROSALINA

Caspian is gone, and it's just me and the briars. Shouts and cries sound through the battlefield. Blood and frost coat the ground. Gritting my teeth, I feel for my mate bond with Farron.

It snaps taut, and I see a flash of gold running up the crest of the hill. He's heading toward Perth Quellos. I need to hurry.

Pushing down the fear shaking my heart, I run across the battle-field. A quick glance over my shoulder tells me Billy and Dom are still engaged with the giant wraith. *I'm on my own.*

A wraith charges me from the side. Instinctively, I raise my hands. The thorns writhe around my wrists and one shoots out, diving into the earth before sprouting larger. The sharp point strikes the wraith through the chest.

I feel the blow as if the thorn were my own hand. *A bargain well struck*, I think.

As I run, two more briars sink into the earth, racing alongside me like twin sea snakes, their backs arching in and out of the ground. A couple wraiths step in front of my path. I skid to a stop, flowing my consciousness into my briar companions. They leap up, jagged edges like spears.

One strikes straight through a wraith's eye socket, shattering the skull. But the other wraith is quicker, slicing my vine in half. A cold shiver passes through me. Physically, I'm not hurt; it's only a phantom pain.

My lip curls back, and I whip my hands down then up, sprouting a terrible, twisting fury of thorns that consume the wraith. It falls to the ground in a tangle of briars.

I'm left face-to-face with a young fae soldier, his sword shaking in his hands. "T-the ... the Below," he stammers. More soldiers look my way.

My thorns have twisted all the way up my arms. Crap. I guess wielding the same magic as the Prince of Thorns isn't the best look.

Come on, Rosalina. If there was ever a time for me to find my voice, this is it.

"I am not your enemy," I call, emulating the same air of command Farron had earlier. "I am the mate of the High Prince of Autumn, and I'm here to aid him."

I don't retract the thorns; instead, more rise around me, and I hold each of the soldiers' attention.

"Please," I say. "Help me get to him."

The first soldier steadies her shaking sword. "I stand with you, Lady of Castletree."

The others eye her warily, then nod. I tighten my fists. "Then let's go."

I take off across the field, flanked by my thorns and the members of the Autumn Guard. My briars shoot out at every passing wraith, plunging through their skulls or chests. My movements are instinctual. *There's so much more to this magic.* Too bad the only person who could teach me is a lying jerk from the Below.

A sudden sharp pain courses through my body, as if I'm struck by lightning. I clutch at my chest, expecting to find a wound, a spear from one of the wraiths. But there's nothing.

Pain continues through me, and I fall to my knees in the mud. The Autumn Guard make a circle around me, and my briars rise to form a protective barrier.

The pain is so intense, I dig my fingers into the mud for purchase. *What's happening?* My heart pounds so hard, it feels like it might burst.

A cry radiates through my mind. *Mother!*

This pain ... It's not my own. It's his. Farron's.

I blink through my tears. There I see him, a glimmer on the horizon, clutching Princess Niamh's body. Dayton is a blur of gold blocking Perth Quellos.

Grief—my own, Farron's—threatens to consume me. *I'm too late.*

The soldiers grunt, crying out as a wave of wraiths surround them. I dig my fingers into Autumn's soil. The thorns around my arms shiver and thrash, new vines breaking off and spilling into the earth, burrowing deeper, growing.

"It's not too late," I whisper to myself. Not for Ezryn. Not for Dayton. Not for Farron. Not for Billy and Dom, and every Autumn soldier fighting to defend their home.

With a deep growl I rise, bringing my briars with me. They burst from the earth, consuming each of the wraiths surrounding us.

The Autumn Guard murmurs a collective thanks, but my gaze is set ahead. To Perth Quellos. To my mate.

"Farron," I whisper, "I'm coming."

85

FARRON

D id it happen to me too? Did the frost creep over my body and steal my will? For I can't move; everything in me feels cold.

Cold as my mother's dead body in my arms.

I'm screaming. I know that, like I know that the sky is blue, and I need air to breathe. But it's a distant thing. There's a battle: ice and cries and blood.

My mother is dead.

"Get out of here, Farron! Go!" Someone's voice. A familiar voice. A voice I love. He wants me to leave. He thinks I'm in danger. Maybe I am. But what does it matter at this point?

My army is falling. The frost has come. And my mother is dead.

"Farron."

There's another voice. Ah, maybe I was wrong. I'm not overtaken by the frost; I'm simply lifeless. I know this voice, and there's no way it would be here on the battlefield. I squeeze my eyes shut.

"Farron, I'm here."

It's so sweet, this voice, like a small drop of sunlight over the ice inside me.

"Farron, look at me!"

I open my eyes. "Rosalina?" Something cracks. I blink, and the breath hitches in my throat. She's here in front of me, dressed in the golden armor of Autumn.

She looks down at my mother's body. "I'm so sorry."

"Get out of here, Rosie!" That other voice. I look up to see Dayton, blood streaking down his cheek. His sword clangs against Quellos's ice spear. He lands death strike after death strike, but nothing kills the cursed vizier. "Take Farron and go!"

I've left him to fight Quellos alone. Gently, I place my mother on the ground and grab Rosalina's shoulders. "What are you doing here? You have to get out of Autumn."

She lifts her chin in defiance. "I fought my way to you, Farron. I won't let you do this by yourself."

"Look around you! The battle is lost."

"No, it isn't." She grabs my hand and pushes something into it. A scroll. "Not while the High Prince of Autumn still has strength in him."

Slowly, I unravel the scroll. A great burst of energy seeps from it, blowing back my hair and sending cold shivers through my skin. "This … This is from a grimoire." I barely get the words out: "This is a death spell."

"Take it from me." Rosalina runs a hand along my jaw, causing me to look up at her. "Not everything that looks evil is evil. Embrace what you are, Farron."

I inhale deeply and draw my eyes over the words. She wants me to use a death spell…

Why shouldn't I? Autumn is the death of life. That's what everyone says. It's what Quellos fears. That Autumn should bring the end of all things, that it should leach and drain and steal.

And yet…

Embrace what you are.

Without death, the threads of life would never tie together to create the binding of the world. The bounty of our harvests would not be as precious; the ground would never be filled with leaves; and we would never see the beauty of embers after a roaring fire.

Yes, Autumn is death.

And I shall become death to save the living.

I stand on shaking legs, holding the scroll with one hand on top, one on the bottom. Rosalina rises beside me, her eyes shining.

The words seem to light into flame as I say the incantation aloud: "Ancient winds and shadows deep, hear our call and spirits reap." Vast power grows within my chest. "Send these souls to their final rest, where earth may claim them and death attest."

A stinging clang shoots through the air as Dayton's sword meets again with Quellos's spear. But Quellos stumbles back. "What are you doing? Stop that!" he snarls.

"In darkness and silence, you will lie, where no living gaze may pry." My voice carries on the breeze like a great echo. "Rest now in eternal sleep and let your souls find peace to keep."

My eyes catch on a cluster of wraiths. They step back, dropping their weapons, blank eyes turned upward. Their frosted bones shiver, pieces of sparkling dust creeping away into the wind. The living dead drift away, back to the soil where they belong.

"Slumber, oh dead, and take your rest. Your bones will crumble, your souls now blessed. Return to the earth and let the living be. And in your final death, you shall be free."

"It's working," Rosalina cries, spinning. Around us, the wraiths look toward the sky. A sense of peace overtakes their frozen expressions as their bodies float away, glimmering like snowflakes.

Reaching for the deepest well of my magic, I speak the final words of the spell: "For death is not the end, but a new beginning. A part of the cycle, forever spinning. Your time on earth has now ended, a peaceful death, a circle mended."

A torrent of wind blows across the battlefield. My soldiers blink and lower their weapons as the poor wraiths, forced to fight even in death, are finally gifted peace.

"No! No!" Quellos cries.

Dayton lunges at him, but Quellos jerks away.

I drop the scroll, panting. My chest feels empty, every reserve of magic I have depleted. "It's over, Quellos. It's time to surrender."

"Never," the snake cries. "It's not over yet, princeling."

Dayton stalks toward him. "You have no army."

Quellos backs up, and there's something frantic and wild in his expression. A cornered animal. "You're right. I have no army. So, I'll take yours."

His green eyes glow with sickly flame; a mist oozes out of his fingers and swirls around his body. His mouth works, but no sound comes out.

"Stop him!" Rosalina cries. "Get the crown!"

Dayton pitches forward, but it's too late.

With utter horror, I look around. The dead are rising again. Not the ones I just set free.

Our dead.

Our fallen soldiers.

And they're turning against the living.

I clutch my chest, as if I could replenish the magic well I've just run dry. No, no, we've come this far. But there's so many fallen soldiers, our own ranks so thin. The deads' eyes blanch as they turn on their own comrades. Horrified screams rise.

There's nothing left—

A horn blares in the distance. A sound as powerful and thunderous as a winter storm.

My feet shake beneath me as the ground trembles. Atop the hill emerges a host of riders, their great steeds varying from polar bears to moose to eagles.

And at the helm, atop a huge reindeer, rides Keldarion.

86

KELDARION

Looking down at the battle from atop the hill, I know we arrived not a minute too soon.

The usually golden field before Coppershire glimmers with white frost. Autumn's soldiers are pushed to the wall, their own dead rising up against them.

And Perth Quellos still lives.

Eirik Vargsaxa, captain of the Kryodian Riders, comes up beside me, his moose glimmering in silver-blue armor. "On your command, my Prince."

With the full might of Winter's most valiant cavalry, I let loose a cry and surge down the hill. The Riders follow me, charging upon the living dead with claw and tooth. An owl screeches from above as its rider lobs flaming arrows. The Autumn troops stagger backward as we flow across the battlefield, their stunned expressions finally registering that we're here to help. They throw their swords up in cheer.

With one hand, I hold tight to the reins of my steed, and with the other, I hack the heads off any wraiths in my path. There's no sign of Farron or Quellos amidst the chaos.

A familiar glint of dark metal catches my gaze, and I usher my reindeer forward. With a single swing, I cleave the wraith facing off against Ezryn in two. His armor is streaked with frost and blood.

He tilts his head up at me. "Little late to the party."

"Fashionably so."

We hold each other's gazes for a moment and then he gives that familiar shake of his helm, the one that lets me know there's a smile deep behind the metal.

"Come on." I hold down my arm to him. "Let's find my vizier."

He swings up behind me on the reindeer. "Is an I-told-you-so in order?"

"If I let you kill him, are we even?"

Ezryn snorts, and I take that as a yes. "I last saw Farron heading for the center high ground."

I redirect my steed and snap the reins. We ride, weaving between soldiers and wraiths alike.

Ezryn's breath is heavy. "You couldn't have told us you were leaving to go get aid instead of just running off?"

My shoulders stiffen, and I'm glad he can't see my face. "I wasn't sure I could convince the Riders to follow me. I didn't want you to count on me if I failed."

Ezryn sighs. "Come on, Kel. We can always count on you."

I stay silent, focusing on maneuvering through the conflict. Two giant polar bears crush a small horde of wraiths beneath their massive bodies, their riders swinging flaming swords at the ones that scramble out. My reindeer leaps over a fallen frosted horse.

"We're never going to find him in this chaos—" I begin when I feel it. That terrible, nagging thing in my chest. That thing I wish I could rip out. *She's here.*

I dig my heels into the side of the reindeer, the rest of the battle fading away as I follow that tether.

"There!" Ezryn yells, pointing.

Up ahead, at the base of the central hill, are our brothers. Dayton fights sword to spear with Perth Quellos, while Farron's got one hand on a scroll, the other desperately clinging to his chest. And beside him, standing radiant and strong, is Rosalina.

That cursed woman.

Fury and terror surge within me seeing her here in the middle of a battle. She was supposed to be in the keep, away from all this!

But Rosalina can't follow orders if her life depends on it.

Which it does right now.

Cursed, cursed woman!

Ezryn growls. "Let's fucking kill him."

I click my tongue and the reindeer lowers its antlers. With a roar, my great steed charges straight into my vizier, sending him flying.

I pull to a stop, and Ezryn and I jump from the animal.

"Kel," Rosalina breathes, and I turn to her. Gods Above and Below, she is beautiful. And despite the battle that rages around us, there's no fear on her face, only determination. I fight the urge to grab her in my arms and—

"It can't be." Ezryn's voice. He collapses to the ground beside a body, and my heart tightens. Princess Niamh.

Green glows from Ezryn's hands, but even I can see it's too late. She's gone. The only consolation is that Quellos's unnatural magic has yet to animate her corpse like the other soldiers.

"You came."

Farron stands before me, a flat expression on his face. I grip him around the back of his neck. "As long as I draw breath, I will fight for you."

"Yeah, well, let's get to fighting then." Dayton stands beside him, body drenched in blood. I inhale. It's his own.

Quellos staggers to his feet.

"Your time is over," I call to him, dragging my sword through the earth.

He bares his teeth and hisses, "Keldarion, cursed one, traitor. Beast of the Briar. I'm liberating Winter from your rule."

"Liberating it with death." I slam my foot upon his spear, shattering it. My family comes up beside me, and I feel their presence like a warm breeze. My brothers. My mate.

Quellos's eyes flash. "Death would be better than serving under a monster such as you."

I kick him in his chest, drawing my sword up over my head. "Then I shall grant your wish."

I swing the blade down—

It smacks hard against ice. Quellos laughs, a shield of green frost between me and him. "Always the fool, Keldarion. I am not like you. I am so much more. I need not Winter's Blessing or the Sword of the Protector, or even life itself. I am beyond it. I am greatness. I am—"

Something shoots forward: a purple thorn vine. I whirl. Caspian? But no. It flies from a coil around Rosalina's wrist. The briar wraps around Quellos's crown and draws it toward her. A horrific crunch sounds through the air. I reach for her but—

But I don't need to. Quellos's green crown lies beneath her boot.

"Everything you say is poison," she snarls to the vizier and grinds her heel harder. A green mist oozes out from the crushed crystal. "You don't get to hurt anyone else." Her expression flashes with darkness. "There is no future for *you* in the Enchanted Vale."

Her vines twist around the gnarled vizier, binding him in a vice of thorns. He struggles against the hold, but without his cursed magic, he's nothing but a weak old man.

I will not suffer this traitor to live. I rise my sword above my head—

Farron grabs my arm. "Wait," he says. "We should take him alive to question him about this sorcery."

With a heavy grunt, I lower my arm. Farron's right. My former vizier can rot in a cell for the rest of eternity for all I care.

"The crown is broken but the wraiths live," Ezryn says, drawing our attention back to the fight. Though the cavalry has handled a great number of them, our troops are retreating, the undead too plentiful.

"There's another crown," Farron says. "Rosalina and I saw someone else wearing one at the war camp."

Ezryn spins around. "No sign of him now. You must use the spell to rest the dead again."

A horrified emptiness takes over Farron's face. "My magic is depleted. I've got nothing left."

A desperate fear spreads throughout us. I turn, staring out at the battlefield. Our soldiers scream, a new panic lacing their features as they are attacked by their own comrades. Many abandon their posts, sprinting toward the city walls.

No, it can't all have come to this. My family has given up everything. I brought the Kryodian Riders to their doom. Farron has lost his mother. There has to be a way for us to fix this—

"Take my magic."

We look to Dayton. Blood paints the blond hair hanging over his shoulders, and his chest heaves, but there's a strength to him, a strength that reminds me of his older brother, the former High Prince of Summer.

Dayton cups Farron's face. "Take my magic, Fare. Take it and end this."

Farron shakes beneath his touch. "What are you talking about? That's impossible."

"No, it's not." Dayton's eyes turn steely. "Make a bargain with me."

My chest heaves as I look between Dayton and Farron. The air is thick between them, as if the ancient magic of the world senses something powerful is about to happen.

"I can't take your magic," Farron breathes.

"Trust him," I say and look down at Rosalina. "Not all bargains are evil."

It was, in fact, a bargain with this stubborn, tenacious woman that gave hope to Castletree.

She smiles up at me, eyes shining with tears. "And not all who make bargains are evil."

The frosted thorns bracelet on my wrist seems to sing, and I wrap my hand around it. But my doubt dissipates as I see the expression on her face. She's looking at Farron and Dayton with pure affection. As if their happiness is her happiness.

There's the *ting* of a sword as Ezryn leaps forward, blocking a charging wraith. "You alone can save us, Farron. It doesn't matter what we say. Trust yourself!"

The wraiths have sensed us, their bodies still fleshy and fae-like. I draw my sword, stepping in front of Dayton and Farron. "We'll protect you."

Purple vines erupt out of the ground, roiling like waves. Rosalina shoots a look over her shoulder at Farron as the thorns swallow up three wraiths. "For the Autumn Realm."

Farron's eyes gleam. "For you all." He places his hand over Dayton's. "Let's make a bargain."

87

DAYTON

I've never made a bargain before. Crazy, I know. All fae make bargains. But I never wanted to be held to anything.

But now, I know I'll do anything to hold on to this.

Magic laces my words, and they sparkle like champagne in my mouth as I kneel down before the High Prince of Autumn.

It's easy to make a bargain, I realize. You just speak from the heart.

"Farron, son of Autumn, I pledge my magic to you. May it always be at your disposal. May you take my power and make it yours; may I be a vessel and conduit; may you siphon my magic and let it flow through you. Through every season and every storm, may I belong to you." Emotion claws up my throat, and I fight to keep sight of him through my blurring vision. "In return, vow to me you will never forget this moment. Who we are now. When you loved me. And when I fucking loved you."

Farron's face breaks in emotion, and he pulls me up, wrapping his arms around me. A turquoise light shimmers around us; the bargain magic hovering, waiting for the agreement.

Farron nods. "It's a bargain, Day. Through every storm and every season."

The space between us shivers and sighs. A string of gold made light bursts from Farron's helm, and a sprig of silver from my blade does the same. They twine together, becoming cuffs of silver and gold, before wrapping around one of my biceps and one of Farron's.

"Take it, Farron," I say through gritted teeth. "Take my magic and save your people."

He cries out, and golden light mixes with the turquoise shimmer. A strange sensation ebbs through me; not a siphoning, but a gentle trickle. I *feel* Farron's touch within me, his own magic coaxing mine out in a gentle sway.

Farron doesn't let go of me as he whispers the spell. The incantation laces itself through the wind, a sigh upon the breeze. Autumn soldiers and Kryodian Riders slash at empty air as their enemies turn to dust and settle back into the earth.

The battlefield is silent.

The glow lessens, and my muscles go slack. Farron catches me before I hit the earth.

"Did it work, Fare?" I whisper, already knowing the answer.

"It worked," Kel says, putting a hand on both mine and Farron's shoulders. "Congratulations. You've just saved your realm."

THE BATTLEFIELD IS in clean up mode. Perth is chained in silver and watched over by Keldarion and Ezryn.

The other soldiers are helping the wounded or collecting the dead. As is the nature of war, bodies litter the ground. But there would surely be many more if it wasn't for Rosalina's bravery and Farron's courage.

Farron was radiant, power ebbing out of him in glowing waves. The ram crown of the High Prince glistens in the afternoon light. His eyes still glow with a radiance that reminds me of his wolf.

I stretch my fingers. He drained me of all magic. I know a visit to Castletree will restore my reserves, but with this bargain, it'll forever be at his beck and call.

A bargain I don't and will never regret.

Autumn is the death of life. Farron always used to tell me that. But now that magic, his magic, brought the natural cycle of the Enchanted Vale back to order.

My heart has never been so full of love for him.

And Rosalina, his mate. She stands beside him, looking like a true Autumn princess, dark hair framing her beautiful face. A painful yearning throbs in my chest when I look at them.

My heart stutters as I focus back on the battlefield. Padraig, Billigan, and Dominic kneel before a body covered in Padraig's golden cloak.

Princess Niamh. I try to push away the sorrow threatening to overtake me. She'd always been like a second mother to me, had comforted me when I lost my own mother ... And now we've lost her as well.

With a sudden stark realization, it hits me hard that among the five of us—Rosie, Kel, Ez, Fare and I—there is not a single mother left.

I turn to Rosalina now, stance strong, but there's worry etched across her face. "What's on your mind, Blossom?"

Her eyes flick back and forth. "I'm concerned," she says. "I thought I saw a figure with a crown like Perth's earlier. Day, he looked like—"

A hacking laugh sounds. Perth Quellos sneers over at us.

"Be silent, you foul creature." Ezryn delivers a swift kick to the chains around his ankles, but Perth keeps laughing.

Rosalina and I slowly approach, and I place a protective grip around her waist. Perth inclines his head, as if offering a secret.

The five of us exchange wary glances. What can he do? He's in chains.

"You've," Perth gives a croaking wheeze, "lost."

A sense of foreboding seeps into my bones, dread that I can't quite explain.

"You're the one bound for Winter's dungeon," Kel growls.

Perth throws his head back, that laugh turning into a sick cough. "I knew there may be a chance I'd fail. How could I not assume that the betraying prince might pull more traitorous tricks? So, I devised my greatest experiment yet."

Kel grabs him up by his robes. "Enough riddles."

"If my army fell," Perth smiles emptily, "I wanted to make sure you and your precious mate fell with me."

I straighten, pulling Rosalina tighter. The air seems to thicken, like a great weight pressing down upon us. The hairs on the nape of my neck stand on end.

"A mortal creature that was already filled with hate and vengeance for the High Prince of Winter," Perth rattles, "was the perfect apprentice for my teachings. He will bring honor to the Green Flame and earn his own retribution by doing so!"

Then I hear it: a series of harsh bangs and the rush of wind. An unearthly chill shudders through me.

To the eastern flank, a hailstorm of deadly icicles bursts upon a platoon of Autumn Guard and Kryodian Riders. Each shard of ice strikes with deadly accuracy, impaling the soldiers. Screams of agony and pleas for mercy cut through the wind.

Ezryn snatches the chains around Perth's wrists and yanks hard. "How are you conjuring this wickedness?"

But Rosalina answers, her voice a panicked cry. "It's not him! Farron, look out!"

Farron blinks rapidly, standing alone now on the crest of a small hill, scroll in hand. "What's happening—"

But he doesn't finish his words. Dark ice crawls up his legs, over his torso, and quickly devours him—like it did to Koop and Flicker.

Farron! My heart constricts. *We'll get him out, we'll get him out.*

A cloaked figure emerges from behind Farron, a deep green crystal crown glowing on his head. "Ah, the first monster that tried to end me. It will be *so* easy to shatter him this way."

That voice. I fucking know that voice.

He throws off his cloak, and I see the twisted features of Lucas. But he's changed, now one of those wraiths. His skull appears fractured, frozen back together by frost. A sickly greenish-blue glow courses over his frozen body. Huge icy mounds grow over his shoulders and arms, and jagged spikes stick out of his chest. What sort of monster has Perth turned him into? And he has one of those crowns...

It's as if I can sense Ezryn and Kel's thoughts as my own. He will die. *Again.*

Keldarion drops Perth in a heap, draws his blade, and storms toward Lucas. "One death wasn't enough for you?"

"Wait, Kel don't—" Rosalina yells.

But he doesn't listen. Kel leaps, sword raised. It connects with Lucas's neck. There's a shimmering clang, like steel meeting stone. Keldarion pauses, blue eyes wide as ice skitters from Lucas's neck onto the sword. It crawls up the blade, then onto Kel's hands, over his arms. He tries to pull away, but he can't break free. He casts one horrified look at us before the ice encases him.

Rosalina lets out a terrible cry.

This monster just took down the most powerful fae in the Enchanted Vale. And he didn't even swing a sword.

Ezryn lets out a furious growl, then nods his helm at me. "Take her and run. I'll destroy the crown."

I stumble back almost instinctively at his command. The battle is in chaos as soldiers are swept away by the hailstorm or flee from the deadly ice shards.

"We can't *leave* them," Rosalina shrieks.

I feel her desperation. Fare, Kel, Ez—I can't abandon them.

Ezryn charges, but he's sheathed his sword, not willing to touch Lucas like Kel did. A powerful blast of fire erupts from his palms. It wavers around his body, then falls away.

"Fire isn't enough. The crown must be destroyed first!" Rosalina calls.

But it's too late. Lucas throws his hand out, fingers extending into terrifying icy claws. They rake down Ezryn's chest plate. An icy shell devours Ezryn before he can scream.

Lucas turns, that crystal blazing a sickening bright green. Rosalina clutches her wrist. Ezryn may have healed the skin, but the scar remains, visible or not. "It's time to shatter your prince," he says.

I stand in front of Farron's frozen body, drawing my double blades. "You will not touch him."

"If you want to be near him so much," Lucas growls, "then be with him in death."

A line of ice, quick and slithery, weaves across the ground then strikes at my legs. I don't even have time to yell before it starts to crawl up my body.

The last thought I have is to swing out my arm, pushing Rosalina away. "Run! Run, Rosie."

She backs away, looking down at her wrists covered in thorns. "Come on, come on, come on."

Nothing happens.

The ice reaches my torso, a cold cutting deep within me.

Rosalina looks from us to the battlefield, but she doesn't move.

"Run!" I yell again.

Lucas steps forward. "Oh, she's not going anywhere."

A great wall of ice grows, closing us in. Trapping her.

Frost creeps up my neck, and I gasp for a final breath.

I wasn't strong enough to save her.

88

ROSALINA

This ... This is what it's all led to?

I heave in a shaky breath and spin in a circle. Lucas's magic encases us on all sides, Autumn's blue sky shut out behind the thick ice.

He stands before me, changed and mutated from the man I once knew. But he's not unfamiliar. It's like his outside finally matches the inside.

My princes are trapped in here with us, their bodies frozen, their pain and fear visible even within the ice.

It really has all led to this.

I'm exactly where I was eleven years ago, trapped beneath the ice, with only Lucas.

"I didn't want it to come to this," he says, his voice all jagged edges. "But that crazy ice faerie gave me a second chance. So, I saved you from those beasts. Saved you again."

I glare at him through my tears. "You didn't care about me then. You don't care about me now. It's always been about what makes you feel powerful."

He gives a cruel laugh. "I don't need to feel powerful. I *am* power." He flexes his fists, green fog lacing through his fingers. "I've always known it, and now I've proven it. Even those beasts couldn't defeat me. Is this what you wanted? To play the role of adventurer, of princess? Fine. Stop fighting and play pretend with me."

Stop fighting. It would be so easy just to follow him, to be his shadow once again. To give up this foolish idea that I have any say in my world.

But that's not who I am anymore; my princes taught me that. And I proved it to myself. My men stand around me, silent sentinels of ice. I rise, trying to feel for the connection of the briars on my wrists. When I saw Lucas, the magic seemed to ebb away from me, lost within my wild fear.

But there's no other choice but to find it now.

Power surges through me, and two thorns break free, tearing through the hard earth and striking up at Lucas like hissing snakes. The sharp briars tear at his arms, ripping past fabric. Black blood leaks from the wound. Black blood like the goblins.

He grimaces at me. I take careful steps, not taking my eyes off him. My briars are alive, coiling up my arms.

I send another thorn-shot up at him, aiming for his head. But this time he's ready, catching it with fingers covered in ice claws. The entire briar crystallizes then shatters.

"What magic is this?" I spit. In all my research, I never read of magic that could rival the High Princes of the Enchanted Vale. A sinister smile creeps up his face. Green mist curls around the crown. *I need to break that damned thing.*

I place my hand behind my back and grow a single sharp thorn, then launch myself at Lucas. Vines wrap around my legs, propelling me higher. I scream, bringing the thorn down on the green crystal.

Lucas doesn't have time to react, and I strike true. The thorn connects. For a single heartbeat I'm suspended in the air—my thorn pressed to the crystal—and my vision fades to black. The world spins upside down, and an image appears before me.

A woman, writhed in shadows, black hair swirling around her like tendrils of smoke. She kneels in a cavern made of massive green crystals. Her hands are splayed out, and her voice echoes in a terrible incantation. She's calling something...

A sense of profound wrongness fills me, something so evil and terrible I can barely grasp it. My whole body goes cold, and the thorn splinters on the still-intact gem as time speeds up. I collapse to the ground.

"Now, Pumpkin." Lucas's rough hands grip me around the waist, and he hurls me across the icy cave. "That wasn't very nice."

I slam against the frozen wall, landing in a heap. My head rings. Distantly, I register that he didn't freeze me, not like the princes. Not because he can't, but because he doesn't want to. I can't squirm in terror if I'm frozen.

Groaning, I try to push myself up, my hands slipping in blood. Where did that come from? I don't get a chance to think before his boot connects with my ribs, and I roll on the ground, crying out in agony.

"I don't mind breaking you," Lucas says. "I've done it before."

I force myself up, crying through the pain, using the frozen body of one of my princes to help me. Farron. Tears stream down my face. I'm just as trapped as them.

Lucas lunges, and I desperately throw out a briar to stop his advance. But it won't hold him for long. Red coats the icy wall as I run my palm along it, trying to steady myself. Distorted silhouettes waver outside the ice cave—soldiers trying to break in?

Lucas's footsteps echo behind me, and I turn, struck by my reflection in the ice. Broken, frightened, helpless. Human.

"There you are," Lucas says.

I try to dodge out of his way, but he grabs me, placing a large hand around both my wrists and *freezing*. I scream. The ice crawls up my arms, over the briar bracelets I bargained for. The only way to defend myself ... Gone.

"No!" I screech, a long terrible wail. Lucas stops the ice as it reaches my elbows, then lifts me by my frozen arms. I kick my feet, and they bang uselessly against him.

"I think your friends are trying to get in."

Still holding me with one hand, Lucas waves his other. The ice around us dissipates, showing the surrounding Autumn soldiers. They let out a collective cheer of victory and race toward us.

A terrible understanding courses through me. Perth was right. We've lost.

Lucas waves his free hand, and that green crystal glows brighter. The crown ... It's funneling magic from that cursed cave I saw. And without Perth and his dead army, Lucas is taking it all. He roars, sending another vicious hailstorm into the soldiers.

"No!" I scream, feeling as if I take each blow to my own heart. Distantly, I see Billy, Dom, and Padraig racing toward me, their eyes wide as they take in the scene, spotting the frozen princes. The only people who could save us.

Now, you know that's not true, a voice, barely audible, scratches at my mind.

Lucas lowers me closer to his frosted face. "Forget this place."

I squeeze my eyes shut. Forget this place ... How could I?

It's so much more than a *place.* I have found more in this land than I could ever imagine. I've found a family. My loves. A purpose.

You were made for this world, Caspian had told me. It wasn't just a jest.

To forget this place would be to forget myself.

And I won't give up on her.

I lift my chin and heave in a breath. "I'm not your captive anymore."

"I beg to differ." Lucas curls his lip over his teeth, and the ice crawls further up my arms. "Look around, Pumpkin. Your princes are frozen. Your army is dead. You're trapped, no magic, no crown. You're nothing. Gaze upon what I have become, so much more than a mere human."

The air seems to crackle, and my skin heats. Words spark in my mind, and I realize, I do have the answers.

They come to me, crashing down like shooting stars.

Caspian's words.

You are no mere human.

Trapped in that human skin.

"You might not be human anymore," I growl at Lucas, "but neither am I." The truth burns bright and golden inside of me.

My mother wasn't stolen by the fae. She *was* fae. And so am I.

Something kindles in my chest: a flash of heat next to my heart. The embers I've smothered to keep from igniting. My own beast within me, slumbering in the dark place I've been too afraid to look.

Even when I knew the truth deep within, I couldn't make myself believe it. Lucas stole my trust in myself. Made me believe there was nothing inside of me worthy of the light.

But he was wrong about me.

I found it when I saw the goodness hiding behind a wolf's smile. When I forgave my father. When I peered into the dark spaces between the briars.

For a moment, it is silent. The Enchanted Vale taking a breath.

Then I look inside of myself and let the fire within rage.

Like a spark cresting atop dry leaves, I ignite. And whatever's catching flame within me is more than my courage. It's something beyond, something deep and ancient and powerful.

I let loose a scream. Images flash before my face: finding the rose-bush, Castletree obeying my command, the briars helping me save the roses. A woman's face, eyes filled with glittering starlight, as she smiles down at me.

I *was* made for this world. I am part of it. It is part of me.

I will become flame itself to protect the ones I love who call it home.

White fire explodes from my body. Lucas screams, shielding his face, but there's no hiding from this. No hiding from me.

Roaring fills my ears: the rush of water, of wind, of earth and fire. It's as if for a single moment, I glimpse the fabric of the universe and the threads that bind it together. The stone beneath me is like a second skin. The wind is the rush of blood through my veins.

And I feel my briars. Not the ones on my wrist. The ones that have not yet been made.

My consciousness reaches into the earth, weaving them into existence the way I had in the Below. The green mist evaporates in sparks of white. One of my briars cracks like lightning, shattering Lucas's crown.

Huge, white-gold thorns erupt from the earth, shattering the icy ground. The tangle of briars slams into Lucas, pinning him down to the dirt. Golden roses bloom along my thorns, beautiful and lethal.

A crack sounds, and ice breaks. I blink, somehow registering their faces amongst my fire and roses.

Kel. Ezryn. Dayton. Farron.

My flames shattered the ice—

I freed them—

Lucas's body lays before me, eyes blank, chest run through by a thick thorn.

I freed myself.

89

ROSALINA

The woman in front of me is very beautiful.

And familiar, too.

She's got dark eyes like mine, though hers are framed by joyful lines. Long, brown hair flows in gentle waves down her back, with a few white strands. Her skin radiates like a thousand diamonds.

Her ears ... They're pointed.

Who are you? I ask.

She only smiles and looks down into her hands. A golden rose blooms from her palm. Slowly, she tucks it behind my ear. *Seek below the surface, Rosalina, and may the hidden beauty of the world be yours. Love is your greatest strength.*

Then I'm surrounded by darkness.

I NEED to open my eyes. There's a battle ... And the princes. Did they get out of the ice? Are they alright?

But I can't wake up. Not yet. Something is different about the world.

Or maybe the world is the same and there's something different about me.

"Rosie? Rosie, come back to us!"

Farron's voice soaks into me like a balm, and his soft hands run over my face. My chest hums at his touch, and my skin seems to bloom beneath his fingertips. Perhaps this new world is not too bad.

"Rosalina!" Rougher hands grab me, shake me.

"Stop it! You'll hurt her!"

I'm pressed to a cold chest, and a strange, keening wail sounds. Keldarion. I inhale a deep breath, and the air feels alive within me, cleansing and cool.

"I can't find any wounds." Another worried voice: Ezryn's. His hand is on my forehead. I have no idea how I can differentiate between each of their touches, yet it's like my skin quivers and heats all at once. I smile inwardly, a strange sense of peace fluttering in my chest.

"Then why isn't she waking up?" Dayton for once sounds serious. "Can you hear me? Open your eyes, Blossom. Come on."

I don't want them to be worried. Though I'm not sure I'm ready for this changed world.

But they're with me. My princes.

I blink, gaze met with the beaming Autumn sun. It's so bright, each ray sparkling like starfall.

Oh. The world is beautiful. The clear sky, the rustle of the cool breeze through the grass, the rich smell of the earth.

And most beautiful of all are the four faces peering at me.

"Hi," I whisper, voice raspy.

Farron breaks out in the biggest smile I've ever seen. Ezryn shakes his helmet in disbelief. Dayton stares down at me with a fervent gaze. And Keldarion...

Keldarion is crying.

"What happened—" I start to sit up but stop.

I feel buoyant. Like I'm less tethered to the earth, a part of me mixing with the air.

"Rosalina." Farron muscles Kel out of the way and takes my hands to help me sit up. I hold on to his gaze to keep my breathing steady.

Have I never noticed how many colors swirl in his eyes? Amber and gold and flecks of bronze. "You did something. Awoke something."

My hand shakes as I bring it to my face. Up my cheek.

To the point of my ear.

"Rosie," Farron says softly, "you're fae."

I clutch my chest. That *thing* inside of me, the embers I'd kept smothered. It no longer feels like embers now, nor the burning inferno as it did when I unleashed my magic. Has this been lying dormant within me all this time?

All this time, I'd known there was more to my mother. More to me. I couldn't let myself believe it. But there's no denying it now.

I turn to Kel. "Did you know?"

He shakes his head. "No. I knew there was something about you because of your connection to Castletree and ability to use the mirror, but I never imagined..."

"Perhaps there is more to learn about your mother than only her location," Ezryn says.

I heave in a shaky breath. The princes didn't know...

But someone did.

Listen carefully, Princess. Trust your own instincts above all else. The world will tell you that you don't belong. That you are a mere human. That you have no dominion over the sway of destiny. They are wrong.

Caspian's words from our dance months ago drift over my mind.

My fingers dig into the earth. What else has he kept hidden from me?

Then I'm being lifted by my waist, tugged close to a warm body, and shaken from my thoughts. "Whether you're human, fae, or goblin for all we care, you're our Rose. And you just saved our fucking lives."

I collapse against Dayton's chest, letting him hold me up. Nearby lies a massive briar patch of golden roses. And speared by a thorn is Lucas Poussin. His crown is cracked, no longer shining with green light.

I meet Farron's gaze and nod. He murmurs the death incantation, enough magic within him to pass one more. Lucas's body drifts away like ash in the wind.

Now you're free too, I think.

I look around the battlefield. Beyond us, a cluster of Autumn soldiers stare concernedly. Others work with the Winter riders to carry injured into the city or marshal with their commanders. There are no more wraiths, no more ice storms.

"Did we win?" I whisper.

Kel pulls me into his chest. "Yes. The frost is gone, and Farron has sent the dead to their final rest."

Ezryn places a hand on Kel's arm. "And the High Prince of Winter showed that there are still those in his realm who will fight for him."

I reach my hand out. They come to me and Kel, and the five of us embrace.

For right now, I hold on to them with everything I can, with every piece of my new fae-born heart.

90

FARRON

The courtyard of Keep Oakheart is done up in gold banners, the trees waving with ribbons. A haunting voice sings a hymn as the last pieces of wood are placed upon my mother's pyre.

I've always heard the peaceful dead look like they're asleep, but not my mother. She lies on her final throne, a sense of purpose on her face even in death. Her eyes are closed, hands positioned over her body. Soon, she will embark on her ultimate voyage, and we will send her to the beyond with our well wishes and thanks.

As is customary at a funeral in the Autumn Realm, everyone is dressed in gold. The late afternoon sun shines into the courtyard, bathing my mother in light.

With the pyre set, small groups approach. Our people tie golden strings onto my mother's wrists, fingers, and ankles, or weave them through her hair. And with that binding, they offer her a final word to transition into the unknown realm.

Rosalina squeezes my hand as we watch. Silent tears streak down my face, but I keep my breathing steady, my body still. When it's Dayton's turn, he takes his time braiding the golden string through my mother's hair. He whispers words of thanks. His eyes flick to me as he does so.

My twin brothers approach with our sister, Eleanor, who has returned from her wardship in the Summer Realm for the funeral. Her usually grim face is streaked with silent tears. My brothers take turns laying their heads upon Mother's chest, offering final farewells.

I force myself to watch as my father wraps her wrists in string. His huge body shakes, and though his eyes shine with grief, he manages his words.

There's no one else. Autumn's dignitaries have gone, the nobles from visiting realms, each of the High Princes, and all of her family.

It's time for me to say goodbye.

My mate and I walk hand in hand to the pyre. Rosalina sinks to her knees beside my mother and gently wraps the string around her wrist. "Thank you," she whispers. "Thank you for raising the kindest man I've ever known. Thank you for teaching him how to love with a strong heart and how love can be his strength. You are eternal within him."

My fingers shake as I try to weave my string through her braid. Rosalina places a hand over mine and helps steady me. I lean down, my forehead touching my mother's.

"Thank you, Mother. I promise I'll do right by you. I'll watch out for Father, Dom, Billy, and Nori. The realm will always remember what you've done. What you've given." My voice tremors, but I feel her strength within me. "Your spirit lives on in the changing leaves, the breeze that rustles through the trees. And though I will never be able to hold you again in this world, I know that we shall be reunited someday in a place beyond time and space, where all is as it should be."

I stand, taking Rosalina's hand once more. "Farewell, former High Princess Niamh, Mother of Autumn. Until my road meets yours, farewell."

Rosalina and I place our hands on the wood. I nod, and flames spark from my hands and hers: orange and white, mingling together, accompanying my mother's spirit beyond this realm.

We retire to the great hall for the life thread feast, a joyful celebration. I sit at the head of the table, Rosalina, George, my father, and my siblings beside me. My father will take over my mother's role as steward as I continue my quest to free Castletree of Caspian's magic-leaching briars. I flex my fingers. So much power returned to me by breaking the curse, but I know it's not the true depths of my magic. I have to help the other princes break their curses so we can destroy the Prince of Thorns for good.

Though I won't abandon Autumn the way I have before. I promised my mother I'd take care of our people. It's a vow I'll never break.

Dayton and his sister sit farther down the table. Delphia, the steward of the Summer Realm, is giving her older brother a glower for the ages as he cracks a joke. My breath catches slightly. I'm always surprised how young she is, only a child, and yet there's a sternness on her face that rivals those three times her age.

I look down at the gold and silver cuff around my bicep. Another bargain, but one so different from what I'd made with Caspian. Dayton has given me freedom over his magic reserve, and all I had to do was promise to never forget that moment with him. As if I ever could: it will be seared in my memory forever.

Kel and Ez sit together at the end of the table with Eirik Vargsaxa, captain of the Kryodian Riders. With Perth Quellos in jail in the Winter Realm, a new steward is required; Kel will have to appoint one soon. He says he's not concerned, but I think things are worse in Winter than Kel's letting on.

The green crystal flashes in my mind. I gathered the shards of it and kept it in a box to take back to Castletree ... for research purposes only, of course. Could I have used a similar magic to save my mother from death?

I turn my attention back to the table. Ezryn sits with his usual poise, but I can tell he's looking around. After the battle, we sent word to all the realms about my mother's funeral. No reply came from Spring. Though his father's health has been in decline for decades, it's unlike him not to respond to a royal summons.

I'm sure both Ez and Kel will have to return to their realms soon. A small part of me wonders if Kel might be inspired by what happened here, by seeing the Riders rally with him. Maybe he'll finally want to break his curse.

Maybe he'll finally accept Rosalina as his mate.

I shake my head, still unable to comprehend that I share a mate with the High Prince of Winter. And that he won't accept her.

I turn to look at Rosalina, and a soft smile crosses my face. She's completely engaged with my little sister, listening with enthusiastic nods as Nori explains the delicate art of taxidermy. I thought she was beautiful the first time I saw her all those months ago in my prison cell. Now, she is radiant. The points of her ears and the new glimmer in her brown eyes seem like they've always belonged to her.

My mate has been half-fae all along. A part of me itches to run to the library to research such power lying dormant. Could our mate bond have awoken it? A mate bond has been known to increase a fae's magic, but not create new magic. Yet the fire she'd used to crack the ice seemed so similar to my own. And what of those golden roses...

Mysteries upon mysteries ... with one in particular that her father is determined to solve. I smile as I look at George, who's brought his maps even to the dinner table. Billy and Dom hover on either side of him, arguing over the best route to take.

George has decided not to return to Castletree with us; he's setting off in search of his wife. The realization that Anya was fae has only fortified his determination to locate her. And Dom and Billy couldn't pass up the chance of being his guides through the wilds.

I take a deep breath and stare down at the table. So many questions lay before us, and I know there won't be any rest for the Princes and Lady of Castletree.

But we'll find the answers together.

91

ROSALINA

Carefully, I place a folded blouse into the bag on my bed. After months in Coppershire, we are finally returning to Castletree. It feels bittersweet, but I know the Autumn Realm will always be home to me.

Strolling through the room, I stop, noticing my reflection in the gold-plated mirror. The pointed ears are still a shock, and I delicately reach up and touch the tips. Physically, that's the biggest change. But inside…

Inside, everything is different. Parts of me have opened up, vast wells of … I'm not sure. Magic? Power? The princes have promised to help me explore this transformation, and I trust them.

The world has changed. Colors are more luminous, and I can perceive the glint of enchantment in the air. My bond with Farron burns so brightly sometimes I think it'll ignite my whole self in flames. And my bond with Kel … Well, that's stronger, too. An insistent tug, an itch that can't be scratched.

"Hey-o!"

"Hello! Rosalina!"

"Rose, dear!"

Three voices call from outside, and I rush to my balcony. Down below—atop horses laden with full saddlebags—are Billigan, Dominic, and my father.

The trees around the burnt library are still unfurled from the battle, but my view is no longer of the ruins. The broken wood is covered in lush moss, the ground now grassy, and there's even a small pond with crystal-clear water. A combined gift from the High Princes. One day, I know Farron and I, will rebuild the library.

Currently, my horse, Amalthea, and Farron's elk, Thrand, graze in the clearing. Thankfully, Thrand's no worse for wear after being frozen in the battle. Farron found him amid many of the other frozen soldiers and steeds and was able to melt the cursed ice. I'll miss them. Perhaps one day Castletree and the lands beyond will be safe enough for them, too.

I turn my attention back to the trio. "Shouldn't you be on your way already?" I yell.

They're about to set off on their own adventure. For the first time, seeing Papa leave doesn't fill me with loneliness. Instead, I'm filled with hope. Perhaps my fae mother truly is out there.

"One more thing!" Papa calls up. "What would you like me to bring you?"

"Just a rose!"

He laughs. "That got me in a bit of trouble last time."

"Trouble of the best kind," Dominic chuckles.

"True enough if it brought you here," Billy adds.

"You two better keep him safe," I say, waving. "Now go before I start crying again!"

"Goodbye, Rosalina!" Papa calls. "I love you!"

"I love you too." I wipe a tear from my face and step inside.

A part of me understands his love and devotion in a way I hadn't before. I would never stop trying to get back to my princes, and he'll never stop searching for my mother.

I return to my packing, placing another sweater in my bag. The corner of a book peeks out. My heart shudders, as it always does, when I see it. Carefully, I pull away the clothes hiding it and run my fingers over the cover.

It's the grimoire Caspian stole from the alder tree. It hadn't been hard at all to control the thorns he gave me, to reach into his armor and switch my book with this. He'd been so focused on completing our bargain ... On *kissing* me.

The material is weathered and rough. Intricate symbols etched across the cover writhe before my eyes. Each time I look, they're in a different place, like the book is alive.

The thorns encircling my wrist, shrunken down to only delicate bracelets, weigh heavily as I look upon the book. The pages are yellowed and brittle, their edges frayed with age. They feel fragile, as if they might crumble at any moment.

I've only had a chance to briefly flip through it. The words are written in a flowing script that twists across the page, defying the rigid lines. It's a book about humans. This passage speaks of the Queen's fondness for people, of their curiosity and ingenuity.

It's strange. I'd been in the alder tree with Farron, and there had been many books that seemed more dangerous. No world-ending spells or dastardly secrets here. In fact, the whole thing seems purely scientific and observational.

But he went to so much trouble for this one book. Why? I have no doubt he'll return for it. I'll have to hide it well and be ready with my own bargain if he wants it back.

A light tap sounds at my door, and I quickly tuck the book deep within my bag. "Come in!"

Keldarion steps into my room, raising a dark brow, the look he always gives me when he thinks I'm up to something. "Rosalina."

I haven't told any of them yet about seeing Caspian on the battlefield or the bargain I made. They haven't questioned the thin thorns around my wrists. Perhaps they think I summoned them myself.

"Almost ready to go?" The Winter Prince strides before me. He's dressed in that simple elegance he excels at, a laced black shirt with tight pants and boots.

"Almost."

He tucks a piece of hair behind my ear, fingers delicately stroking the point.

"If I've always been half-fae, why did I look human?" I ask softly.

"I'm uncertain." He shakes his head. "There are illusion spells, but to physically change your appearance for so long requires a magic beyond what I understand. But we'll find the answer, I promise."

I place my hand over his.

"Oh! Ah!" An awkward sound comes from my doorway: Farron, eyes wide and hands jittery. "I didn't mean to interrupt."

"Come here, Farron," Keldarion says.

Farron grits his teeth, looking like he really regrets entering my room at this moment. But I hold out my hand to him and relish the feeling as his fingers weave into mine. He might still be awkward around Keldarion but having both my mates close settles an ache in my chest.

Keldarion places a large hand on my shoulder, and the other on Farron's, then holds both our gazes. "There is a tether between the three of us now. Do you feel it?"

Farron swallows, throat bobbing. "Yes."

"I feel it," I say.

"High Prince of Autumn," Keldarion lowers his forehead to Farron in a sort of surrender, "you are mate of my mate, and I swear I will protect you from this moment to my dying breath."

Farron flushes deeply. "Uh, yeah. Same, Kel."

Kel turns to me, and his eyes blaze. "Rose, I will never send you away again. You have saved me and saved the Autumn Realm. Without a doubt, this is where you belong forever."

My heart sings at his words, at the devotion in them. "Kel," I say, feeling the unbreakable tie between all three of us. "Farron broke his curse. He freed his people in Castletree. Together, we could—"

Keldarion straightens. "The events here have only strengthened my resolve. I'll help the others to break their curses and hope that is enough to heal Castletree. But this curse will lay upon me forevermore."

He turns to leave.

"Kel!" I yell angrily.

He waves a dismissive hand. "Do not be sad, Rosalina. Now your other mate may satisfy your base needs."

Farron lets out a long sigh. "He really is infuriating, isn't he?"

I loop my arms over his shoulders. "Sure you're not regretting being my mate *forevermore* with all that icy baggage?"

"I'll take you whatever way you are." He drops his nose to nuzzle against mine. "Forever with you doesn't sound too bad. And now I don't have to continue my secret research on extending human life."

I giggle as his lips drop to my pointed ears. There's the rustle of wind as a gale brings a tumble of golden leaves. "I love you, Farron."

"In the starlight way," he says.

"In the starlight way."

KEEP Oakheart's halls are lined with Autumn nobility to bid the residents of Castletree goodbye. They whisper that their High Prince is a wolf guardian, that the other High Princes are blessed with the same magic. It's good enough gossip to keep the curse under wraps for now.

Marigold, Astrid, and my princes wait by the door that will lead us back home.

Farron explained Castletree is still too weak for us to keep the door open, allowing the staff to come and go as they did before the curse. But it won't be closed permanently anymore. Already these halls have been dusted and polished.

Dayton gives Delphia one last hug, spinning her up in the air while she grumbles. But when he goes to put her down, she wraps her arms tightly around his neck.

Farron groans, squeezed in the tight embrace of his father.

"I'll be back soon," he grumbles, squirming out, and quickly bestows his little sister Nori with a kiss to the top of her head, which she bears well.

Padraig straightens, wiping his watery eyes. "Thank you, High Princes of Castletree, for all you have done for the Autumn Realm."

ELIZABETH HELEN

Then he gives me a broad smile I can't help but mimic. "And here we have the Lady of Castletree, whose bravery has saved my son. Has saved us all."

"There is nothing I wouldn't do for Farron," I say, "and for the Autumn Realm."

"Ey, there it is. Because you're not just the Lady of Castletree anymore." He opens his palm, revealing a simple golden leaf. "Mate of the High Prince, a courageous defender. Rosalina O'Connell, Princess of the Autumn Realm."

He drops to a knee, and akin to leaves falling from a tree, the rest of the nobility follow suit, one after another. Suddenly, everyone is bowing and I'm the only one left standing.

My princes incline their heads with the utmost respect. Farron stands and takes the leaf from his father's palm. Delicately, he moves the hair from behind my neck and threads the leaf onto my necklace, so it falls perfectly next to the moonstone rose. "Princess of Autumn," Farron breathes, "will you lead us home?"

I touch the golden leaf, feeling in my heart the magic of this place: the crisp nights, blazing bonfires, the forest of a thousand colors, the bravery and legends of these people.

"Woven together," I say, looking out at everyone.

"Woven together," Padraig and the others say. He rises. "You will always have a place in the Autumn Realm, Rosalina."

Tears brim my eyes as I leave behind this new home for my other one. With a heavy heart, I turn toward the great door and grip the handle. I feel the magic of Castletree calling me as I pull the door open. Farron clasps my hand, and Dayton holds his. I reach out for Ezryn's gloved hand, and he follows suit to take Keldarion's. I step onward to Castletree, to home, woven together with the princes who make it so.

92

THE PRINCE OF THORNS

After all these years, I still haven't figured out if the citizens of Winter *enjoy* their realm being this damned cold, or if they've all just lost feeling after ages of serving under the iciest bastard in the Vale.

I breathe hot air into my palms and rub them together, but it does little to chase away the chill in my bones. Ah, well. Won't be here long.

I'm never long on the surface these days.

My feet thud on the hard stone floor of Frostfang's dungeon. Several guards squirm and press against my thorns, which bind them to the wall. I wave a hand and the thorns grow to cover their heads, saving me from listening to their bothersome cries.

A shame, really. I don't get much time up here nowadays, and I hate to spend it in this frozen vault. Hate spending it running errands for *her*.

She walks in front of me, long black hair swaying behind her like a cape. Each step radiates with the command she asserts over everything, whether it be stone tile or fae. She's beautiful and terrible in the way a lightning storm is beautiful and terrible.

Sira, Queen of the Below.

My mother.

"I don't want to be here any more than you do."

I shiver at the smoothness of her voice.

"Don't you think I have better things to do than free idiots from this freezing wasteland?" she continues, not even deigning to look back at me. "It was the perfect opportunity for you to take Autumn. You could have swept in while they were in turmoil. You already forced your brothers and sisters to fight the night of your little party—"

"The goblins," I snarl, "are not my brothers and sisters."

She snorts, then finally turns to look at me. I'm caught in the serpentine green of her eyes, the sly smirk. "My perfect boy," she murmurs. "My perfect, pathetic boy."

She turns on her heel and we continue down the hall. Instinctively, I reach into the folds of my tunic for the book, but it's not there. Of course, it's not there. Because Rosalina took it. My only solace is I doubt she understands the magnitude of what she possesses.

Not that it's of particular importance to anyone but me. *The only fae that could change her form, truly transform herself…*

Ah, well. I'll retrieve it soon enough. It's always fun to pay my little Rose a visit. And I haven't yet beheld her now that she's unleashed her true form.

At least a part of it.

Sira stops before a cell and snaps her fingers, drawing me back to the present. I sigh and send a surge of thorns cracking through the ice, ripping the door from its hinges.

Huddled in a corner is the withered shape of Perth Quellos. His defeat has left him a husk of a man.

"Who are you?" he breathes, backing further against the wall. "Caspian? The Below has come to kill me—"

"Oh, don't be dramatic." Sira examines her fingernails, filed to talons. "I saw a lot of potential in you, ice sorcerer. I thought you could be of assistance to me. Who did you think delivered those crowns to your doorstep, after all?"

Quellos blinks. "T-they were gifts from the Below?"

Sira steps toward the fallen vizier and studies him with a cold gaze. "I have use of your talents. But you'll need to be educated so as not to fail me again." She offers me a sweet smile. "I don't take kindly to failure, do I, pet?"

"No, Mother," I respond flatly.

"I won't serve a master," Quellos hisses, and I'm almost impressed by the passion left in him. "Especially one from the Below."

Sira sniffs. "Come now. We all answer to someone."

A shudder passes through me as I think of who my mother answers to. The Green Flame.

With a sudden spin and flick of her raven-black hair, Sira walks back toward the broken door of the cell. "Offer your allegiance and services to me, and in return, you shall have revenge against those who shamed you. I will gift you power greater than even that of the crown. Or..." She narrows her eyes. "Stay here. Rot in this cell, knowing that brute Keldarion rules over what should be yours."

Quellos's chest heaves. Sira waves for me to follow her out of the cell. We start to exit—

"I'll do it. I'll serve you," Quellos cries. "And then I will have my retribution against the beast prince."

I nearly laugh, imagining this pitiful old man enacting any sort of justice upon Kel. Instead, I smirk. "You'll have to get in line."

Sira raises her chin to me. "Send him to my sanctum. I'll begin his re-education when I return Below."

I swallow my anger as I weave my briars around Quellos, who sobs and struggles against their touch. With a rough hand, I direct the thorns spiraling down through the earth, taking Quellos deep Below.

"Where to now, Mother?" I drawl with mock sweetness. She knows the more magic I use on the surface, the more it drains me. Already, I feel the thick wave turning my blood to sludge.

"We need to check on your sister."

"She's not my *real* sister," I say, simply because I know it annoys Mother so much.

Sira snatches my jaw, nearly piercing the skin with her sharp nails. "I let you disparage my sweet babies, but do not speak ill of my adopted daughter. She's accomplished more in twenty-five years than you have in centuries." She flicks my jaw away and mutters to herself, "Ungrateful boy. Thankless wretch."

I rub my face and summon the thorns. Thankfully, it's not far to Spring.

I think I'll make it before the black rot takes me.

The thorns carry Sira and I quickly beneath the surface, and I maneuver us up to the vast cavernous Hall of Vernalion, the throne room of the Spring Realm.

We erupt into the hall. I stagger out of the briars and collapse on the floor, gagging up sludge. Trails of black drip from my eyes and nose. I need to get back to the Below...

Sira steps over me, heels clicking. "Well, well, well. Things seem to be going swimmingly here."

I look up, fighting to see through the film covering my eyes.

Prince Thalionor, Ezryn's father, and steward of Spring has collapsed to his knees, head hung low, hands in chains behind his back.

And dressed in armor of blackest night, wearing an eerie helm with sharp metal crests on the brow resembling a great horned owl, is Kairyn, Prince of Spring. Ezryn's younger brother. And he's currently crushing the head of a princeguard beneath his boot.

The rest of Prince Thalionor's princeguard lie in pools of their own blood, their skulls all caved in.

My stomach turns, and I struggle to my feet.

That's when I see her lounging across the massive metal throne made of various helms. Her body is angled to the side, one leg draped over the arm of the throne, a silver goblet in her hand.

The Nightingale smiles at me, blue eyes flashing with mirth. "Recovered from your party, big brother?"

I say nothing.

Kairyn's chest heaves as the man dies beneath his boot, and he staggers over to stand beside my sister, like a dog returning to the foot of its master.

The Nightingale runs an idle hand down Kairyn's arm, eyes never leaving mine. "I heard your little goblin assault on Autumn was practically useless. I tried to help you that night, but you wouldn't listen. Now here I am, right on track to deliver the Spring Realm."

Something twists in my chest, and I unconsciously grab my wrist, fingers drifting over the mark there.

"Come on, Caspian, why the long face? You should be delighted." The Nightingale gives a lilting laugh. "We're going to kill the High Princes. And their," her blue gaze meets mine, "thorny little princess, too."

Her threat doesn't go unnoticed. She knows of Rosalina's power. Her price will be high to keep that from our mother.

But as the pull of the Below finally becomes too much to take, I sink within my briars and fall down into the deep.

I'm going to have to be very careful about my next moves.

Betrayal is a dangerous game.

And I haven't quite decided who I'm going to betray yet.

Thank you so much for reading Woven by Gold! We hope you enjoyed your second adventure in the Enchanted Vale.

Reviews help others find our book. They are vital to indie authors like us.

You can leave a review on Amazon here:

You can leave a review on Goodreads here:

THE ENCHANTMENT
CONTINUES IN...

FORGED BY MALICE

Beasts of the Briar Book 3
OUT NOW

ACKNOWLEDGMENTS

Rosalina says that the Enchanted Vale makes her feel alive. That is the simplest way we can describe creating this series: a joy so powerful it makes our own lives shimmer with magic. Thank you so much to everyone who has been a part.

A huge thank you to Anne, Beate, Camille, Carlie, Charlotte, Jamie, Kaylee, Khepri, Natasha, Olivia, Renee, Sarah, Tatjana, Taylor C., and Taylor G. Writing a book takes a village. Thank you for being part of ours.

With all our hearts, thank you to the readers around the globe who took a chance on Bonded by Thorns and have welcomed Rosie and her princes into their hearts. The bookish online community is one of the most loving, encouraging, and happy spaces to be. We're so grateful to be a part of it. A special thank you to Hailey and Lindsay, two wonderful friends we've met because of our love of smutty books, Pedro Pascal, and Taylor Swift.

And finally, thank you to our friends and family who have championed our stories since the very beginning. To Mom and Dad for reading everything, even the twisted stuff. To Graeme for letting us steal his ideas and talking us through how a siege works. To Auntie Jo for her #jowatches and always taking care of us. We love you so much!

On to the next one!

Elizabeth + Helen

Also by Elizabeth Helen

Beasts of the Briar

Bonded by Thorns

Woven by Gold

Forged by Malice

Broken by Daylight

Novella

Prince of the Arena

ABOUT THE AUTHORS

Elizabeth Helen is the combined pen-name of sister writing duo, Elizabeth and Helen. Elizabeth and Helen write fantasy romance and love creating enchanting adventures for their characters. When they're not writing, you can find them snuggling their cats, exploring their rainforest home, or rolling the dice for a game of Dungeons & Dragons. You can connect with them on TikTok, Instagram, or Facebook.

Facebook Readers' Group

Join our Facebook Readers' Group to interact with like-minded bookish people, get behind-the-scenes info on the creation of our books, receive sneak peeks for Book 4, and chat all about the Enchanted Vale and the fae princes!
facebook.com/groups/elizabethhelen

AuthorEizabethHelen.com

facebook.com/elizabethhelenauthor
instagram.com/author.elizabeth.helen
tiktok.com/@authorelizabethhelen
amazon.com/author/elizabethhelen
goodreads.com/elizabeth_helen

BONUS STORY

PRINCE OF THE ARENA

Before the curse, Farron travels to the Summer Realm to watch Dayton compete in the Solstice Games.

Read this Dayton and Farron spicy and sweet bonus chapter exclusive to newsletter subscribers.

ElizabethHelen.SubStack.com

PLAYLIST

Spoilers ahead!
Scan the code with the Spotify app.

Trøllabundin | Eivør Pálsdóttir *(Staring at the rosebush)*
Possibility | Lykke Li *(Rose's sad-girl-dumped-by-older-man era)*
The bioluminescence of the night | James Horner *(Seeing Ez)*
The Mandalorian - Epic Version | Samuel Kim *(It's time for Spring's melt)*
It's an Ultimatum | Sonya Belousova, Giona Ostinelli *(Kel vs the 3 princes)*
Oracle | Timmy Trumpet *(Dancing around the willow tree)*
Everybody (Backstreet's Back) | Backstreets Boys *(The princes arrive in Orca Cove)*
Labyrinth | Taylor Swift *(Returned to my mate)*
Home | Alan Menken *(Home at Castletree)*
Soldier, Poet, King | The Oh Hellos *(Seeing Rosalina's library with Farron)*
Experienced Hands | Joseph Loduca *(Dip in the hot springs)*
The Cello Begins | Neal Acree *(Cas comes to dinner)*
The Story of the First Witcher | Bear McCreary *("Who did this to you?")*
I Am Merida | Patrick Doyle *(Entering the Autumn Realm)*
The World is Ahead | Howard Shore *(Exploring the Autumn realmlands)*
Flaming Red Hair | Howard Shore *(Billy and Dom pull Rosalina into a dance)*
Noble Maiden Fair | Emma Thompson, Peigi Barker *(Farron and his mother feels)*
Snow on the Beach | Taylor Swift, Lana Del Ray *("You knew I would feel you.")*
Only Love Can Hurt Like This | Paloma Faith *(When you're rejected by two fae princes in one night)*
Throne | Saint Mesa *("Keldarion and I both look to the throne")*
My Jolly Sailor Bold | Ashley Serena *(The mermaid arises)*
Eat Your Young | Hozier *(Ezryn satisfies his woman)*
Eye of the Storm | Bear McCreary *(Farron is missing)*
Fools | Lauren Aquilina *("I'm glad he's here. At the end of it all.")*
Geralt of Rivia | Sonya Belousova, Giona Ostinelli *(Kel protects his family)*
A Thousand Years (feat. Steve Kazee) | Christina Perri *(Rosalina and Farron complete their mate bond)*
~~**A Claim to the Throne** | Max Richter *(Farron returns to Coppershire)*~~
Forever | CHVRCHES *(Rose, Autumn, and Summer)*
Breath Of Life | Florence + The Machine *(Meeting Caspian on the battlefield)*

PLAYLIST

The Fire Within | Within Temptation *(Farron lays the dead to rest)*
Transformations | Alan Menken *(Rosalina is fae)*
The Last Goodbye | Billy Boyd *(Niamh's funeral)*
Everytime You Leave | Sonya Belousova, Giona Ostinelli *(Mate of my mate)*
Kylo Ren's Theme | Fake Hypocrite *(Taking the Spring Realm)*